This book is dedicated to my true love. May I be lucky enough to find you in our next life and finally be able to call you mine.

Special thanks go to my sisters, Erica and Sarah, who have help with character naming, as well as various design aspects throughout the book.

PROLOGUE

My name is Fisonma. I am the leader of the Elder Council, governing body over a realm not known to most humans. Those who are chosen to find themselves in our presence call this land the Astral Realm—a land just past the edge of "normal" existence. For untold ages, we have governed this realm in peace, but it has not always been so.

Far longer than anyone can recollect, this land was actually under the control of the shadows—people consumed by power and hatred. It was that corruption that tarnished the city now known as Nimost. The darkness coming from their thoughts and actions was so intense that it began to corrupt the Elemental Towers and the powers of the Elementals themselves. During this dark time, the people suffered greatly, and far too many perished as the power was used to destroy instead of to sustain life.

Only when things had become too unbearable was something done. Great warriors arose, each hearing a silent plea for help. These warriors were led by one who was blessed by the Light itself. Light so pure that this person became the legendary White Angel. However, darkness gave birth to its own Angel, one so full of hate that almost all light was destroyed by his very presence. With tenacity and a solid purpose, they were able to eventually drive the shadows away from the Towers and south to a land now known as the Shadow Lands.

These great warriors were the first Guardians to the Elementals, and an age of peace was allowed to be brought forth. Sadly, the White Angel had perished fighting the Angel of Darkness. A tower was still erected in their honor, representing the hope and peace that we currently reside in now.

Unfortunately, that peace is once again threatened. The Guardians are ever vigilant, dealing with the threats as they arise, but it has become painfully clear that another great war is on the horizons. The armies of the Shadow Lands are becoming more brazen in their actions, their people filled with an unquenchable hatred because of tales that have been handed down. Now, more than ever, faith in a legend has never been so important. I just hope we are able to find our champion before the darkness can corrupt its own.

CHAPTER

1

The Beginning of a Legacy

"Senia?"

The voice of the nurse drew the soon-to-be mother from her thoughts. "Sorry."

"No harm," she said with a warm smile. "We're ready to induce your delivery. Is there anyone here with you?"

Senia thought for a moment as she stared out the window into the empty morning. Her parents were out of the state on business, and the man she thought she loved hadn't turned out to be what she had expected. Scrunching her brow, she gave a slight smile, her hands absently rubbing her abdomen. "I'll be fine on my own," she replied softly.

The nurse gently took her hand and motioned for her to follow. "The staff in the labor ward will be there for you if you need them," she said as the two stepped into the elevator.

The ride to the fourth floor was completed in silence, but as the two stepped out, she saw the look of intrigue upon Senia's face. "The staff here keep the environment as peaceful as possible to ease in the deliveries. Soft music, an inviting atmosphere. Even the paints are chosen for each room by our head OB."

One of the midwives came up while the two were talking and smiled, and she hugged a clipboard close to her chest.

"Senia?" she asked, already knowing the answer. "We've been waiting for you. The doctor already picked out your room and wants us to make you as comfortable as possible."

The nurse looked at her watch and tsk'ed.

"I have to return back to the main floor. Do you have everything you need?" she asked, looking at the midwife who flipped through the charts.

"Yes, ma'am. I believe we're all set on this end. Thank you for bringing her."

The nurse nodded and took Senia's hand. "Be strong dear. I'll check on you in a couple of days, once things have settled down."

Before she could thank her, the nurse was down the hall and in the elevator.

"Come now," the midwife said as she led Senia to her room, painted a tranquil blue, which contrasted her airy nature, and a large window that nearly consumed the far wall. "Beautiful, isn't it?" she asked, catching Senia staring at a stormy ocean scape painting beside her bed that showed a massive wave seeming to engulf an entire civilization. "It was donated by a local artist."

"Very beautiful," she replied as she slid into the bed. Pulling the blankets up just under her abdomen, she rested as she was hooked to the various machines, and soon the baby's heartbeat filled the room. "Is that her?"

"It is," the midwife answered with a smile. "It's strong and very healthy sounding," she added as she gave her an injection into the IV in her right arm. "This is going to help you go into labor. Before you know it, we'll be ready to start pushing." She jotted down things onto the chart, records of what was being done. "The doctor will be in soon to check on your progress."

And with that, she drew the curtain and exited the room.

Senia rested her head into the plush pillow and ran her hands over her swollen belly. Her touch was met with vibrant kicks and movements. It was those little movements that helped solidify the bond the two shared even with so much separating them. "I was beginning to think you didn't want to come out," she said with a soft laugh. "Not that I'd blame you . . .," her voice trailed off as she stared out the window into the late morning sky.

She'd lost herself to her thoughts before a sudden kick brought her back and a slight hint of blush flared across her cheeks.

"I'm sorry, love," she said as she rubbed the area where she'd been kicked and continued. "I don't blame you for not wanting to come out, but I'll always be here with you to protect you, and so will your grandparents. They can't wait to see you."

In time, with her soothing voice, the movement slowed until it ceased completely, but Senia wasn't without pain. The medication she was given had started her contractions, and she winced as the sudden surge of pain ripped through her body. Shortly after the contraction subsided, a knock echoed lightly against her door, the sound of footsteps following shortly after.

"Senia?" came a questioning voice as the door closed.

"Yes?" she replied, sitting up a bit and pulling the blankets further up her body.

"Oh good," came the answer as a man poked his head around the edge of the curtain, drawing it back. He adjusted his glasses and flipped through her chart. "I'm Dr. Northwood. I'm going to be delivering your daughter today."

He glanced from the chart to the machines, watching the contraction monitor, nodding, then going back to the chart and jotting down notes.

"How much longer?" she asked, wincing through yet another contraction.

"Well, I'll have to see how far dilated you are, and we should know more then."

She nodded, and the doctor checked how far along she was.

"This is promising. You're farther along than I'd expected you to be." He stood up and tossed the gloves away before jotting onto the paper once more. He then adjusted the medication she was getting and closed her chart. "I have to go get some things ready, then we'll be back, and within the next couple of hours, we should have a baby." He turned and walked toward the door. "Get some rest, I'll be back soon."

And with that, the door closed, and she was in silence once again.

"Not much longer, my angel," she said softly as she felt some minor kicking, but it was drowned out by yet another contraction.

She shifted to ease the pain it was causing in her back, but it was little comfort. The contractions were more painful and coming quicker. She was beginning to think that pain control would have been a better option to the natural birth, but as she was about to request any medication, the doctor, a nurse, and two midwives entered the room.

"How are you feeling?" Dr. Northwood asked as he sat on a stool at the end of the bed.

"A lot of pain," Senia panted.

The doctor nodded and lifted the sheet, checking dilation. "Well, you're fully dilated, so we can break the water and start the delivery."

She nodded as each midwife held her hand, dabbing sweat from her forehead as the doctor broke her water. She gasped, feeling the rush of fluid and tried to sit up. "What was that?"

"It was just your water breaking," he replied, glancing over to the machines and nodded. "All right, I'm going to have you push. When you do, tuck your chin down, and bear down with your abdominal muscles, can you do that for me?"

"Uh-huh," she panted, feeling another series of contractions.

"Okay, push," he instructed, everyone bracing as she bore down, pushed to the count of ten, then letting her head fall back against the pillow. "Again," he said, giving her a chance to rest to prevent her from getting dizzy. Again she pushed, then a third, and finally a fourth time before he told her to stop. Her face was red as her head fell back again and the nurse put an oxygen mask on her just for a little extra help. "Okay, rest easy. I'm going to suction her nose and mouth."

It only took moments, and she was pushing once more, but this time, there was a slight problem, and Senia had no problem in letting the staff know about it. "Does it always hurt this bad?" she screamed.

"No, but I need you to stop pushing," the doctor said. "Her shoulders are stuck."

Senia's brow twitched in annoyance. She growled as she fought back the urge to just push for all she was worth and get her out, no matter what would happen to her. Just as she was about to do so, however, she felt the pain lessen and vaguely heard the doctor's instructions to push. And push she did. With a gnarled scream and a final push, the baby was out, and Senia went limp with exhaustion.

For safe measures, she was kept on the oxygen.

"You did wonderfully," one of the midwives said softly.

"She's absolutely beautiful," the nurse said as she wrapped the fussing baby in a blanket. "We're going to take her to the nursery to get cleaned up, weighed, and measured. We'll bring her back when you're more rested all right?"

"Thank you," Senia breathed, her eyes sliding closed as sleep took her.

Hours passed, and early evening had begun to set in. Senia now sat in front of the large window, Tara bundled and resting fitfully. Their beautiful and peaceful morning had begun to turn dismal and gray with the threat of an incoming storm.

"I feel something ominous in the clouds," she said softly, drawing her daughter closer to her chest. "How about this for your first storm, Tara?" she asked as the clouds suffocated what remained of the day and the distant roll of thunder echoed around them.

She was so drawn into the storm that she almost missed the knock on her door and turned in time to see the nurse enter her room. "I'm sorry. I didn't mean to startle you."

"No, it's okay. I was just watching the storm outside. It's so . . . dark," her voice trailed off as she looked back out the window only to see that the storm had completely surrounded them.

She chose to stay quiet about her feelings concerning the energy of the storm for fear of being branded a fool or overreacting.

"Well, that's the reason I'm here," the nurse admitted. "We're taking all the babies back to the nursery. They're calling for some fairly extreme weather, and it will be easier to care for them if the power goes out, if they're all in one area."

"I understand," Senia replied as she placed a gentle kiss upon Tara's head then handed the dozing infant to the nurse.

Once the two were gone, Senia took a blanket from her bed and sat back in the reclining chair she had set in front of the window. It looked black as night, even with the time of year, it should still have at least two more hours of daylight. As soon as she sat down, it was like the storm had her complete attention, its energy wrapping around her and forcing her to watch what was to unfold.

Her room lit up, dimly at first, but in time, it would light up bright as day. She watched as lightning snaked across the underbelly of the clouds like reaching hands searching, grasping for what they sought. She watched as thick bolts struck the ground with such ferocity that showers of sparks sprayed in various directions.

"This is insane," she breathed.

There should be fires everywhere with as many strikes as were hitting the ground, but it surprised her that there weren't. Again the skies lit up, and she could see the raw powers of the wind. Trees bowed under the pressure, some cracking as they tried to resist their bend. This in turn sent splintered shards of wood to the four corners of the winds. The building shook under the power of each crack of thunder, but what she found so strange was that even with the powers of the winds, the storm seemed stationary.

"How is that possible?" she whispered, completely entranced.

She was so taken by the storm that she was unaware that the power had gone out, and that the screams of another woman were echoing down the hall, masked by the roaring thunder. But suddenly, the storm stopped. Thunder still echoed, and the clouds still lit up, all be it internally unlike before, but Senia was drawn in enough that she could feel the energy building. She didn't dare blink, and even her breathing seemed to slow. She seemed so in tune to the storm that she could feel the oppression, the need for release . . . the darkened hatred. "What is it waiting for?"

Somewhere in the depths of her mind, she thought she heard the cries of a baby coming into the world. This seemed to be the catalyst the storm needed, and suddenly it was like the maw of hell opening. Torrents of water flooded down from the skies that lit up with fiery fury while thunder threatened to rip through the ears of all who listened. Through the blinding light that filled the skies, she could see the slow roll of the clouds as they moved on, but as they did, the dread that filled her continued to grow, and with a searing crack of thunder, powerful enough to shake her to her core, she dove from the chair, ripped from her transfixed state, and was instantly under the blankets, where she waited out the remainder of the storm.

Two days later, Senia found herself standing in front of the large pane window. Her nerves had finally settled, and she was looking forward to going home the next day. Everyone was extremely nice, but she was starting to feel closed in. Cop mentality, she called it. Or that was what she was blaming it on. As she stared off into the distance, she searched for any signs of the storm's wrath. A fallen tree, busted buildings, tossed cars . . . something. Something that would tell her that she wasn't losing her mind. But there was nothing.

"It's frighteningly . . . perfect," she mumbled as she began chewing nervously on the nail to her right thumb. But she knew what she saw. Churning winds, drowning seas of water, lightning that should have set the whole city ablaze with furious hatred. But what was lain before her was serene perfection. "It's not right . . . it can't be." Or had the storm taken such a hold of her mind that . . . "No way," she said, shaking her head furiously, refusing to believe something so outlandish. "That's just insanity," she said with a sound nod as she spun on her heels and walked to the nursery to retrieve Tara for some quality time with her daughter.

"We have a beautiful indoor garden in the center of the wing, if you want a change of scenery," the nurse said as she handed Senia her daughter.

"That sounds nice," she said with a smile as she stared down into the endless emerald pools of her daughter's eyes. "Would you like that, Tara?" she asked as she brushed some brunette locks from her face.

She received a contented squirm and what she could only assume was a smile and that was that. She thanked the nurse and was on her way. Moments later she was in the mid of the most wonderful thing she'd ever seen. So many varieties of plants and trees. Fragrant flowers filled the room with the most relaxing scents. Ponds and small waterfalls added to the atmosphere. Perfection topped it with the small speakers planted in various places that played songs from various species of birds since keeping real ones just wasn't practical with parents bringing new babies in here.

Senia finally started to relax, forgetting the events the night that her daughter was born. Sinking back into the bench, she closed her eyes and took in the sounds and scents around her.

"Excuse me."

The voice startled Senia from her thoughts as her head shot up, her sapphire eyes flickering open to behold the voice's owner.

"I'm sorry. I didn't mean to startle you."

Senia focused on the woman before her. Tan skin, jet black hair, dark, striking eyes, eyes that seemed to pull her in. Her mind was momentarily lost, but she shook her head quickly and sat up straight. "No, you're fine," she assured with a smile. "This place seems to have a life of its own, almost enchanting."

"It is quite amazing how they managed to create such a sanctuary in a place like this," the woman said as she took the seat Senia offered after scooting over. "I'm Yukino, by the way," she said, holding out her hand.

"Senia," she replied, taking the offered hand, her eyes shifting to the child she was holding. "He's a handsome little guy."

Yukino smiled with pride. "Thank you. This is my son, Darius. He was born the night of the storm." She then caught sight of the little girl and was just as fixated. "She's beautiful."

Senia blushed and stared down at her daughter. "This is my daughter, Tara. She was born just before the storm started moving in."

"Aww, they're practically twins," Yukino said as she held Darius so the two could see each other.

Hours passed as the two conversed, sharing childhood stories and various portions of their past. They'd even found out that they currently lived just houses from each other.

"You should come over some time," Senia said as she stood to stretch.

"We will," Yukino said with a warm smile. The two bade their farewells. Senia returned to her room to pack and rest while Yukino remained in the gardens with Darius, humming softly, a tune she was taught when she was young.

Months passed. The two were discharged and returned home to lead their respective lives. Each made good on promises made to visit, and the two quickly became close friends.

One balmy day in the middle of summer, Senia stood in the kitchen washing some plates after a lunch visit from her parents. A jug of tea sat steeping in the window, and Tara was in her room napping. Days off were a rare and welcomed thing for her, and she planned on making the best of it.

"Today would be perfect for a swim.," she mused, staring out at the inviting crystal waters of her pool. Tara was old enough now that she could stay in the play pen and keep busy. "Well, that's that then," she declared to the window in front of her. "Time for a much needed swim.

She walked to her room and put on some music, sliding some of her favorite CDs into the multidisc changer then hitting Play and Shuffle.

"Better," she said as she rummaged through the drawer she kept all her suits in until she held one up in her hands. She inspected it, scrunched her brow, then nodded. "This'll do," she declared as she changed.

Standing in front of the full-length mirror, she inspected herself. She'd lost most of the baby weight she'd put on, not that she gained much, but the way she looked in the crimson bikini she'd chosen for herself pleased her.

"Not bad," she said as she plastered her hands on her hips.

Turning up the music, she switched the speakers to play both in and outside so she had something to listen to while she swam. Tying a wrap around her waist she grabbed some quilts and a few toys for Tara to play with, taking them outside and setting them in neatly.

Just as she'd made it back into the kitchen and had reached for the jug of tea, she heard the doorbell ring. Tilting her head, she tried to figure out who'd be paying her a visit. She wouldn't see her parents again until she dropped Tara with them the next day, and she wasn't expecting anyone. Securing the wrap around her waist, she threw on a loose button down shirt and headed for the door.

"Senia!"

"Yukino!" Senia replied with a laugh. "How are you? Come in, come in," she said, nearly dragging the two into the house. She shed the shirt and tossed it over the back of a plush recliner then motioned for her to follow. "What have you been up to? I haven't seen you guys in a while."

"I'm sorry. The company I work for was being faced with a huge lawsuit, so the entire legal department was made to work overtime to get everyone ready. We only finished a couple of days ago—by the grace of whatever being rules the universe." The two shared a small laugh before Yukino took notice of her friend's attire. "Oh, I'm sorry. I didn't realize you had plans. I can always come back later."

"No way," Senia said with a shake of her head. "With the weeks you've had, you need this as much as I do."

"But I don't have a suit or anything," Yukino said.

"That's okay. You can borrow one of mine." She'd let her get no further and dragged both her and Darius down the hall to her room. Once there, she swept Darius into her arms and opened the drawer that contained all of her swim suits. "Here, take your pick."

"Are you sure?"

Senia began to laugh. "Of course. Now hurry, it's not like this perfect day will last forever." With the speakers still echoing the music, Senia began dancing in slow circles with Darius while Yukino rummaged around, looking for a swim suit that she liked.

Yukino stood suddenly with a slightly upturned brow then slowly looked over her shoulder. "You seriously have a pink swim-suit?" She could only hold the seriousness to her face for so long before erupting into a fit of laughter.

"Yeah . . . about that," she began with a hint of flush to her cheeks but Yukino only shook her head.

"It's okay, I've done stupid stuff too," she said, calming the laughter as she continued looking. She then held up a sleek black one piece with a deep v cut in the front, low cut in the back, and cut high over the curve of the hip bones. She looked it over and nodded. "What do you think?" she asked as she turned around seeing Senia and Darius dancing again.

"I like it." She beamed before turning Darius around. "What do you think kiddo?" to which they got content cooing as the response. "I guess that settles it."

"As long as this is the only aspect of my wardrobe that he chooses. Gods only know what he'd decide on for every day wear." Yukino then disappeared into the bathroom to change. She listened to the music as she adjusted the suit until it fit perfectly then exited, rolling her eyes at the whistles Senia was teasing her with. "I'm so glad you approve," she sneered, taking Darius from her and resting him upon her left hip. She then looked up to one of the speakers before they left the room to grab towels, Tara, and their drinks. "I really like the music you have playing. What is it?"

"Just a mix of different bands that I've always been able to relax to." She then leaned over Tara's crib and scooped her up. "Even though crime is going down, the violence behind it seems to be getting worse so the music really comes in handy for relaxing."

"Well, I'm glad you have a positive outlet." Yukino said as the two entered the kitchen. Senia grabbed the jug of tea and the glasses while Yukino grabbed the metal cylinder of ice. Between the two of them, they managed to get everything outside and where it was supposed to be without dropping anything.

"We make a good team," Senia said with a grin as they put the kids in the play pen.

Yukino nodded as the two walked to the edge of the pool. While Senia opted to diving right in, Yukino decided to wade in. Senia emerged running the flats of her palms through her hair to press out some of the water just as Yukino quickly dunked under. "I have a question," she said as she surfaced, the water running down her face only to rejoin the collective body of water they were in. "if you don't mind, that is."

"Not at all, what's on your mind?" Senia asked as she swam over to her friend.

"I know it sounds dark, but, with your line of work, do you ever think of the possibility that Tara might lose you?"

Senia folded her arms as she propped them on the edge of the pool and thought. "Well, it's always a possibility," she began, listening as the cd changed and a bit heavier set of music began to filter through. "But I try not to dwell on it, especially at work. A distraction like that only escalates the chances of that becoming a reality instead of a constant thought."

She watched Yukino nod, but she then smiled and splashed her with a swift sweep of her arm through the water. "Besides.," she said as Yukino wiped the water from her eyes, "if anything were to happen to me, I have plans lined up so that Tara is well taken care of."

Speaking of the kids made the two look back over toward them, especially since they really hadn't made too much noise. "Oh, how adorable," Yukino said softly. Tara had curled up against Darius and fallen asleep as had Darius fallen asleep curled up around her.

The rest of the day went smoothly. Senia fixed them a light dinner and the two reclined in the lawn chairs as the sun began to dip into the horizons, awakening the creatures of the night, their songs lighting up the evening. "This was definitely a perfect day," she said as she stretched out.

"It really was. Thank you so much for having us."

"Think nothing of it," Senia replied with a wave of her hand." I'm just glad you agreed to it," she finished with a large grin.

The stars were beginning to reveal themselves in the heavens and Yukino gave a soft sigh as she sat up. "It's starting to get late. I should get going. The briefing for the trial is tomorrow."

"That's fine," Senia replied as they scooped the children into their arms and headed into the house. "I should probably go that way myself. We have a drug raid set for some time tomorrow," she said with a roll of her eyes.

Yukino slid her clothes on over the swimsuit while Senia put Tara down for the night. "I'll wash this and bring it back," she said as her friend emerged back into her room.

"Nah, keep it. For some reason, it looks way better on you."

Yukino blushed as she held Darius. "Only if you're sure.," she began only to be cut off with a nod and a laugh as they walked toward the door.

"Don't worry, you saw the contents of the drawer. I won't miss it."

Quick chatter of upcoming plans faded into farewells for the night. Senia watched as Yukino faded into the darkness of the night before shutting and locking her door, but as each retired for the night, neither of them knew just how intertwined their lives would become in the years ahead.

CHAPTER

2

Blurring the Lines

A s the years passed, the bond between the four only grew stronger.
They considered each other family, and even Senia's parents had
taken to Darius and offered to watch them on the days they would
take away from the office. One spring morning, Senia and Yukino
decided to take the kids to the park. While the children ran around,
on, and through the various toys provided, their parents sat and
talked. Senia stared up at a passing cloud, the odd silence catching
her friend's attention. "Something up?" Yukino asked.

Senia seemed reluctant to answer but there were things on her
mind that she wasn't sure about. "Can I ask you something?" she
asked, finally lowering her gaze to her friend, flickering between her
and Tara.

"You know you can ask me anything." Yukino assured, leaning
forward a bit, giving her full attention. She noticed the gaze and her
own trailed to Tara before fixing back to Senia.

Senia's voice fell, her tone hushed, her eyes darting, making sure
that there was no chance anyone could hear what she was going to
say. "I . . . I think there might be something wrong with Tara."

Yukino sat up, her brow creased as she took in what she had just heard. "What are you talking about? She seems fine."

"Well, that's just it," Senia confessed. "I'm not really sure what's wrong, but lately, she's been asking me about these doors that just don't exist, asking if I know where they go. When I tell her that she's just seeing things, or it's just her imagination, she starts getting upset. She'll say I'm calling her a liar, or that I don't believe her." She paused as she looked back to see Tara and Darius still playing. "It's getting to the point where I'm starting to wonder if I should take her to a psychiatrist."

Yukino arched a brow at the extreme measures she was willing to take and softly shook her head. She'd always felt that there was something special about Tara, and the tales that were being spun before her now only cemented that suspicion into fact. "Before we get that drastic, why don't you let me talk to her. Maybe an extra set of ears would help gain some understanding and find how best to dissolve the situation."

Senia's eyes lit up and she clasped her hands over Yukino's. "Would you mind? I really don't know what to do about this, and it just seems to get worse."

"Shh, just let me take care of things, okay?" Yukino's voice was calm, and Senia seemed to relax almost instantly. Moving from the current topic, the two talked about possible plans for the summer.

Unaware of what was going on, Darius and Tara ran around, under, over, up, and down whatever they could, racing down a bumpy slide, across monkey bars, leaping over tires, before finally ending at the swings. Tara leaped into hers first, closely followed by Darius, each determined to out swing the other. "I'm gonna go higher!" she declared as she kicked her feet as hard as she could.

"No way," Darius said as he too kicked his feet as hard as he could. "You're a girl, you can't win."

"Says you." She scowled. "Besides, I'm older than you."

"But that doesn't make you better."

"Well, it should." Tara was so caught up in their debate that she didn't notice the door before her until she'd almost made good on her declaration. But once her brain registered what she was seeing, her feet stopped kicking, and she began to slow, swinging lower and lower as she stared.

"What is it?" Darius asked, his gaze following hers as he too slowed his swing down to match hers.

Tara just pointed at the area in front of her. "There, do you see that?" she asked, fear and hope fighting inside of her, begging silently for validation that she really was seeing these . . . doors.

"You mean the door?" he asked. "Of course I do. But you sound pretty surprised that you see them though."

"No," she began, staring at the ground, still swinging lightly. "It's not that. I've seen them for as long as I can remember, but Mom doesn't see them. She tells me I'm imagining them, but when I try to tell her that I'm not, she gets mad and tells me to stop. I didn't think anyone else could see them, so I started thinking that it was just my imagination."

"Nah." The ease in which he spoke of this put her at ease and the two once more resumed their competition as to who could swing higher. "Mom calls it a special sight, stuff that only a few people have, so people who don't have it don't understand it."

"Why just a few?" Tara asked as she leaned forward and back, gaining speed to go higher.

"Not sure." Darius replied, trying to match her movements. "But Mom says that because not many people have it, that we shouldn't talk about it."

"Not to anyone?" Tara asked, fearing that they would now be in trouble for doing just that.

But Darius just laughed. "No, just with other people who have that special sight too."

Tara's brows merged. "So how will I know who I can talk to about this?"

Darius just shrugged. "I don't know. Mom says that you just know."

Tara rolled her eyes. "You don't know much, do you?" she asked with a grin that just fueled his attempt to beat her.

"More than you," came the quick retort, and the competition was back in full swing.

"You wish," Tara said with a roll of her eyes.

"Betcha I do!" he argued back.

"Okay, fine. Then where do these doors go to," she asked, her eyes boring into him for answers.

Again, Darius shrugged. "Mom says they go to this place called the Astral Realm, but she says I'm still too young to go there." The last part was said with a scowl of his own as he dug the toe of his foot into the sand on a downward thrust which sent a spray of sand out before them in the upward arch.

"Sounds interesting," Tara said, seeming to let the subject fall for the time being.

"I'm sure Mom will talk to you about it, especially once she finds out that her feelings about you were right."

"That'd be nice having a grown-up who actually believes me." The conversation ended there and the two moved on to more exciting topics, focusing on what they could do over the upcoming spring break.

That night Senia and Tara met her parents for dinner. Talk was business as usual, which bored the child to tears and she began to fidget more than half way through the meal. "Tara please behave." Senia said in a low tone.

"I'm bored," she said, her voice hinging on whining.

"We'll be going soon, I promise." Senia assured. "Just please . . ."

"Is everything all right, dear?" The sound of her mother's voice broke the scolding and Senia looked up.

"Sorry, Mom. Tara's just getting tired."

"We can always talk later," her mother said, touching the back of her husband's hand. Her father nodded and paid the check.

Farewells were made and the group parted their separate ways. Senia headed toward their house and sighed, looking in the rear view mirror at her daughter. "You've never acted like this with your grandparents. What's up, kiddo?"

"I'm just tired," she said halfheartedly. In truth, since she and Darius talked at the park, all she could think about were the doors that they see and this Astral Realm place that they led to.

"We'll be home soon," she said as she focused on the road again.

Minutes later they were pulling into the drive. Tara yawned as she got out of the car, her eyes droopy and her feet were shuffling against the pavement. "You really are tired." Senia said as she scooped Tara up and carried her off to bed. She helped her change and tucked her in, kissing the top of her head. "Sleep well my angel."

The next morning Senia dropped Tara off with Yukino. Darius ran out the door waving. "Tara!"

"Hi, Darius!"

"Thanks so much for watching her Yukino. Mom and Dad got called in for some board meeting and I couldn't call off work."

"Think nothing of it," Yukino assured as they watched the kids run inside. "This will give me a chance to talk to Tara."

"That would be great." The two hugged, and Senia was off to work.

Yukino walked back into the house and into the kitchen. She retrieved some drinks and breakfast for the three of them. The smells of bacon cooking with eggs, hash browns, and toast began to drift throughout the house closely followed by the sounds of soft singing. "Wow, your mom has a really pretty voice," Tara whispered, hearing the movement approaching closer until Yukino appeared with their breakfast in hand.

"All right you two." Yukino started as she set down the tray and began dishing up their breakfast. "Eat up." They each took their plates and began to eat. Yukino herself sat back into the couch, regarding the girl that sat before her. "Tara?"

Tara looked up and blinked several times. "Yes, ma'am?"

"Your mother asked if I would talk to you." She chose her words carefully. She didn't want to say something that could possibly upset her. "She says that sometimes you see things."

Tara was a little prepared for this thanks to her talk with Darius at the park and just nodded. "Darius says he sees them too. He kind of told me about them."

"Embellished with his own imagination I'm sure," Yukino said light heartedly.

"Thanks," Darius said with a scowl, ignoring the giggles from his friend.

Returning to a semiserious state, Yukino decided that this would be a good time to teach the both of them. "The doors you see, do you know what they're for?"

"Not really. Darius mentioned where they go, but nothing really more than that," Tara answered, turning her body to fully face Yukino.

She nodded, her mind darting between thoughts. "Well, the doors we see here, lead to a place called the Grey Plains."

"The Grey Plains?" Tara asked. "Darius said it went to something else."

"One step at a time dear," she said in a soothing tone.

Tara nodded, her hands folded in her lap. "So what are the Grey Plains?"

"For those who can see the doors, whether it be through conscious sight or through meditation, the Grey Plains are used as a form of travel. Most people use them to check on loved ones, though there are the few who use them for darker intentions."

"Hurting people?" Tara asked.

"I'm afraid so," Yukino replied. "But that's talk for when you're a bit older."

"What do they look like?"

"Gray, duh." Darius said before he started laughing.

"Darius," his mother warned, her look being enough to quiet him. "The Grey Plains is an area covered in a rolling fog. There's no day, no night. If you remember what it looks like during a rain storm, that's pretty much what the skies look like there."

"Soooo, if all the doors lead to one place, why are there so many?" Tara asked.

"Because each door leads to a different place throughout the Plains."

"Ohhhh." Tara sort of understood, but she was very eager to hear more.

"The Grey Plains border a place known as the Astral Realm, a land much like here, but time goes by much slower than it does here and the use of energy and the powers of the Elements are quite common."

Tara's brow quirked. "Huh."

"Most here would call it magic."

"Ohhh! I get it now!" Tara exclaimed, quite proud that she was grasping what she was being told. "So why can some people see these doors and others can't?"

"There's so many reasons that people give. The most popular school of thought centers on the idea that people with heightened mental senses are the ones who are able to see these doors."

"Mental . . . senses?" Tara asked.

"Like being a true psychic, or an empath," Yukino explained.

Tara's eyes lit up. "So I'm psychic?"

Darius laughed. "Don't be stupid."

Tara glowered and pegged the side of his head with a ball that was on the floor. "Shut up. How do you know I'm not?"

"All right, you two, please." Yukino asked. Only after they settled down did she continue. "Like the doors here, there are many doors in the Grey Plains, each leading to different places within the Astral Realm."

"What does that look like?" Tara prodded.

"It's different, ever changing. There can be dead forests, endless chasms, rolling dunes, empty plains. It really all depends on which door you enter through."

"So can everyone who sees the doors here, go through the doors to the Astral Realm?"

"I'm afraid not," Yukino said with a slow shake of her head.

"Well, why not?"

"The Astral Realm is an intense place. A lot of fighting takes place there. Only those with a purpose there will be allowed through."

"Have you been?" Tara and Darius asked in unison.

"I have, but those are stories that you don't need to hear."

"Awwwww." They both pouted, once again echoing each other.

"No," Yukino said again. "Now, the last thing I'll tell you before we stop for the day, is that no matter what, do *not*, enter through the doors until I've been able to train you, especially how to protect yourself while you're there."

"I promise," Tara said, raising her right hand.

Yukino smiled. Such promise the both of them held. She would be proud to teach them both. But she figured that was enough information to bombard them with for one day so she allowed them to play, ending with the art of finger painting. Late afternoon brought the familiar sound of Senia's car pulling into the drive. "Tara," Yukino called over her shoulder.

"Mama!" Tara exclaimed, running for the door, arms outstretched to reveal the paint coating her hands.

Senia laughed as she stepped out of the way and patted the top of her head. "Go wash up honey." The two watched as Tara and Darius raced to see who could get to the bathroom first. Tara squeaked in and closed the door with her foot and the two women watched as Darius ran face first into it.

"You cheated!" he declared.

"Whatever," came the reply from behind the closed door. "You're just a sore loser, especially since you ran into the door." The end of her sentence was met with a fit of giggles and answered with a growl.

Senia had to laugh before taking the chance to speak with Yukino. "Did you get a chance to talk to her?" Her voice was hushed as she spoke, knowing Darius was still in the hall, pounding on the door, demanding to be let into the bathroom.

"Everything is taken care of," Yukino assured just as the announcement that Darius was going to break down the door brought them from their conversation. "Darius!"

But it was too late. Darius was already charging the door, shoulder tucked down as he prepared for the encounter. But just as he was about to hit it, Tara opened the door, leaping to the side to avoid the collision. Everyone watched as Darius tripped over his feet and sprawled out across the bathroom floor. Tara just blinked and stepped past him. "Idiot," she said, shaking her head before running up to Senia and hugging her tightly. "I missed you, Mom!" she exclaimed with bright eyes.

Senia smiled and wrapped her arm around Tara's shoulders. "Well, why don't we head home so Yukino can clean Darius up, hm?"

"Okay," she said before hugging Yukino tightly. "Thank you," she said with a warm smile.

"You're very welcome Tara," Yukino replied, waving as the two left before she tended to her son.

When Tara and Senia got home, Tara bolted from the car and into the house. The two had decided on pasta for dinner, and Tara went digging through the pantry for the noodles and sauce while Senia got the bread and the meat balls from the freezer. "Thank you for your help. Why don't you go read the new book I bought you. Dinner will be ready in about an hour."

"Okay." Tara skipped down to her room and flopped onto her bed. Grabbing her book, she began to read, but the words seemed to slip through her mind as it was constantly drawn by the conversation with Yukino earlier in the day. She soon found herself staring outside through her window, her eyes fixated upon the door nestled within the trees just to the right of the pool. "As soon as I'm sure Mom's asleep," she whispered, leaving the sentence unfinished.

She knew she'd promised, but the pull was too great, especially for one as young as she was. "Besides," she said to the window in front of her. "Why shouldn't I see what I'm going to be getting myself into?" So the matter was settled. Once Senia was asleep, she would see just where her door would lead her.

Dinner went smoothly. Senia hated bringing her work home with her so she always focused on Tara, asking her an array of questions both to distract her and because she was genuinely interested in her daughter's life. "What did you three do today?"

Tara went into a detailed account of what happened, omitting the talk about energy and the Astral Realm, but as the evening wore on, she could tell that her mother was getting tired. She'd even caught her head bobbing. "Mama, why don't you go lay down. You're falling asleep."

"I'm sorry, honey. I don't know why I'm so tired."

"You're working a lot. Let me take care of putting dinner away and the dishes. You need rest."

Senia sighed as she pushed from the table and kissed the top of Tara's forehead. "You're too grown up for being as young as you are."

"Am not." Tara just grinned and started laughing.

"I was lucky when the Gods blessed me with you," she said before heading to her room.

Tara just rolled her eyes. "Oh, quit." But all she heard was her mother's soft chuckle echo down the hall.

She made a face as she turned to the sink, putting the dishes in before putting the remainder of their dinner away.

"Cold spaghetti for breakfast . . . yum!" she exclaimed happily.

She finished the dishes and ran the dish washer and shut the lights off before creeping down the hall to her mothers' room. Poking her head into her room, she listened to the soft sounds of her mother sleeping, excitement growing with each soft snore that fell upon her ears. But she would wait.

"Just a bit longer," she whispered, backing to her room. There was no way she wanted her mother to wake up for this.

When she figured enough time had passed, she crept from her room and down the hall. Leaving the lights off, she made her way to and through the kitchen, leaving the back door open so the sound of it closing wouldn't wake her mother. Skirting the edge of the pool, she made her way to the small cluster of trees where the door was hidden, her door.

"No turning back," she whispered as she reached for the door.

She gripped the handle, turned it, and flung the door open, her jaw falling at what lay before her.

CHAPTER

3

Nowhere to Hide

Fog spilled around her feet as she stared through the door. A whole new world was now opened to her. It took all her will not to squeal and end things before they could even begin. Taking a few breaths to quell the growing excitement, she stepped through, guided somehow by some unseen force. Dead tree stumps arose from the mists casting crawling shadows that seemed to twist and reach as the fogs rolled through in silence.

"How creepy," she whispered, as if something unseen would hear her. "But wonderful too."

Her feet continued to move on their own accord as she strived to take it all in, sweeping her fingers through the mist, against the rough bark of the trees. But then she saw it, another door. It seemed to emerge from nowhere, looming over the fog and casting its own reaching shadow, calling to her in silence, beckoning her ever closer.

She came to stop before the door, staring up at the ornately carved frame. Vines and flowers decorated it, giving an inviting air, calling to her, urging her to continue. It was this feeling that coaxed her to pull on the handle.

"Nothing happened here, so what could happen through there?" It was perfect logic for a kid, and it was all she needed to let the door swing open as she stepped out of the way. Tara saw nothing that even closely resembled her home.

Stepping through the door she took stock in what she saw. The moon shone very full and very bright, revealing to her what looked like a lifeless landscape. Dead trees broke through a parched, cracked earth, their gnarled branches reaching for salvation that was long since denied them.

She caught some movement from the corner of her eye and spun quickly though she saw nothing living. All that surrounded her were the twisted shadows cast from the haunting sphere above her. She shuddered and drew back. "Their shadows almost look alive." It was enough to make her blood run cold, but not enough to break the pull that continually led her toward destinations unknown. It felt like someone was there, even though she couldn't see them. "Where are you!" she shouted to empty space. "Where are you taking me!" But her echoed voice fell once more into silence.

Her shoulders slumped in disappointment as she continued on her way. "This is nothing like what Yukino told us. There's nothing magical about this at all."

She'd expected mages, wizards, dragons—things from myth and legends. Not dead trees in the middle of a desert. Time crawled on. Things looked so much alike that she had actually quit paying attention. Instead, she just stared at the ground, looking up only when she felt that nagging feeling that she wasn't alone. She hadn't even realized that things were beginning to show small signs of life instead of the hollow skeletons she'd seen when she'd first arrived. Instead of the sparse trees that dotted the landscape, trees were now growing in small groups with tufts of grass around them. It was one of these patches that caught her attention as the blades tickled the underside of her foot since her eyes hadn't really registered their presence.

Now, she paid attention, looking around to see the steady changes. She saw that not only were the trees looking more lively, but that more were growing together and that the small patches of grass that were nothing more than spotty at best, were now more pronounced, spreading over wider areas. But the further she walked the less light she saw. Chancing a glance skyward she saw the overhanging branches blotting out the moonlight.

"They look like hands," she said with a shiver, but they permitted just enough light that she could find her way without falling. After a while she could see the break in the trees and beyond that, the bright light of the moon. Filled with relief, she broke into a run, stopping only when she breached the tree line, gasping at the sight that lay before her.

What she saw was nothing short of amazing, something that should have come from an elaborate fairy tale. A lush meadow stretched out as far as she could see, stirred by only the slightest breeze which carried on it, the faint scent of flowers. The faint sound of a running stream echoed through the silence, the first sound since she'd begun her exploration. She gave a relieved sigh, for even this small sound brought ease to her tense energy. But what had stolen her breath and made her stare in awe, was the sight of a large lake. From her current position, it appeared to be at least a good mile away, though through sheer size it appeared much closer. The surface of the lake rippled and glittered against the light of the moon like it was reflecting off millions of gems.

She took a couple of slow steps forward. "Darius is never going to believe this." Her voice was half giggles, a combination of excitement and nerves. She still hadn't seen anyone yet and that thought began to bother her some. But if this place was as vast as Yukino had told her, she was sure to find someone sooner or later. She started walking again, still guided by an unseen force that led her to an outcropping of rocks that overlooked the entire meadow. "It's huge," she breathed. As she sat down she realized that the pull she'd been feeling no longer had a hold over her. Her brows merged as she looked around more carefully. "This is kinda weird," she said as she ran her hands along her arms. "Why would I be led here?"

No sooner had she spoken those words that a warm aura surrounded her, setting her fully at ease. "Perhaps it was your fate to find this place," came a voice from behind her.

With the energy around her, she wasn't afraid. She simply rose to her feet and turned around to behold the man standing before her. He was tall with long, unbound silver hair. "Who are you?"

The man chuckled and gave a deep bow. "Forgive me. Allow me to introduce myself. My name is Arcainous."

Tara watched as strands of silver hair fell into his face and over his shoulders, staring at him with a sense of wonder.

"I'm Tara," she finally replied, hands placed firmly upon her hips in triumph. She studied him closely, her brows creasing as she fixated upon his eyes. "What's wrong with your eyes?" she asked, leaning in closer to further inspect them, her eyes squinting as she continued to study him.

Arcainous had leaned in, looking at her just as intently, until she asked about his eyes. He stood upright and tilted his head as he regarded what he was asked. "There's nothing wrong with my eyes. They have always looked like this."

Tara's brows creased further. "But people's eyes aren't supposed to look like that though." She'd seen enough to know, and this fact, in her mind, made her an expert as to how people's eyes should appear.

"I'm Lycan," Arcainous replied.

"You're . . . like-in . . . what?" she asked, the vacancy in her gaze revealing her lack of knowledge about the Lycan race.

"No," he said, trying not to laugh. "Werewolf."

But all this did was warp the conversation into a whole new direction as the look of unmasked horror crossed her face. "You . . . you wear clothes made from wolves?" Her eyes grew round, glazing over with tears while her lip began to quiver. "I don't think I like-in you anymore!" she shouted.

Arcainous was dumbfounded at this point. How could this child have absolutely no knowledge of his race? Most everyone who traveled through these lands knew of his clan of wolves and what they were. He gave a gruff sigh and ran his fingers through the long silvery strands of hair hanging into his face, but before he could explain further, he found himself interrupted. "Arcainous!"

The two turned to see someone else running toward them. Tara studied him, noting that he resembled Arcainous, though he looked much younger with flowing black hair bound tightly at the base of his skull.

"Belzak," Arcainous strode forward to meet his companion. "What's going on?"

Catching a brief glance of the child, Belzak lowered his voice. "The scouts found an open door leading from here to the Grey Plains."

"Noteworthy," Arcainous said as the two returned to where they'd left Tara. "But that's not too much cause for alarm."

"Perhaps. But they explored further and found an open door from the Grey Plains into the physical realm." Now this, was much more cause for alarm. Some of the things that wander through the Realms did not need to be set loose on the physical plain. Only then did he openly acknowledge the child standing just behind Arcainous. "Who's that?" he asked, with a sweep of his head in her direction.

Arcainous stepped back and held his hand out. "This is Tara. She's a visitor to our world."

This didn't catch his attention much. There were many who traveled into their world for various reasons. All had a purpose, but he was surprised that someone so young had found their way here. Belzak nodded to her and smiled before returning to his previous conversation. "What do you want us to do?"

"We need a group to track through the Grey Plains to make sure no one has gotten out, and if they have, destroy them. Send another group to the physical plain to make sure things have gone no further."

"Right away." Belzak replied. He was about to change and warn the others when the sound of low growls caught everyone's attention.

What they all saw first were several pairs of glowing red eyes staring at them. "This isn't good." Arcainous said as he and Belzak moved closer, blocking Tara from what was now before them.

"A trap?" Belzak asked.

"It looks that way," Arcainous answered, though he couldn't really figure out why the two of them would be ambushed, or by whom.

"What would they be after?" Belzak asked.

Arcainous looked over his shoulder to see Tara cowering behind them, shrinking back as the eyes began getting closer. Hounds began to materialize from the shadows, the moonlight only adding a depth to the glow that their eyes emitted. Tara saw that they were much larger than even the largest dog she'd seen at home, almost the size of young bears that she had seen at the zoo. Fur bristled over pronounced muscles as snapping jaws opened to reveal fangs yellowed from lack of care, but razor sharp all the same.

"Enough!" The voice from the shadows depths drew everyone's attention from the hounds that had stopped as ordered. Displeased, they curled their upper lips over their gum lines, showing the full length of their fangs as a white foamy mucus dripped onto the ground. "I see you have found my prize." The owner of the voice emerged slowly, mounted upon the back of a black stallion whose eyes glowed just as red as the hounds. Steam billowed from flaring nostrils and as he pawed at the ground with onyx hooves his teeth gnashing upon the bit in his mouth. Tara looked past that though to the most frightening detail about the horse. She stared in complete horror as she watched any and all light as it was absorbed and destroyed by his very body as it attempted to reflect off of his coat.

"There is no prize here." Arcainous's voice was low, hard, and even.

Belzak's mind was racing, trying to remember who this was. His head finally snapped up and his eyes flickered. "Durion," he growled. "One of the champions of the Shadow Lands' armies."

"I am," he replied, his form shrouded in the darkness of crushed light. "And you two must be the leaders of the Realm Watchers, Arcainous and Belzak." He shifted and stiffened, sensing the irritation of his hounds. "Who you are is of no consequence to me however. I am here for the child, nothing more."

"What do you want with a child?" Belzak demanded. "You have enough minions."

"Why, her innocence of course," Durion mused, the smile evident in his voice. "Who do you think left the doors open, allowing my hounds to wander into the physical plain?"

Both Belzak and Arcainous looked over their shoulders. Tara wasn't moving, petrified with fear she didn't even hear what was going on between the three until the order was given to attack and grab her. Only then did she release an ear splitting scream as she fell to the ground, curled into a tight ball behind Belzak. Both men, within an instant, had abandoned their human forms only to take on their true forms. Large wolves, equally as big as the hounds that were now attacking, their snarls echoing in the once quiet space.

The grind of snapping bones made Tara whimper and twitch as the power in Arcainous's jaws came down upon the neck of one of the hounds, crushing it and killing the hound instantly. Belzak in turn sank his fangs into and through the leg of another hound, rendering it useless and unable to battle. "Get her out of here, Belzak," Arcainous ordered, blood running from his maw before he went for the throat of a third hound, ripping it from the flesh and hearing nothing but gurgled whimpers before another lifeless form hit the ground with a sloppy thud.

"You can't take them all on by yourself," Belzak protested as he reared onto his hind legs, grappling with one of the hounds only to have Arcainous tear through the hound's abdomen, eviscerating the hound completely. The sopping sound the hounds intestines made as they hit the ground made Tara turn green with the threat of vomiting.

"Don't argue with me!" he snarled.

Belzak backed down and crouched down before Tara. "Come on, kid. Climb up and hang on tight."

Tara did as she was ordered and clung for dear life to the fur on the back of his neck and the two darted off like a bullet through the trees. To his relief he could hear the sounds of some of the hounds behind him, but most significantly, he could hear the thunder of onyx hooves crushing the ground behind them. Belzak knew that now Arcainous would have a chance against the hounds that stayed behind, especially now that Durion was chasing them instead of lingering behind. Avoiding the trails that Tara had taken, he pushed forward, winding through trees, taking any abnormal pattern he could think of to try and throw the hounds off his scent. As they drew closer to the door, however, they watched as the trees dwindled into the spotty reaches of death that Tara had encountered when she'd first entered.

This left them open for attack but just as the hounds had broken through the trees the snarling of wolves echoed closely followed by whimpers and yelps as the hounds were ripped to shreds.

"Sometimes it pays to run in a pack," Belzak commented as he continued forward but all Tara could do was bury her head into the back of his neck and shake as sprays of blood revealed themselves to her sight. As the sounds of death faded Belzak listened for the sounds of Durioun's mount, but heard nothing. He knew the black rider was too smart for the pack as fragmented as it was, so the remainder of the trip toward the Grey Plains was done in silence and with as much speed as he could force from himself. Seeing the open door was nothing short of welcoming and as he raced through it he whirled around and slammed it closed.

Only then did he stop, his lungs heaving and burning as he struggled for breath. His muscles quivered from exhaustion, but he looked over his shoulder to see Tara still clinging onto him. "What were you thinking?"

Only now did Tara dare look up, seeing the rolling fog surrounding them. "What do you mean?" she asked, her voice quite small, the horror still etched across her face.

Belzak watched his temper as he continued his questioning. "What brought you here?"

"I don't know. I was curious."

"Have you been trained? Did you know you're supposed to make sure the doors are closed after you walk through them?"

"Uh . . . no. I'm eight. Besides, why is that so important?"

Why was . . . ? Really? The muscles encasing his eyes began to twitch. "Those things that are chasing us," Belzak began. "If you think they're dangerous here, they're deadlier in a world where they can't be seen."

"I didn't know."

"That's right, you didn't know." His voice was becoming harsh as his frustration began to surface.

"I'm eight!" she yelled. "I'm naturally curious!"

"This isn't something for you to be curious about!" he yelled back. "You shouldn't have come here alone. You should have had a guide for at least your first few years."

She glared, her cheeks now hot with anger at having just been yelled at by a dog of all things.

"You're not around kids much, are you?" she asked, her voice dry as her brows merged.

Belzak was caught off guard with the question. Of course he wasn't around children, but before he could say anything, the echo of growls once more resonated through the fogs. More hounds emerged, skinnier and faster than the ones they'd found earlier. In his current state of fatigue out running them would be a chore at best.

"Hang on. This isn't going to be as easy as it was last time." When he was sure she was secured, he was off again, darting through the fogs and winding around the dead tree stumps that jutted through the fog. Snarling and snapping jaws could be heard gaining behind them, but Tara just kept her head buried in the back of his neck, holding on for all she was worth. As they ran for her freedom Belzak couldn't help but wonder what had happened to Durion. There was just no way he would go to this kind of trouble to get her, just to run off.

Not long after the chase had started, Belzak saw the open door. "Oh, thank the gods," he huffed, but as he reached it, something tripped him and he sprawled out across the ground. This of course, sent Tara tumbling over the top of his head, landing unceremoniously in her backyard.

She scrambled to her hands and knees, turning around just as the mass of hounds attacked. "Belzak!" she shrieked, reaching her hand out for him.

He snapped his jaws, crushing the throat of one hound while his claws tore into several others. He looked back, his eyes piercing into hers, changing them forever. "Run!" he snarled, just as he was swallowed into the mass of hounds, the release of energy slamming the door shut.

She sat there, shaking, listening as the sounds of battle thrummed against the door, unsure of what was happening to who.

The entire ordeal held her frozen, her muscles completely detached from any form of mental process. If she could move, however, her movements would have taken her straight back to the door to try and help Belzak, even though she didn't know what she could do. It was only when she heard the barking of a neighbor's dog that she bolted to her feet and nearly flew into the house. Tearing down the hall, she dove onto her bed and under the covers where she curled tightly into a ball, holding herself just to keep her trembling down to a minimum. She wasn't sure how long she was there, but as she strained to listen all, she heard was silence. It was that moment where she decided to poke her head out from beneath the one thing that might have been keeping her safe.

It was the worst mistake she could have made, at least to her. As soon as her head cleared the blanket she heard an unmistakable growl. Her body froze, unwilling to turn her head, knowing what she would see. But as she had stated earlier, children were curious, and she slowly turned her head. The color drained from her face as she came face-to-face with a huge bulldog. His eyes were the same as the hounds but this particular dog wore a spiked collar firmly around his neck. Her voice was now lost to her as she tried to scream.

Franticly she searched for a way to escape and as she moved to leap through her window she saw the shadow of a man standing there, waiting for her to do just that. Only then did she find her voice and let out a blood curdling scream. Trapped, she scooted back into the corner of her wall, caught, with no means of escape.

She dared a look to where she saw the dog, and to her relief, it was gone. She fled from her room and headed to the one place she felt safe, her mother's room. But as she dove for the bed and the warmth of her mother she found only the chill of empty sheets. Her mind reeled at her mother's absence, unaware that she had been called out on an emergency shortly after her trek had begun. With no safety to be found anywhere she fled to her mother's closet, hiding in the furthest corner under a pile of clothes, and there she stayed until her mother found her the next morning.

As the morning dragged on the police continued combing the backyard, especially the flower bed under Tara's window. Tara clung to her mother for all she was worth as another officer approached. "Thanks for coming out so quick, Mark." Senia was holding Tara close. "Tara's absolutely terrified about what happened."

Mark nodded and crouched down to look at Tara. "Hey, kiddo." Mark decided to work on building some trust before questioning her. Tara watched him and smiled some, remembering him from several squad parties. "Did you see what the person looked like?" he asked, keeping his voice even and low. Tara just shook her head furiously and held back onto Senia. "Do you remember how tall he was?" he asked, hoping that they could get some useful information from her that would help them.

This, was something she could help with, and she pulled from her mother and Mark, climbing onto her bed. Even with the sun lighting everything, she could still see Durion's outline as if he were standing before her now. She swallowed hard as she stared at the faceless figure before her and reached for a black marker. With trembling hands she began to trace the outline Durion had left imprinted forever in her mind. When she was done she let the marker fall from her hand, uncapped, as she moved from her bed back to her mother's side. "That's him," she said quietly.

Mark knelt down beside her and rested a comforting hand on her shoulder. "That's a great job Tara. Are there any details that you can remember?"

Tara shook her head slowly before staring at the ground. "He was covered in shadows. That was all I saw."

"That's fine. You did great," Mark assured. "But I need to talk to your mom for a bit. Is that okay?"

Tara nodded and watched as he led Senia into the hall to talk. This left her with the outline of the most terrifying person she'd ever met now drawn on her window and the techs that were photographing the image. As she sat on the bed she knew that they would never find him, even with the molds the techs outside were making of his feet. There's no way to catch someone that they couldn't see.

"Senia?" The alarmed voice of a woman could be heard from the front door. Tara's head shot up suddenly as she flew from her bed, down the hall and through the door.

came back. The road would be long, but she wasn't going to push her. For her to survive an attack by one of the top champions for the Shadow Lands. There had to be something about her. Something that would make itself known in the future, or so she hoped.

CHAPTER

4

A Time to Grow

It took well over a year for Tara's nightmares to stop, but it was a welcomed relief when they did. The trauma associated with her ordeal
wove a tight shroud around what happened. She no longer remembered Arcainous or Belzak, nor did she remember her encounter with
Durion. Everything from that night was erased from her mind. With
such a wall built around her mental senses, Yukino focused on teaching Tara how to meditate while she trained Darius how to protect
himself while traveling through the Realms.

"All right, Tara, go ahead and center yourself like I've taught
you. Let your mind be at rest but be mindful of the energies around
you. I'm going to get Darius started on his training."

Darius was standing by the door into the Grey Plains. He found
that it was an ideal place to train as well as travel. Not much happened there so Yukino allowed him to venture through and practice
as he saw fit. "I'm ready, Mom."

Yukino nodded as she opened the door. "I want you to work
on your barriers like I've taught you. Around, through the ground,
a perfect sphere. Yours still break once they hit the ground. When

you've gotten that down, work on moving with it, will it to move around you as you move."

Darius nodded and looked at his mother. He wanted to ask again what had happened to Tara, but he was tired of always getting the same answer: "It was nothing," or "Don't worry about her, she's all right now." This secret had created a form of "sibling" rivalry between the two where he was always out to prove that he was the best and the fastest at learning. He always looked at her now with a sort of distain even though the two were now being trained in two different fields of the same thing. He began forming the energy as he'd been instructed and worked on pushing it through the ground. Yukino nodded and closed the door after complementing him on how quick he was able to bring the energy together for the shield. He smiled, his pride bolstered, but as the door closed, he abandoned the shield, letting the energy disappear. He had his own things he desired to work on, such as devising a way to pry all wanted information from his childhood friend.

As Yukino walked back into the house to check on Tara, she saw her staring off into space, tracing symbols absently in the air and whispering words that seemed too advanced for someone her age. "Tara?" Her voice was low and even, trying not to disturb her and jar her from something that could be important to her. But Tara did respond, her head turning as she stared with glossy eyes. "Tara, are you all right?"

"What are these pictures I'm seeing?" Tara asked. "And the words I see with them are so strange." She wasn't scared. In fact, it was quite the opposite. What she saw intrigued her. She was still in her meditative state and looked back in front of her, tracing another image in the air, repeating a separate set of words.

Yukino's eyes widened and she ran to the counter, grabbing paper and pens. Kneeling down beside her she placed them before her. She watched as Tara wrote and drew. "Those look like runes." She took one of the papers, studying it as Tara continued.

"What are runes?" she asked, her gaze still fixed upon the papers before her.

Yukino set the paper down, her features becoming thoughtful. "Runes are symbols that mean different things depending on the words written with them. Some are made to protect, while others can be used for guidance."

"Do people hurt others with them?"

"They can," Yukino admitted.

"Why did I see them?" she asked as she slowly brought herself into a more conscious state.

"Well, what were you thinking about?" Yukino asked, as she scooped the papers together and put them into a book for her.

"I was thinking about being strong enough to protect everyone close to me," Tara replied.

"Well, a person's desires can take on a form and expression that helps that person fulfill them." This brought a new understanding to Tara who was happy in the knowledge that she might soon be able to protect those who she held dear.

The two flourished and excelled in their training. By the time the two were thirteen, Darius had succeeded in creating several barriers to serve many purposes, some minor attacks using the manipulations of the energy around him, and was finishing his tracking and how to stay hidden. Tara had mastered the art of creating runes, allowing her meditations to show her what she needed to know. She had come out of the shell she'd created around herself even though the block remained firmly in place around her senses.

One winter day the two were walking home from school, their banter back and forth starting out as their typical picking at each other, though it quickly escalated. "Why won't you tell me what happened to you when we were eight."

Tara sighed. *Here we go again*, she thought as she hung her head. "I don't know what you're talking about," she said, shooting him a look.

"You do too." He shot back, his gaze hard as stone. "All you have to do is look at your eyes. They aren't normal."

"They are too!" she hissed. With her mental sight blocked, her eyes appeared just like everyone else's, but Darius and Yukino could see it quite clearly, though Yukino had long since stopped bringing it up.

"The shape is different, the color, everything! I thought I was your best friend, but I guess I was wrong."

This stung Tara quite deeply, and she stopped at the base of the drive to Darius's house. "How could you?" she said, her tone wounded. "You are my best friend, at least I thought you were." She lowered her head and walked past him to the house where her mother was waiting.

Darius grabbed her arm and pulled her back. "Hey, wait a minute."

Tara winced at the pressure placed upon her arm and tried to pull free. "Let me go!" she ordered before finally yanking her arm free. Darius glared and shoved her, causing her to cry out as she fell back, drawing the attention of their parents. Tara had just shoved him back as they ran outside to break things up.

"That is quite enough out of you two," Senia scolded.

"He started it!" Tara protested.

"Stop. I don't want to hear it," Senia interrupted while Yukino scolded Darius.

The two were grounded that very night. Senia sat on the phone with Yukino, the two trying to find where the tension had started between them. "What could have gotten into them?" Senia asked. "I haven't seen them act like that ever."

Yukino sighed heavily as she glared back over her shoulder at a sulking Darius. She knew what the fight was about and Darius knew there would be hell to pay for the constant fights he was starting about it. "I think maybe we should get them involved in activities to keep them distracted."

"I think that's a great idea, Yukino. Finding something tailored to each of them. They're getting ready to start high school, why not sports? They both show an athletic ability."

"That sounds like a wonderful idea."

"I'll stop by the school on my way home from work tomorrow then and get the sign up information. We'll have to get physicals and stuff, but we still have enough time to figure all of that out."

"I hope this works. They've been so close for so long. I'd hate for something trivial to tear them apart," Yukino said with a soft sigh.

The two talked for a bit more as Darius stomped off to his room.

He sat on his bed, staring at the wall with fixated anger. *Friends don't keep things from each other,* he repeated over in his head. He held onto that thought, obsessing over it, letting it fester within his mind. It was the type of thoughts and energies that Yukino tried keeping them from, but tonight, Darius held tight to that dark seed, letting it take root. He would become strong enough, and whether Tara liked it or not, she would tell him what happened, one way or another. And so started a dangerous trek down a very dark path.

CHAPTER

5

Lost and Found

Along with new challenges, high school presented the two with its own opportunities and adventures. Senia and Yukino made good on their promise, however, and the two were introduced into the athletic department. They each tried several sports before finding the ones that suited them the most. Darius settled on wrestling and football while Tara took to soccer and tennis. While their athletic schedule was demanding, their academics far from suffered. The rivalry that existed between the two fueled their studies, each trying to best the other which only pushed them to the top of their class by the time their freshman year had ended.

The summer didn't bring relief from work like it did for their classmates. Tara and Darius spent the beginning of their summer in intense training with Yukino. Tara spent hours in meditation, focusing on her energies which gave birth to more runes. She kept detailed notes and instructions in her journal of how to cast what she'd created. She'd finished three complete journals, surprising herself and impressing Yukino. They also held the vast amount of shields she'd managed to create, how to summon them, and how to maintain them if she was casting something else. Some even had little sketches as to how they appeared to her as they were cast.

Darius stayed outside in the yard to work on his Astral travels, but to also stay away from Tara. His school work kept him busy, but when he would do this, the thoughts from the past would often resurface. Yukino had taken to going into the Grey Plains to train him further, allowing him to sharpen his skills. He'd learned to shield other people, mirroring the inside of the shield so that if they attacked it would reflect back and injure the caster. Now he learned to reflect attacks and attack on his own using his mother both as a target as well as a teacher.

They trained hard because the second half of their summer was spent at school training for their respective sports. Practice was grueling though both of them did well enough to go against the varsity teams so no slack was given. Tara flopped down in front of her bag before downing a bottle of water.

"You're holding up well."

A voice from behind her startled her slightly, and she turned around.

"Um, thanks," Tara replied, shielding her eyes from the sun. She squinted, trying to recall the name of the girl that stood before her, but it failed her.

"Morgan," she replied, plopping down beside her.

Tara nodded and took in the girl's fair complexion and long raven hair held together in a tight bind at the base of her skull

"Tara," she replied, her voice fading.

For some reason, the way that Morgan tied her hair struck a buried thought within her, but she couldn't bring it to the surface.

"Yeah, you were the buzz of the soccer team. It's not often that a freshman even gets considered to train with the varsity team."

"Is that good?"

"Beyond!" Morgan exclaimed with a wide grin. "Coach has been talking about making you part of the starting squad."

Tara blushed. "I'm glad he thinks I'm good enough."

Morgan made a face, laughed, then waved her hand as the two watched the football team take the field to practice.

The two stayed to watch them practice. Tara because Yukino was her ride home, and Morgan because the quarterback Tyler, was one of her best friends. After about an hour though, Morgan's mother came to pick her up. She and Tara said their farewells and Tara decided to get some tennis practice in just to hit the ball around.

Afternoon had set in by the time the football team had finished with practice. It was coming closer for cuts and things were starting to get a bit ruthless. Everyone had taken notice though about how well Darius was doing against the first string and his place on the varsity team was looking promising. "Not bad."

Darius took off his helmet, facing the person who had spoken to him and nodded. "Thanks. Tyler, right?"

The boy gave a smug grin and nodded. "The one and only."

"You're a good quarterback," Darius commented, running his fingers through his hair, trying in some vain attempt to put it in place.

"You're not so bad yourself," Tyler said as he poured some water over his head and down his face. "It was pretty intense watching you run the ball. It was like everyone was just bouncing off you as you plowed through 'em."

Darius just laughed. "Well, Tara always said that running into me was like bouncing off a brick wall."

"Tara?" Tyler asked. "You mean the girl who's always around you."

"Yeah. She and I have been friends since we were small."

The two walked, talking sports and work outs. After a quick shower and change they emerged outside the gym. "So where is she?"

This he wasn't sure about, and he looked around before hearing several grunts echoed only by the smack of a ball hitting the wall. The two headed around to the side of the building and found Tara assaulting a tennis ball, hitting it as hard as she could before moving with the ease of a cat to hit it once more. "Wow, what'd that ball ever do to you?" he asked, watching as she gave it one final beat, causing the poor thing to pop before falling to the ground with a lifeless thud.

"Nothing," Tara replied, turning around to size the two with an innocent smile.

Tyler shook his head and laughed. "Remind me never to get in the way of one of your swings." But before Tara could answer, he clasped his hand on Darius's shoulder. "See you at practice, man." He then turned and headed toward his car.

Darius walked up to the deflated tennis ball and picked it up, tossing it a few times into the air before catching it. "What's on your mind?" he asked, holding the ball in view.

"Nothing," she lied.

In truth, she was thinking about the flicker of the image she'd see when Morgan sat beside her. "Shouldn't we get to the parking lot? Your mom should be here soon right?"

The topic was dropped for the time being, but Darius wasn't going to let it go so easily. That night, Tara sat on her bed with her journal in her lap. She drew what she could remember, then jotted some notes down beside it. It frustrated her that it nagged at her mind and she finally resigned herself to the fact that she might have known her in an earlier year of school.

As the summer neared its end, so did the seemingly endless practices that they were made to endure. But as the camps drew to their close, they noticed that people in suits, or polo shirts and slacks started hanging around.

"Who are they?" Tara asked as she slid her shin guards on.

"College scouts," Morgan replied. "They always come around toward the end of the summer, watching all the seniors to see if any of them look promising for what they want. If they find someone, they go to the games and watch them more. If they're impressed, they try offering them a scholarship to get them to go to their school. If you ask me though, I don't think half of them care about academics as much as they do about sports."

Tara watched as they gathered, clip boards in hand as they tapped pens against their chins. "They seem too uptight if you ask me."

Morgan laughed as they took to the field, each doing their best to show that they were a cut above everyone else. But every time that Tara had the ball she always seemed to be able to weave between everyone with great ease, always putting the ball where it needed to be. "She's pretty good."

The coach looked to his left where the voice had come and arched a brow. The man who had approached him was around mid to late thirties, military build with very short, spiky sun-blond hair. "They all are. Just who are you talking about?"

The man pointed his pen directly at Tara just as she arched, hitting the ball into the air with her chest before leaping into the air, turning sideways and kicking it with such force that the goalie dove out of the way to avoid getting hit. "Her."

"That's Tara. She's going to be a sophomore when the school year starts."

"Is that so," the scout said as he jotted a few things down.

The coach nodded. He never really did like his girls being exposed to the scouts from the colleges, but every year they would flock around the high schools like vultures on a rotting carcass. He looked at his watch before blowing his whistle. "Bring it in girls!" he shouted. He watched as the girls ran in from the field. "Tara," he called, waving his hand for her to join him.

Tara looked over at Morgan who shrugged and joined the rest of the team, sipping on a sports drink. Tara jogged over to where her coach and the scout stood and wiped her face off on her jersey. "Yeah, Coach?"

The coach stepped aside and motioned with his left hand. "This is . . .," his voice trailed off, realizing that he didn't even get the man's name.

The man chuckled and stepped forward extending his hand. "The name's Raiden."

"Tara," she said as she took his hand. The instant she did though, it was like a wave of energy crashing over her. Blurred images from some forgotten dream flashed before her, too quick though for her to see anything clearly. For just the smallest second she felt disoriented with the onslaught but she quickly regained herself and smiled. "It's nice to meet you," she said before joining her team and running the cold drink she was offered across the back of her neck.

As the team cooled down and stretched the football team came onto the field for their practice. The attention of the scouts soon shifted as well and they were once again jotting down notes. Tara noticed that Raiden was placing the same focused attention onto Darius that he had studied her with and as she watched him it was as if he was looking through him, or at least into a deeper portion of him that no one else could see.

"Something on your mind?" Morgan asked, seeing the intense look on Tara's face.

"That Raiden guy, have you seen him before?" Tara asked as she broke her stare.

Morgan shook her head as she chewed a piece of gum. "Nah. But not all the same scouts come every year," she said with a shrug.

Tara nodded and looked back to the field just as Darius was running with the ball toward the goal. It was nothing new, but as he swept his hand across his chest she watched as players went flying, almost as if they had bounced off a rubber ball. But she knew better and her gaze flew to the side, studying every inch of Raiden. If he saw it he wasn't letting on. All anyone seemed to see was that he had plowed through half of the defensive line to score a touchdown.

After practice was over Tara stood with Darius waiting as they had every day prior for Yukino to come get them. She looked around, making very sure that they were alone before she turned to him. "You idiot!"

Darius narrowed his eyes. "What?"

Tara's hands were plastered on her hips as she turned to face him. "What were you thinking?" Her assault made the look in his eyes darken and for a brief moment she stepped back, but she wouldn't relent. "You used your energy to break through that line. I felt the pulse of it from the sidelines! Even the scouts were staring at you."

"So?"

Tara blinked as her hands fell back to her sides. Never before had she heard him speak like this, nor had she ever seen him misuse his energy. "You always treated your gift with such respect," she said softly. "How could you—" But before she could get much further, she was quickly cut off.

"Oh, don't start," he snarled. "I know you do the same thing." But just as she opened her mouth to counter, he cut her off as he continued. "I've seen you slam the ball down the sideline in tennis. I've seen the power behind your kicks in soccer! So don't you *dare* stand here and preach to me!"

Tara's eyes widened. Yes, they'd had their share of spats, all friends did, but never before had he spoken to her in such a manner, and it had left her momentarily speechless. Her jaw clenched, as did her fists, her eyes boring into Darius's. "I might use my energy," she began, her voice even, "but I keep a tight handle on it. I use it as an outlet, and no matter what, I *always* keep things fair." She was shaking by this point, and without giving him a chance to react, she spun on her heels and stormed off, ignoring his shouts of her name as she made the mile walk to her house—alone.

The rest of the summer passed slowly for Tara. She was grateful for the lapse in their training with Yukino due to their sports, but she was looking forward to the school year starting so she could lose herself in her studies and her friends. Yukino and Senia could see the obvious difference though neither Tara nor Darius would admit to it let alone tell what had happened. By the time school started, the two were no longer on speaking terms. Darius turned in on himself, becoming darker in nature, while Tara focused on an even balance of her studies and sports.

One night as Tara walked home from a tennis game, she couldn't help but feel a bit uneasy. She kept seeing flickering images from the corner of her eyes, but every time she would look, there would be nothing. She sighed softly knowing that it was increasing and would just be another entry for her journals. Sitting on her bed she pulled her journal out and tried sketching what she'd seen. When she looked at it, she saw that it was part of a door. Lifting her head, she quirked a brow. "Huh."

She didn't tell Yukino what she'd seen. She figured that she had enough to worry about with Darius's constant shifts in energy that were insanely palpable. But that didn't mean she didn't miss him. She'd become so attached to him over the span of their lives that each passing month they went without talking felt more like a year to her.

So she decided that she would stop by one of his football games, just so she could see him and perhaps settle some of the nervousness that had made its home in her stomach.

The night of their homecoming game was when she decided to go. She was upbeat as she associated with friends, talking about the dance that she had opted out of going to. Promising to catch up with them later, she watched as people filed in through the gates. She stared at them for several moments before a deep breath calmed her and she herself headed in. Her eyes scanned the bleachers before lighting up and she darted up the steps, sliding to a stop as she sat beside Yukino and threw her arms around her.

"Well, hello there," Yukino said with a smile as she hugged Tara. She sat back and took her in, seeing differences in her energy. She regarded her thoughtfully before turning her attention back to the pregame show. "You know, Darius hasn't been the same since the two of you quit talking," she said, bringing an edge of seriousness to the conversation.

Tara frowned. She didn't have the heart to tell her about everything that had happened between them that fated summer day. Yukino was always so proud of him, so she kept it to herself. Instead, she gave a light smile, turning her attention back to the field.

"I miss him too," she said quietly, closing her eyes in focus before opening them once again.

Yukino gave a knowing smile. "You're using your energy to hide yourself."

Tara blinked and blushed at having been caught. It was true though. The small sessions of focus were spent manipulating her energy into, and reinforcing a double mirrored shield, keeping her energy in and other people's energy out. "I wanted to surprise him," she admitted. "And I didn't want my presence to be a distraction."

"I know he'll be happy to see you," Yukino said with a reassuring smile. "The two of you have been together since the day you were born."

Tara nodded and leaned in to her for a tight hug before their attention returned to field. The game had most everyone on the edge of their seats. The lead switched quite frequently, much to Tara's surprise and only then did she take some mild interest. It seemed that he'd taken her words to heart, she'd just never seen it until now. But as expected, they did win. Darius was able to run the winning touchdown with just seconds to spare.

The roar of the crowds was almost deafening and Tara held her head. There would be several parties, lasting well through the night. She watched as the football team relished in the cheers before she felt the nudge of her side. "Go see him," Yukino said as she rose to her feet and exited into the parking lot.

Tara moved to the side of the bleachers, watching as the team slowly began to filter toward the locker room. Darius brought up the rear, speaking with Tyler. The two were laughing before Tyler broke from the conversation and ran to catch the rest of the team. Tara took this moment to act and leaped silently over the railing. Keeping several feet behind Darius she let her shield crumble, allowing the pent up energy to rush outward and surround him. She knew it had reached him when he stopped suddenly. "Darius . . ." Her voice could barely reach over a whisper as she stepped toward him, managing only a couple of steps.

Darius kept his back to her, eyes facing straight forward as if he hadn't heard her. He could feel the pain in her energy as it retreated, a prelude to what she was about to do before he spoke as a smug look crossed his face. "You never were good at hiding things from me."

It was the acknowledgement she needed and as he turned to face her he was met with a full tackle. He caught her with ease and as she buried her head into his chest he couldn't help but smile. "I don't want to fight anymore." Though her voice was muffled, Darius heard her clearly and his arms encircled her shoulders.

"How easy it will be to get what I want from you," he thought. "I don't either," he said softly. He stared down at her, his gaze softening. Taking her in for a moment, he soon rested his lips against the top of her head and closed his eyes. "I'm sorry," he whispered. "I never meant to hurt you."

"I know," she mumbled, her arms tightening around his waist. "Just promise we won't fight like that anymore."

"I promise," he assured. But as they held each other in the quieting night they were unaware that an brewing battle was being waged, the purity in her heart trying to defeat the growing darkness seeded in his.

Things quickly went back to the way they had been in the past. They attended each other's games and were completely inseparable, much to the delight of their friends who now found it quite fun to pick on them. "It's about time the two of you made up and got back together."

Tara quirked a brow. "We're not together Morgan," she corrected, though Morgan just gave her ear to ear grin as she bit into an apple.

"You could have fooled us," came the snickering voice behind them.

Darius glowered at Tyler, smacking him in the back of the head as he sat. "She doesn't need more ammo," he stated flatly.

The look that crossed Morgan's face was eerily innocent, which made everyone take notice. "Well . . ." But before she could get more out, her eyes darted over to Tara, who had promptly pinched her lips shut, her brows now creasing in a scowl as she got the hint.

The rest of the day went by with the four of them driving around poking fun at each other and just enjoying each other's company. When evening finally fell, Tyler was pulling up to their street. "See you two at school," he said as the two climbed from the car. The group waved before Tyler drove off to take Morgan home.

Tara leaned into Darius as they headed home. Tilting her head back, she stared into the sky, watching as the horizon shifted from a brilliant shade of fiery deep purple, to a deep sapphire blue, and finally into the black of night where stars had already started shimmering as they made way for the rise of the moon. "It's peaceful tonight," she said, not really wanting to break the tranquility that surrounded them.

Darius looked down at her as he wrapped an arm around her shoulders before his gaze shifted skyward. "It is." His voice was calm, and she leaned in closer to him, feeling his arm tighten around her. The two continued their walk in silence as they reached Tara's driveway. The two stayed outside for a moment, enjoying everything around them before heading inside. The look on their parents' faces, however, made Tara wish they had stayed outside. "Mom?" Darius asked, seeing the sorrow etched in his mother's features.

Tara looked between her mother and Yukino, alarm growing with each passing glance. "Mom?" Her question repeating Darius's as she clung to him.

Yukino glanced up at Senia whose hand was clasped on her shoulder for support before looking back to their children. "Um." There really was no easy way for her to break the news to them. "The company I work for, well, they've opened a branch in Osaka Japan." Tara's face blanched with swift understanding as she continued. "They are transferring me as the head consultant for the legal department."

"Wha—" It was all Tara could muster as her throat tightened.

She and Darius were finally getting back to how things had been and now it was being taken away. The ground seemed to fall out from under her feet and it felt like she was going to fall. She looked up to Darius for support, but all she saw was a rigid statue, and the sudden chill made her shrink away, feeling very much alone.

"They're going to let him finish out the school year . . ." But everything that Senia was saying barely registered. In fact, Tara wasn't even sure that she'd heard anything that was being said. All she knew now was that she was losing the one person who she trusted with everything, the one person she knew she could turn to. She was losing a part of herself.

Yukino rose to her feet, exchanging looks with Senia before reaching out for Darius. "We should get home, it's getting late." She didn't want to leave, but she figured that their prolonged presence would do more harm than good. Reluctantly, Darius followed his mother, leaving Tara standing in a void she desperately wanted to escape.

The rest of the year seemed to fly by quickly, too quickly. Morgan would often say that it didn't come quick enough however. She was looking forward to graduation and starting college the following fall, awarded a partial scholarship for her feats in soccer as well as in her studies. Tara watched in silent agony as the final minutes shrank into seconds before the final bell would ring. When the bell did ring, Tara felt everything inside of her collapse. It would only be days now before she would lose the person that had been the closest to her since they were born.

The day of the move found the four standing by the cab that would take them to the airport. Their things had already been packed and already in transit to their new home in Japan. "I feel so bad for them," Yukino said as she watched the two say their farewells.

"It's not your fault," Senia replied. "You're doing what's best to give Darius a better life."

"I never thought I'd be taking them away from each other. We've become family and your parents have always been good about watching Darius when we've both had to work."

Senia just smiled and hugged her tightly. "We are family," she said softly. "And it's not like we can't visit each other."

As the two adults talked, Tara stood with Darius, her arms folded tightly across her chest. "It's not fair." Her voice was on the edge of breaking as she stared at him with doe like eyes.

Darius held her, running his fingers through her hair. "It'll be okay." He was trying to sound reassuring, always keeping his fingers entwined through her heart and her mind.

"I'll never see you again," she whimpered, burying her head into his chest.

"We can video chat at night," he said as the warmth of his breath seeped into her scalp.

"Except that night is day over here," she retorted, her voice defeated as she stared at the ground.

He sighed, realizing that, for the moment, nothing he was going to say would make things any better for her. Instead, he placed a single finger beneath her chin. He lifted her head, forcing her gaze to meet his as he leaned in and kissed her. She stiffened almost instantly, her mind racing for an explanation to what had just happened. She finally allowed herself to relax into it and he smiled as he felt her body sink against his. He brushed the pad of his thumb beneath her eye and held her gaze. "Now, nothing is ever written in stone. Just because I'm going there now, doesn't mean that I'm never going to come back."

"I guess." She pouted out her lower lip and sighed.

"Now, now, no looks," he said as he kissed her forehead, just as Yukino's voice broke in.

"Darius, it's time to go . . ." She hated saying it, and the look she saw on Tara's face as she clung to him only made her feel worse.

"All right," came the call over his shoulder.

He then looked back at Tara, taking her in, staring into her eyes where he memorized the animalistic characteristics they had taken on that unspoken night. He knew the separation would be a cruel blow to her. He was sure that if he played his cards right, all the information, all the secrets, he would know everything he wanted. With a final kiss and a lingering embrace, the two parted. "I swear I'll keep in touch," he said before getting into the cab beside his mother.

"Tara . . ." Senia reached for her daughter only to feel her pull away.

Nodding slowly, she decided that Tara needed some time alone. Tara knew her mother was always there for her, but having her world just vanish from her, she didn't want anyone around her. However, her solitude would give way to much more than she could ever imagine.

6

Trapped by Memories Forgotten

Can You See Me?

Do you see the lone star in the night time sky
The one with the lavender hue?
Can you see it? Can you see me?
As I'm watching over you
That shooting star you wish upon
Streaking through silent air
Can you see it? Can you see me?
I'm racing to come see you
My arms are empty without you
My heart pains when we're apart
Can you see it? Can you see me?
I want to say that I love you.

Tara stared at the screen of her computer. The poem she'd just finished bore everything she held for Darius. As she hit the Send button for the email, she could only hope that he not only liked it, but felt the same for her.

"I got my school info earlier today," Darius said one night while they were on the phone, saying nothing about the emails he'd received from her.

"Oh?" Tara asked, her head tilting. "You don't sound impressed," she added, grinning at the hinted scowl she could hear in his voice.

"You're enjoying this." He could tell she was trying not to laugh. "I just won't tell you then," he said with a smug grin.

Her eyes widened as she sat up straight. "Hey, that's not fair!" she protested. But even as she protested she could hear his laughter coming through and she sulked into her chair. "Oh that was mean . . ."

"I know," he said with a smile. "But did you want to hear about it. It's way worse than back there." His eyes rolled as he spoke, focusing on the wall or out the window.

"Sure," she said as she flopped onto her bed. "How different can it be anyway."

"Well, for starters, the school days are longer. You have to wear uniforms. You have to change your shoes for these weird slipper things before you go into the building. You stay in one class room while the teachers rotate between classes, but the worst part, is that every time the teachers come in, you have to stand and bow to them."

With everything that he was telling her, Tara couldn't help but start laughing. "It says that in all the info you got from the school?" she asked between fits of giggles.

"No," Darius replied with another scowl. "The info from the school were my classes, uniform, school hours and rules. The rest of the info I got was from a new friend I made out here."

"Oh?" Tara asked with an upturned brow. "What's her name?" she asked with a tease to her tone.

"*His* name, is Vonspar."

"Oh, relax, I was teasing," Tara replied with a sigh. She looked over her shoulder and nodded before sitting back up. "Hey, could you get online? My mom wants to talk to yours."

"Hello, Darius," Senia said as she was handed the phone. A few words were exchanged while Tara got onto her computer. She then exited the room, her voice fading into the distance as she and Yukino talked about how things were going out there.

lost2shdw: So what r u doing this summer for sports?
FwRoOlSfT: *shrug* dunno. Think I might stay with soccer. Mom wants me to get my driver's license which will take time from sports.
lost2shdw: ROFL, you, driving? Should warn people to stay off the sidewalks.
FwRoOlSfT: *scowl* oh har har. Shut it, Mr. lost2shdw. How emo LOL. Where'd u come up with that n e way.
lost2shdw: I like this name. Urs makes no sense.
FwRoOlSfT: *eye roll* does 2 >_< ne way, I have to go. I have an early morning.
lost2shdw: Same. V and I r hanging out. I'll ttyl.

He logged off quickly, leaving Tara to stare at her computer screen. "He sure is acting odd," she sighed before pushing from her computer. She sat in front of her vanity, staring at her reflection as she brushed her hair. "I'm sure he just has a lot on his mind." It was almost like she was trying to convince herself that settling into a new place, a new country, was the reason for his distance toward her. "Things will be the same again once he's settled in," she said as she let the braid she'd put her hair into fall down her back. Satisfied with her answer she slid into bed, falling into a restful sleep.

The next day Tara made the mile walk to the school while her mother headed for work. She walked into the gym seeing the usual crowds of kids gathered around the sports signup sheets giggling and staring. The girls would talk about the guys and who would be hotter in which uniform, though, the guys seemed more focused on the cheerleaders. Tara just rolled her eyes and waited till the crowds thinned enough for her to put her name on the sheet for the soccer team. She had just finished writing her name when she heard the office door open. Turning her head, she saw her tennis coach and jogged up to meet her. "Hey coach!" she called with a wide grin.

"Tara, hello," her coach greeted with a warm smile. "Come to sign up for the usual?"

Tara leaned against the wall and frowned a bit. "No, just soccer this year," she said, much to the displeasure of her coach. "My mom is wanting me to take some driving classes to get my license, so I'm only able to go for soccer this year."

The coach nodded. "We'll be looking forward to you trying out the next season then," she said as she headed off for lunch.

Tara slung her bag over her shoulder and headed into the locker room. The quiet was welcome as she changed into a loose shirt and a pair of running shorts. "Might as well get a good run in," she said as she tied up her hair, grabbed her MP3 player, and headed out for the track. The first round of track tryouts were just coming to an end so she took to the track to run while they rested. Tucking her ear buds in securely she began, starting out at a jog then breaking into a sprint just for some energy release, then returning back to the steady jog.

She could feel eyes watching her, boring onto her like some lab specimen. She figured it was just another coach trying to get her to join their team. The irritation fueled her energy and before she knew it, she'd cleared the mile run in just over three minutes. Rolling her head, she looked around, searching for the eyes that had watched her. She saw someone from the track team staring in her direction and shrugged as she downed some water and sat on the grass to stretch, ear buds still firmly planted.

Only a looming shadow broke her concentration, and, as she lifted her head, she focused on the stupid grin and sighed in frustration. "Can I . . . help you?" she asked, hooking the chords around a single finger before pulling them from her ears in annoyance.

He continued looking at her even as her brows began to merge. "You're pretty fast. Even our fastest track runner can only clear the mile in just over four minutes. You took almost a minute off his time."

"Okay," Tara replied coolly as she stood, brushing the grass from her shorts and legs. "And?" she asked with a disinterested shrug of her shoulders.

"Ever think of joining the track team?" he asked, keeping her pace easily.

Her agitation was growing with each step she took, but she tried keeping her temper as even as she could. "Hadn't planned on it," she replied sharply, eyes forward. "I have enough going on."

"Oh, I know. I have a couple of friends on the JV soccer team, so I'd watch you practice while I waited for them."

Tara found this more than just a little creepy, and as they reached the locker rooms, she turned. "Is there something else? You're starting to get a little . . . stalkerish."

"Not really. I really just wanted to introduce myself," he said as he extended his hand.

Tara just looked at his hand then back at him as he tried saving face by running his hand over his dark military buzzed hair. "Aaanyway . . . My name is Toran."

Still she remained quiet, and he sighed in the temporary defeat and turned to walk from her. Just as she was about to walk into the locker room, however, he glanced back over his shoulder. "By the way, nice eyes wolf!" he shouted before continuing toward his car.

Tara's eyes widened as she stood frozen. "Creep!" she shouted just as he reached maximum ear shot. She wasn't even sure he heard her, but what he'd said had shaken her. How was he aware of her online name? Not even Darius had figured it out. She had to explain it to him, which was embarrassing. Scowling, she turned and strode into the locker room. She had planned on showering here before heading home, but she decided against it and instead went to her locker.

"What a jerk," she glowered as she flung her locker open, grabbing her things and changing just as she heard the giggling babble of the cheerleaders echoing into the once silent room.

When the captain of the squad rounded the corner and saw her, she waved, and the girls with her said hello. Tara smiled and greeted them before slinging her bag over her shoulder and heading out. They weren't a bad group of girls. Most of them were friendly enough, but she still thought they were all just a bunch of air heads.

Her walk home was spent wracking her brain as to how Toran knew her online name. "I don't think we have any friends in common," she said as she looked up at a single cloud hanging in the sky. She decided to see if perhaps he'd found and added her and lay the whole thing to rest just to get it out of her mind.

When she was about a block from her house, however, she began to feel a bit uneasy. She stopped, looking around her as she felt the feeling bear down on her. She wondered if it was Toran. The intensity in the energy reminded her of his leering gaze, but she saw no cars moving, nor did she hear any. There were no other people out either, that she could see anyway. This gave her the needed push to get home, and to do so quickly. As soon as she cleared the threshold, she closed and locked the door, pressing her back against it as she took in several deep breaths. Within the walls of her home she felt at ease and gave a relieved sigh as she headed to the kitchen and grabbed the phone, calling her mother's cell to let her know she was home.

"Did you get to talk to your coaches?" Senia was standing in front of her locker getting her sting gear together.

Tara walked in small circles before leaning against the counter. "Yeah. They're looking forward to having me back next season if I'm up for it."

"That's good. Oh, just to let you know, I'm going to be home late," Senia said as she put her gear in the trunk of her car and got in. "We're setting up a sting and I'm not sure how long we'll be."

Tara pursed her lips at the mention of a sting. She always worried when they did things like that. "Just be careful, Mom."

The unease was evident in her voice as she spoke. "Are you okay, honey?"

Giving things a quick mental run through, she wondered if what she felt outside was some form of insight. "I just feel a bit uneasy," she admitted.

"I'll be careful," she promised.

"I wish you didn't have to do this."

"Everything will be fine," she assured. "I'm only support, not part of the main team."

While this did make Tara feel a bit better, she still couldn't shake the lingering feeling nagging at her. "I'll take care of dinner and set a plate aside for you when you get home," she finally said, trysting to distract her brain.

"Thanks, honey. I'll be home when I can."

"Don't worry about me. Just focus on staying safe, okay?" She smiled as she stared out the window into the backyard, overhearing her mother talking to Mark. It was nice seeing them becoming closer, though, she did have to end the conversation with her mother so she cleared her throat. When she once again had her mother's attention she laughed. "I'll see you when you get home. I love you, Mom."

"I love you, too dear," Senia said before clicking her phone closed.

When Tara set the phone down the grin on her face was ear to ear. "They're so cute," she laughed as she reached into the fridge for a bottle of water.

Spinning the top off, she tilted her head back and downed nearly half the bottle before she needed to take a breath. The light hearted mood she now found herself in made her forget about the feelings that awaited her outside her front door and in her own mind. Walking into her room she set her water on the dresser and looked around.

"What to do, what to do," she mused.

She wanted a shower to get the sweat and grime from the morning off her skin, but as she pulled one of her drawers open, she nodded a bit as she pulled out her light blue two piece.

"Yes, I think a relaxing swim is in order." Tying her hair up, she grabbed her water and headed into the hall to play her favorite cd into the backyard.

Taking a towel from the closet, she headed into the backyard, closing her eyes as the music seeped into her thoughts. Releasing a contented sigh, she set the towel and water aside before diving into the pool, feeling the chill of the water against her skin. Letting her head bob just over the surface of the water she cleared the water from her eyes before pushing from the wall with enough force to give her the momentum to start swimming laps. She swam until her body gave out and she was literally dragging herself from the pool into the hot tub. Sinking into the now frothy bubbling water she let the jets work their magic while she took another sip from her water bottle. The pulsing water melted the fatigue from her calves and moved against her back relieving any stress that might have knotted her muscles. As her eyes closed, she thought about her meeting with Toran. He wasn't normal by any definition, but stalker seemed to be a perfect classification for him. She sighed, sinking further into the water as the end of her breath added to the bubbles around her.

When her skin had gone beyond the stage of pruning, and her muscles had finally yielded to the massage of the jets, she finally got out of the tub and turned it off.

"No better way to relax," Tara said as she looked at her shriveled fingers and scrunched her nose. But her time in the water wasn't over. A shower was needed before the chlorine from the pool did its wonderful green number to her hair like it had when she was younger and refused to wash her hair after a swim. She tossed her towel onto the washer as she walked into the house and locked the back door behind her.

About an hour later, the bathroom door opened, and Tara emerged clothed in a pair of baggy shorts and an oversize T-shirt, her hair wrapped tightly in a towel. She turned off the music as she walked down the hall, opting for the background noise of her TV as she sat on her bed long enough to find something to watch. She was about to give up when she suddenly stopped on her favorite ghost hunting show, surprised that it was on so early. "Not going to question a good thing," she said as she rose to her feet, tossed the remote onto her bed, and fired up her computer. She waited as everything came to life, connecting here and there to what it needed to. As her messenger loaded, she watched as a few screens popped up. One was from Morgan, letting her know that she'd gotten settled into her new dorm, while another was from one of her old tennis partners. As she replied and cleared things away, she found that there were no new friend requests, but she also found an IM from Darius. All it said, was that they needed to talk, and for some reason she could feel her stomach sink yet again.

"Great," she sighed before tilting back in her chair, staring at the ceiling as she undid her towel and roughly ran it over and through her hair.

She didn't want to think about what it could be, so she didn't. She focused on the TV until her hair was nothing short of a mess. Pushing to her feet she blinked at herself, catching a glance in the mirror that rested over her desk then headed into the bathroom. Tossing her towel over the shower rod she reached for her brush and began the process of taming the wild mane that framed her face, looking at her reflection with an almost vacant gaze. All she could do was stare into the reflective glass, her gaze focused upon itself, through itself. Her mind seemed to be on a different plane, mulling over thoughts unknown to her conscious mind and it was that separation that caused, just for a split second, something she'd been told she possessed to come to light. Her brush fell from her hand as she saw it, the sound it made as it hit the floor bringing everything back to the present, her eyes once again her own.

Her brows merged. "What was that?" Her voice was distant, almost a whisper as she retrieved her brush and set it down. Forcing her mind to maintain the image she saw she quickly tied her hair back and returned to her room. Sitting in the center of her bed she took her journal and opened it to the next open page and began sketching. It was a close up of her eye, the way she'd seen it in the mirror. Shadowed around the edges with an almost glowing amber iris. When she was done, she stared down at it with a scrutinizing gaze.

"It's me, but not," she said as she set the book on the bed and looked at the picture intently. She was so focused on the drawing that she almost missed the chime come across her computer letting her know that she'd just received an IM. Looking over at the screen, she rose to her feet and flopped into the chair at her desk.

lost2shdw: U there?
FwRoOlSfT: Yeah, wut's up?

lost2shdw: Nothin'.
FwRoOlSfT: How's your mom?
lost2shdw: fine

Tara's brow creased in annoyance. "Why is he being so standoffish," she grumbled. With a sigh and a scowl, she typed out another question, hitting the buttons on her keyboard a bit harder than she'd meant to.

FwRoOlSfT: Alllllllrite then. How's ur new friend out there. Von . . .
    something or other.

She remembered his name quite well. She was simply trying to get something other than a one-word answer from him.

lost2shdw: fine

Tara gripped the edge of her desk, glaring. She had enough to do without worrying about a stupid game they played when they were kids and got mad at each other.

FwRoOlSfT: U kno wut? 4get it. I'm done playing this. If all ur
    gonna do is give me one-word answers, then u can jst tlk 2 me
    when u feel like tlking in a complete sentence.

Tara sat for a few moments, waiting. With her tone, she was sure that would elicit a response, but when none came, she shook her head in defeat. She pushed her chair back, but just as she was about to stand up, another bleep came across the screen. "Now he replies," she grumbled as she wheeled back to her desk.

lost2shdw: Is there n e thing u want 2 tell me?
Tara arched a brow in confusion. "What is he talking about?"
FwRoOlSfT: Uh . . . no. Y?
lost2shdw: C, I think u do.
FwRoOlSfT: Xscuse me?

lost2shdw: U heard me. I was unpacking some books for my mom, and I came across her last progress journal that she was keeping on us. It has some interesting things in it.

Tara's jaw fell open as she stared at the screen.

FwRoOlSfT: U didn't!
lost2shdw: I did.
FwRoOlSfT: How cld u betray ur mom like that!
lost2shdw: How funny that u shld bring up betrayal, you lying witch.

What the—Tara was stunned to say the least. He had nerve speaking to her in such a manner.

FwRoOlSfT: What r u tlking about? What lie did I tell u *this* time?
lost2shdw: The only lie u evr told me.
FwRoOlSfT: I NEVER lied 2 u!

Several moments passed without a reply, so she assumed that he'd finally grown up and dropped the subject, realizing that he was being childish. But the old adage of what happens when you assume something was about to rear its ugly little head. She was just about to push from her char and go about the rest of her afternoon when another chime brought up the once closed conversation between her and Darius. She reached over to close the window again, but it was as if something was drawing her to read what was being posted to her. A word-by-word account of what Yukino had written about that unspoken night. Every horrifically vivid detail that was posted found its way into her mind's eye as flashes of images, faces, blood . . . It all began punching holes into and through the barriers that had been reinforced for years. By the time he'd posted the last of what Yukino had written, it was as if the breath had been pulled from her lungs.

lost2shdw: Do u still want to stick to your story about not lying to me?

Tara shook in her chair. If that had, in fact, happened, why could she not remember any of it, or was he being intentionally cruel? But if he was, the question was why.

lost2shdw: Yeah, that's what I thought.

But Tara was not about to allow herself to be treated like this. Not by anyone, and especially not by him.

FwRoOlSfT: Oh, just SHUT UP! Stop dwelling on something that supposedly happened 8 FREAKING yrs ago! No, y'know what? Y don't u tlk to me once u grow up some and can stop acting like such a damn child!

But Darius had what he wanted, the information he'd sought for so long. "With this, there's no need for the charade." And with that decided, his fingers moved easily across the keyboard.

lost2shdw: I wouldn't bother waiting for me. I'm nvr speaking 2 u again. We're thru.

And with that, he logged off, leaving Tara to sit in the aftermath of what he'd created. She leaned back in her chair, arms folded across her chest as she stared blankly at the computer. Words and images raced through her mind, jumbling into a mass of such disarray that she finally just closed down her computer and flopped down on her bed. She stared at the TV, not even paying attention to what she was watching and as one program ended into another she found herself able to doze, though it was anything but restful.

When she awoke, the sun had begun its descent toward the horizon. She sat on the edge of her bed staring at the floor, her head swimming with everything that happened only hours earlier. Shaking her head she passed it off as a mood and headed for the kitchen to start dinner. Opening the fridge, she rummaged around for something to fix. Her brows merged in thought as she saw the chicken that had been thawing and her eyes brightened as she grabbed it.

Tossing it onto the counter she continued to search until a small pile of food had amassed on the counter. She then hit the pantry where she grabbed seasoned breading and marinara sauce. Breaking an egg into a dish she beat it with a fork before adding milk, salt, pepper, and a generous amount of hot sauce. Putting the chicken in to soak she made the bread coating, mixing different spices with bread crumbs and set that aside.

"This should be good," she said with a small smile.

At least it was offering her a distraction as she poured some sauce into the bottom of a small baking dish, breaded the chicken, then put it into the oven to bake. As the chicken cooked Tara went about making a salad with all the fresh veggies she and her mother loved, however, the broccoli was left out for her to steam. With about ten minutes left on the chicken, she pulled it from the oven and put more than just a generous amount of cheese over the top before putting a bit more sauce around the bubbling pieces and placing it back into the oven. By this time the water in the steamer had begun to simmer so she pulled the broccoli from the fridge, putting it in the basket after lightly salting the water. Grabbing plates and silverware she got everything set up and made the salad, finishing just as the ovens timer went off. A spoonful of sauce on each plate and each getting a chicken breast. She watched as the cheese ran down the chicken and Tara couldn't wait to eat.

First came the broccoli though, divided evenly between the two plates, and salad on her plate. Cooked salad just didn't sound appealing. Tara wrapped her mother's plate, first in plastic wrap, then in foil, putting the oven on warm and setting the plate on the center rack. "Now we eat," she exclaimed as she dug into the chicken. "Gooey cheese," she mumbled as strings of it hung from her lower lip. "Nothin' better." She was going to enjoy her evening, so thinking about what happened earlier in the afternoon wasn't an option, but as she looked at the clock on the stove, she couldn't help but wonder how her mother was doing. She didn't dare call, knowing that things could be pretty intense around now, but she didn't worry any less.

When she was done eating, she cleaned the dishes, shut off the lights after leaving a note for her mother about dinner, turned on the porch light then headed to her room for bed.

Unlike earlier, Tara couldn't shake the unease, so she left her T V on, grateful for the background noise as she drifted off into a troubled sleep. Several hours passed before she awoke to something on her television. Rubbing her eyes she stared, confused and only a bit disoriented. "Mom has to be home by now," she said sleepily, seeing that the clock read just after two in the morning.

Shuffling down the hall, she went to her mother's room, pushing the door open only to see the empty bed. Alarm grew steady as she went to the kitchen and saw that the oven was still set to hold. She turned it off and retrieved the food, leaving it on the stove to cool before putting it in the fridge and went to check the driveway. She looked out the window and saw nothing. Her stomach dropped, expecting the worst to have happened so she raced down the hall to her room to check if she'd missed any calls. When she picked it up it began to ring and she dropped it with a startled scream. Seeing the number across the screen, she scooped her phone back up and answered. "Hello?"

"Tara? This is Mark. I didn't mean to wake you."

"Huh, no, it's fine," she said, her head shaking a bit. "Where's my mom? She hasn't come home yet."

"I'm on my way over there to get you. There's been an accident."

"What?" Tara could hardly believe what she was hearing. Her hands trembled as she pressed for details. "What happened? Is she all right? Where is she?"

"Easy, Tara. I'll explain everything when I get you, okay? I'll be there in about five minutes."

Tara heard the line go dead as the phone slid from her hand onto the bed. A million things were racing through her mind as she threw on whatever was in her reach which amounted to her warm up pants from soccer, a tank top and hoodie. She shoved her keys, wallet, and phone into her pockets and stepped into her shoes just as she heard the bell ring. She ran down the hall and threw the door open, her pleading eyes staring up at Mark.

"Where is she?" she begged, stepping into the night air as Mark led her to the car.

Mark pulled onto the street and drove. He didn't know where to start, or if he even wanted to, but her constant gaze pressed enough and he relented.

"The sting didn't go quite as planned. Your mother was part of the first group that went in."

"What!" Tara's voice interrupted the conversation. "She told me she was support tonight."

But Mark slowly continued. "Somehow they were tipped off about what was going on, and they were waiting for us." As they passed under a streetlight, he could see the horror across her face, but still she pressed for more, and again he gave in. "They open-fired as soon as we went in. We were still able to take them down, but a lot of damage was done as well. A bullet hit Senia, but I don't know where. I don't know anything else except which hospital they took her to."

"Is she alive?" Tara's voice sounded on the edge of shrieking, but she was trying so hard to be strong and composed.

"The last I saw, yes, she was. But I heard the EMTs talking, and things were looking kind of grim."

The rest of the trip was made in silence. Mark wasn't sure that if he said anything more, if it would make things worse, and Tara just didn't trust her own voice to say anything further. Once they arrived Tara fled from the car and through the sliding doors to the Emergency Department of the hospital, ignoring Mark's calls for her to wait. She was running so fast that she almost ran into the desk at the nurses' station and as one looked up she stared with pleading eyes.

"Please, I'm looking for my mom . . . where is she . . . ?"

Tears starting running down her cheeks as the nurse brought up the patient lists. "What's her name?"

By now Mark had arrived and placed his hands on Tara's shoulders. "Senia. She was brought in from the sting."

The nurse did more typing and the smile on her face began to droop into a frown. "She's on the fifth floor in surgery. If you go through the elevator here, you'll see their station when you get off just to the left."

Tara nodded and ran with Mark close behind her. The elevator couldn't move fast enough for her and as the doors opened it was a repeat of downstairs.

"Please, ma'am, I'm looking for my mom. The lady downstairs said she was up here." Tears were running quite easily now as she silently pled for the answers she wanted.

Mark emerged behind Tara just as the nurse was about to ask for her name, but remembering Mark from earlier she rose to her feet. "You must be Senia's daughter," she said as she rounded the station and motioned for them to follow her.

"How's she doing?" Mark asked, his arm wrapped protectively around Tara's shoulders.

"I don't know. The doctors haven't come out since they brought her in."

When they reached the waiting room, she offered them a seat. "I'll let them know you're here, and one of them will come out to talk to you." She then disappeared from sight. Slowly though, other officer's families began to filter in and Tara could see just how wrong the sting had gone.

Moments later doctors began to file in, each giving different news to the people they spoke to. Some was wonderful news, things that could be fixed easily, but some news was much worse with no chance of the happy ending that many sought. It was all very overwhelming to Tara, and as she looked to her side, she saw that Mark had left, offering condolences to other families, leaving her very much alone as a doctor approached her.

"Tara?" he asked, catching her off guard a bit.

Tara jumped some and stared up at the man in front of her. "Yes?"

The doctor sat beside her and rested a hand over hers. "I don't know what all you know of your mother's condition," he began.

"Just that she was shot." Mark's voice flanked her from the other side, and for a moment, she felt relief, knowing she wasn't going to have to hear this alone.

The doctor looked up and nodded. "Well, yes. She was shot twice. One was a through and through, which shattered her femur. The second grazed the left side of her skull."

"So she's okay then, right?" Tara asked. "I mean, if it just grazed her."

But she was cut off. "The area in her skull that it hit was not ideal. I'm afraid that it fragmented a portion of the skull cap, leaving pieces . . . well . . ." He was conflicted in continuing, telling such terrible things to someone so young. "She's currently in a medically induced coma, but you can see her if you would like."

Tara was shaking visibly as she nodded. "Yes, please."

The doctor motioned for a passing nurse to take her to the ICU unit, watching as they disappeared before he finished talking to Mark. The trip to the ICU unit was silent. Tara didn't want to talk, and the nurse wasn't about to push it.

When they reached her room, the nurse paused and placed her hand on Tara's shoulder. "She's going to have machines hooked to her. Some are to help her breathe, and some are to monitor how she's doing."

Tara nodded, really just wanting to go see her mother and be at her side. "Just let me know if you need anything child."

"Thank you," Tara answered softly. As she entered her mother's room she could hear the beeps of the machines, the puffs of air that another one was making as it maintained her breathing. So many tubes, machines, there were even multiple IVs hanging, forcing fluids into her to keep her hydrated and to fight potential infections. It was all too much to take in, so much so that she hadn't even taken in her mother's condition. The bandages, the discoloration . . . She suddenly felt violently ill and had to force herself to walk to the chair beside her mother's bed. Once she sat down she could feel the weight of everything on her. "Oh, Mom," she said softly, taking her hand and rubbing her cheek over the back of it. She tried to stay strong, tried not letting anything show, but eventually the tears broke through and she cried silently, clutching Senia's hand tightly.

She wasn't sure how long she'd been alone, but she jumped as some movement startled her. She rubbed her eyes and squinted only to see Mark coming into focus. "Sorry, kiddo. I didn't mean to startle you."

"No . . . you're fine . . ." She was drained, and it showed. Her eyes were faded and her voice was small and distant.

Mark had her sit back down and sat on the other side of the bed, studying her, studying Senia. "Your grandparents are on their way."

Tara just sank back into the chair, suddenly feeling so small in it. "I want to go home," she said softly. She was feeling very overwhelmed, and if she had the chance, she'd run.

"I'll take you home, just as soon as they get here. I promise. But you shouldn't be alone." His gaze now focused more on her as he studied her intently. "Would you rather go with your grandparents?"

Tara shook her head. Something was pulling her desires to return home. Safety perhaps, but that's where she wanted to be. "I have to go home," she said, her eyes shifting from his prying gaze. "I have to make some calls for her."

He wasn't happy with the decision she'd made, but he had to sigh in defeat. In her state, he wasn't going to push anything with her. He looked at his watch then leaned forward in his chair just as Senia's parents walked into the room. "Oh dear," her mother breathed, covering her mouth with her hand.

"Grandma." Tara rose to her feet, tears streaking down her cheeks again as she ran forward feeling the warmth of protective arms around her.

"Oh, Tara," her grandmother said soothingly, kissing the top of her head. "You look so tired."

Tara just nodded. "I am," she said softly. "I'd like to go home. This is way too much."

"Of course, dear. You shouldn't have to be subjected to this," her grandmother said, smoothing the hair from her face. "Mark, could we impose on you to take her home?"

"No trouble, ma'am." He walked over to the two and held out his arm for Tara, who willingly joined him. "I'll let you know when she's home and safe," he assured.

The two left, leaving Senia in the care of her parents and the hospital staff. The ride home was made in silence. Tara was still quite numb from the whole ordeal so Mark respected her need of silence. When they finally pulled into the drive, Mark put the car in park and once more studied the girl in the passenger seat. "Are you sure you're going to be fine on your own here?" he asked, concern evident in his voice.

Tara forced just the hint of a smile and nodded. "I'll be fine," she assured as she opened the door. "Just make sure that my mom is taken care of."

She didn't leave much time for an answer before she closed the door and headed into the house. She left the porch light on for the moment, turning on several lights in the house as she headed for the phone. She took the phone into her room, pacing back and forth as she dialed Yukino's number. She listened as the phone rang and rang and rang, silently pleading for her to answer the phone. When she heard the answering machine activate her heart sank and she started to cry again as the beep signaled her to begin the message.

"Yukino . . . it's Tara. Please call when you get this. It's Mom, she's been shot."

Hanging up the phone, Tara was unaware that on the other side of the line, Darius stood watching and listening as the message played, a dark gleam glinting from his eyes as he smiled, his finger brushing, and finally pushing the button that would erase the message left by his former childhood friend, reveling in the break he was sure would come.

"Soon enough you will know the embrace of the Shadows," he promised, turning on his heels and stepping out, disappearing into the afternoon that awaited him.

7

Enemies in the Shadows

Tara paced the length of the hall, her mind abuzz with thoughts that had no end, no beginning, just mass. Images tore through her mind's eye, bandages, blood, bruises, and machines. It was too much for her to handle, and she feared a mental snap was just around the corner. She reached for the phone, her thumb moving over the keys to dial Japan once again when she heard it. "Tara . . ."

Tara froze as the phone fell from her hand, but not even the sound it made as it crashed to the floor drew her attention. "It's happened," she whispered. "I've finally snapped."

"Tara?" The voice sounded as if it were all around her, holding a sorrow to it with the lack of recollection. "Tara . . . don't you remember me?"

Tara decided this was a sick joke and spun, her eyes darting as she searched for the owner of the voice. "Who are you?" she demanded. "Where are you! Come out!"

"It's me, Belzak," the voice said again. "I know you remember me, you have to remember me. I know it's been years to you, but the gaze we shared that night . . . You have to remember."

"Belzak?" she repeated his name, but there was no recollection. "I'm sorry, I don't know what you're talking about, or who you are, or how you even got in this house. The fact that I can't see you . . ." Her voice dropped as she began to laugh. "I think I'm finally losing it." But even as she spoke his name she could feel a warmth radiating throughout her chest, almost as if a forgotten memory was trying to make itself known.

"I saved your life when you were just a child." There was then a long pause before he spoke again. "I wonder if it's been so long that you've forgotten."

"If you're who you claim to be, then why don't you appear? Come out of hiding," she insisted, her arms folding almost snuggly across her chest.

"I can't," he began.

"Then I am imagining this," Tara retorted with a scowl.

She tried to move, tried to walk to her room, her sanctuary. There she would feel human again, there music awaited her that would ease her mind. But as she tried to move her right leg to begin walking, she found that she could not. It was as if she were glued to the floor.

"I can't because I was injured severely that night. I can project my voice to you, but I can't appear to you. If you'll just go to the door by your pool, the door that led you here. Please, you'll see that I am who I say I am."

Things were quiet for a moment before she chose to speak again. "There is no door in my backyard. I think I'd notice one." But even as she protested to everything that was going on, her body finally decided to work, though it had its own mission. Feeling the mobility of her limbs once again, she tried walking down to her room, but her feet had other ideas, leading her through the kitchen and into the backyard. As he spoke, as they spoke, fleeting images flickered through her mind's eye, memories of a life forgotten it seemed, just out of reach from her conscious mind.

"Your heart remembers," he said, his voice seeming ever closer. "You just have to go through the door."

"There *is* no door!" she snarled. She held her forehead in her hand and sighed harshly. "I can't believe I'm having an argument with myself," she spat, her shoulders shaking as if she was trying not to laugh at herself again for what was going on.

A heavy feeling hung in the air, her mind and her soul warring at the validity of everything going on around her, and before she knew it, she had held out her right hand, reaching for something she couldn't see. Until her hand moved through a thick energy. Her hand stopped midway, her eyes fixated upon a single point as large chunks of wall fell away from her mind. She watched as a door slowly began to appear before her, only drawing her hand away as it began to solidify. As it appeared completely before her, the last of the wall fell from her thoughts and everything came rushing back.

A startled gasp fell from her lips like stepping into frozen water from the hot day. Floods of memories returned to her. That night, the door, leading through the gray mists that was the Grey Planes, all centering on that one moment where they faced Durion. Now she remembered. His voice, his face . . . that final gaze they shared. "Now you remember."

His voice startled her from her thoughts, and she spun around, half expecting to see him there, but she realized she was alone.

"Belzak," she whispered, and he could tell in the change of tone that her memories had returned. "I thought you were dead. Watching you become engulfed in the sea of hounds . . ."

Everything was running together now and she felt a bit faint with such a heavy onslaught of newly released energy, but even as she sat down, it was almost as if she could feel the energy behind an unseen touch as it ran over her cheek.

"I am quite fine," he assured. "But the injuries were bad enough that they have bound me from leaving."

"What happened to Arcainous?" Her body flinched as she remembered the horrible fight just before Belzak had raced her away.

"Oh, he's just fine. But we'd love for you to come visit us. Just go through the door."

His voice was so coaxing, always pushing for her to go, ever since he'd first called to her. "All right."

She did want to see them. She had to make sure they were okay. Pushing back to her feet, she placed her hand on the door, feeling it yield to the pressure from her hand. Stepping through, she closed the door, walking through the rolling mists.

"Okay, I'm here. Where are you?" she called into the vast emptiness.

"You have to venture into the Realms. I told you, my injuries were grave enough to bind me there."

Tara sighed as she walked, but it didn't take long until she reached another door. Pushing it open, she stepped through, kicking it closed behind her. But what she found this time was not the moonlit forest and lake that she had seen her first time here. She found herself on an empty street, lit only by a cold moonlight. Looking around, she saw that she was alone.

"How odd that a town would have no one out." She walked down the street, peering into empty windows, seeing only darkness. "Belzak!" she shouted, hearing only the echo of her own voice. "Belzak, where are you!"

In a separate part of the Realm, a sphere appeared before a group of three, her form clearly evident within it. "Must we really stand by and allow this to happen?" Arcainous asked, clearly displeased.

"This is the only way we'll know," Raiden said as he rubbed his chin. "I sensed something about her when I first met her, but there was a rather well-placed wall around the depth of her mind. If you ask me, this all should have happened much sooner."

"With Durion as your first Astral encounter, coupled with what she had to witness happening to Belzak, I think she's more than proven herself," Arcainous replied "And it would explain the wall her mind built to protect her. I'm surprised it didn't last longer."

While they talked about how fair this was or wasn't, the gaze of the third figure remained upon the sphere, watching as she continued wandering aimlessly down the streets, looking for the one who had brought her there.

"For the sake of the Light!" Arcainous protested. "She's in the middle of the Shadow Lands! She's already gone against Durion, must she be made to suffer more?"

Raiden looked at Arcainous with a cool expression. "She did not face Durion. You and Belzak protected her. If she is in fact what we suspect, she must face her trials alone. The others have, and have endured much worse to obtain their titles, as must she."

There was no arguing. He knew what Raiden said was true, and he fell silent, staring into the orb, into her eyes where he saw the gaze of his old friend. Losing Belzak was not only a great loss for the Watchers, but for the Realm as a whole.

Irritation was making itself at home in Tara's mind as she peered into more windows and looked down more alleyways. Each time she found nothing. "What kind of town has no people, no signs of life?" she asked as she ran her hands along her arms to warm the chill creeping around her skin. "If this is a game," she muttered, "it's far from funny—BELZAK!" Her voice echoed off the walls of the buildings around her then faded into silence, offering no reply. "Oh, that's it. I'll just find my way back to the door and go home. I have enough to worry about without having to deal with this on top of it."

The three watched as Tara spun around only to freeze as the fine hairs on the back of her neck stood on end. She let it affect her for just a moment before nearly stomping off, but as she moved, Raiden caught movement at the bottom of the sphere. When they focused, it vanished, but it quickly appeared again, and Raiden took a step back. "This isn't good."

Arcainous lifted his head and stepped forward. "What isn't?" he asked as he peered into the sphere.

Shrouded hands lifted, pulling down the cowl of a cloak to reveal curly copper hair spilling over the shoulders and down the back of the third member of the party. "Vampires," she replied, her cool silvery eyes flickering to the other two.

"Elder Fisonma," Arcainous said, his voice holding great respect. "How can you be sure who or what that was? They were nothing more than blurs across the bottom of the orb."

"Every being, whether physical or Astral, has its own energy signature, much like people from the Physical Realm have their own fingerprints to tell them apart." She then lifted her arm, pointing at the blur as it appeared once more and dragged it to an empty space beside it. "A vampire's energy signature is soft edged, which is why they are good at manipulation and camouflage. A broken aura edge allows them to take in energies around them."

"So if we can match the energy, we'll find who is following her," Arcainous said.

"In theory, I'm sure," Raiden said just before three faces appeared beside the sphere.

"Just as I feared," she said with a sigh. "There couldn't be anyone worse following her."

"Dante, Gabriel, and Malik," Raiden said.

Arcainous's brow arched. "They're the three most powerful vampires in the Realms. We have to go help her!"

"I want to see how she handles them," Fisonma said. "They are still nothing compared to Durion, so she should fare well if our assumption is correct."

While they talked, Tara continued storming through the city, trying to make her way back where she had come from. Occasionally she would hear footsteps behind her, but when she turned around, she saw nothing, no one. Merging her brows, she headed off again, walking a bit quicker as the footsteps started again, keeping perfect time with her. Again she spun around, swearing that she'd seen something from the corner of her eye. Planting her hands on her hips she glared into the darkness. "Come out!" she demanded. "You're not cute, you're not funny!" Still there was no answer, but now she was aware of the presence near her. Glaring in frustration she spun around to leave only to leap back in surprise. "Who are you!" she demanded.

"We are as old as time," Malik replied.

"We are time," Dante added.

"I'm not impressed," Tara shot back.

She had long passed the threshold for childish games, and as she stepped back from them, she drew the index and middle finger of her right hand beneath her chin and stared forward. "Bound by honesty and the quest of true knowledge, I call you forth!" The rims of her irises began to glow as she visualized what she wanted and where. "Rune of Truth!"

Everyone watched as glowing symbols appeared upon the chest of each vampire, burning through their cloaks, pressing for and through the skin, their aim, the heart, the birthplace of all truth, all lie, every intention. "She has nerve . . ." Raiden said, his voice dropping to nothing more than a low mumble.

"I'll ask you again," she said, jaw set, hand outstretched toward them as she fed the energies of her rune. "Who . . . are you!"

Though stunned for only a moment, the three soon regained themselves, and with a sudden gust of energy, her runes lay shattered on the ground between them.

"You are strong, but your power means little to us," Gabriel said as he slowly stepped forward, his eyes glowing an eerie shade of amber, which cast a sickly look around his eyes, though the tips of his fangs revealed through his cruel smile remained shrouded in the shadows of his hood. As was the case with the other two as they followed behind. "Coming with us will be so much easier now than in the long run," he said, extending his hand outward toward her.

"Not a chance!" she shouted as her fingers began tracing spirals through the air. "Bound by the steadfast earth, I call upon you! Runes of binding!" She watched as the ground gave way, releasing tendrils of energy that wrapped around the legs and arms of the three, giving her enough time to run. As strands were broken, others broke through to take their place, which gave her greater distance. She tore through the streets, dodging between buildings, doing anything she could to displace herself to them and make herself scarce. The only problem was that now she was very lost. She had no idea how long she'd been running but she couldn't sense anyone around her so she ducked into a dark alleyway, pressing herself tightly against the wall.

"This isn't right!" Arcainous shouted as they watched her hide.

"She has to face them," Raiden insisted.

"Can't we find another way to test her?"

"Stop, both of you," Fisonma said, watching as both backed down. "She's done well so far. She needs to see this through to the end."

Arcainous could make no arguments. All the Guardians had their own trials testing their will, strength, awareness—many traits to ensure they were the best protectors for the Realms. Reluctantly, he set his personal feelings aside and stared into the orb, barely able to make out her form concealed in the shadows. "Be safe," he whispered.

Tara pressed as far into the wall as she could, wishing she could push through it. She did what she could to slow her breathing but even the roar of her heartbeat seemed loud as it echoed within her own ears. Now that she was safe she could reflect on her runes. She never thought she would ever have to use them. She knew they were there to protect her, but she thought they were there in an energy sense, not in a physical one. She strained her ears as the thrum of her heart died down, listening for any sounds of her pursuers but heard nothing.

"I need to get out of here," she breathed, daring to push from the wall, but as she stepped into the haunting moonlight, she found that she should have just kept running.

She screamed as she came eye to eye with Gabriel, who wrapped his hand snugly around her throat, hoisting her into the air. "You thought these little tricks of yours would save you?" he asked, allowing her the first full glimpse of his face as the moonlight betrayed her and fell upon the gnarled features.

"You are so weak," Dante said as he and Malik flanked their leader.

"Just give up," Gabriel said as he threw her back into the alley and onto the cold ground. "It will be much easier for everyone involved if you do."

"Without her protection you'll be ours in time anyway," Malik said with a deep chuckle.

"Quit running from your destiny," Gabriel said as he again extended his hand to her.

"My destiny is what I make of it!" she shouted, rubbing her throat. "No one will shape it but me!"

Gabriel sighed and waved his hand. "I've had enough with the games. Take her, but leave her living. Vonspar has plans for her."

Tara's eyes widened as she scrambled back. "Vonspar . . . oh no . . . Darius," she breathed, but they were suddenly upon her like the strike of a snake.

Her mind went blank. She couldn't recall any of her runes to protect her and Arcainous and Raiden watched in horror as she was suddenly consumed by the shadows.

"Get her out of there!" Arcainous begged. But before anything could be done, the three were startled by an intense flash of light.

"What was that?" Raiden asked as the three looked closer into the orb.

When the intensity of the light faded, they saw a domed shield of ice energy surrounding Tara, and the three vampires sprawled out around her. Fisonma looked closer, segmenting out a portion of the shield to appear on a separate space below the profiles of the vampires. "Do you see what I'm seeing, Raiden?" she asked. Concern and intrigue hung heavy in her tone.

"You don't think . . .," Raiden began, tracing the white swirls that were mixed into the energy.

"It's very possible," Fisonma said.

"What's possible?" Arcainous asked, but before anything could go further, the sound of exploding energy turned their attention back to the sphere in enough time to see the shards cut into the once again mobile trio sending them fleeing into the night uttering their curses. "Get her out of there!" he demanded, and this time Fisonma listened. With a wave of her hand, a door appeared behind Tara, emitting a warming white glow.

Tara spun around and cowered back. After what she'd just gone through, it could be nothing more than another foul trick, but the energy emitted from the door made her dive through it without a second thought. She soon found herself sprawled on her bedroom floor, and when she looked up, she watched the door fade away. "Wait, the doors don't do that . . ." She leaped to her feet quickly and looked around. "What's going on!" she shouted as the sphere the three watched went dark.

"We have much to do, Raiden." Fisonma said.

"Will anyone care to explain?" Arcainous asked.

"When we're sure," Raiden said. "If we're right, this could change the future of everything."

Arcainous stared at the dark sphere, his only link now to who Belzak used to be. He often wondered if he knew his fate, but that was something to think on for another day. So much had happened and much needed to be done and he exited the room with a fresh picture of those haunting eyes burned into his mind.

Tara paced around her room, sat down on her bed, then was up pacing again. She felt caged and her mind wouldn't shut down. Running her hands over her arms she felt moisture. Thinking it was only sweat she paid no mind until she felt the thickness of the fluid. Only then did she dare look down only to see blood smeared down her arm. She sighed and pulled her shirt off, tossing it to the floor before heading in for yet another shower. As she cleaned her arm, she inspected the damage and found a semi deep cut, wondering if it was from her confrontation. As the spray washed any evidence of her encounter from her body, events were falling into place that would change the course of her life forever.

CHAPTER

8

Family Tie

Yukino stood in her kitchen, leaning against the counter that overlooked their backyard. Nestled in her hands was a half-drunk cup of tea, steam wafting in small curls as each sigh cooled the surface. For days now she had been having unsettling dreams and a nagging urge to contact Tara and Senia.

"Something isn't right," she said as she set down her cup. She knew well enough to trust her instincts, and right now something grave was crossing her mind's eye. With their number on speed dial, calling took no more than seconds. "I just hope they're home," she said as she listened to the phone ring.

Tara rolled over and stared at the phone as it began to ring. Hoping it was good news from the hospital she scooped it into her hand and accepted the call. "Hello?" Her voice was marred by a cat-like stretch before she again settled into her bed.

"Tara?" Yukino asked, not really recognizing her voice. It sounded so different, soft, defeated, drained. "Honey, you sound horrible. Is everything okay?"

Tara stared ahead, dazed at just how easily Yukino could read her. But it didn't take long for the floodgates to open and tears that she was sure no longer existed began flowing. She began talking, relaying everything that had happened to her mother, omitting things that had happened between herself and Darius. "I've been calling and leaving messages," she finally said as she finished filling in what had happened.

"You did?" Yukino's brow arched as she flipped through the message and call logs, finding nothing. She shook her head slowly and let out a silent sigh. "How is she?"

"It's still touch and go," Tara admitted. "Her leg is healing just fine, and the doctors are kind of hopeful now that the swelling in her head has gone down, but they won't know anything solid until she wakes up."

"I'm so sorry we're not able to be there to help you, dear," Yukino said as her eyes scanned toward the front door, knowing Darius would be home soon.

"It's okay," Tara assured. "Mark and my grandparents have been really great about making sure I'm okay."

The two talked for only a few moments after that before Tara had to go. Yukino gave her their best before hanging up and setting the phone down. Even with bits of information she knew that something wasn't right and she was slightly irritated.

"How could he be so careless," she wondered. Not long after she'd sat down, she heard the front door opening. "Darius." Her voice was flat and even as she rose to face him.

"Hi, Mom," he greeted though his brow soon arched as they faced each other and he could visibly see the irritation etched into her features. "Um, what's wrong?"

"I was hoping you could tell me," Yukino said as she folded her arms loosely across her chest.

"What are you talking about?" Darius asked with a growing scowl.

"I just got off the phone with Tara," she answered, taking note of the darkening look across his face. It was that look that gave her all the answers she needed. "So you have been deleting her calls and messages."

"So what if I was!" he snapped back. "It's not like it's our problem. They aren't even family!"

Yukino gasped at the outburst, and in a matter of seconds, she was across the room, and the back of her right hand had found its home against the side of his face before Darius even had a chance to react. "How dare you speak of them like that," she chastised. "They are family. Just because we don't share the same blood doesn't make them any less family than you and I are."

Darius was stunned that his mother had actually struck him, but as he rubbed the side of his face, he decided that he was no longer going to take any of this. "Family?" he asked, his gaze bearing down onto his mother. "Family doesn't hide things from one another," he growled.

Yukino was unfazed by the look she was receiving, and her arms once again folded. "I don't know what you're talking about," she replied coolly. "I've never hidden anything from you."

"Haven't you?" he asked as he strode to a set of shelves, retrieving one of the progress journals she kept on them.

"What are you doing with that!" she demanded. "Those notes are private and not for you to read!"

"Oh, so now you remember," he said, swinging the book side to side between his fingers. "That night, she traveled, and you kept it hidden."

"Her experiences are her own!" she challenged. "I don't tell her about your travels and experiences, and hers was enough that her mind blocked it out."

"You're always making excuses for her," she snarled. But before she could say more, he threw the book to the floor and stormed from the house.

"Darius!" She called to him, but it was no use. He was already gone. She sighed as she knelt down, picking up the book. "What has gotten into you lately?" she asked as she ran her palm over the cover of the book to cleanse his energy from it before replacing it onto the shelf.

He stormed down the streets, hands shoved deep into his pockets as he uttered curse after curse under his breath both toward his mother and to Tara. "How could she side with . . . with her?" he growled, each anger infused second passing adding more energy to the growing seed within the depths of his heart. The more the anger consumed him, the less aware he was that he was being watched until he found himself running head first into Vonspar. Unaware that it was him, his first reaction was to snap.

"Hey, watch where you're—oh, hey, V." His tone dropped dramatically as he looked at his friend.

"Hey yourself, D," Vonspar replied, brushing himself off and taking in his friends features. "To what do I owe the honor of this little . . . head-on collision?" he asked, peering into the eyes of his friend.

"Yeah, sorry, 'bout that," Darius said with a lopsided grin, his tone becoming almost sheepish.

"Problems on the home front?" Vonspar asked as the two began walking down the street.

"You could say that," Darius answered.

"Girlfriend?" Vonspar wanted to see the look that crossed his face with this question.

He wasn't disappointed as he saw the darkness in his face. "Don't have one."

Playing this up, he tried to look surprised. "But you two seemed so happy, I mean, aside from the distance and all."

"Yeah, well, I found out that her and my mom were keeping some pretty important things from me, so I told her that everything I felt for her was just a game."

Vonspar read his energy as plain as words on paper, and the gaze that crossed his eyes was very sinister. "A game, huh? Did you ever have any feelings for her?"

Darius looked skyward, thinking back on his life back in the states. "Nope, can't say that I ever did. Feelings of betrayal, but never anything physical. That was all an act to try and get the information I wanted from her."

Vonspar stopped suddenly and turned to face Darius, a devious grin crossing his lips. "What if I told you that I could help you exact revenge on them for what they've done?"

Darius stopped, curious as to what he had in mind. "What were you thinking of?" he asked.

"Something grand enough to let them feel what they've made you feel with this grievous act of betrayal," Vonspar explained. It was a bit over dramatic, but if he could sink his claws into his soul.

"I'd say, bring it on," Darius answered.

As the two shook hands, the seed that had taken root so long ago wrapped itself around his heart as it worked to suffocate the light Tara had planted before they left.

While one light was being extinguished, on the other side of the world, another was becoming stronger. The phone continued to ring as Tara dove across her bed to grab it. She held her breath as she listened to the voice on the other end, her eyes lighting up as information was passed along.

"You're kidding, right?" she asked, not sure if she should believe what she was hearing. "Really? That's awesome! Of course! I'll be there just as soon as I can!"

CHAPTER

9

New Directions

Tara sat on the edge of her seat, eyes glued to the road while Mark drove as fast as legally possible. Evening had begun to set in as they reached the hospital but Tara didn't care.

"Come on, Mark!" she exclaimed, already out of the car and bouncing around.

"She's not going anywhere," Mark told her, failing at the attempt of a joke when he received the oddest upturned brow in response. With that though, she was gone, almost sprinting to the doors.

"Where's the fire?" he called as he tried to catch up, doing so only because she was waiting for the elevator. He took this chance to study her, seeing the anticipation etched into her face, the hope that filled her eyes which only grew as the numbers lit up, coming closer to them. He had to laugh though as the same process was repeated once they were inside and heading up.

"What's so funny?" she asked, brows merging into a scowl.

"You look like you're waiting in a long line for the restroom," he teased, rubbing his arm as she slugged it.

Shortly after, the doors opened, and she was gone. She waved to the nurses on duty, their voices only a mumble to her as she skidded to a stop in front of Senia's door, almost missing it. "Mom!" she exclaimed as she dove for the comfy chair beside her mother's bed.

Senia smiled, resting her hand upon Tara's head as she rested it on the bed.

"Hello," she said as Mark finally entered the room.

Her voice was a bit raspy from the tubes that had been down her throat and from simple lack of use, but as the three talked her voice continued to get stronger until it was like nothing had been wrong at all. Prospects were looking good for her being able to come home soon, but work was an entirely different story. There was still swelling around her brain, so if she was able to go to work, it would be purely a desk job. That was a far point though as they sat and enjoyed each other's company well into the night.

Days later it was time for soccer camp, and as Tara walked to school, she couldn't help but notice how time seemed to be going by so fast.

"It's probably everything that's going on," she said to herself as she reached the school grounds and headed in to the locker room to change.

Emerging through the door, she stood in the shadows of the building, watching as kids ran on and off the field, most showing off for the scouts which led to a few injuries.

"Really," she mumbled as she jogged out to the field to join the rest of the varsity tryouts.

The team quickly fell into its routine, feeding off of a collective energy, each member of the team put to the ultimate test by the rest until the coach called the game. Exhausted, the team jogged in from the field.

"You've gotten better over the years, if that's possible."

The voice made Tara stop in her tracks, staring at the man just off to her right.

"Me?" she asked,

Raiden nodded and approached her. "Yes, you," he said as he flipped through pages on his clipboard.

"Um . . . thanks," she said warily.

"Have you given any thoughts to college yet?" he asked, watching her with great interest.

"Somewhere local," she replied, not really interested in the whole college subject. She had the school year to figure it out anyway.

"That's perfect," he said as he began to scribble some notes. "I'm from the college in the city. Your grades are simply outstanding, and I'm sure we could offer you a full scholarship."

Tara blinked and stared at him. It would be easier on her mom; she'd be close enough so she could take care of her. "Uh, sure."

"Great. I'll just need to talk to your parents. You know, discuss the programs, have our academic dean come out and go over the school as a whole."

Tara stiffened, and Raiden could feel her energy solidify into a shield around her. "Yeah, I don't know when will be a good time to talk to her." Her tone had even changed from unsure to almost distant and cold. "She's a cop, so . . ."

"That's fine, just have her call me when she's available," he said, trying to be reassuring as he handed her his card.

"Yup." It was all he would get out of her as she jogged back to the locker room to change. As she again reached the shadows cast by the building she could feel a pair of eyes bearing down upon her. Her skin crawled as she recognized the leer, and as she looked over her shoulder, she saw Toran and a couple of his friends staring at her.

"Creep," she muttered with a glare to return his stare before disappearing into the building to change and head home.

The rest of the summer passed by fairly quickly. Senia had come home and before Tara was aware, school had started. "I wish I could clone myself," she groaned as she slumped into her seat.

"Oh? Why's that?"

Tara looked to her left to see that the goalie from her soccer team had heard her mumbling and she offered a sheepish smile. "Well, with soccer, academics, and driving classes . . ." She omitted caring for her mother from the chain of things to do for the simple fact that she hated people knowing anything personal about her.

"No social life, huh," she said dryly. "I couldn't do it."

"Yeah," Tara said with a small laugh. "Such is the price paid by being a senior though, right?" The two shared a laugh before settling back into the academic routine as the teacher walked into the classroom.

* * *

Mark studied her as he drove her home from her driver's test. Night had started to fall and he could tell that Tara was starting to fall asleep. "How are you holding up?" he asked, brows creased with concern.

"I'm doing all right," she assured, leaning back into the seat with her newly obtained license clutched in her hands. She was excited, but exhaustion was winning the fight this night.

"You look a bit worn out," he admitted.

"A little," she confessed. "It's just hard seeing Mom do nothing, but wait while they decide whether or not she can go back to work."

"You're too young to worry about that. Why don't you let me and your grandparents take that on. You have enough on your plate as it is."

"I can handle it," she lied, trying to convince herself more than she was trying to convince him. She stared out her window, signaling the end of the conversation and before Mark was aware, he could hear the light snoring coming from the passenger seat.

"When you're older you can take on the world," he said softly as his eyes returned to the road. "But until then, let us handle the big stuff." The rest of the ride home was silent. When he pulled into the drive he nudged her shoulder gently to wake her. "You're home, champ."

Her head rolled lazily to the side as her eyes drooped open. "Champ?" she asked, her lips scrunching into a disapproving look. "What am I, six?"

Mark couldn't help but laugh as the wit he was so used to began to return. "I could have called you tiger, or sport if you'd prefer."

Tara sat upright and stared. "Eww . . . no, thanks," she said as she pushed the door open with her foot. Standing, she stretched, feeling her back adjust before releasing a loud sigh. "Did you wanna come in and see everyone?" she asked, noting the presence of her grandparents' car in the drive.

"Not tonight," he answered. "I've got the early shift and I need to let everyone know that she's doing all right. Maybe next time."

"All right. Good night, Mark."

"Night, kiddo."

Kiddo? She shut the car door and watched him drive off. "Well, I guess it's better than champ," she said with a mock shudder before heading inside.

Tara's grandmother was waiting by the door when it opened. "Hello, dear."

"Hi, Grandma." Tara smiled, easing into the warmth of a welcomed hug.

"How was your day, Tara?" she asked as she led her to the couch and took her books.

"It was all right," she answered as she sat down, looking around the room. "Where's Mom?"

"Sleeping," came the reply from the kitchen.

Tara looked over the back of the couch seeing her grandfather doing the nightly dishes. "Grandpa," she protested. "I can do those later."

But he would have none of it and simply waved his hand at her, making her sigh and snuggle against her grandmother. "You've had a rough few weeks. You need to take a break for yourself," her grandmother said soothingly as she ran her fingers over her hair.

Even as Tara tried protesting, it was quelled as her grandmother placed a finger against her lips and shook her head.

"We put a plate of food in the fridge for you," came the voice from behind them.

Tara looked up to see her grandfather drying his hands on a beige hand towel before tossing it over his shoulder. He then leaned over the couch and kissed the top of her head and looked at his wife.

"We should get going, let her do her homework and eat."

She nodded and rose to her feet with Tara.

"We'll call later to see how you're doing," she assured as she kissed Tara's forehead.

Tara saw them off, waving as she watched them pull onto the road and into the darkness before turning off the porch light and locking the door. She headed into the kitchen, grabbing her food from the fridge and nibbled on it as she walked down the hall to check on her mother. Allowing her eyes to adjust to the darkness, she soon saw the outline of her mother, asleep on her side, her ribs rising and falling with each peaceful breath. Satisfied, she silently closed her door and returned to the kitchen to finish her dinner and wash her plate.

Turning off the lights as she went, she grabbed her books and headed into her room to study. When she turned on her light, however, she was greeted by a large stuffed wolf sitting on her bed. "Looks like Arcainous," she said as she tossed her bag onto her bed and hugged it tightly to her. "I miss him," she mumbled as she buried her head into the top of the plush fur. She was still tired from the week, so with the weekend upon her she decided that her homework would wait. Instead, she curled up on her bed with the wolf and fell fast asleep.

School continued to keep Tara busy, and even with her license, Mark was still over taking as much care of her mom as he always had. Before any of them realized though, the holidays had come, and Tara was getting ready to go on winter break.

"Mom!" She emerged from the kitchen, wiping her hands on a towel having just put a sheet of cookies into the oven to bake. It was well into the morning, and Senia hadn't emerged from her room yet. "Mom, are you all right?" she asked as she walked down the hall.

Knocking on the door got no response, and as she opened the door, she could tell something was wrong. From her space in the doorway, she could see the sheen of sweat covering her face, and by the time she reached her mother's side, she had her phone out, dialing for EMS.

She shook Senia's shoulders, calling to her, patting her cheeks before shaking her shoulders again. "No, she's not waking up," she told the operator. "She's all sweaty, and she feels like she's on fire, but she's shaking." She listened to the dispatcher, nodding and shaking her head off instinct before verbalizing her answers. The sounds of sirens drawing closer made her look back over her shoulders. "They're here, I have to go," she said, tossing the phone to the bed before racing to the front door. "Please help her," she begged as she led them down the hall, stepping aside to let them do their job.

"Has she been acting or feeling out of sorts lately?" The question drew her from the deluge of thoughts that had flooded her mind as to what was wrong.

"Huh, oh, um . . . well, I know she's been more tired than usual the last few days, but we all thought it was because of the physical therapy."

"Tara?"

"Mark!" Tara ran from the EMT, running down the hall, nearly tripping over her feet as she clung to him.

"Hey," he said, resting his hands on her shoulders and pushing her back enough to look at her. "What's going on?"

"I don't know." Her eyes were darting around, watching people going in and out, carrying bags, meds, and things she didn't recognize. "She won't wake up." While the two talked, one of the EMTs came out to talk to them. They had her on oxygen and were taking her to the hospital. They couldn't give her any explanation and could only pack Senia into the ambulance before rushing away leaving Mark and Tara standing in a state of shock in the living room.

That night they were told that she'd come down with a cranial infection and would have to be hospitalized for a few days while they fought it off. The days passed slowly and Tara would often look at the calendar, counting down the days, hoping that her mother would come home. The holiday was spent at the hospital, but Senia was awake and talking so no one really minded.

"I'm sorry about this, everyone," she said in a timid tone.

"Quit worrying, Mom," Tara assured.

"What she said," Mark added as he leaned in and kissed her cheek. "You just need to focus on getting better."

School had already started again by the time Senia was allowed to return home, and soon winter had given way to spring. With the change in the seasons talk soon focused on prom and as girls giggled about who they'd like to have ask them Tara could only cringe. To her it was just another day and she had no desire to attend.

"So given any thought to prom?"

Tara flinched, her gaze narrowing at the back of her locker before slamming it shut. "Not even a passing one," she replied coolly, averting her gaze from Toran's direction, but as she tried to step past him, he planted his palm firmly against the locker next to hers.

"You don't need to be so rude about it," he began, his gaze once again bearing down onto her. "I was going to ask you to be my date."

Tara blinked several times before erupting into a fit of laughter. "You're kidding, right?" she asked, looking upon him with a quizzical stare. "Have you learned nothing from our previous encounters?" she said, her gaze taking on a more serious nature. "Even if I was going," she began, putting emphasis on the word *was*, "there's no way I'd be caught dead going there with you." She stepped past him and stormed off only to stop suddenly as he grabbed her arm. "Hey! Let go!" she snapped, but as she spun to face him, she came face-to-face with a look that was truly dark.

"You don't have to act like such a stuck-up bitch," he snarled.

She'd make him regret those words, and her eyes took on a danger to them that nearly matched his own. That look alone made him loosen his grip slightly. "You haven't seen bitch yet, coward," she hissed, yanking her arm free of his grasp. "Touch me again, and you'll see just how nasty I can be."

And with that, she spun around, heading to her next class and leaving him to sweep up a bit of his ego.

The rest of the year passed quickly. Tara accepted the scholarship that Raiden had offered her, but Senia had also gone back to the hospital with another infection that the doctors couldn't find the cause to. Tara focused through it all, acing her finals with help from her grandparents and Mark. With them out of her way she felt like she could breathe for the first time in over a year.

Tara pulled to the curb as she reached her house, seeing that everyone was over. She sat in the cab of her truck for a few moments. It was going to be so different no longer coming here every day after school, but as she stared at the back of her mother's car, she gave a small but sound nod. She knew what she wanted to do with her life. She was going to study medicine so that perhaps what was happening to her family wouldn't happen to another. Exhaling the thought from her mind, she slid from the truck and slung her bag over her shoulder. Heading into the house, she smiled and waved to everyone. "Hi."

"Well, hello there, honey," Senia said as she rose to welcome her daughter home.

"I have some interesting news," Tara said as she slid her bag from her shoulder and took a seat. All eyes were soon upon her, making her nervous. She never got used to it even though she knew she'd have to quite soon. "Well," she began, "first off, I've aced my finals."

"We knew you would." Her grandfather beamed.

Tara smiled warmly before taking in a slow breath. "Secondly, I've been named valedictorian for our graduating class."

She hadn't even gotten the phrase finished before everyone's voices merged into a single mass of mumbling words. "Oh, sweetie, that's wonderful!" Senia squealed. Tara blinked repeatedly as she was hugged. Hearing her mother squeal like a kid was just plain wrong, on so many levels, but she let them have their moment and just thanked the Gods that they weren't in public.

The last month flew by, too quickly it seemed, and before any of them knew it, they were all standing outside the building where they were to graduate, dressed in their caps and gowns. They filed in through a side door while Tara and the salutatorian took their seats on the stage, accompanied by selected faculty and key speakers. Tara stared blankly into the crowds of people. So many of them. She never thought her class was as large as it was, but seeing them all together in one space.

The principal called things to order, saying just how proud he was of those graduating. He seemed a bit long winded, telling them that he knew that great things awaited them in life and things of that nature. Others followed and Tara finally zoned them out and sighed. A large door was about to open in her life, in all of their lives, and she was sure that many of her classmates were thinking about the very same thing. She wasn't too far gone from the program though and when her name was called she rose calmly to her feet and approached the podium. Waiting for the applause to die she smiled as she looked over those before her. Insight, inspiration, words of encouragement. That was what her speech consisted of and even those in the audience were moved by her words.

"She's very wise for her age," Mark said as he gave Senia's hand a gentle squeeze.

Senia just smiled. "She always has been," she replied with silent pride.

The salutatorian was the next to speak. Though not as moving as Tara's speech, his was just as insightful, and after his speech was done, the two were excused to join the rest of their class. They then filed out to either side of the stage as the presentation of their diplomas began. Tara shifted from side to side, listening as the girl beside her compared this to being herded like cattle. While she was right, it was something Tara wished not to dwell upon. It was supposed to be Darius standing beside me, she thought as her mind drifted off, tuning the goings on out completely. Her thoughts quickly centered on her second family, wondering what they were doing, and wondering if Yukino was going through this same ordeal with Darius. She was so wrapped up in her thoughts though that she almost missed her name being called.

Rushing forward, she smiled while her picture was taken as she accepted her diploma. She waited for the girl she was to walk with, the two descending the steps, and once more taking their seats to watch as the rest of their class received theirs. This gave her the perfect time to zone, and that was precisely what she did, tuning everything out until the principal approached the podium for the last time. He once more gave a little speech, stressing again how proud he was of them before he asked them to stand. With a few more words he soon announced them as graduated and the air was alive with a sea of caps. Tara tossed hers only to catch it between two of her knuckles by the corner. With a swift flip it was once more upon her head, the tassel now on the other side of her head.

Turning around, she watched with widened eyes as the group of students merged with the group of family members, creating a single mass that made her cringe. For a brief moment, she had lost sight of her family, her eyes darting from side to side before freezing forward. As she searched she could feel a gaze raking over her, causing the hairs on her arms to stand. Turning her head to the right she found the cause behind her unease, locking stares with Toran. His arm was slung around some blond that she didn't recognize, but he soon let it drop, much to her dismay. She was trying to figure out what he was doing until he saw the slow deliberate paces he was taking that would lead him to her, but his movements were halted as the presence of two uniformed officers came from the other side.

She grinned, watching him slink back to the blond who was now lecturing him and spun around. "Mom! Mark."

Senia opened her arms, hugging her tightly. "We're so proud of you," she said softly

"You made quite the speech, Tara. Had a lot of the parents moved to tears," Mark added with a grin that was returned with a light laugh.

"Where are Grandma and Grandpa?" Tara asked, still very aware that Toran's gaze hadn't left them.

"Your grandmother wasn't feeling very well, so they left after you received your diploma. They wanted me to tell you though just how proud they are of you." Senia's smile was soft and warm, but even Tara could tell that something wasn't right behind it, and she feared that she was getting sick again.

"Can we go?" Tara asked. "The noise is starting to make my head hurt."

"Of course, dear," Senia replied, wrapping her arm snuggly around Tara's shoulder.

The three walked toward the exit, though she could still feel Toran's gaze cutting through her. Once they were outside though, it lifted, but even as they escaped into the night, none of them knew the changes that would greet them in the near future.

CHAPTER

10

Breaking Point

Summer flew by quickly for Tara with campus tours and packing consuming most of her time. Before she knew it, she was standing at the foot of her drive with her mom and Mark, truck packed, and the engine rumbling low in the background. She stared at her mother for a long moment before speaking. "Call me if you need anything. It's not like I'll be far."

Senia smiled, keeping a perfect poise for this new adventure in her daughter's life. "I can handle myself, dear," she assured.

"I'm sure you can," Tara started, leaving the phrase unfinished as she exchanged glances with Mark.

"Don't forget to let us know when your games are," Mark piped in, trying to ease the situation.

Tara smiled, allowing the subject to drop for the time being and hugged them tightly. "I will," she promised before sliding into her truck and pulled out onto the street. As she drove off, she looked into her rearview mirror, and she watched as her mom leaned into Mark, laying her head on his shoulder. She smiled, happy that she had finally found someone she could spend her life with.

"I swear, if they don't get married soon," she said, laughing at the empty-ended threat as she turned up her music.

Summer gave way to fall, and with fall came the throes of college life. Scheduling her classes an hour apart gave her ample time for studying, homework, and tutoring where she needed it. This also freed up her afternoons and evenings for soccer and an attempt at a social life. Taking the field though was like second nature to her. She moved with a feline grace across the field, her quick yet deliberate moves proving without a doubt that she'd earned her place on the team.

One night after practice she was passing by the large fountain in the middle of the campus when she felt a sudden shiver race the length of her spine. She stopped and dropped her bag, spinning around, expecting to see someone behind her, but saw nothing. The feeling of being watched grew stronger, and as she peered into the darkness, she realized that not even the sound of nocturnal creatures that she would normally hear resonated through the darkness. She closed her eyes, reaching out with her energy in an attempt to locate the source of her discomfort. She found nothing more than the trees and brush that surrounded her. Scowling at her defeat she grabbed her bag, slung it over her shoulder and headed off once more.

As she continued walking though, the feelings continued, even growing a bit stronger and more daring as the sounds of rustling leaves echoed behind her. She spun around, thinking it was a sick prank, but again found nothing, so she kept walking, choosing to ignore the sounds behind her. She didn't realize it, but her pace had quickened to the point that when she saw the light of her dorm building, her heart was pounding in her chest. Reaching the small quad, she saw that for a weekend, there were only a handful of people.

"That's odd," she said under her breath as she climbed the stairs to her room. "Usually there's more people than that, especially on a weekend."

Once inside the safety of her dorm, she flipped on the light and let her bag slip from her shoulder to the floor with a thud. A quick survey let her know that she was alone, most likely for the night. Her roommate was never one for staying around once the sun went down. She wasn't going to complain about it though. Having a roommate made her meditation and rune work kind of hard, so she took the solitude where she could get it. She opened the cabinet above her desk and retrieved several white candles, placing them in a precise way before lighting them. Taking in several deep breaths she allowed her body to calm down, feeling her nerves settling. When she was centered, she stepped back and took a seat in the center of the room. She reached out to the energy of the room, feeling it, allowing it to form in her mind until she saw everything perfectly, even seeing herself as she looked around.

When she reached the depth of meditation, she desired she pushed back to her feet and held out her right arm. Her fingers curled, leaving one extended as she began tracing in the air. "Bound by light and protection, I call you forth." Her eyes shot open, as did her hand, as an image began to appear before her. "Rune of protection." Her words finished, she watched as the image of a shield came fully into view, glowing brilliantly. She then moved her hand to the window, repeating the process, over and over until every possible entry point into her room was covered. Returning to the center of the room she knelt down and placed her palms on the floor as a larger shield appeared, mirroring itself onto the ceiling, creating a dome of protective energy.

When things were done to her liking, she lifted her head and looked around, admiring her handiwork with a nod of satisfaction. She pushed to her feet, expelling a tired sigh, and returned to her desk. Picking up each candle, she thanked the energy for protecting her and showing her what needed to be done. She then lightly puffed out the flame before replacing them back into the cabinet. Killing the lights, she slid into bed, assured that she would be protected from whatever was in the darkness, and with that, she fell into a fitful sleep.

By the night of her first game, the events of that night were nothing more than fragments of a forgotten dream. Raiden stood in the front of the bleachers, arms folded across his chest as he watched the game progress. He listened as some of the parents discussed their girls, and others that were on the team. He listened until the chatter began turning into gossip and with a disgusted look, returned his attention back to the field just as someone from the other team tripped one of their best runners. Tara leaped easily over her but stopped to help her up as the ref called some fouls.

"You okay?" Tara asked as she helped her hobble back to the sidelines.

"I'm fine." Her tone was defeated as she waited for the sports therapy crew to show up and check her out. She then pulled Tara closer, her eyes darting before she leaned up to whisper against her ear. "Kick their asses for me."

Tara stood and grinned, thrusting her right arm out, giving a thumbs up and a wink. "Gladly," she replied with a smile so devious that it drowned out her usual innocent nature.

"Come on!" the coach called out, clapping his hands together firmly. As Tara jogged back onto the field the call was made and they would get a penalty shot.

The team stood on the field to discuss what they were going to do. "Okay, Jaz, you've got the best throw," Tina said. "Toss it to Tara."

"They've been all over me tonight." Tara scowled.

"Yeah, I know." Tina sighed, but she was still confident. "We're tied, but we're at the end of the game, so we need to pull out some interesting stops."

"What do you mean 'stops'?" Jazmine asked.

"We're going to rally around Tara." She then looked at Tara only. "When you get the ball, do a swift kick back to Mia. We'll all be around you so it will hopefully confuse them. When you've kicked it back, just take off running like you have the ball with you. If it works, Mia, Jaz, Kelly, and I will be able to run it down for a goal while everyone else keeps our opening, well, open."

"Sure thing," Kelly said with a sound nod.

"Should be interesting, at the very least," Tara added with an evil cackle as they spread out to the field.

Tara puffed her cheeks full of air as she looked around. She could feel a pressured gaze as if everyone's eyes were fixated upon her. The ball was thrown, and the plan rolled into motion. Tara broke free, her feet going through the motions of having the ball, but not even midway down the field she realized that they were no longer following her. Stopping, she saw that her team was in the middle of a struggle to keep the ball.

"Ugh." She raced down the field, sliding into the fray on her side to kick the ball. She then flipped to her feet and grinned as she joined the rest of her team, staying close to Jazmine. "Go down the field," she whispered.

"Huh? Why?"

"Just trust me," she assured. She then watched as Jazmine disappeared behind the fray and almost missed as the ball was coming into play closer to their goal.

Getting back into the mess, she weaved between players with an agility that surprised most, and when she found the ball, both she and the girl controlling it kicked for it at the same time. The crack of their shins meeting echoed across the field and even into the bleachers, but as the girl fell, everyone turned to see the soccer ball sailing straight for Jazmine.

"Ohh yeah!" Mia shouted as the group raced the length of the field.

"It's all you, Jaz!" Tina shouted, watching as Jazmine side kicked the ball, barely making it between the goal marker and the goalie. The crowds soon erupted in cheers as time was called and they were announced the victors.

"That was brutal." Kelly huffed. "This better get easier from here."

Raiden smiled in satisfaction, turning to regard Senia and seeing how the sickness had ravaged her body. "Tara did well tonight."

Senia looked to her side and gave a frail smile. "She always does well in what she puts her mind to."

Raiden nodded and stepped down to talk to the coach just as Tara emerged from the crowds. "Mom!"

"You were fantastic." Senia beamed.

"Bet you could go pro," Mark chipped in.

"Nah," Tara said with a blush racing her cheeks. "I just do this for fun," she claimed. "Besides," she said with an adopted look of thought. "I'm going for a medical degree," she announced, hands resting on her hips in triumph. She then took the time to look intently at her mother, her hands falling to her sides. "Mom, are you all right? You don't look so well."

Senia insisted that she was fine, claiming fatigue, and discussing it no further. But when she started coughing Mark pulled her aside, wrapping a blanket around her and ushering her away quickly. Tara tried to chase after them, but they drove off before she could reach the car.

She stood, glaring into the darkness, hands curled into light fists as she watched the tail lights disappear into nothing. "You know . . ." The voice broke her thoughts, quelling the growing anger before it could rise. "She's trying her best to be strong for you."

Tara's heart did a triple beat, leaping into her throat as she spun around. "Raiden . . ." Her look was less than pleased as she swallowed, dispelling the lump and putting her internal organs back where they should be.

He just smiled, standing beside her as the two stared out into the darkness. "I see our faith in you was well placed." He cast a side glance to her to gauge her reaction but got none. He nodded and looked back out into the night. "How about a lift back to the dorm?" he asked.

Tara arched a brow and turned her head some. "No, thanks."

It was weird that he would offer her a ride, and as she looked back into the awaiting night, she scrunched her brow, wishing that she had driven herself to the field as the watchful feeling began to creep around her once more.

So he continued as if she had said nothing. "I know you can sense it," he pressed, watching as her body froze, her fingers curling tightly around the front of her jersey.

"sense what," she asked, feigning ignorance.

"The shift in energies," he replied.

Tara blinked. This came too easily for him to discuss. This bothered her a great deal, but with enough coaxing, and a bit of curiosity on her part, she finally gave in and followed him to his car.

I'm going to regret this, she thought as she tossed her bag into the back seat and slid into the passenger seat in front. "So how do you know about energy and stuff?"

"It wasn't a coincidence that I found you," he continued, ignoring her outright as he got into the car and started the engine. Any hopes of a conversation after that point were doused though, and the remainder of the trip was made in silence. Tara stared out the window as he pulled into the dorm parking lot and pushed the door open quickly as soon as he came to a full stop. As she leaned over the seat to retrieve her bag, he took a firm hold of her wrist, startling her, "Whatever happens, always have faith in the Light."

"What?"

"It will never fail you, but you have to believe in it."

Tara stared blankly. Her back was starting to hurt with the odd angle she was standing in, and the rose-quartz pendant that she had started wearing had slid from her jersey and was now swaying in the open air. "As you can see. I have faith in my own protection."

Raiden was beginning to lose his patience. Why did they never listen when he sought them out? "Your shields are strong, but they will do little against the things you have been seeing lately."

Tara pulled away in fear. No one knew what had been going on lately, so how could he guess it so easily? She closed his door firmly and backed away, heading back to her dorm, ignoring anything else he was saying to her as she tucked her pendant back into her jersey.

Once she reached the quad though, she was roped into socializing with a few girls from the team who were hanging out, still celebrating their first victory of the season. When she was done fulfilling social obligations, she excused herself for the night and headed to her dorm, where she found her roommate passed out on her bed. She changed quickly and sat in the center of her bed, her MP3 player playing a classical score as she unwound from the day's events. She lost herself to the beat of the music, releasing her mind until she finally fell into a fitful sleep, wrapped in the warmth of an energy that was not yet her own.

The remainder of the season passed by slowly. With all the close calls they had, they still managed to remain undefeated and even went as far as to sweep their championship games. But in their rise to the top Tara noticed that her mother made it to less and less games, eventually becoming nonexistent. It had been obvious to the coach that she was distracted, but she took the growing irritation, forcing it through her system and using the energy to drive her to her limits with an increased focus.

To celebrate their flawless streak, the Dean of Students hosted a banquet in their honor. Tara had received a couple of awards and several announcements of recognition for her part in aiding the team, but outside of that, the evening was extremely uneventful, and she found herself getting very bored. "Where's Mom?"

"She hasn't been well," her grandmother confessed.

Tara felt that the lack of communication was more than just a bit underhanded. "Why didn't anyone call?"

"She didn't want you to worry."

Tara's brow twitched. She could have made the argument that by not keeping her in the loop about what was going on would make her worry more, especially when she was looking for her mother at each of her soccer games, but being in public, she thought better of it and just sulked deeper into her chair, her arms folded tightly across her chest. As the night wore on, she paid enough attention to get through the endless supply of conversations and questions.

When it was finally over, she walked out to the parking lot with her grandparents. The small talk seemed strained, but she was also still feeling a bit wounded having been left out of, to her, some fairly important goings on at home. She watched them drive away and leaned against one of the small pillars.

"Finally, a moment of peace," she mumbled.

As she stared into the night sky, she reflected on what had been going on. The nights where she would feel watched were becoming more and more frequent. She tried to call Yukino many times to ask her about what was going on, but every time she did, the number would be disconnected, or it would be the wrong number. She'd also contemplated retreating to the Grey Planes to find her, but there were no doors in the area that she could see, and going home whenever she needed to travel was just out of the question. It didn't help either that she had never really been trained how to travel. Her sight had been lost to her for so long that she wasn't entirely sure how to navigate without winding up in the same mess she had the last time. "Too many things to try and explain to too many people." She sighed.

"Oh?" came a voice behind her.

Tara spun around, releasing a flying backhand that was easily caught, but when her eyes focused, she scowled and yanked her hand free. "Raiden," she hissed. "You scared me."

"Far from my intention," he chuckled. He moved to stand beside her and stared off into the night with her. "You seemed a bit out of sorts at the banquet, so I thought I'd check up on you."

"You seem to check up on me a lot," she stated flatly.

"I check up on all my recruits," he answered evenly.

Tara's brows merged. Too easy. Tara spun to face him, hands upon her hips as she craned her head forward to stare him in the eyes. "Do you now?" Her voice was even and cool as she spoke, but it was obvious that there was no way she believed him.

"Yes."

But that was as far as he would allow him to go. "I don't see you giving anyone else rides back to the dorms, checking up on them. And you always seem to show up when things get—"

"Unsettled?" he interrupted, finishing her sentence.

"I was going to say strange," she answered, her eyes squinting. "And just how do you know about that anyway?" she questioned, instantly regretting that question. Only two people in her life knew about her "gifts," and she would have preferred to keep it that way.

But Raiden just laughed and patted her on the top of the head, which made her scowl. "Rest easy, Tara. The shadows hide nothing this night." He left it at that and bade her good night, leaving before a new line of questioning could begin.

Tara stared off in the direction Raiden had driven in before eventually heading back to her dorm. "How could he have known?" she asked, rubbing the flats of her palms along her arms.

The multitude of answers intrigued and frightened her, so she pressed it from her mind. If she was going to be safe for the night, she wanted to enjoy that feeling and as she slid into her bed for the night she thought of nothing more than a love from the past, a single tear slipping from her left eye as she clutched her pillow, surrendering to the restless sleep that awaited.

Weeks passed and nothing out of the ordinary seemed to have happened. With soccer over, she quickly fell into an academic routine, filling her afternoons with various work outs to replace her soccer practices. It was an unseasonably cold day in spring that found Tara in one of the gyms just off the main weight room. Here they kept large punching bags as well as other equipment that the wrestlers and football teams would often use. She moved to the back of the gym to avoid too much interaction. She hooked her MP3 player to a small speaker and turned it on before she began punching one of the larger bags. It was a great way to release any frustration that had built up with everything that was going on at home, the lack of contact with her mother, and Raiden's convenient appearances.

She broke free from the bag and moved into her old martial arts katas, going through them over and over before she even broke away from them, absorbed by the energy of the music where she began working with her own energy.

She was so focused, so drawn in, that she was unaware that, for several minutes now, she was being watched. "You know . . ." the lighthearted voice began, breaking the hold Tara's music had on her. "If our energies existed in this world, you would have destroyed the gym by now." She then began to giggle as she eagerly awaited a reaction.

Tara paid her no heed, which made her stalker a bit upset. When energy was mentioned, she only paid a mild interest and allowed herself only the slightest glance, recognizing her instantly as the girl from her high school graduation. She thought it odd that, through all the running around she'd done on campus, she had never crossed paths with her until now. Not that she wasn't grateful. Closing her eyes, she again focused on the music, allowing herself to again be drawn in and her movements once more regained their fluidity. An act that angered the blond who was now stomping and pouting like a spoiled child.

"So?" Another voice interjected itself into the conversation, his eyes piercing into their prey.

"She doesn't even know I'm here," she whined, stomping her foot solidly while her clenched fists landed rigidly at her sides. "What's so great about her anyway!" she demanded.

But Toran only patted the top of her head. "Our reasons are our own. Not to be known by a mere puppet."

Her smile faded, and she glared. She hated being reminded that all she was, was a tool. She'd always hoped that if she could please Toran and do well enough in the tasks he'd given her, she would eventually be more. "Hmph . . ." She turned from him and folded her arms across her chest, going into full tantrum mode, offering him nothing more than the silent treatment.

Knowing he would no longer get anywhere with her, Toran soon turned his attention back to Tara and cleared his throat, loud enough that he knew she would hear him. Tara felt the chill of the invading energy and whirled around, throwing out both of her arms. It was true what had been said. Their energy had no effect on the physical plane of existence, but the intensity of her energy sent a gust of air rushing past the two. The girl ducked behind Toran who only chuckled as he fixed his hair. "Well, hello there to you too."

Tara glared, her gaze becoming hard as ice. "What are you doing here?" she growled.

His gaze remained neutral. "I don't believe I have to explain my actions to you," he began.

"You do when your actions bring you within breathing distance of me!" she hissed.

Toran sighed and shook his head, placing the palm of his hand over the girl's mouth as she opened it to start chastising Tara. "If you must know. I was in town on business. I finished early and decided to check on this one here." He removed his hand from her mouth, casting her a glance that warned her to keep quiet before gently patting the top of her head.

Tara watched the display with disgust. "Like . . . some kind of dog? Uggh . . . Y'know, whatever. Just get out!" she snapped before spinning around to gather her things.

The girl began to pout again, but Toran just ushered her from the gym, assuring his voice was loud enough for her to hear as they left. "It's a shame, really." The cruelty was evident in his smile. "I guess you really aren't interested in what happened to your mother." The girl giggled, but as Tara spun around, the two vanished through the doors.

Tara scowled as she wiped the sweat from her face. "He's always trying to get under my skin!" Even though she was shouting, her voice was muffled by the towel. "And it always works," she growled, offering the bag beside her a final punch before retreating to the locker rooms for a much needed shower.

Shoving everything into her locker, she retrieved another towel and slung it over her shoulder but just as she was about to close the door, a blinking light caught her attention. Tilting her head, she retrieved her phone and opened it. She was surprised that she'd missed a phone call since she wasn't expecting any. Her eyes lit up with the possibility of it being Yukino but as she played back the voice mail delight gave way to dread and hope surrendered itself to despair. The color drained from her face and her legs began to tremble under the weight of her own body. Over and over the words echoed, stealing away any light. She hadn't even realized that her phone had slipped from her hand and was now laying shattered on the locker room floor.

CHAPTER

11

Escape

Tara slowly began to come around. Her vision was blurry, and the voices around her seemed to be a jumbled mass of noise. She couldn't really move, but as her vision finally decided to come back into focus, she could see the face of her grandmother looming over her. Darting her sight from side to side told her that her grandfather was also there, accompanied by Raiden and a few people dressed in white. She let her eyes settle back onto her grandmother and let out a soft groan as she tried to sit up. "What happened . . . ?"

"Oh, thank the stars you're awake!" her grandmother exclaimed as she hugged Tara tightly. "Raiden found you passed out on the locker room floor."

She wasn't going to say just how creepy that was. She seemed to always be on some unknown watch list, but the look she shot him said enough. She winced as she rubbed the goose egg on the back of her head and sighed. "I had the worst dream," she mumbled. She then started laughing at just how insane the idea of her mother being dead was. "I dreamed that Mom—" She quit talking as soon as she mentioned her mother and saw the look that crossed her family's face.

"I'm afraid that is no dream," her grandfather said, clearing his throat.

"Huh?" No, this had to be wrong. It made absolutely no sense. Her face twisted, refusing to accept that her mother had lost. She had always fought and won against the string of infections that had plagued her since that fated night. "But . . . she's so much stronger than that." Her voice was suddenly small and distant as her world started to implode. Her mind seemed to break, raking over every detail until every piece settled upon one name, one face. Her body began to shake as everyone began to notice the sudden drop in temperature. They rubbed their arms and even went as far as putting jackets on, questioning if the air had been turned on. "Bastard," she hissed.

"Tara?"

Her eyes were frozen with a look that was unmasked hatred as she looked past everyone. "That bastard!" she seethed. "He killed my mother!" Raiden watched her closely, feeling the pulse of energy coming from her in waves. It twisted and contorted itself as it fed from the brewing hatred that was beginning to manifest itself within her heart. It would be something they would have to teach her to keep under control before it could be used against her. "I'll kill him!" she growled.

"Tara!" Her grandmother was shocked at how hostile she'd become but as she placed a hand upon her arm to calm her she drew it back quickly from the bite of her energy. "We've arranged travel for Yukino to come out," she said, hoping the news would somehow make things a bit better.

But it didn't make things better. Yukino coming meant that Darius would come, and she wasn't sure she could stomach seeing him after what had happened between them. After a moment though she dropped her head and nodded, staring at the sheets as she gripped them till her knuckles were white. She didn't even look up as Mark rushed into the room, feeling herself fall into him as he hugged her.

Her mind was focused on nothing short of vengeance and the outside world hardly registered to her.

"I came as soon as I heard," he said, speaking with her grandparents. He turned his attention briefly to Raiden, thanking him for helping her and for taking care of her. He then turned his attention to Tara. "We will get the person responsible for this," he swore.

No, you won't, she thought, her muscles twitching once again. "It's not fair," she snarled through clenched teeth.

"I know," he answered quietly, rubbing his hand along her back trying to quell the growing anger he could feel rising within her.

"Excuse me." A voice broke the heaviness of the moment as the charge nurse poked her head into the room. "I'm sorry, but visiting hours are over."

Tara pulled from Mark and looked at the nurse with a squinted gaze. "What do you mean visiting hours? I'm not staying here."

"It's just over night," her grandmother said.

"No!" Tara protested.

"Tara, please," Mark said as he stared down at her.

"Miss, we aren't sure how long you were unconscious. It's precautionary only, strictly for observation," the nurse assured.

"I said I'm not staying. That's final! There's nothing wrong with me!"

The sorrow that filled her grandparents' faces was enough to quell the storm for the moment, and she slowly relented, heaving a heavy sigh of defeat as her shoulders dropped. "We'll be back first thing to get you," her grandfather promised.

But she was silent, the hard glare returning once more to her eyes.

"I'm sorry, dear, but I'm worried about that lump on your head," her grandmother told her.

She just nodded, feeling each embrace and hearing as each person left the room save one.

"Raiden." She spoke his name just as he was about to leave, leaving only them in her room.

"Yes?" he asked, leaning against the door jam.

"Why?"

"Why what?"

The look she shot him was one of warning. She'd had quite enough of his games. "You know why what," she growled. "Why are you always around when something happens?"

Raiden sighed as he pushed from the door frame. "There are people after who you are, and people trying to protect you from them." But he would say nothing past that.

"What are you talking about?" she demanded.

All she would get was a shake of the head as a response. "This is neither the time nor the place to discuss that." And without another word, he was gone.

Tara huffed, glaring daggers through the now empty room, her arms folded rather tightly across her chest as she fell back into the pillow. "This discussion is far from over, Raiden," she vowed.

The wake was a quiet, intimate gathering. Close friends, family and colleagues gathering to mourn the loss of a light taken too early from this world. The procession to the actual burial though was nothing short of overwhelming. It seemed like everyone had turned out for it. Motorcycles led the way, their lights flashing while bagpipers played Amazing Grace. But as she looked out over it all, what left the most lasting impression on her was just how everyone seemed to come together. "How can one person's death make such an impact in people's lives."

"Your mother was a very special person."

Tara looked up to see Yukino looking back down at her with a tender smile. She sighed then looked back out at the car that carried her mother's casket, shrouded with the US flag. "She was," she said softly, the two disappearing into the crowds as they made their way to the burial site.

The funeral itself was taxing on her ability to cope with what was going on. The community had taken care of everything and remained to show their support to the grieving family, offering their condolences, or even sharing a fond memory they had of her Senia. Tara remained quiet through it all, keeping close to the protective embrace offered by Yukino. "I don't want to be here," she said after a while. Her voice was quiet, lost, and subdued as reality finally caught up to her. Her body shook as the coffin was lowered into the earth and tears slipped down her cheeks as the flag was folded and presented to her grandparents.

"I know honey." Yukino whispered, kissing the top of her head. Tara seemed relieved when she saw that she'd come alone, dreading any form of interaction with Darius. Yukino explained that Darius had taken off shortly after Senia had been shot and had never returned. She stared down at the young woman, seeing the mask she worked so hard to uphold, but she could see through the cracks into the turmoil that lay beneath. The echo of gun fire signaled the end of the funeral and Tara just stared as she watched people file through, some giving their parting words, while others set fresh flowers beside the head stone.

A meal was planned at Tara's house after the funeral and the turn out almost rivaled both services. Tara was as social as she needed to be, but there was only so much she could take and she quickly reached her limit of the 'poor dear' comments and people talking as if she weren't there, asking just how she was going to get on. It was like, without her mother, she was nothing, and the thoughts started to make her angry. "Like I'm not my own person," she growled, ducking down the hall to her room. As she pressed her back against the door she heaved a sigh. "I can't do this," she said, letting the back of her head hit her door.

She stood there for a while before pushing away and crossing to her bed. Flopping down, she reached onto her nightstand for one of her journals and a pen, opening to a blank page. She stared at it, unsure of what she wanted to write, or if she even wanted to write at all. But as thoughts of her mother emerged, memories of her smile, the soft nature of her voice, even the loving energy that always seemed to surround her even toward the end when she was losing her fight. She hadn't realized that as she thought back on these things, her hand had already begun to move across the paper. When she was done she realized that her hand was shaking from the exertion of energy.

Diamonds in the Moonlight

A tear falling to join a diamond sea
Crying only in the presence of the moon
A facade of strength you are forced to bear
Though secretly you're not that strong
Where are the arms that promised to hold you
In your greatest time of need?
They are withdrawn, laughing, watching in shadows
As you stumble along on your own
Fear not young child, you're never alone
The moonlight will guide your way
Taking your hand and wiping your tears
Away to that diamond sea.

As she replayed the words, they did and did not make sense. This wasn't what she wanted to write at all. Her thoughts were only of her mother, the definition of unconditional love, so why was she writing of her own personal betrayal? She did know though, that somewhere, Darius was hiding, laughing as her world was slowly taken from her. The move overseas had changed him and she was painfully aware of that change, even from so far away. Staring at a past picture of the two of them, she hoped that her mother would continue to guide her, even if it was from some beyond place. But those thoughts merged with ones of a darker nature. Thoughts of Toran, the words he said, the cruelty he seemed to delight in, and the very real possibility that he was the one responsible for her mother's passing. These thoughts fueled a new energy within her, a heated anger and deep desire for revenge, emotions that she couldn't quell, emotions she wasn't sure she wanted to quell. And before she was aware, this energy coursed through to her hand, which had begun moving across the paper once more.

Elemental Fury

Let nature's fury take the wrath
Of an unbridled elements heart
The flurry of passion, raw emotion
Burning through brilliant eyes
Haven't you seen them? The streaks through the
heavens?
Of bloodlusts battles born?
All to relieve the pent up hate
Of betrayals emotionless lie
With skies rent asunder and energy drained
The storm will soon subdue
And natures rage saved for another day
To cleanse the heart of the moon.

When she was done, she stared down at the paper, her eyes reading, but her mind not registering what she was passing into it. The toll on her energy was severe and as she looked around her room with tired eyes only one thought remained to her. "Escape. Just for a little bit. I need to get away from these people." But if she went back through the house to get to the backyard she knew there would be no escape, only endless conversations and more sympathy. Her gaze then fell to her window and as she pushed to her knees, she slid it open, poking her head through and looking around. Only a handful of people lingered on the porch and with the cover of night she was confident she could make it to the door unseen.

Easing herself from the window, she crouched down in the brush, watching, timing every movement precisely, waiting till backs were turned before making her way to the other side of the yard, ducking into the small groups of trees, taking great care not to make much noise, if any at all. She saw that her only problem might be that the door to her salvation rested just outside of the reach of the light cast by the lighting in the backyard.

"The things I do for some alone time," she grumbled before clamping her hands over her mouth as soon as the words fell. She looked around, barely even breathing as she waited to see if she'd been discovered. Sighing in relief she saw that she was still safe and continued to slowly make her way until she felt the wood of the frame brush across her arm.

She stayed crouched, reaching for the door. She turned the handle quickly, a bit too quickly though because as the door opened, she lost her balance and fell through. The noise she made as the door closed was enough to draw attention, but she was already through so it was chalked up to nothing more than a rabbit running through the brush. Standing up Tara brushed herself off.

"Really? All of that just to go through a door?" She sighed in frustration and just started walking, hands shoved into her pockets. She was still a bit shaky from the expulsion of energy so her movement was a bit sluggish. Her mind wandered, remembering how her mother looked in the casket, the echo of the gun fire as they put her into the ground. "At least she isn't suffering anymore." But it was little comfort to her as Toran's face appeared in her mind's eye. The cruelty in his face, the darkness in his eyes.

Something about him always seemed to bring out the worst in her, and this was no exception. As she continued thinking about him she found that her hands were balling into fists and her thoughts were becoming darker, contemplating the perfect revenge. The more she thought about it, the darker the thoughts and ideas became until a shadow began to appear through the mists. When she reached it she saw a door more ornately carved than any other she'd seen thus far. Gnarled vines covered in thorns framed the warped and faded wood. She stopped and stared at it. She had learned that a door to the Astral Realm only appears when it is desired to. "But I wasn't planning on going." Her brows merged as she turned to walk away only to find that her limbs would not cooperate. "No, we are *not* going to do this again!" she shouted with growing irritation.

In true stubborn fashion, however, her body remained held where it was, refusing to yield. "There is no reason for me to go through," she argued, trying to pull her leg from where it was so she could continue her walk, but it was like she was glued in place, only able to move if she were stepping toward the door. She exhaled heavily and stared once more at the door. "Or is there a reason you appeared," she said as she reached her hand toward it. Just as her fingers brushed the door it opened, the force of the air sucking her through with a startled shriek as the door slammed behind her. She leaped to her feet quickly and looked around. Where she found herself was nothing short of decrepit. Dead trees darted the barren landscape. Overhead lightning broke the darkness as thunder shattered the silence, releasing torrents of rain. "Wonderful."

She began walking around aimlessly, searching for that pull that always seemed to lead her where she needed to go. But this time she felt nothing, no pull, no guidance.

"Why am I here?" she asked, shielding her eyes as a bolt of lightning struck the ground several feet from where she stood.

She quickly abandoned her thoughts of revenge, replacing them with thoughts of finding a place to escape the weather. The more she searched, the less those dark feelings existed, and the less the desire existed, the more she began to feel that familiar feeling. She let go and allowed her feet to guide her, her body lost to the storm around her.

She was focused on keeping herself warm, rubbing her palms over her arms and wringing out what water she could from her clothes. She hadn't even realized that her wanderings had taken her to a more densely grown forest until she realized that the storm had seemed less than what it was before. Looking up she could just see the glow the lightning offered as it lit up the skies above her, outlining the tops of the trees shielding her.

"Better than nothing," she muttered as her teeth began to chatter.

In time though, the rain subsided, and the echo of thunder was nothing more than a soft roll in the distance. But even with its passing, she could still hear the sounds of water. "A river?" she asked with a tilt of her head, straining her ears to listen for a moment. "That way? I think?" she said to herself, flicking a fingertip to her left. She listened for a moment longer, sure that she was correct, then headed off.

In time she broke through the forest line, and as she expected, she found herself standing on the bank of a river.

"I wouldn't really call this a river though," she commented to the air around her as she crouched down to take a drink. "More like brook." Whatever it was, it brought her peace and soon the sound of the running water did its intended job. In spite of the cold, her muscles relaxed and she sat where she'd once knelt. "It's like the water is taking away all the anger," she mused, casting her gaze in the direction the water flowed. "Maybe this was the release I needed after all."

Even the overwhelming feelings of dealing with the passing of her mother seemed to fade. It still hurt, but she found it much easier to deal with instead of feeling like the entirety of the situation was going to swallow her whole.

Only the chill of an uprising wind drew her from her contemplation some time later. Standing, she again rubbed her hands over her arms. "There has to be a place I can go to get warm." And as if on cue, that tugging feeling returned to her, taking her further down the length of the brook. Time had been lost to her, as had distance, but as she rounded a bend in the water, the stillness of the night was marred by an odd noise. Her brow arched as she took refuge behind some brush and watched. Whatever it was, was in terrible pain, but as it moved, she could make out the form of a wolf. From the other side of the fallen form she could see the briefest glimpse of two sets of ears followed by whimpering and whining. The noises on the bank seemed to draw the attention of other creatures in the forests as unfriendly snarls, growls, and howls began to fill the distance.

She looked again to the wolf and the pups, seeing if she would try and move them but she was now motionless and the whimpering was drawing the surrounding sounds closer. Growing bolder, she moved from her hiding spot and crept closer, stopping only when she was about two or three feet from the trio. Only then could she see the pool of blood that they lay in. Just by the volume that was shed she knew their mother was either already gone or was on the brink of passing. Her heart went to them as the pain of her own loss ripped through her heart again.

"It isn't safe for you here anymore," she said as the growls continued ever closer. She was reaching for them when a flurry of movement and the sound of snapping jaws had her falling backward screaming for all her lungs were worth.

When she dared to open her eyes, she came face-to-face with the mother, lips curled, fangs bore, and the most dangerous growl rising from the hollows of her chest. It was obvious that in spite of her condition, she would protect her children with her dying breath. But as she took in the features of what she was sure to be her end, an odd thing occurred. Their gazes locked and Tara found herself unable to turn her head let alone avert her eyes. The mother's posture softened and she slumped back to the ground, always holding her gaze. "You, you're a watcher, are you not?"

The voice was echoed, and it took about a minute for it to register to Tara that she was hearing the voice in her head. "Um . . . no, sorry, but I'm not a watcher," she answered nervously. "I'm actually just passing through."

"You have the eyes of a watcher," the wolf continued.

"It happened a long time ago," Tara said, running the tips of her fingers over the lower part of her left eye socket. "I couldn't even begin to tell you how," she confessed.

"It matters little no," the wolf told her, her head falling back to the ground. The two pups slowly circled from behind their mother and approached Tara, staring intently at her. "My time here is coming to its end. They will not survive. Please, I beg of you, take care of and protect them."

"But," Tara stammered, trying to find her words to protest, "I'm from the Physical Realm." But she stopped, hearing the hollow ring of those very words. The Physical Realm, the place where she had lost her mother to a senseless act of violence. The place where the greater part of her heart had turned on her. No, she decided. It was no longer her home. "I'll . . ." But before she could commit, the gaze was broken, and she was still. Knowing she was gone made the pups whine and howl in distress which only fueled those who were hunting them. She realized just how close they had gotten during the course of the conversation and her eyes widened. "Too close," she said as she leaped to her feet, memorizing their mothers face as she scooped the two into her arms. "It's time for us to go," she said as she ran into the water, following its path just as the first of what ever creatures were hunting broke through the trees. But she wasn't going to look back, even as some of them began to follow.

"Thank the Gods for soccer," she huffed, shifting the pups under her arms as gravity tried pulling them into the water. More than once she slipped on the rocks, landing solidly on her back at least twice, but each time she got back up and forced herself forward even as their pursuers abandoned their chase. When her muscles finally threatened to betray her she broke through the forest entirely. With exhaustion setting in, she nearly landed face first into a large lake as she tripped over an extended tree root. Regaining her footing quickly, she looked around, recognition sinking in.

"I know this place," she said softly as she took several more steps forward. Her arms went slack and the distraction of two wolf pups splashing into the water drew her from her memories. "Oops, sorry, guys," she said with a bashful smile. Kneeling down she picked up the now scowling duo and walked toward the overhang where she had first met Arcainous and Belzak.

"It seems so long ago that I met them, almost like a distant dream." The two siblings squirmed, desperately wanting free so they could shake the water from their fur. They soon got the chance when she reached the alcove and, to her surprise, found a cave carved into it. "I'm sure I would have noticed this if I'd looked around," she commented, her brows merging as the two wiggled free and furiously shook themselves dry before starting their whimpering for food. She went into the cave and found a well-worn fire pit with wood stacked against one side, complete with flint and tinder. "Well, this should do well to keep us warm." She stacked the wood and tinder, striking it, and praying. She blew as gently as she could, given her body's frozen state, but sighed in relief with the ease that the wood caught. The crackling soon filled the cave with a growing warmth and allowed her to better see what was around them.

Against the other wall rested crudely made fishing poles. "Of all the things I never learned to do." Tara groaned, blaming that on the lack of a father in her life, but at least she knew there was the possibility of fish in the lake. "Well." She took one of the poles and exited the cave. "No time like the present to learn." As she emerged into the moonlight, she was met with the circling and jumping duo. "Yes, I'm going to try and catch you something to eat," she assured. Sitting on the shore she tried to mirror what she'd seen while surfing through her TV but as she tried to throw the line forward she felt it snag. "What the . . . What could it get stuck on?" Frustrated, she turned around only to see the line in one of the pups' jaws. "Let go, you goof. How am I supposed to catch anything if you're trying to eat the line?"

The pup whined and came up beside her to lay down. Tara rested her hand on the pup's side and studied it. With fur the color of the moonlit night, images of mystery and elusiveness began to fill her mind. "Luna," she mumbled softly, looking into her eyes to see the glow of the moon reflecting in them. "Yes, Luna suits you," to which she got a happy yip in return. Again she threw the line back, and time after time it would snag, or become a new game. As she studied the second pup she saw that the shade of his fur reminded her of the mists of the Grey Planes, as did the ease of his movements. Images of stealth and agility filled her mind and she again smiled. "Myst, I told your sister. If you keep playing with the line, I'm not going to be able to catch anything, and all of us are going to go hungry." He looked up at her and whimpered, settling into the grass, waiting patiently for his dinner.

Shaking her head she again cast the line, pleased when she heard it hit the water with a light plop. Cast after cast yielded several fish of various sizes and when Tara was satisfied with the amount that she'd caught she rose to her feet and called for the two to follow her back to the cave. It had warmed up since lighting the fire, but she was still chilled to the bone from the rain. She set the fish on the ground for the pups to eat before peeling herself out of her wet clothes, laying them out before the fire and praying they would dry. With them eating and her skin slowly warming she took the time to study the two closer. Combined, the two looked strikingly like their mother and images of the rolling storm again flowed through her mind. Startled, her head lifted and as she looked outside a single word fell from her lips. "Arashi."

Her eyes returned to the fire, her gaze staring into and through the flames as her fingers began moving. Curling and twisting, her mind drifting away from conscious thought. In such a detached state her energy became malleable, a thing to be touched, and her fingers began working. She sighed after some time and stared down at her hands, her brows arching at what lay within them. Glittering against the light of the fires flames rested two identical sets of linked hoops. Hanging upon the center loop rested a mirrored image of their mothers face. Lifting them to the fire she inspected the glass like creations. "But they're cold as ice," she mumbled. "But they don't melt when they're close to the fire." Not that she was going to argue a good thing. She called the two over, watching as the two fought over the final fish before abandoning it to her call. "I think, these are from your mother," she said softly as she slipped one over each of their heads watching as it reflected the flames light.

With a scratch behind their ears she patted the ground. "It's time to sleep," she told them. "We have a long day ahead of us. We have to find a place to go." With only a minor protest, the two finally settled down and curled up around each other, sleep taking them quickly. Tara leaned forward and watched them. "Where are we going to go?" she wondered. She'd never had to be responsible for anyone before, not even when her mother was sick. There were always people stepping in and taking care of everything. She was just learning to take care of herself. "I'll figure something out," she promised. The stress she now found herself under fought with the cold and fatigue she was feeling, surrendering only after more wood was added to the fire but her sleep was anything but restful.

Hours later her body became very aware of a pair of eyes watching her. She didn't dare open her eyes just yet, but as she became more conscious of her surroundings she could feel something heavy and warm laying over her. Her mind shot out, seeking out Luna and Myst only to recoil as she discovered the owner of the gaze watching her. "The wolves are fine," the voice assured. As if on cue, the sounds of happy yips came from the mouth of the cave as the two played. "They've been up for several hours playing."

Tara sat up slowly, her eyes drifting open to see the woman sitting between her and the mouth of the cave. "How did you find me?" she asked warily, but her voice interrupted their own conversation as the pups bounded into the cave and leaped into her lap licking her face happily.

"I often walk around this lake," she replied. "It's a very peaceful area to get away and think."

Tara's brow creased. "So this is your cave? I'm sorry. I didn't mean to intrude," she began. "But with the storm and—"

But the woman just shook her head. "This cave isn't mine," she assured. "I've never seen it used actually," she confessed.

Tara wasn't sure why, but she felt that she could trust this woman. There was something about the energy she possessed that seemed to make everything right. "I'm Tara," she said after a moment of silence. "And these two here are Luna and Myst." She pointed to each one respectively, scratching the top of their heads. They responded by bucking their heads back and licking her palm vigorously. "I guess they're hungry."

The woman noticed the change in Tara's expression. "What's wrong, child?"

Tara sighed as she slid into her still damp clothes, scowling at the cold against her skin. "I hadn't planned on staying here. I'd only really come here to escape, but I can't leave them here alone, but I can't bring them back with me either."

Luna whined, moving to sit with the woman who began to inspect the pendant around her neck. "Did you ever think," she began, once more seeing the small white swirls of energy dotted throughout the rings, "that this is where you are meant to be now?"

There was silence as Tara thought about this, her fingers running absently through Myst's fur. "What do you mean?"

"Hmmm, how should I put this?" Her eyes closed as she filtered through her own mind for just the right words that wouldn't send her running. "There is growing strife everywhere, as I'm sure you're very aware," she began. "Here as well as in your world. You were a light to your mother and those around you, but with them gone, perhaps it's time for you to be a light for others, like these two pups, for example." When her eyes had reopened, she found herself staring at a very startled, slack-jawed young woman.

"How . . ." Tara couldn't make her mind form any complete sentences. Fear and irritation gripped her. *How do so many people know so much?* she wondered. "Why do you know so much about me?" Her throat was tight as she spoke, giving her voice a harsher edge to it than she meant for it to have. "I don't even know who you are."

"Oh." An embarrassed flush spread across the woman's pale cheeks. "Please forgive me. My name is Fisonma."

"Fisonma," Tara repeated.

"Yes," she replied with a warm smile, leaving that part of the conversation.

"Okay." Tara studied her closely, her eyes squinting. "But that still doesn't tell me how you know so much about me."

The smile faltered. She was so full of questions that just weren't so easily answered, and now Fisonma understood Raiden's frustrations. But if her path was in fact what she had seen, then she was right to be cautious. She gave a soft sigh before answering. "All I can tell you right now is that it is my job to know."

Her brow twitched. "I am so sick of people telling me that," she snapped. "You said it, my soccer recruiter said it . . ."

"Please, be calm." The pups had started to whimper, sensing the growing distress, and Myst had begun to paw at her arm while Luna stayed close to Fisonma. "Why don't you come with me? The wolves will have plenty of food and a place to run around where they will be protected."

Tara was on the edge of anger. If she lived in such a wonderful place, then why didn't she just take them? But as she looked down at Myst, staring into his eyes. She heard the soft whines, the fear that she too would leave, just as their mother had. Her shoulders fell as she scooped him into her arms, rubbing her cheek against the top of his head. "Go with you where . . ."

"A place you will be safe," she assured. But before Tara could make another of her famous comments, she continued. "While you are there, we will be able to further your training in rune casting, if you so desire."

Tara stared. The question how once more hung on her lips, but there was no point in asking only to get the same replies as earlier. "If I decide to go," she said slowly, running her fingers over the side of Myst's head, "I'll need to go back to my house and get a few things."

"I can arrange that for you if that is what you wish," Fisonma answered as she exited the cave followed by the two pups and lastly by Tara herself.

"I don't know how long it will take me to find the right doors again," Tara confessed. "Or that if I do, that I'll find my way back here. It could take a while. Are you all right with waiting?"

"There is no need to hunt for any doors," Fisonma told her.

"But how else will I be able to get back?" Tara asked.

But Fisonma would only smile as she turned from her. Her voice fell to nearly a whisper as words flowed like the stirring of a light breeze. Her fingers moved effortlessly, creating such intricate patterns that Tara wasn't even sure she was seeing what she was seeing. But in time, a door began to materialize before them. Framed in white and very much full of life unlike the door that had led her here. "That door," she breathed as pieces of her prior experience here began making sense but also began to raise more questions.

Fisonma interrupted quickly, wanting to divert the brewing line of questioning before it could surface. "We should hurry," she told her. "Staying in one place for an extended time in the open is unwise."

Of course that brought up another line of questioning, but she wanted so much to be in dry clothes so she didn't question it. She crouched down and stared at the two curious pups. "Now, you stay here all right? I'll only be a moment." They sat there, watching her as she went through the open door. Turning their heads, they glanced at each other, back at the door, to each other once more, then trotted happily after her, much to Fisonma's amusement. Everyone knows after all, that in puppy speak, when you're told to stay put, it's an open invitation to follow Mom through and explore. With a single graceful leap, Luna was on the bed, face-to-face with the stuffed wolf that her grandparents had given to her. Startled, she began to growl, her fur bristling.

"Oh, you're so tough." Tara laughed as she pulled a dry shirt over her head, tucking it into a clean pair of fleece lined jeans.

Luna snapped at it, confused that it didn't react to her until Tara yanked it up by one of the front legs, bonked her on the head with it, then tossed it into the bag she'd once kept her soccer gear in.

"See? It's not real." She folded her clothes neat and tight, creating a base for her journals, writing utensils, her metaphysical items such as candles and incense, and a few other odds and ends that she was sure she was going to need while she was there. Last to be placed in was a picture of her, Senia, and Mark, taken at her graduation before she had become so violently ill. "I'll find the one responsible for this," she vowed before zipping up the bag and ushered Luna back out the door. "Myst . . . c'mon you." When he failed to show, she dropped the bag to the ground and turned to go back into her room just as he darted out from under the bed with one of her cleats clamped tightly in his jaws, but as he tried to escape, he ran over the remote to her TV, turning it on.

"Ohhhh no, you don't," she scolded, crouching just as he ran past her. With an easy motion, she retrieved the shoe, spun, and tossed it back under the bed just as a report was coming across the news about the disappearance of a local college student. She paid only the briefest attention as she returned through the door and closed it. But as she retrieved her bag and headed for places unknown, the screen on her TV came into full focus, her picture splayed for the nation to see, the reporter calling it a kidnapping given the nature of her mother's death.

12

Nimost

To Tara, the trip was less than exciting. Every time she tried bringing up the door Fisonma summoned, comparing it to the door that had appeared when she was attacked by the vampiric trio, Fisonma would change the subject, pointing out various towns that they would pass, or rattling off the name of a vale, forest, or lake, telling her who or what it was named for. Every time she questioned the amount of information Fisonma seemed to know about her, all she would get were the same cookie cutter answers she'd gotten earlier. She scowled and started the age old line of questioning. "When will we get there?" she asked, shifting her bag to her other shoulder.

"It shouldn't be much longer," Fisonma answered, her mood always light as the pups kept running circles around them.

Tara fell silent again, staring at the ground until what seemed like hours had passed. Leaning back, she felt her back pop in several places. "Are we there yet?" It was obvious that she was getting annoyed.

"I'm afraid not," Fisonma confessed.

"How much longer?"

"Tara," she sighed softly and stared up into the sky, drawing the hood of her cloak over her head. "Time as you know it really has no meaning here. The sun and the moon move as fast or as slow as those who govern time dictate."

"Wait," Tara interrupted. "There's someone who governs time?"

Well, at least her irritation has gone down, Fisonma thought. "So the tale says."

"What tale?"

"There is a tale that has been handed down for as long as the Realms have existed. There is said to be a being that governs the flow of time, a neutral observer of the affairs that go on. This being dictates when the sun and moon rise and fall, the length of time between them, et cetera."

"Do you believe it?" Tara asked, casting an upturned glance toward Fisonma.

"Believe what, the tale?" Fisonma stopped and turned to face Tara. "There are things even in this realm that are hard to explain, or simply have no explanation. It helps to have something to believe in. It makes our jobs much easier in the long run."

"Jobs?" Tara's brow arched.

But Fisonma just smiled and started walking again, leaving Tara to catch up. "All you need to remember, is to have faith, and to believe. Everything else just falls into place as it should."

Tara of course scowled and looked back to the ground, running into Fisonma and falling to the ground as she stopped. "Oww . . ." She rubbed the top of her head and looked around.

"We're here," she said happily, extending her hand to help Tara to her feet.

"Where?" Tara groaned as she was pulled to her feet. Looking out in front of her, her hand fell from Fisonma's as she stared in awe. "Wow . . ."

"Breath taking isn't it?" Fisonma asked, standing beside the young woman.

"No one could ever hope to dream up something so . . . radiant." Tara breathed.

Before them, nestled in a deep valley, rested a city. Groups of buildings dotted the outskirts, growing larger and more frequent the closer to the center they got. But in the center, encased in a ring of which Tara could only assume was water, resided eight large towers surrounding one that stood in the center. The city itself seemed to give off a peaceful glow that could calm any energy. "Welcome to Nimost."

"Nimost? What's that?"

"Nimost is a holy city. Capital to the Realm of Light, and home to the Elementals," Fisonma explained.

"Elementals?" Tara seemed to be more interested than she had been since she left her room and started her journey here.

"Powerful beings whose talents, in the right hands, can be used to create and sustain life. But you will learn more of them as time passes," she assured.

Tara rolled her eyes. Yet another cookie-cutter answer, she thought with a heavy sigh, though the notion did intrigue her. "What did you mean by holy city?" Tara asked as they continued walking.

"Well, it is exactly as I said. Many people from the lands through-out this Realm travel to the temples here to pay their respects to the Elementals, giving thanks, asking for protection, and guidance . . ."

So it's like church, she decided with a scrunched-up face. That comparison didn't sit well with her at all, so she decided to focus on the two pups as they practiced their hunting skills on each other. Stalking and pouncing, gnawing as they playfully went for the others throat, only to leap up and become the prey for the other. "So all those buildings are temples?" Tara asked, lifting her gaze from the wolves.

"Not all," Fisonma answered. "There are forges, smith shops, schools."

"Wait, schools?" Tara interrupted.

"Yes."

"For what?"

"Various things," came a reply from behind them.

Spinning around, Tara caught sight of a large silver wolf, recognizing him instantly. Her eyes brightened as she ran forward.

"Arcainous!" Reaching him, she threw her arms out and around what she thought would have been his furry neck, but instead they wrapped around his waist, but the warmth of his arms as they surrounded her was welcomed, and she rested into him, glad to see that no harm had come to him after their only meeting. "I was so worried," she whispered.

But he just smiled as he looked down at her before stepping back, his hands catching her arms loosely. "My, how you've grown," he commented, taking note of the change in her eyes. His smile faltered slightly as a silent prayer went out to his friend.

"You haven't changed at all," Tara remarked with a small smile. She then looked back to the outlying areas past the towers. "So what kind of schools are they?" she asked.

"Well," Arcainous began, "there are schools that train in magic, fighting, armor smiths, and weapon smiths. There are schools strictly for study, and schools that prepare you to work in the temples."

"Wait, magic?" Tara asked with an upturned brow.

"Yes," Arcainous answered.

Her eyes squinted. "Like . . . poof be gone magic? 'Cause, that's kind of lame."

Fisonma now indulged herself a small laugh at Tara's expense. "No. The magic we speak of would be the magic of your world's fairy tales. But it is very much a reality here."

Tara's jaw hung open slightly. "Seriously?" She so desperately wanted to see it.

"Seriously." Arcainous replied with a chuckle.

"The students stay in dorms built near their field of study, and if a student is good enough, they are chosen for an apprenticeship where they will master their craft. Most will take that back to the towns they have come from to further better their people," Fisonma explained.

Tara nodded and continued to follow them, crossing one of the bridges that led to a path winding between two of the towers, their sheer size making her feel like nothing more than a grain of sand on the beach. "Welcome to the home of the Elementals, their

Guardians, and their armies," Arcainous said, smiling at the look of awe clearly splayed across her face.

She stepped out from the two and simply stared. Her gaze befell a tower seeming to be carved from the face a grand mountain, following the natural features as it soared skyward. Boulders of various sizes surrounded the base leading to pebble covered areas with statues carved from stone depicting strength and hidden beauty. Surrounding these were granite benches, their legs curling and disappearing beneath the pebble flooring.

Another appeared almost normal with the exception of the glowing orange aura surrounding it. Tara stared at it long enough, that she could feel the heat radiating from it in waves, even as she stood on the other side of the courtyard from it. Occasionally, she could swear she caught a glimpse of bubbling magma or some other super-heated substance appear and then disappear from the surface around the tower.

Tara's gaze soon settled upon a most magnificent sight. A tower carved from rock as red as freshly shed blood. Statues of dragons in various colors rested perched or curled around the tower as jets of flames spewed forth from their open maws, vaporizing into nothingness. "That is the tower of the Fire Elemental," Fisonma told her as they watched while open pockets of natural gas shot flames into the air around the perimeter of the tower.

Tara just nodded wordlessly, her eyes falling upon a tower carved from shimmering onyx, black as a lightless night. Her head tilted, wondering how something so dark could exist in a place that was supposed to exude such light and peace. But just as she was about to ask about it, thick bolts of soundless lightning struck the many tiers of the tower, many of them snaking down the body of the tower to give it an almost ghostly glow. "That would be home to the Lightning Elemental," Arcainous told her, seeing the look of confusion crossing her face.

The next tower she saw amused her. It was almost a white blue color, and as her eyes lifted, she saw several rings of clouds moved by an unfelt wind. It was almost as if staring at the tower would remove any trace of ill energy. "The tower of the Air Elemental?" Tara asked, looking up at Fisonma.

"Indeed, it is," she answered with a smile. "You are familiar with your elements."

Turning slightly, she took in the next tower, her eyes widening. Such chilling beauty rose before her, jutting from the ground like a crystal cluster. She took in the shimmering frozen ground surrounding the tower itself. "Wow . . ."

"Beautiful, isn't it?" Fisonma asked, resting her hand upon Tara's shoulder.

But Tara could only nod, finding it hard to tear her gaze from that tower to look at the next. The two took note of that as they exchanged glances while she looked at the next tower which resembled nothing short of an oasis in the desert. The roar of waterfalls echoed to her now as they fell from various points in the towers face, pooling, and trickling into streams that fed other pools where various species of fish and other aquatic animals swam about freely.

Coming full circle, her gaze fell upon what to her was the most unique tower. It appeared to be made from the trunk of a very old and extremely huge tree. The roots extended out, disappearing into the ground while flowering vines wrapped themselves around the length of the tower. Gardens, trees, even a variety of wildlife inhabited the area surrounding the tower, and the sweet fragrance of flowers seemed to reach her as she took in a drawn-out breath, closing her eyes as she eased into the scent.

But in the center, almost as a beacon of light, was a single tower. A brilliant white and nowhere near as elaborate as the others. In fact, to Tara, it was quite plain, but the energy radiating from it was so peaceful, that it began drawing her in until Fisonma stepped up to stand beside her and looked upon the tower with her. "Do you remember what I said when we first arrived?"

"About what?" Tara tore her gaze reluctantly from the white tower to look at Fisonma.

"What I mentioned earlier about the Elements."

A small streak of red ran across her cheek bones. "No," she admitted sheepishly.

Fisonma gave a soft sigh, but she knew this was quite a bit for Tara to take in at once. "When used properly, the Elements are able to create and sustain life. That is what the towers represent, and why they appear as they do." Tara nodded before feeling a gentle pressure upon the small of her back, urging her forward. "Come, there is someone that I would like you to meet."

After assuring that Myst and Luna were still with her, she looked up, her eyes brightening. "Belzak?" Her tone was hopeful, but the hope was dashed with a single glance from Arcainous.

"I'm afraid that Belzak is lost to us," Arcainous told her.

Her heart sank as her mind returned to the night that he'd led her back. She didn't want to believe that he was the one who had led her to harm, but if things were as Arcainous had told her . . . No, she decided. She would believe in him until she saw things for herself. And even then, who's to say that she couldn't bring him back to his senses. She did have his gaze after all. There had to be a reason for it, and it was that very gaze that fell to the ground, catching glimpses of paws as the two pups wove around the three as they walked. She heard the idle chatter between Fisonma and Arcainous but paid little attention until a third voice joined the conversation. "Well, I didn't expect to be seeing you here so soon."

That voice . . . No. Even here he was stalking her? Her body froze as the muscles in her face began to twitch. "Tara?"

But Fisonma's voice was lost to her now. All she heard was the rushing of her energy against her eardrums, feeling it rise from her feet to gather in her upper arms and shoulders, begging for a release that she was all too willing to grant. Even Arcainous could sense the air around them becoming colder as she bled the warmth from it, drawing it into herself and adding it to the swelling mass. "Tara!" he shouted, trying to shake her back to reality. "Snap out of it this instant!" he ordered.

She would have none of it though and shoved him to the side with a power that betrayed her slender frame. When her head finally snapped up, her eyes were glowing an icy blue. "You!" Her voice growled as she threw her arms out, delivering the much needed release, all watching as waves of energy raced forward.

145

Fisonma and Arcainous watched as Raiden easily erected a barrier which became visible once the energy hit and began freezing around it. "I don't understand why she's acting like this." Arcainous confessed as the two watched the glow in her eyes warp, becoming tainted as a symbol began to appear in the center of the barrier. "A rune?" he asked. Fisonma nodded as they watched her fingers flick, causing its destination.

Shards of ice flew, several cutting into Raiden's arms and chest, one even slicing his cheek, but he paid it no mind and simply brushed the finer dust from his clothes. "I was always curious about what you could do," he commented as he ran his fingers over his cheek, drawing them back to examine the blood pooled upon the tips. "However, I would suggest we begin with training you to control your temper to keep your power in check."

She so desperately wanted to be calm for the sake of the two she swore to protect, but even as their whimpers and whines reached her ears, the overwhelming presence Raiden seemed to have in her life had finally hit the right nerve. "Why!" she demanded. "Why are you here! Why are you always around me!"

Fisonma could feel the growing stress and stepped between the two, her aura radiating a feeling of peace that slowly chipped at the anxiety Tara was feeling. "I believe I can explain that." Turning to face her, she continued. "You see, we have been watching you since your first visit to the Realms when you were a mere child."

"Yeah, because that doesn't sound stalkerish at all." Tara growled, folding her arms tightly across her chest.

"We have a good reason," Arcainous cut in, only receiving a livid scowl in response.

Her brow arched as she spun swiftly to face him. "Is that so?" Fisonma's aura was losing the battle to calm her, and she soon stood on the edge of surrendering to the Shadows that had begun brewing in her heart, much like that had grown in Darius's. "This . . . should be good."

But confronted with the question only made him fall silent. He diverted his gaze to Raiden and Fisonma before lowering his head. "It is not my place to reveal such information."

Tara's head shot up and her demeanor became hard as stone as she threw her arms into the air. "What a shock!" she shouted. "No one seems to be able, or willing to tell me anything!" Spinning on her heel, she began to storm off, her fists clenched tightly at her sides.

"Tara!" Fisonma called out to her, even going so far as to follow her, but she was stopped when Arcainous took hold of her wrist, motioning with a silent shift of his head to Raiden.

"No!" Tara shouted, but she soon stopped as she felt something strange wrapping itself around her right arm, pulling back to keep her in place. Looking down at her arm she saw a tendril of energy wrapped around it and as her eyes followed the tail, she could see that she was on the receiving end of Raiden's whip.

"You need to settle down and stop acting like a damned child," Raiden ordered.

This of course did not sit well with Tara at all, but even as her energy tried to freeze the tail of the whip to allow her to escape, all she saw was her own energy being drained into it instead. "Let . . . me . . . go," she seethed through clenched teeth. Failure to yield resulted in her tugging against the whip trying to free herself, but she found that the more she struggled, the more her strength failed her. "What's going on!" she demanded, alarm setting in.

"Just calm down!" Raiden demanded, but it was to no avail. She struggled until there was nothing left of her energy.

"Raiden, stop!" Fisonma ordered, but they could only watch as gravity won over her. Her eyes rolled back and soon she was nothing more than a crumpled heap on the ground. Luna and Myst were the first to reach her, the two sniffing at and licking her face in a vain attempt to rouse her. With that failed they sat and soon began to whine and howl as they began the possible mourning of yet another mother.

Raiden dispelled the whip as the three approached. "I'm sorry, Elder." His voice took on an odd note of respect as he addressed her. "But I saw no other recourse."

"It's all right," she said, trying to be assuring. "But I've never seen anyone last so long against you. Usually your whip has them subdued in mere moments." Never have they seen anyone falter. They had always yielded before it could get to this point.

"Perhaps then, there is validity to our assumptions?" Raiden asked, steadying himself against a pillar. For even as his weapon drained the projected energy, he was very aware of it. He could feel it, and even a bit of his own strength was drained, used to bring down the woman before them.

"It is possible," she replied softly as she knelt down to comfort the wolf pups. "Shh, there, there. She's only sleeping." Her voice was calming, and the two were soon content, once again scampering about as if nothing had happened.

Arcainous lifted her into his arms and stared at her face. "Even in sleep she is confronted by turmoil."

"We must give her time," Fisonma said. "Her past has been nothing short of traumatic."

"But do we have time?" Raiden asked.

"We will have to make the time," Fisonma replied.

"Where are we going to put her?" Arcainous's voice broke into the conversation, drawing attention to the woman he held.

Fisonma closed her eyes in thought. At present, Tara's energy wouldn't allow her through the doors of the White Tower, and it was too volatile for her to reside with any of the other Guardians. "Where are Aaronel and his armies?"

"On patrol," Arcainous answered. "Scouts say that they are well past three days from Nimost."

"We will keep her there then." Fisonma decided, the three heading toward the tower that housed the fabled Ice Elemental.

* * *

Tara looked around, seeing that she was consumed in complete darkness.

"Where am I?" she asked, clasping her hands over her mouth when she heard the strange echo that it held. "Am I dreaming?" But none of her dreams had ever felt like this and she soon began to wonder if perhaps it was something worse than her dreaming. But as she began to entertain the thought that she could, in fact, be dead, the area before her began to clear until it came into focus. Just in time to see a small child spilling into her line of sight and out a door that was opened behind her.

"That's me!" Her voice revealed the shock and her body trembled as it hovered there, growls closing in on her from all sides. "Run!" she shouted, drawing her head back in confusion. "But I did run . . ." Her brows merged, but her eyes soon shot open. "Belzak told me that! Just . . . before . . ." She left her sentence unfinished, knowing what she had seen next on that night, but she was to relive that again to a much deeper degree. "Belzak!" She shouted his name, as if the vain shout of his name would somehow change what happened, but her voice faded into nothing as the sounds of growls and snapping jaws descended upon her. She cried out as she felt invisible fangs sinking into her flesh, radiating pain through to her core. When she was sure she could stand no more, and the threat of passing out met her, the snarling stopped, and all fell eerily quiet.

The silence and the shadows caved in around her, compressing her as she floated there. Doubt and regret flooded both her mind and her heart as hazy images appeared briefly to her. A decrepit city, dead forests littered with bones, neglected by the Elements themselves. She saw dank swamps with noxious green clouds floating over the foul waters. Her nose curled in disgust but her vision soon went dark again, leaving her to hang in limbo, the pain from the previous attack spreading through her like a poison.

"Is this what you went through?" She looked around as if expecting an answer, but all that came were more images. Abandoned towns, prisons that reeked of death and rot, and people who were filled with such hatred that it made her want to hide. Their features were twisted as their yellowed eyes stared at her, through her, revealing their hidden desires of revenge. The energy she felt was nothing short of evil.

But things once again went dark, though the chill of the energy lingered around her, leaving her to wonder if they could in fact, see her. She wanted so desperately to wake from this living nightmare but as she tried, she fell further into the vision until one last image came to her sight. Different from the others, this one held the small glimmer of hope. Green grass flanked by trees that were very much alive.

"Perhaps he is all right after all," she breathed as she clawed her way against the darkness around her. A building came into view but with the promise in front of her, the feeling around her still was that of dread and despair. Steps led to a building with shadowed figures waiting for them and her hope began to fade. "Darkness can't exist in hope." But as the sight drew closer she stared up at one of the figures, fear gripping her instantly. This was no vision of hope.

"No," she gasped, clamping her hands over her mouth in fear that she would be heard. A hooded head lifted revealing a deep crimson gaze. "Durion . . ." Her heart thrummed in wild panic, her only desire being to free herself of her newfound hell. But she couldn't move. Her gaze was fixed, unblinking, unwavering, held fast as his gaze pierced directly into hers.

"Hello, child."

Her face paled as everything again went black. That gaze, malice defined. Now pulled from the hold he'd had, her body shot up, startling Arcainous and the two pups. With eyes still closed, her body still gripped in sleep, she released an ear splitting scream. Arcainous reached her side, shaking her shoulders. Her eyes opened, but the look within them was wild and unrecognizable. "Tara! Tara, can you hear me? Tara, please, wake up." But her eyes just rolled back into her head and she went limp in his arms and was asleep once again. He didn't dare leave her, but Fisonma needed to know what had just happened. Leaving the pups with her he departed to relay the news.

When she finally did wake up she was almost freezing and burrowing under the heavy blankets was doing no good at all. She let her gaze roam the room taking note of the shimmering walls that almost appeared to be carved from pale blue clouded glass. What she could see of the floor appeared to be white granite, and she dreaded putting her feet on it. On the far wall a gentle breeze stirred heavy velvet curtains to reveal a spacious balcony and allowing what she could only assume were rays of the afternoon sun to dance across the floor. Luna and Myst slept sprawled on the foot of the bed making any escape harder if she wanted them to stay asleep. Maneuvering first one leg, then the other, she was finally able to free herself and stepped onto the floor. Her toes curled with the chill beneath them but she eventually adjusted to the temperature and ventured forth through the curtains and onto the balcony.

From where she stood, she could tell she was in the crystalline tower. Moving to the far end she leaned over the railing, just able to touch one of the crystals that jutted from the base of the tower. It was smooth, like polished glass, slick as warming ice and just as cold.

"Beautiful, isn't it?" The voice behind her startled her enough that she almost lost her footing, sending a prickly feeling straight through her spine to the base of her neck.

She whirled around, her hands once more gripping the railing she was once leaning over. "You scared me," she hissed with a glare.

"It wasn't my intention," Arcainous apologized, ignoring the look as he moved to stand beside her, looking out over the grand courtyard. "This tower is home to the Ice Elemental and its Guardian."

"Ice Guardian?" The look on Tara's face softened as she turned to look out at the other towers once again. "And they're okay with me being here?"

"Well, presently, there is no Guardian to this tower," he confessed.

"Then who protects the Elemental?" Tara asked, turning to face him as she leaned against the railing.

"His name is Aaronel. He's the Captain of the Ice Guardians armies." But before she could begin with her next line of questioning, he looked down at her, staring into her eyes. "You didn't rest well, did you?" he asked. His question was direct, too close to the point, and she looked away saying nothing. He could feel the wall presenting itself again to protect her as he rested his hand upon her shoulder. "I ask, because you woke up screaming." He paused, searching her face for answers. "You sounded terrified, but you passed out again shortly after."

Tara just shrugged, rolling her shoulder from beneath Arcainous's grip. "I'm sure it was nothing," she lied. She wasn't about to reveal what she'd seen in that waking hell she was forced to endure because of Raiden.

Arcainous sighed, watching as she turned from him, walking to the other end of the balcony and falling silent once again. He opened his mouth, ready to chastise her himself, but the door to her room opened shortly followed by the servants startled scream at being tackled by two very happy, and very hungry wolf pups. Arcainous disappeared back into her room, scolding the two who were now fighting over a large steak, even though another hung off the edge of the cart that rested in the center of the room.

Now alone, Tara looked around, taking a seat in a nearby chair. "Had he always been there watching me?" she wondered aloud. Closing her eyes, she shook the questions from her head before resting it on her arms which were now folded on the surface of a table. Her body once more desired sleep. Simple, dreamless, quiet, sleep. But just as she felt her body surrender, her chair was jarred, drawing her quickly from the edge. Groaning, she looked down to the tug of war over the steak and sighed.

"Honestly, you two . . ." Leaning down, she snatched the slobber covered slab of meat. "Eww . . ." She scowled, tearing the meat along the puncture marks their fangs made then tossed half to each pup. "You two really are going to have to learn to share." But her words met deaf ears as the two were off once more, hiding on each side of the balcony to enjoy their prize. She just sighed and shook her head, staring down at her hands. "Ugh . . ." She turned them over and was about to wipe them on the legs of her jeans when another presence stopped her.

"Here's a towel for your hands."

Seconds later, she caught the tossed linen and wiped her fingers clean.

"Thanks," she said as she tossed it onto the table.

"You have a way with them," Arcainous commented as he set a plate of food on the table in front of her. "Now, eat. After what you've been through, you will need your strength."

"I'm not hungry," she muttered, casting a disapproving gaze to the table and the food.

"You can eat willingly, or I can always feed you, if that is your desire."

The idea of being fed by anyone, let alone a grown man, was unpleasant enough, and she relented. Leaning forward, she plucked two grapes from their stem. One she promptly ate while the second was used as a projectile, bouncing off the center of Arcainous's forehead. "If I have to eat, then so do you," she said as her elbows found their home on the table's edge.

Arcainous caught the grape as it fell and set it back down on the table, taking a seat across from her. Taking a bit of cheese and bread, he pressed the two together, his gaze lingering over the woman before him. She had grown so much from the curious child he had met so long ago. Slowly, he began to prod at the wall she had erected, and in time he was able to break through. He saw her posture relax and the two were finally able to fill in the gaps since their last meeting. She'd even told him that she was given a stuffed wolf she named after him for their likeness. But even as they sat and talked, in the Physical Realm, a desperate search was still continuing.

CHAPTER

13

Reunion

Yukino sat in front of her computer as she did most days when she wasn't working. Her fingers moved easily over the keyboard. The sound each key made as it was pressed was the only sound in her now empty house. He had dropped out of school and vanished completely. The friends he had that she could find hadn't seen him, or if they had, they were quite tight lipped about it. In spite of all the dead ends, she kept the hope alive that he would return to his senses and come back home. She leaned back in her chair and rubbed her eyes. They were blood shot with fatigue and her joints ached from the hours that she would spend searching for him.

She let out a sigh as she extended her arms far over her head. Her back gave way and popped, releasing the pent up energy that was trapped in her joints.

"Where are you, Darius?" she said with yet another sigh.

She returned to the missing persons' website that she had placed his picture on to see if perhaps there were more leads, or any information at all. Her shoulders dropped in disappointment though when she found that nothing had been added, nor had there been any recent views of his information. Her heart sank within her chest and she wondered if he was, in fact, a lost cause. Defeated, she moved the mouse to close out the page, but when she clicked it, the arrow moved and selected the tab for the newest additions to the database.

Her brows merged at the misclick, but as she went to close it once more, her body froze. A dreaded chill raced along the length of her spine as pictures and information revealed themselves to her. "Oh no," she whispered. Her eyes raced the length of the text, ending with the suspicion that she went missing the morning after her mother's funeral. "Police are calling this a kidnapping?" she read aloud. "How absurd. She didn't leave the house at all." Or at least to her knowledge, she didn't. She'd had to leave early to return home and couldn't find her to say her farewells. "But where would she have gone?" she asked herself, racking her mind with possible places she would have gone, but everything logical would have ended with her appearance. "Where did you go?" she wondered aloud, leaning forward and staring at the image staring back at her. There was one way to find out something general about it, and she quickly pushed to her feet.

Crossing the room, she turned on some very mellow classical music then lit some candles she had set out across a small table in the center of the room. Sitting cross-legged, she closed her eyes and let her mind relax and sink into the count of the music. Centering herself for meditation came to her like second nature and took only seconds where with Tara it would often take hours. Her mind, once cleared, focused on the picture of Tara that she'd seen on the site, the repeated question of 'Where are you.' echoing in her thoughts. Slowly her vision began to clear as images began to appear. First a door, opening to a raging storm, followed by the image of a pack of wolves racing along the grasslands. Her brow creased as she tried to put the cryptic images together before the feeling of warmth enfolded her, guiding her with its gentle pull. She knew the feeling instantly, and as her meditation ended, her eyes flickered open. "Why do I need to look there?"

"Maybe I should see if they might know where she is," she wondered aloud as she pulled on a short denim jacket.

Grabbing her keys, she gave the house a final look-over to assure things were off and extinguished before closing the door behind her. As she drove, the images again replayed in her mind. There was no sense to be made about the storm unless it was metaphorical for the turmoil existing in Tara's life. The wolf pack was a bit easier to try to make sense of. She wasn't capable of changing form like the Watchers did, but she did have the imprinted gaze from one and she wondered if that's where she should start. Her mind was pulling against itself as she pulled into the park. Looking around, she could see that it was quite busy and that she would be waiting for just the right moment to fade through the door.

She'd searched for one closer to her home, but this was the first one she could find and it would have to do for now. She strode past chatting mothers and fighting children, their behavior reminding her so much of how Tara and Darius would act. The memory tugged at her heart, but her gaze never faltered and remained level. And then, she found it. In the middle of an empty field often used for sports practices, she found the key that would hopefully bring her the answers that she sought. But even now, on this sunny day, small children ran back and forth playing tag, or tossing balls around. She thought she'd even seen a Frisbee sail effortlessly through the air. With all that was going on, there should be no reason for her to hesitate, but every time she reached for the handle, she would feel eyes upon her, or a child would run before her and say hello before laughter carried them off into the distance.

"I am going to have to find another door when this is over with," she decided. But well over an hour had passed since she'd reached the door, and people were beginning to whisper, wondering if perhaps she was some predator or something. This made her brows merge with disgust but the waiting paid off. A rather small window presented itself and she eagerly took it. But as she stepped through, the window was closed and as she vanished through the door, a small child ran off to tell his mother about the disappearing lady he'd just seen.

"Now that that's out of the way," she said as she smoothed out her blouse. She looked around for a moment before she began walking, her steps hitting the ground with great purpose, knowing exactly where they needed to go. She knew that the ease in which she traveled made most green with envy, including Darius, who always strived to best her at something she'd done for much longer than he'd been alive. She found her second door easily enough and as she opened it, she stepped into the warmth that Nimost's energy had to offer. "I just hope she's here." Her eyes scanned the length of the White Tower as she crossed the bridge leading to it. "If anyone would know how to find Tara, it would be her."

Seeing someone approach made the guards take notice as they moved to block her path. "No one is allowed through without express permission from the Elder Council." The harshness in the Captains tone made Yukino's eyes narrow. Never before had she been prevented from entering and now would be no different.

"I'm here to see Elder Fisonma," she said, hardly acknowledging that he'd said anything to her.

"And I told you."

"I'm well aware of what you said." Her voice was now quite curt as the argument ensued about whether or not she would be allowed to pass.

The guard standing with the Captain squinted a moment before his eyes widened. He'd seen a painting of this woman standing with Fisonma once before in the tower. "Um . . . Captain . . ."

"Not now!" he snapped, flashing a glare toward the guard before directing his attention back to Yukino. But as he did, the air around her rippled and a set of deep green robes appeared over her clothes bearing the symbol of Nature embroidered in gold on the front.

"I am Priestess Yukino," she began in an almost angry tone. In truth it was just harsh enough to get her point across. "I am a personal scout to Elder Fisonma and it is urgent that I speak with her, sooner rather than later."

The Captain was now tripping over himself as he scrambled to get out of her way. "My . . . my apologies," he stammered.

Yukino strode past him and through the doors, entering the grand hall. "Now where would she be," she wondered. Soon though she found a passing servant who was able to direct her to one of the many libraries where Fisonma would often go when she needed to think. As she entered the spacious room Yukino found her in the center, her eyes distant in deep contemplation, but the smile she received told her that her visit was expected. "Elder." She gave a deep bow before approaching the table where she sat.

"Why so formal my friend?" Fisonma asked as she rose to her feet to greet her, her white cloak swirling effortlessly around her as she moved. "To what do I owe the honor of your visit?" she asked, sweeping her arm to the side, motioning for her to sit.

"I came to seek your help," she admitted, taking the offered seat as Fisonma returned to her own.

"You're looking for the girl and your son."

"Uh, yes." She was always surprised with the ease in which Fisonma was able to pin point the subject of a conversation. She read emotions and energies with too much ease, and some would often swear she could also read a person's mind. "Tara more so however," she admitted. "I believe she possesses a great gift that will aid us in the future."

"I've not seen you wrong yet," Fisonma said with a warm smile. "That's why I chose you. But while I cannot help you find Darius, I can tell you exactly where Tara is." It wasn't that she was trying to be cruel, or that she didn't want to find him. Truth be known, Darius held the same promise that Tara still held. But once a person chooses to surrender to the Shadows, they become lost to her sight.

Yukino gave a sigh of relief with the prospect of finding at least one of them. "Please tell me she's all right. I didn't even realize she was missing until just a bit ago. Coming here was my first, well . . ."

"Insight?" Fisonma asked. "You were wise in following what you saw." But with the look that she received she couldn't help but laugh. "Don't worry about Tara. She's fine, now, though she was a bit tired from her standoff with Raiden."

Yukino nodded. "She didn't—wait, she's here?"

Fisonma nodded. "She's in the tower of the Ice Elemental. Arcainous is watching over her and making sure she's resting."

"Thank the Gods." She sank into the chair and sighed. With the load removed from her mind she lifted her gaze in question. "Wait, did you say she attacked Raiden?"

"Quite well, in fact," she answered. "Though, he did finally have to resort to using his whip to subdue her."

Yukino cringed. "I remember that whip. We've watched many falter to its power, but I thought she would have been smarter than to attack him."

"I believe that his constant presence around her put her under a great deal of stress, compounded only by losing you to the move, and losing Senia." She then leaned forward resting her chin on the backs of her hands. "I think we made a mistake separating Tara and Darius though." Her voice was full of regret as she made the statement. "But they were both losing their focus."

"We wouldn't have done anything different if we had to do it again," she assured. "I just hope we can pull Tara from the edge."

"There is something rare in her energy," Fisonma admitted. "But we need to calm the rage building in her heart. I would hate to lose her to the Shadows."

"I think she'll be fine once she's had time to grieve the loss of her mother."

"If that is so," Fisonma began, her voice lowering to just above a whisper, "then you must help me keep something secret." The look that crossed her face was nothing short of ominous.

Yukino in turn became concerned as she leaned in. "What secret?" she asked. "How serious is this?" But even after moments of silence she received no answer. "Fisonma!"

"Serious enough," she finally admitted, startled as if drawn from a deep thought. With a heavy sigh she waved her hand with a single fluid motion, closing and locking the doors and assuring that they were alone. Only then did she dare continue, even though no one knew of Tara's arrival to Nimost. "What must be kept from her at all costs is the cause of her mother's death. What led to the string of infections."

"The shooting?"

The look on Fisonma's face was grave as she nodded, explaining what she had seen in great detail. "This was planned when she was still rather young."

The look on Yukino's face was one of disbelief. "Are you certain?"

"I can only hope this is one time that I am wrong, but all I have seen leads me to the one conclusion." Sitting back, Fisonma brought forth an imaging sphere. Within it was the image of the pendants that Tara had made for the two wolves. "She creates such beauty when her heart and mind are calm."

"She created those?"

"She did." The image then went dark but the sphere remained. "If she knows what really transpired to bring her here, her hatred would drive her past my sight."

"I was unaware that she had such a level of power," Yukino confessed.

"This is nothing." Fisonma circled a finger along the sphere, allowing an instant replay of her encounter with Raiden. Yukino leaned forward, studying the new rune with concern before watching it explode. They then watched her struggle with his whip, ending with her collapse. "I believe that with you here, she might be calmer, easier to train."

Yukino nodded slowly. "Her new rune concerns me." She adjusted herself in the chair before she continued. "Up until that moment, all of the runes she'd created were used to protect. She often showed me her journals which is how I know this. But this. This rune does make me worry greatly."

"So you'll stay then?"

"I will. I can't fail her like I failed my son."

The two rose but Fisonma was at her side in an instant, her hand resting upon her arm. "You did not fail him. Our destinies are chosen by the fates. Those who run from them are often lost, never able to find their way back." But that was enough talk of dire things. With a wave of her hand the doors opened once more and the two walked from the Tower, their conversations turned toward more pleasant topics from their past.

"I still can't believe you let me reside in the Physical Realm."

"Your gifts would have done us little service here," Fisonma told her, drawing the hood of her cloak over her head once more. But as they approached the walkway leading to the Ice Tower, it was apparent that the Tara was feeling much better than she had when she first arrived.

She sat on a railing, watching as Arcainous tried teaching Luna and Myst the finer points of hunting but the presence of new energies caught her attention and her head shifted slightly. "Yukino?" No, this had to be a cruel trick, but as they drew closer she realized that it was no trick. "Yukino!"

"Tara!"

The two watched as she leaped from the railing, almost gliding over the ice. "Are you sure she doesn't skate?" Fisonma asked with an upturned brow toward her friend.

"Certain," Yukino replied just as she was tackled in a rather tight hug.

"I'm so glad to see you." Her voice was muffled, but the words still rang through quite clearly.

"Not half as glad as I am to see you," Yukino confessed, her palms running the length of her back.

Pulling back, Tara tilted her head as she stared up. "Why?"

"The news has been saying your disappearance after your mother's funeral was a kidnapping."

"My what?" Tara was confused. "But her funeral was like what, yesterday? Isn't saying I was kidnapped a little premature?"

Yukino's smile softened. "Dear, the funeral was days ago."

"Eh?"

Fisonma sighed as she brushed a stray lock of hair from her face. She thought that training her would be easier than this. "Child, do you not remember what I told you on our journey here?"

"I do now.," she mumbled. "Time as I know it to be has no meaning in this Realm of existence." Her voice mirrored Fisonma perfectly with the exception of her mood coming through.

This of course, made Yukino laugh which drew Arcainous's attention. This in turn gave the two wolves the opening they sought. Myst flew from the shadows, leaping effortlessly onto his back while

Luna's tiny jaws went for his throat. "Okay, I think that's enough for now," he said as he shook the two to the ground before returning to his human form. Approaching the group, he bowed to Fisonma and smiled. "It's been awhile, Yukino."

"Indeed it has," she replied. Tara took this as a sign to tune out and sat on the ground, greeting the two pups that scampered up to her. The yips drew her attention and she crouched down eyeing Tara, but also seeing for herself the pendants that dangled from their necks. "And who are these two?"

"Luna and Myst." Tara answered. She didn't look up, but instead, kept her attention focused on the two, scanning for any wounds that might have been received during their training, rubbing their sides vigorously when she found none. "I'm taking care of them," she continued as she ushered them off to play. But she would say nothing further. The details of what had happened were too personal but were written down in one of her journals. Not even Fisonma knew what had happened on the banks that stormy night.

Fisonma turned her attention once more to Yukino and touched her arm. "Your room has been prepared in the White Tower."

"You're too kind. I could have stayed in the temple."

"I wouldn't hear of it," Fisonma protested. Tara took the introduction of small talk as her cue to leave them to their conversations and beckoned the two pups to follow her back to the tower. But even as she began to settle into her new life in Nimost, she was unaware of the ordeals that lay before her.

CHAPTER

14

Of Ice and Fire

Tara was sound asleep when the form of a large wolf landed upon her. Her heart leaped into her throat, leading to a flurry of motion that sent the wolf yelping as he landed sprawled out onto the floor. In a blur of movement, she was crouched on the bed, watching as the wolf slowly returned to the human form of Arcainous. "What in the nine levels!"

His chuckling cut her off and the daggers again flew from her gaze. "You can handle yourself well enough," he admitted. "But that exercise was to help you to avoid the initial encounter, to be prepared, even in sleep."

"You ass!" she snapped, launching a pillow sideways at his head.

The commotion began to rouse the two sleeping pups, who were none too happy at being awake before they were ready. "This was an exercise for you two as well." Arcainous announced as the two made their way over to the bed. "You're going to have to protect her as you get older." This of course meant little to them and they soon sat on the floor, whining that they were hungry.

"Great," she mumbled as she fell back onto the bed, rolling over and burying her head under a pillow. "You made them whine, you get to feed them."

"They'll have to eat on the run. You're going to be late for your first day of classes."

Her head poked from beneath its confines, her hair nothing short of a wild mess. "My what?"

"Your first day of classes." Arcainous said as he began tossing clothes onto the bed for her to change into.

Tara glared at the selection of clothes that lay on her bed. "Yeah, I'd rather die than wear that." She then went to her bag and got out a pair of black jeans and snug black top. She disappeared to change and brush her hair, returning only after it was secured upon the top of her head in a high pony tail. "These are clothes," she said flatly before pointing to the dresses and robes that were on the bed. "Those . . . not so much."

He sighed and tossed a pale blue cloak at her. "Then at least put this on," he grumbled. Grabbing her arm and some food for the pups he led her from the tower. "We're going to be late." The irritation in his voice was evident and he shifted into his wolven form. "Get on," he ordered.

"Aren't we moody," she huffed as she got onto his back, holding the two pups close to her chest. He gave a low growl before lurching forward, but she was expecting nothing less and was able to hold on easily. "Better luck next time!" she shouted, pressing her legs firmly into his sides.

The look he threw over his shoulder was enough to quell any more comments that she had stashed away and the remainder of the trip was done in silence until they came up to a large building. "We're hear." His voice was flat and she'd just managed to get off his back before he returned to his human form.

"Ah, Arcainous." The two looked as a woman approached. She wore a simple pale blue dress, the same color as the cloak Tara wore, but the cloak she wore was white, fastened at the neck with a series of crystalized snowflakes.

"Who is that?"

"That is Cetsia. She's a priestess from the Temple of Ice."

"Arcainous. To what do we owe the pleasure of a visit from the great Watchers."

"Cetsia," Arcainous replied with a bow. "I'm here only to bring you a new student." He swept his arm to Tara as he again rose. "This is Tara. She's come to us from the Physical Realm, a prospect of Yukino."

Even to the instructors Yukino was known. "Her skills in detecting deep promise has proven invaluable." She then turned her sapphire gaze to the woman beside him. "Well, hello, Tara." But Tara just nodded, unsure of what to think about the whole thing. "Is there anything you'd like to ask me before classes begin?"

"Why am I here?"

"Well, I can't answer that. I don't know why you're here."

"Shocker."

"Tara," Arcainous hissed.

"What?" She spun around to glare at Arcainous. "I think if I'm going to be forced to be somewhere, I have the right to know why."

"No one is forced to be here," Cetsia interrupted.

"Actually . . ." Arcainous gave her a quiet gaze.

"Ahh . . . I see." She then turned her full attention to Tara. "So you're the one. Fisonma sent word about you. I am nothing more than a basic instructor. I will be giving you the basic knowledge of everything you will need to know, then your advanced classes will be chosen for you depending on what your strengths are proven to be."

Arcainous clamped his hand over Tara's shoulder and gave her a stern look. "You listen to what she has to say." He then handed her a bundle and stepped away. "That's your food for the day for both you and the pups. I'll be back when classes are over."

"When will that be?"

"When they are over." And with that, he returned to his wolven form and was gone before protests could be made.

"Come, Tara." She then looked at the two pups who obediently followed. Once they were in the class, Tara took a seat in the back while Luna and Myst curled up under the desk, finishing the nap they were so rudely interrupted from. Once the class was settled, Tara was able to look around as Cetsia made her introductions. There were people of various ages and some of them she could have sworn were Elven, but their ears were hidden by their long, straight hair. "Now that introductions are made, let me give you an overview of the class. I will be giving you the basics of the Elements. This means that I will be telling you how a person's element is decided. In spite of what many think, a person's element is determined at birth, but it can take years for it to manifest itself."

Tara leaned in and propped her chin in her hands. Cetsia turned her back to the class and began drawing diagrams on a white board. "There are so many ways that a person's element is decided. The Physical Realm would have you believe it is ruled by which Zodiac you are born under. If this is true, those born under the fire signs would by default, be fire elements. But that is not the case is it." Her gaze then fell upon Tara who soon felt the entire gaze of the class upon her.

"I don't know," she muttered, hating that she was put on the spot like she was.

"You were born under the fire sign Leo, were you not?"

"Yeah."

"And yet you are an Ice Element."

"I guess."

Cetsia turned her attention to the class once more. "Purists teach that true astrology is what determines a person's elemental fall. But that will be another class for those who are interested. It's not a class required for you to progress further. Now, no matter where you hale from, the four basic elements are universal. Earth, Fire, Water, and Air. But there is also a ring of Outer Elements." She once more went to the board and expanded upon the diagram. "Ice, Plasma, Lightning, and Nature. Each is a perfect split of their two base elements." emphasized by the lines leading from each outer element to each of its base elements.

"Now, most people will be a single element with tendencies of a second. Like, a person will be a water element with tendencies of either air or earth. But there are those born under the influence of a single element. Those are considered pure elements, but only belong to the four basic elements." One of the students rose their hands to ask a question and Cetsia pointed toward him.

"Why are only the basic elements pure?"

Cetsia went into detail as to why that was and how outer elements couldn't be pure because they were a combination of elements. Anything after that just seemed to bore her. Many sessions went like this, reviewing everything so that it was understood flawlessly, but always introducing new information after the old was reviewed. She'd even gotten better at her daily wake up attempts. He'd gotten the best of her most times, but she was slowly able to at least move when he would leap onto her bed. Toward the end of her class the powers of Light and Dark were introduced. "Everyone chooses, no matter their element, which will influence them. But that does not make it finite."

"Why not?" one student asked as she twisted several strands of her fine blond hair around her finger.

"Corruption is quite easy," Cetsia explained. "If a seed can be planted, those who choose the Light can easily fall into Darkness, but it is harder for those who embrace Darkness to surrender their ways and come to the Light."

"Well, why?"

Tara blinked. Even she knew this one, too well she knew that. Her deepest fears were that Darius had done just that, embraced the darkness that her heart fought so hard to extinguish. Her body shivered then as a flicker of his screen name appeared before her mind's eye. Propping her chin into her palm she wondered if he was in fact, confessing to her that he had surrendered to the Shadows. "It just is," she muttered.

The girl looked back and scowled. "What do you know Outsider," she snapped.

Tara leaned back in her chair, turning her attention from the girl, which only fueled her irritation. "More than you know," she replied, her tone still holding the evident boredom. The two growing wolves sat and took notice, baring their fangs as they growled in warning. Only then did Tara seem to pay attention, watching as the girl shrank back in her seat. She scratched the two behind the ears, soothing them once more. "Hush now." Her voice was soft, holding an almost motherly tone. "She's not worth it." Her statement was said with enough of a bite to get the message across, and her gaze drilled a hole into the back of the blond's head.

"Enough!" Cetsia slammed her open palm onto the desk, grabbing both of their attention. She took a seat on the edge of her desk, watching the entire class. "Hanna, you of all people should know that where you are from has no bearing on what you can become." She then looked around, making eye contact with each student. "Remember this if you remember nothing else. As long as our mission is one and the same, our personal background is moot. Someone of another Realm could rise to be Elder, while someone from the lowliest gutter could rise to be a Guardian. Make your friends, do not push them away because of a petty difference. There might come a day where your very lives might rest in the hands of those sitting next to you." She then looked out the window and saw that the sun had reached beyond its half-way point through the day. "Class is dismissed. Remember to start studying. Classes will resume three days from now for your final exams."

The downtime was spent with her nose in the notes she had taken, memorizing even the most minute detail, or as much as she could. But when she walked out of class she was satisfied that she had at least done well enough to pass. "So?"

Tara cast a side glance. "What?"

"You know what?" Arcainous said, his arms folded loosely across his chest.

"Oh, you mean my final?" There was an under tone of sarcasm to her voice as all expression faded from her features.

"Yes, your final."

"Well . . ." She paused and stared up at his face before quickly turning away to walk toward the doors. "If you want to know so badly, you should have taken it." A triumphant smirk crossed her face, feeling the scowl of his burning into the back of her head.

Cetsia walked out, hearing her comment and sighed, her head shaking softly. "She passed with flying colors Arcainous."

"Really?"

The introduction of yet another voice made Tara stop and turn around. "Yukino!" She hadn't seen much of her since she started her classes, so she was happy to see her.

They all watched as Tara ran and gave her a tight hug. "She has quite the grasp on the basics and fundamentals of the Elements." Cetsia commented. "I assume we have you to credit?" Cetsia asked, her gaze shifting to the Priestess. "Either way, I suspect she will advance quickly through the remainder of her classes."

But by now, she was lost from the conversation, focused on the two wolves at her side. The three soon raced outside into the late morning sun, the rays warming her skin from the chill of the air in the classroom. "She seems much happier than when she first arrived," Arcainous remarked as he watched her disappear.

"I believe that directing her focus away from everything that troubled her allowed her mind and heart to clear," Cetsia said, her gaze shifting to Yukino. "Of course your presence helps quite a bit as well."

"I think the fact that she knows I'm here for her to come to is help enough. She really hasn't sought me out," Yukino said with a soft smile. "I believe she is trying to prove to everyone around her that she is capable of doing this on her own."

"I just hope she is better tempered when she meets up with Raiden. He is ultimately the one who will be overseeing her training, no matter where she falls." Arcainous groaned.

The classes to follow bored Tara to tears. Beasts of the Realm which included variations of animals she was already familiar with. The bears, however, looked rabid with bats even bigger than the bears. She did learn though, that the webbing from the bats wings, when harvested properly, could be used as weather proof sheltering

Next was a herbology class. Too much information for her to take in at once. Never before had she taken so many notes and drawn so many diagrams. She vaguely remembered their instructor telling them that different combinations could heal a wound, or be used as a lethal poison to coat a blade or arrow. In spite of the vast amount of information, she managed to pull through with high marks, allowing her to move on in her classes.

Her favorite class, however, was the class given on the dragons that existed in the Realm. "We are unsure just how many different breeds exist, but we have many catalogued." Alexia then brought up an image sphere and began going through the breeds they were aware of. Some looked hard as stone with spikes like rock formations jutting out at the base of their wings which Tara thought was quite impractical. The spikes at the end of their tails however . . . Others looked like serpents, dragons from Chinese lore. "We call them Ancient Dragons because of the scales that fall around their jaws giving them the appearance of a beard. They are also the hardest to seek out, keeping to the most secluded areas of the Realm."

Still more dragons appeared through the sphere leaving Tara entranced. Some that looked like they were from her medieval fairy tales, while more still looked like combinations of sea creatures with wings. The arm of one of the young men in their class shot into the air, waiting patiently to be called on. "Do the Elemental Armies have dragon riders?" he asked, flicking stray strands of jet black hair behind his shoulder, revealing to Tara, if even for a split second, the hint of a pointed ear. It was almost enough to break the trance the dragons held her in.

Alexia was hesitant to answer the question but the rest of the class joined in with pleading eyes, wishing for an answer to the question. Reluctantly, she caved and took a seat on the front of the desk, her hands resting upon her knees. "Well, the Guardians do each possess a dragon unique to their element and a rider is chosen with great care for each dragon."

"Well, how is a rider chosen?" another student asked.

"I don't know what is required. If you're good enough, you're approached by the Watchers, the Elders, the Elemental Guardian, and Raiden."

But before anyone else could ask any questions Tara raised her hand. "Um, what kind of dragon is that?"

Everyone turned their attention to the sphere which had still been cycling through their database, stopped on something that looked like living death. "That . . ." Alexia rose to her feet and drew the image from the sphere, allowing the class a better view. "This is a bone dragon. Born of necromancy, they serve the Shadow Lands."

"Necromancy?"

"Death Magic," Tara said flatly.

This made the young man in front of her who'd asked about the dragon riders turn and stare at her. "Just how do you know about Death Magics?"

Tara rolled her eyes at the implication in his voice and leaned forward, locking gazes with him. "Where I'm from, things that are considered in the Dark Arts are popular with kids looking for some new way to get attention or to defy authority." She then leaned back, her tone revealing her boredom with the conversation. "Yukino briefly mentioned it while she was training me and taught me how to protect myself against it." She then signaled the end of the conversation by rising to her feet as class ended and walked out the door.

The rest of their time in this class was spent learning the signs of dragons in the area, how to avoid them, and how to kill them, should avoiding them fail. After their last class was over, Tara lingered, watching as the rest of the class filed out into the halls. Alexia approached her and sat on the desk beside her. "Is something on your mind? Usually you're the first one out the door."

"I had a question actually." Tara admitted, taking her gaze from the window, knowing that Luna and Myst would be cross with her being late.

"What's on your mind?"

"The dragons, and their riders," she began.

"Like I told Ander, I don't."

"That wasn't what I was going to ask," Tara interrupted. She then leaned forward, not even sure herself how to ask what she wanted to know, but she figured she'd muddle her way through it. "I know dragons aren't immortal, since we've gone over the various ways to kill them, so I know that there just isn't one dragon for each Elemental."

Alexia sat up and nodded. "I think I know what you're trying to ask. You see, when a rider is chosen, they are imprinted to a hatchling. They stay together always, training and becoming familiar with the movements of the other."

"So there is more than one rider?" Tara asked.

But Alexia shook her head slowly. "A new rider is chosen when something happens to the current rider or their dragon."

"What do you mean?"

"The bond created between a rider and their dragon is so strong, that forcing another upon them has been known to drive the dragons mad, and the riders are usually unable to trust a new dragon."

"So what happens to them?"

"Well, some riders are allowed to join the armies. But those who are too mentally gone are retired to estates here in Nimost where they are allowed to live out the remainder of their days as a celebrated hero."

"And the dragons?" Tara pressed.

But this question Alexia seemed quite reluctant to answer. "They are allowed to live out the rest of their days in peace in fields north of the city."

"Where?"

But Alexia shook her head. "I shouldn't have even told you what I have about them. Besides, the area is under a constant patrol of elite soldiers" She then rose to her feet and held out her hand. "Come now. I'm sure you have better things to do than to ask me about flights of fancy."

Tara nodded, pushing to her feet and exiting the class just as Cetsia and Yukino passed by. "Well, hello, Tara."

"Hi, Cetsia," Tara greeted with a smile, hugging Yukino tightly when she saw her.

"You're here awfully late," Cetsia commented, exchanging glances between Tara and Alexia.

"I was answering some questions she had concerning the drag-ons of the Towers." She then smiled. "She's so curious." Her gaze then shifted to Yukino. "I suppose we have you to thank for that curiosity?"

But she just laughed and shook her head. "She's been like that since I first started working with her."

Tara made a face then looked at them. "So which class is next?"

Cetsia thought for a moment. "Advanced Elements," she said with a nod. "There, most everyone will be separated into their classes."

"I thought we already were in a class."

"You are, but you'll be separated into your fighting classes. Warriors, archers, rogues, mages, and the almost elusive, illusionists."

"Is that what happened to the people who quit coming to class after herbology?" Tara asked.

Cetsia nodded. "They showed the skills to become alchemists and were pulled from your class so they can be further trained. If they are lucky, and prove themselves better than all others, they will receive an apprenticeship with one of our master alchemists."

"What happens to everyone else?"

"They return to their villages where they can use the knowledge they gained here to better the lives of those around them." Alexia answered.

Tara just nodded and rolled her head to pop her neck. "Hey, since you're still here," Cetsia began, "would you like to see where your class will be tomorrow?"

This struck Tara's interest. "Sure."

"Is the teacher still who I think it is?" Yukino asked.

Cetsia and Alexia just smiled. "It is."

"And he still asks about you." Alexia added, finishing Cetsia's statement.

Tara stared at Yukino, studying the blush she was trying so desperately to hide and nodded to herself. When they exited the back of the building though, her look changed and she started glancing around. "Um, where are we? Why are we outside?" By now, Luna, and Myst had found her scent and followed it to the field in which they stood, nipping at her hand until she fed them.

"This is our classroom."

Everyone turned, hearing the duel voices speaking in perfect unison. "Trista, Tristan, how good to see you."

Trista smiled. "To what do we owe the honor of such a large group visiting us?"

Cetsia stepped forward, her hand sweeping to where Tara knelt as she finished feeding her wolves. "We thought we would show Tara where her next class would be starting."

Trista leaned forward, meeting Tara's gaze. "So this is the buzz around the school."

The look that crossed Tara's face was one of confusion. "Huh . . ."

But she just laughed and shook her head. "Nothing." She then looked at her brother, then back at the group.

"So when did you start helping with the class?" Yukino asked.

Trista thought for a moment and shrugged. "Just after you left actually." Tristan answered, though it was obvious who his smile was meant for.

Tara thought it was cute, but it did make her miss Darius, or the Darius she knew before her mother was shot, and her gaze fell to the ground. Before anyone could ask about it though, she pushed to her feet. "Yukino, I need to get going. These guys are getting hungry and ate what I had left for them."

Yukino smiled and hugged her. "All right, dear. Good luck in class tomorrow."

She just nodded and turned to the twins. "I'll see you at the start of class."

"We look forward to it," Tristan said with a shallow bow.

Tara cracked a partial smile before waving to the rest of the group. Giving a short whistle, she headed off with her two charges leaping happily as they followed after her. "Is she okay?" Alexia asked.

"I think she's still trying to find her place," Yukino replied with a sigh.

"She looked so heartbroken for a moment," Trista commented with a glance over her shoulder.

The five continued their discussion as Tara reached the center point of Nimost but as she crossed the path that would take her to the Ice Tower, she stopped suddenly. "Fisonma."

"I hear congratulations are in order."

"For what?"

"How you've been doing in your classes. I hear you have top marks."

Tara just shrugged. "It's an old habit. I was always competing against Darius." Her gaze shifted to the side as she continued. "It was almost like a sibling rivalry." But her gaze once more fixed upon the Elder just as Arcainous joined them.

"Ah, Arcainous. I was going to come find you."

Tara's brow creased. "What's going on? Something feels off."

Fisonma's look became sullen. "You are more perceptive than Yukino gives you credit for," she began. "The armies of the Ice Tower are returning to Nimost. They will be here before day's end. Unfortunately, this means you will have to stay in the dorms for the remainder of your classes."

"What?" Her gaze shot between Arcainous and Fisonma. Suddenly returning to the Physical Realm didn't sound like a half bad idea. "What about Myst, and Luna?"

"Things have already been arranged. You'll have a room to yourself, large enough for the two wolves. You'll be quite comfortable."

"And just think." Arcainous interrupted. "You won't have to worry about me waking you up in the morning."

"I'll be sure to count my blessings," Tara replied dryly. Her arms folded instantly and her gaze returned to Fisonma. "Can I at least get my stuff?"

"I've already had it sent to your dorm." She then turned to Arcainous. "The scouts have information you'll need to hear as well, so I will need you with me." She then bowed and took her leave, heading to the White Tower before Tara could say another word.

Tara just stared, trying to figure out just what had happened when Arcainous approached her and rested his hands on her shoulders. "I have to go, but I'll come see you later." But he got no reaction from her until he leaned in to kiss her forehead. She pulled away, moving to stand behind Luna and Myst. He just stared at her and shook his head before taking his leave.

She just stared off into the distance as the day began to fade. "At least back home I felt like I belonged somewhere." She heaved a sigh and lowered her gaze to the ground. She wanted to stay and catch a glimpse of this captain who was returning, but she didn't want to be anywhere around the Towers right now. Shaking the thoughts from her head she scratched the two behind their ears. "C'mon, you guys, let's go and get you fed."

The prospect of food made the two happy and they circled around her the entire way back to the dorms. The head Mistress of the building was polite and gave her the directions to the room she would be staying in, slipping her two wolves a treat when she was sure Tara wasn't looking. As she looked through the open rooms she could see two to three people per room. It gave her an insight as to how big the rooms were, but also gave her something else to feel out of place about.

"Are they trying to isolate me?" she asked as she finally found her room and pushed the door open.

Luna and Myst ran in ahead of her, their noses telling them of the feast that had been set up for them while their things were being moved. Turning on the light revealed a room big enough for the three of them. Heavy curtains covered a picture window where a desk and chair rested. On another wall stood three book cases and a closet while on the opposite wall were two very plush and full pillows for the wolves to sleep on.

"Yeah," Tara said as she stepped into her room. "I don't see you two using those much."

The two looked at her, scraps of meat hanging from their jaws before going back to their meal.

Tara shook went about unpacking her stuff—again. Her clothes were hung in the closet, separated by what they were, with the dresses Arcainous thought himself clever to hide hidden in the back. The few books she brought with her were placed in order on one of the book shelves while her meditation items were placed with care on the desk. Lastly came the picture of her, Mark, and Senia which she placed on the table with a small lamp, and the plush wolf that got tossed onto her bed. "Well, at least I'll be close by," she said after a while, sitting heavily on the edge of her bed. "And now you two won't have to worry about trying to fit under my desk."

In spite of the positive spin she was trying to put on everything, it just wasn't working and she just sighed, lowering her head as her fingers slid through her hair. Luna leaped onto the foot of the bed, resting her head in Tara's lap, her soft whines drawing her from the downward spiral of thoughts. Looking into the calming moonlit eyes Tara smiled softly and ran her fingers over the side of her head.

"You two are so good."

Myst soon joined them, sitting before her with his chin rested upon her knee, receiving the same kind affection as his sister.

Tara was oblivious to the rising commotion and sounds of footsteps racing down the halls. The only indication to her that something was amiss was the sudden sound of low growls rising from the hollows of Luna's chest as her eyes fixated upon a figure standing in Tara's doorway. Tara lifted her head, her bangs falling over her eyes, hiding the blue haze they had taken on.

"Can I help you?" She had recognized the girl as the one from her basic elements class who'd dared to call her an Outsider, so seeing her just was not the highlight to her evening.

The girl took several timid steps into Tara's room, her gaze fixed upon the wolves. "Um, Tara, right?"

Her voice was small, and Tara wondered what was so fearsome about the three of them. "Don't worry about Luna and Myst, they won't hurt you," she said as she pushed from her bed. Myst quickly took her spot, and the two curled up in the center of the bed, their eyes always watching.

"They're very beautiful wolves," she said, trying to break the ice as swiftly as possible. The two took notice of the compliment and sat up, puffing out their chests. "It's obvious that you care a great deal for them."

"I made a promise," was all she would get as a response as she moved closer to inspect the duo. She then caught a glimpse of the woven chain around each of their necks and gasped.

"Those are the most amazing things I've ever seen." She slowly reached out to touch the pendant around Myst's neck, drawing her hand back swiftly when the frigid chill of the ice raced through her fingers. "Are those ice?" Tara just nodded, her arms folded against her chest. "Wow. How often do you have to remake them?"

"Never," Tara answered flatly.

"C'mon. Everyone knows that ice melts eventually."

Tara hated being questioned and her glare became quite evident. "Look, did you want something?"

The girl stiffened quickly and looked at her. There was a moment of silence before she spoke again. "I heard you were moving into the dorms. I wanted to come and apologize for the comment I made to you, about you being an Outsider. Cetsia was right. In the end, we're all going to have to count on everyone, and well, I'd rather know I've not given anyone a reason to abandon me when it comes down to it all."

A selfish apology, Tara thought. How . . . predictable. She was about to say something when another girl came to an abrupt stop in front of her door. "Aiya! Come on!"

The look on Aiya's face changed like the snapping of fingers. "Oh Tara, you have to come with us!"

The delight in her eyes was almost nauseating. "Go where exactly?"

"To greet the armies of the Ice Tower." the girl chimed in. "Almost everyone goes. It shows our respect for what they do, and it's a way for us to show ourselves to them in hopes of being chosen to fight with them in the future."

"Not to mention it's a great way to scope out the Captains and the rest of the hot guys," Aiya added with a gleeful giggle.

Tara's brow arched, then twitched. Even here? "Stupid schoolgirls," she muttered low enough under her breath that the girls thought she was only clearing her throat. "I'd really rather not."

But the protest was met with deafness as Aiya's friend grabbed Tara's cloak and Aiya grabbed her by the wrist, hauling her off leaving the two wolves in a moment of peace to rest and eat. "It gets pretty cold at night." Aiya said as she pulled on a dark green cloak. Her friend wore one the color of crimson and she just shrugged, draping her own over her shoulders. By the time they reached the towers, a group had amassed but they were able to worm their way to the front. "Is it always such a mad house?" Tara asked, feeling herself being squished around a bunch of people.

"Overall, yes."

"Look! It's Aaronel!" Aiya's squealing voice broke through the conversation and the two looked to where her wagging finger was pointing.

"Who?" But Aiya was caught up in the fandom of the returning armies so Tara turned to her friend for answers.

"Aaronel," the girl replied. "He is the Captain of the entire army sworn to protect the Tower of Ice."

"The whole army?" The astonishment was as clear in her voice as it was in her eyes.

"Mhm." Her smile was warm, welcoming the change to an intellectual conversation. "He was chosen by Marcus himself."

"Marcus?" Tara asked, her eyes soon scanning the sea of armor. "Which one is he?"

But the girl only shook her head. "You won't find him among the army." Her gaze then joined Tara's, watching as families were united and others were greeted by the other officers of the towers. "Marcus was once Guardian to the Ice Elemental."

"What happened?"

"No one knows for sure. A lot of rumors, but the most common was that he was ambushed by the Shadow Lands and killed on sight."

Tara's jaw hung open. "How horrible."

The girl nodded. "Patrols were sent out but found nothing."

"Nothing?"

She shook her head. "No signs of camps, no footprints. It was like he'd just up and vanished. That's why there are so many rumors surrounding him. Some say he's being held prisoner, while others think he was corrupted by power and turned to the Shadows. But no matter which rings true, the only truth we have, is that the Tower of Ice sits with no Guardian."

"Ugh! Is that all you two are going to do?" Aiya's voice broke into the conversation. "You missed everything." There was a sudden pout to her voice as her finger found its home pointed at Tara. "You especially should have been paying attention."

Tara's brow arched as she turned her attention. "Um, why?"

"Because Aaronel and Elder Fisonma were watching you. A bit too much if you ask me."

"I wouldn't pay any mind to it," Tara assured, and the three were once more on their way to the dorms. "I'm sure they were watching someone else anyway."

When the three reached Tara's room, the two girls stopped. "Thanks for coming with us," Aiya said with a grin. She then waved and darted off to her room.

The remaining girl shook her head slowly. "I honestly don't know if she'll make it through classes or not." Realizing she'd said that aloud, a deep blush made its home across her cheekbones. "I'm sorry," she said with a deep bow. "I didn't mean to say that aloud. I should be going. My name's Christine. Chris for short. Let me know if you want to get together and study some time." And with that, she was gone.

Tara stood in the hall for a moment before slipping into her room, locking the door behind her. Making her way to the desk she pulled the curtains aside letting the light of the moon bathe the floor, showing her that the two wolves were curled up, sleeping soundly on their own beds. She nodded, smiling softly as she changed and crawled into bed, passing out as soon as her head hit the pillow.

CHAPTER

15

Revelation

Tara sat up slowly and rubbed her eyes. A quick glance of the area told her that she was not in her room. Thinking it was nothing more than a test, she stood up and brushed her hands down the front of her clothes but even after her eyes had had ample time to adjust to this level of darkness she could still see nothing, no outlines of objects, not even the faintest source of evening light.

"Where am I?" But the echo that resided within her voice gave her the undesired answer.

"Belzak?" Her call would go unanswered though as it faded into the blackness that engulfed her. The cold that began to embrace her shortly after was proof enough that this dream was not of Belzak's design. Rubbing her hands along her arms she began to walk, slowly at first, but the more she walked, she realized that it was nothing but flat, well, nothingness and her pace began to quicken as she called out in random intervals only to hear the echo of her voice drown in the vast darkness.

The more she moved, however, the more she felt stationary, but she attributed it only to the lack of any form of objects around her to use as marking.

"The lack of light doesn't help either," she muttered under her breath. She stopped and listened, straining to hear anything, but there was nothing but deafening silence that nearly made her ears ring. "I've always hated not being able to wake from these." She sighed, rubbing her temples. "Hello!" This time, however, her voice was not met with silence. As she strained her ears once more, she could make out the faint sound of hissed whispers. Her brows merged as she focused on the sound, listening as it drew close and retreating as it became aware of her concentration upon it. "Who's out there!" she demanded.

All that replied though, were more incoherent voices, their games of far and near continuing as their pursuit in taunting her ensued. "This is irritating," she grumbled, her hands planting themselves firmly upon her hips. "I'll not be intimidated by a bunch of cowardly whispers!" she shouted. Her shouts were only met with something she could only assume was laughter. Even as her voice portrayed an air of confidence, her nerves were becoming very aware of things around her. She could feel the energy crawling along her skin, brushing against her hair, and whispering into her ear.

Although she was feeling overwhelmed by the sudden sensations, she wouldn't give them the pleasure of hearing her scream, or even jump. As things seemed like they were going to close in around her, however, she remembered the words that Raiden had told her the night he'd dropped her off at her dorm. "No matter what, believe in the Light. It will protect you as long as you have faith in it."

"What in the world am I remembering something from *that* loon for?" He was the last person she wanted to think about at the moment. All the stress she felt when she was around him, always around her, always there when things seemed to start going wrong. Whatever, it was worth trying. Anything was if it would mean ridding herself of this horrid feeling. Oddly enough, to a degree, she did believe in it, and the more she held onto that thought, that belief, the warmer she became. She closed her eyes allowing herself to become calm, focusing on the warmth that seeped into her as she curled one hand over the other, holding them in almost prayer like fashion. "I do believe," she whispered, even as the shadows continued to creep around her. As her eyes shot open, her arms shot outward which caused the energy to expand out around her. "Into the light I demand you emerge!"

As the words fell from her lips, the most brilliant light filled the area, eradicating the darkness around her. She could see the shield that protected her, and the shadowy tendrils that awaited her on the other side as they attacked the barrier repeatedly. Drawing her gaze forward once more she beheld what she could only assume were four beings, the darkness that filled them devouring any source of light giving them an almost deformed appearance. "Who are you!" she demanded, her voice strong even as she felt their leering gazes pierce through her.

"When you fall from grace . . ." the voice echoed. ". . . you will be ours."

Grace? Really? She started to laugh at the sheer lunacy of the idea that she of all people would be touched by grace. She was forced from a place she'd begun to think of as home, ostracized by her class-mates, and just plain isolated. How was that grace? "What are you talking about! What grace?"

The cruel laughter began once again, chilling her as they mocked what they believed was complete stupidity before they decided to speak again. "You can always just surrender to us now. Our power is so much stronger than yours."

Tara's head tilted at this proclamation. She looked around, see-ing the tendrils that were still attacking her, burned or broken by the light that protected her. She then looked back to the four and tried not to laugh." Yes, your power is *so* much stronger than mine, mm." Her head nodded as she spoke and her arms folded loosely across her chest. "And yet, the powers of four cannot overpower that of one." The amusement left her face, her voice filling with an icy bite as her eyes hardened, matching the leer in her would be attackers.

At her mocking a loud crackle echoed as the pulse of the ten-drils attacked at once and repeatedly. She flinched only at the echo of the continuous crack, but she would not cower before them. This only seemed to fuel the malice they held toward her. "Mark our words . . ."

"No!" she shouted. "You mark mine!" Her voice lowered to a seething clench in her jaw as she continued. "I have been put through nothing short of a waking hell. I didn't run then, and I will not run now!"

For a time there was silence, as if her declaration had stunned them. When they did speak again, the hatred in their voice was palpable, cutting through to Tara's core. "Never say never." they warned.

"Empty threats," she snapped. Through the simplicity of their words, however, the threat was evident, and very real. More silence followed, however, before the four vanished, leaving her to stand in the warmth of the light that had protected her. The echo of their cruel laughter was now the only sound around her.

* * *

Tara woke with a start, sitting up in her bed, her eyes adjusting to the pale moonlight as it bathed her floor in its glow. She rubbed her forehead, looking around when she noticed that Luna and Myst weren't on the foot of her bed. She found them curled up in their own and gave a soft sigh as she moved to the book case to grab one of her journals and took a seat at her desk. She had enough light that she could write without turning any on and began to recount what she remembered. When she was done, she rested her head in her hands and rubbed her eyes.

"This is madness," she mumbled. Her body felt old and worn as she slipped silently from her room and into the cool night air. Staring into the moonlight she found a comfort she had sought since everything had begun with her mother, with Darius. "Why are they all looking for me," she said with a heavy sigh.

"Who?"

Tara looked to her left, a bit surprised to see Raiden standing beside her. The look across her face was displeased but she just stared back up at the moon. "I don't know," she admitted.

"What are you doing out so late?"

"I could ask the same thing," she replied, glancing at him from the corner of her eye, taking note of the film of sweat that covered his exposed flesh.

"Training," he answered simply. "What about you."

"I needed the fresh air to clear my head." Suddenly wishing the spot light away from her, she continued. "Who were you training with?"

"No one in particular," he replied with a shrug of his shoulders.

"Sounds like someone in particular," she countered. She knew this game of his, she'd been a player long enough, and she felt that she deserved some answers.

But he just laughed and stared up at the moon with her. "You'll know soon enough," he assured. He then looked to her, studying her, taking note of her tired appearance. "You really haven't been sleeping well, have you?"

It was more a statement of fact than a question and Tara looked up at him. She was beginning to feel very much like a lab specimen instead of a person. "Is it that obvious?"

"A little," he admitted. "And you need to be well rested for your classes that are coming up. From here on out, everyone will be separated into their respective classes to further their training."

Tara just nodded as she lowered her gaze to the ground. "I really don't feel like I fit in anywhere actually." But she instantly wished she could take it back. She was only ever open with her mother and Yukino, and vulnerability was not her cup of tea. Too many bad things happened when she was. But when she felt the warmth of his hand on her shoulder, she looked up to see an unexpected look of ease on his face.

"Don't worry. We'll all be watching you. We will make sure you are placed exactly where you need to be. When this happens, you'll find that you fit in much better than you think you do now."

This did give her a measure of comfort and she felt fatigue creeping upon her. Pushing from both her perch and his grasp she turned and smiled. "Thank you Raiden." She gave a quick bow of her head and was off.

Raiden watched her leave, a bit surprised in her actions. He'd half-expected her to lash out against him like she had when she first arrived. "Maybe she's finally growing up," he mused, but as he retreated for the evening, he couldn't help but notice the distance in her energy. "Something other than fitting in is bothering her." His brow scrunched as he looked over his shoulder at the dorm. He would have to talk to Fisonma and Arcainous. With Yukino on yet another scouting endeavor, they were the only hope of getting through that shell that she always had around her.

Raiden's words held true. The following days were nothing short of brutal. Learning combinations and counters of elements. It was also true that they would be separated further. Several people had already been pulled from the class who had shown no talents for the magical arts and another one still had been taken out after almost flawlessly sneaking into class while running late. This of course, left the mages who soon found themselves deep in the practices of drawing out the powers they kept within them, forming it to their will to either attack or defend. "Heart and desire are key." Trista said one balmy afternoon as they all stood with small spheres in their hands.

"The more you believe in your powers, the more powerful they become," Tristan added as he wielded an attack toward a kid next to Tara. She watched as a flimsy barrier of water appeared around him but the attack quickly over powered him and he found himself sprawled on the ground

"You have to be more serious than that," Trista said, lobbing a roaring sphere of fire toward Tara. Her mind buzzed as the sphere fell from her hands, shattering as it hit the floor. Throwing her arms out in front of her she turned her head to prepare for the impact. But the impact never arrived, and there were murmuring voices around her. Opening her eyes slowly, she looked from the corner of her eye to see a flame flickering in a crystalized tomb. "Impressive." Trista said with a smile, the class watching as the flame began to grow, threatening to break the ice that surrounded it. "You'll have to do better however."

Tara let her arms fall, her eyes fixed upon what hovered between them, staring, lost as her eyes faded to the pale blue of her element. "I will do better," she mumbled as she extended her arm. Everything that Yukino had taught her had begun to flood back to her and everything began making the most perfect sense. Extending her energy out, she realized that this sphere was nothing more than an extension of the energy that resided within her and as she closed her hand into a fist, the ice condensed around the struggling flame until it was extinguished. Only the shatter of ice drew her from her focus, seeing the shimmering shards upon the ground, her eyes once more their sparkling emerald hue.

Tristan stared in surprise, glancing quickly over his shoulder into the distance. There, Fisonma stood with Raiden and the seven Guardians, each watching for prospective mages. "Why isn't Aaronel here?" Wella asked as she brushed stray strands of teal hair back behind her shoulder.

"I agree," Nao replied. "He is acting head over the Tower of Ice."

Fisonma extended a pointing finger toward Tara. "She is the reason he is not present."

"You're not contemplating what I think you are." A man's voice interrupted the conversation and the group parted to allow him through. He was broad and well-built with a gaze as cold as the earth he protected.

"Anon, how nice of you to join the conversation," Fisonma replied, looking back to the practice.

"Her powers are unchecked and wild. Her energy is destructive."

Fisonma looked over her shoulder. "Yes, I can see that. But need I remind you that the Elementals are the ones who choose their Guardians." This statement caused Anon to step back and quiet down as the group watched the remainder of the practice. "If she would only open up about what's going on." She sighed. "She would have so much more control."

As things wound down and the group was to take their leave for the day, the form of a large wolf emerged over the rise. "Elder Fisonma . . ."

"Arcainous?"

Returning to his human form, he approached the group and bowed. "Elder, I have something you should read."

Taking the books, she flipped through the pages, her eyes scanning the words. "Arcainous, where did you get these?"

"Raiden came to me with concerns about Tara, so I went to her dorm to see if I could find anything."

Fisonma nodded, her mind seeing every vivid, horrific detail that was written. Every dream, every encounter since she was small. There they were, revealed for all to see. "Durion?"

The mention of his name drew everyone's attention. "Why are you bringing his name up?" Elexis asked as she tried to peer at the pages.

"Tara had an encounter with him when she was a child," Arcainous admitted, recalling the account to the best of his recollection. "When Belzak raced her away it was the last I saw of them until she was brought here, but she doesn't talk about her past."

"I can see why." Wella said with a shudder.

"An encounter with Durion wouldn't be at the top of my list of things to discuss." Ashton added.

"But why are the generals of the Shadow Lands so interested in her?" Anon asked.

"I don't know," Fisonma admitted. "It is something I will have meditated upon for some time now. Perhaps the rest of the Elders may have some clues." She then looked at Arcainous. "Return these to her room. All we need is for her to falter now and fall."

Arcainous nodded and was off. The rest of the group looked back to the parting class, watching as the twins approached. The Guardians discussed potential recruits before taking their leave to watch the fighters before ending their day. "We have much to discuss." Tristan said as he, Trista, and Fisonma walked through one of the vast fields that surrounded the campus.

Arcainous stood by Tara's door as she came down the hall. "What are you doing here?" she asked with a tilt of her head.

"I came to see how things were going," Arcainous replied evenly as he followed her in to her room, much to the delight of the two waiting wolves.

Tara set her things down and looked around. She couldn't pin point it, but something felt off, and her brow scrunched. "Things are fine," she answered, her voice distracted as she moved to her bed to kick off her shoes.

Arcainous looked around the room and into the open closet, seeing the clothes he'd picked for her shoved as far to the back as humanly possible. "Why are the clothes I sent hung all the way in the back?" he asked, hoping to draw her prodding mind from the fact that he'd been in here only moments earlier.

Tara laughed and looked at her closet. "Because those are not clothes."

"They certainly are," he protested as he pulled out a simple blue dress that rested off the shoulders.

"Um, no. I wouldn't be caught dead wearing a dress."

"And why not?" Arcainous asked. "I think you'd look stunning."

Luna and Myst just sat, their heads moving from side to side as the argument over clothing continued. "If it's so stunning, you wear it," Tara retorted with a wicked grin.

Knowing he was going to lose this debate, yet again, he placed the dress back into the closet and closed the door. "You're going to have to wear one eventually."

"Not if I can help it," she stated matter-of-factly.

"It'll happen, mark my words."

Mark my words. Tara's body froze. *Mark our words*. Their words came back to her, their haunted hiss of laughter echoing in her mind. Why now?

"Tara?"

She shook her head and rubbed her temples. "Sorry, I'm a little tired I guess."

"If you need to talk—"

But she cut him off with a shake of her head. "I'll be fine," she assured. "I just need some rest."

He approached her and cupped her chin gently into his palm. Lifting her head, he was able to stare down at her face, into her eyes. The time for mourning his friend had long since ended, but within her eyes there was a measure of comfort. "You know you can come to us with anything don't you?"

The look in Tara's eyes was just this side of confused. "You really shouldn't worry about me," she said as she pulled away slowly.

"But I do, we all do."

She just gave a faint smile. "Once class is over, I'll find out where I do, or don't belong. If it turns out that I can't cut it here, I'll just go back to my world and make a new life for myself, Luna and Myst."

But all he could do was shake his head. He couldn't confront her about what he knew, what they all now knew. "Don't cut yourself short," he said, kissing the top of her head. "You've always been full of surprises."

Tara just grinned and sat on her bed. "You talk as if you really know me."

"Don't I?" he asked

"A little I suppose." She would give him that much.

He just shook his head. "Get some rest then."

She watched as Arcainous left before plugging her MP3 player into a tiny speaker. Selecting some calming music to listen to, she fell back onto the bed. His touch seemed to linger and her fingers traced the outline of his hand absently. "Worry wart," she mumbled, turning onto her side and was soon fast asleep.

16

Divided

The morning of their final came as a shock to all of them as they were woken up just before dawn and told to convene outside the dorms. "What's going on?" one of the girls whined, clearly displeased at the early hour in which they were made to rise.

Tara knelt on the ground, rubbing the sides of Lunas neck vigorously. "Not a clue," she replied. "They just pounded on the door saying to pack a couple of days' worth of provisions and get down here as quick as possible."

"Well, this is just dumb," the girl complained.

"Is that so?" Everyone looked up to see Tristan and Trista approach, each dressed to the nines in the armor of their element. They almost looked like they were ready for war.

"What's going on?" one of the students asked.

"We've been called to go on a scouting mission south of Nimost," Trista explained.

"There have been reports of activity from the Shadow Lands," Tristan added.

"Um, don't you think that's just a bit too advanced for us?" Tara asked as she rose to her feet.

"Your role in this is strictly observational, nothing more," Tristan told her.

"If anything happens, Tristan and I are to handle it."

Tara studied them closely. Something was up, she could sense it, as could the wolves who had moved closer to her, their ears flattened against their heads. The group followed the twins to one of the temples. "What are we doing here?" Tara asked as a group of priests emerged from the doorway.

"Thank you for seeing us so quickly," Trista said with a deep bow, Tara's question going unanswered.

"We heard about your mission," the Priestess replied. "We are happy to see you and give you our blessings in your endeavor."

A girl in a crimson robe caught Tara's attention and she squinted to better see. "Christine?"

"Tara!" The girl ran up and hugged her tightly. "Thank you so much," she whispered.

"Um . . . for, what." Tara asked as she stepped back.

"The conversation we had when we went to see the armies of Ice. It made my convictions to be a priestess concrete."

"I'm glad," she replied with a genuine smile. "What about Aiya?"

Christine frowned. "She washed out like I'd feared. I don't know specifics though." She then looked back to Trista and Tristan. "I'd like to give her a personal blessing if that's all right."

Trista smiled. "I have no objections."

Christine bowed her head in thanks before turning back to Tara. "I owe you so much," she began as she placed her hand upon her shoulder. Her eyes closed as she saw the words she wished to speak, however, the warmth that enveloped her gave birth to something neither of them would understand. "Let the strength of the fires lead you. Let the searing flames burn those who threaten the peace you strive to protect." As she spoke, Tara could feel the most welcoming warmth surrounding her. Watchful and protecting as it formed an armor of energy around her.

When the blessing was done, Christine was bewildered but pleased. There was a set blessing that they were trained to give, but the words she spoke were nothing even close to the blessings she learned. "Thank you, Chris," Tara said with a warm smile, drawing the priestess from her thoughts.

"Come back to us safely."

"I will," Tara promised.

"Safely?" Christine asked herself with a squinted brow as she watched Tara join the rest of the group. "How odd . . ." Her voice trailed off as she returned to her prayers. "Of course she'll be safe. They all will."

Tristan bowed his head. "Thank you all." He then turned back to the small group of mages and nodded. "Let's go, everyone."

"Stay alert," she said softly, her hands resting upon the tops of the wolves heads. She drew her cloak closer around her as they headed out into the brisk morning air. Time was lost to them all as they picked their way along the ever changing landscape. Through groves of trees, across open meadows, and along large bodies of water.

"I don't see anything."

Tara glared. Why couldn't that girl have just stayed back at the dorms. All she'd been doing since they left Nimost was complain. But just as she was going to say something about it, Tristan brought them to a stop. "Let's stop here for breakfast. Make it quiet and quick. Trista and I are going to poke around ahead to see if we're still on the right trail."

Tara sat against the trunk of a nearby tree, pulling out chunks of meat, tossing one to Luna, and the other to Myst. She, however, was content to take a few sips of water from one of the many bottles she'd brought with her. She laid her head back against the trunk and stared up into the sky, her mind wandering back to the blessing she'd received from Christine. Focused on her words, the energy returned, enveloping her in a calm warmth.

"But she looked so puzzled," she murmured. She herself was a bit confused at the nature of the blessing. She wasn't striving to protect anything let alone peace. They were going on a scouting run and that was all. She dismissed it though and closed her eyes, dozing for a bit while Luna and Myst curled up beside her.

Time found the group well rested. Most had taken naps while they waited for the twins to return, but even as the sun continued its trek across the sky they found that they were still without instructors. "Something isn't right." Tara said, looking around as she pushed to her feet.

"What do you mean?"

"They aren't here. They should have been back by now." She gathered her pack together and headed off in the direction she'd seen them go, beckoning for the wolves to follow her.

"Where are you going!"

Tara turned slowly. She hated being questioned, especially by someone so insignificant. She stared coldly at the girl who'd done nothing but whine and complain since they day had begun, her voice low and even as she spoke. "I'm going to go find them."

"We were told to stay here!" she protested, stomping her foot solidly. Her actions and pouty nature were starting to remind Tara of the girl who was always with Toran.

Tara was on her in the blink of an eye, her hand flying as the echo of her slap drew everyone's attention. "All you've done since we gathered this morning is whine and complain. You're purposely slow, and you're holding us back!" Her jaw was clenched, each word spoken acting as a dagger as she continued. "Your whining is a razor to our morale. How you ever made it this far amazes us all!" Turning from the girl, she strode to the center of the group, holding each and every student's attention. "You are all more than welcome to stay here if it pleases you, but I'm going to go find them."

She spun on her heels, taking the path she'd seen them take with Luna's and Myst's noses to the ground. "Wait!" The three stopped and looked back. Approaching her was about half a dozen of her classmates, each shouldering their packs as they ran to catch her. "We're coming with you."

She had to admit her disappointment in just how few had come, hoping that the entire class cared enough to want to find their instructors. But she would make do with what she had. "Fine. But stay close, and move quickly." Turning her attention back to her wolves she gave a sound nod. "You're up guys. Find 'em!"

They needed no more incentive and their noses were to the ground once more. The girl stood with a smug expression, her arms crossed, clearly scorned by her encounter with Tara. "They won't find anything." The laughter that followed was nothing short of hateful but it was quickly cut short as the bay of low howls filled the clearing. Tara looked back with a smirk before the group headed off, led by the sibling canines.

The group weaved this way and that, the miles passing countlessly beneath their feet. Sparse vegetation soon gave way to more densely grown groups of trees and shrubs. This in turn became nothing more than a large forest which choked out almost all the light of day. "It's oddly cold here." one student commented. "I don't like it here."

Tara looked around, absently running her hands along her arms. Even in such a densely grown area, the chill seemed almost unnatural. "Everyone, keep your guard up," she said softly. "This doesn't feel like a regular cool spot caused by the shade of the trees." Of course this was taken as an ominous bit of news. Everyone began to huddle together just as a strong gust of wind raced through the trees. Luna and Myst crouched close to the ground, their noses lifting as they tried to find the scent once again. Only the sounds of their whimpers gave away their failure and they once again pressed their heads to the ground as the wind continued to blow.

"What in the world is going on!"

All anyone could do was exchange glances and shrug their shoulders. "Hey!" Tara tapped one of her classmates on the shoulder. "You're an air mage right?"

The boy nodded. "Yeah."

"Do you think you can shield us from this until it stops?"

"I can try," he replied. He closed his eyes and held his arms out. His fingers began moving as if on their own accord as silent words fell from his lips. Forming the energy around them to his will he began to weave the air together to create a dome around them, allowing them to wait out the remainder of the weather.

"Wow, that's impressive," one of the girls beamed.

"It's nothing," he replied.

Tara looked around, her brow creasing as she listened to the wind continue to hammer against the barrier around them. "I have a sinking feeling about this," one student mumbled as she sank deeper into her cloak.

"We all do," Tara said with a comforting smile. "But we have to find Trista and Tristan. If it was one of us lost out here, I think they'd be doing the same thing, facing whatever they had to in order to find us."

The girl took a deep breath and nodded. "I know, but this wind . . . We really can't do anything until it subsides."

This did cause a problem, but as Tara looked around she could see a light breaking through the brush behind them. Again the familiar tug took her and she began to make her way slowly. "I think this is the way we need to go," she said, her finger pointing to a possible salvation. Anything was better than staying where they were and as the group made their way closer to the break in the brush the wind began to die down until it stopped completely.

Nothing about this seemed natural to the small group that hovered on the edge of concealment and exposure. If they were being led to this spot, it was possible that their instructors awaited them just on the other side of the tree line. But their nerves had a solid hold upon them, and darker thoughts of a possible attack were never far from their minds.

17

Frozen in Memories

No one really knew how long they had hidden there. Luna and Myst stayed close to the ground, their muscles tense as they looked around. Their noses twitched, constantly taking in the scents around them, but not even they could sense anything amiss. Tara lifted her head, slowly followed by the others, each staring into the clearing. From what she could tell, where they were seemed to be the end of a long vale, flanked on either side by the forest though no one could see the end opposite of where they hid. "Too perfect of a place for an ambush," Tara whispered.

Further conversation fell short, however, as their collective gaze fell upon a figure laying no more than a few yards from their current location. "What is it?"

"I can't tell from here," Tara answered with a shrug. They watched, waiting for any signs of movement, of life. But minutes passed with no revelation, nothing, and Tara slowly began to creep forward.

"Is that wise?"

Tara looked back over her shoulder with a nervous laugh. "Probably not." Even from this distance it didn't remind any of them of either of the twins. The form had no cloak, no armor. Not even the hair was like theirs. "But we won't find them by just sitting here like scared mice," she continued. "And if this person has seen them . . ." She didn't have to go further, especially given the alternative of this person being caught in a scuffle between the twins and some darker force. The group was all nodding and gathering behind her. As they broke into the clearing the silent commands began. Each mage followed the directions they were given, branching out around the outskirts in case anything were to happen. Even Luna and Myst stayed several paces behind her, crouched and poised to attack.

The echo of her heart raced through her ears as she finally reached the fallen form. At first glance, nothing seemed to be amiss. No blood, no signs of a struggle. Nothing to validate the tense energy that they all felt. Assuming the person was simply asleep, she allowed herself a small sigh of relief, but as she reached out her hand to rouse them, her body froze. She was suddenly aware of a new energy that Luna and Myst had already picked up on. The two growled, bearing their fangs even as she motioned for everyone to stand their ground.

Returning her attention to the form before her, Tara began to feel a great unease. "What's going on," she whispered. The response she received though chilled her to the bone. Faint, but unmistakable, the sounds of hissed laughter rustled faintly through the air. Flashbacks flooded to the surface of the nightmare she had days prior. She shook her head sharply, wishing to rid her mind of those thoughts as she reached with a shaky hand once more to the form lain out before her.

Nothing felt off as her palm found its home on the figures shoulder. The flesh was warm, but there was no sign of life. No pulse, no breath. But the skin was still malleable. It didn't have the waxy appearance or texture that most people had when they had passed on. Cyanosis hadn't even threatened to set in. She sat back on her heels, staring intently, shifting her gaze to the area around her. "This isn't right," she breathed, suddenly feeling the need for escape.

She turned, her hand raising to signal the group to fall back to the brush when everything came caving in around them. "Tara! Behind you!"

"Huh?" Tara turned, seeing the once prone form now standing upright. She cringed, the empty-expressioned face reminding her of the horror movies that she and Darius used to watch. Before her, however, it changed, twisting and contorting into something new entirely, something from the depths of her childhood nightmares. Her throat tightened, suffocating any hopes for a scream. Her muscles locked, refusing to let her run or even try to scramble out of the way. *How? Why?* Her mind raced with the questions as crimson eyes pierced through her own. Before anyone could react, however, the hound lunged, pinning her to the ground before the yellowed fangs sent a searing pain coursing through her which gave birth to an ear splitting scream, the scream that started everything. In an instant Luna and Myst were in action, leaping onto the hound, their fangs sinking into both bone and flesh even as others emerged from the shadows of the forest.

"Get 'em!" Tara wasn't even sure who had given the order to attack, but the same voice sent out the order to protect her.

Tara winced, her jaw clenched as she rolled onto her knees. She clutched her arm feeling the fire that raced through her veins. It almost made the heat of her own blood seem cold as it soaked into her clothing. "I . . . don't understand it." Her voice was almost panicked. "How could they have found me? When?" Her mind raced wildly from thought to thought, unable to settle on one thing for more than a second at best, but as she felt herself descending into madness, the snarling of her wolves drew her back from the brink. Her eyes hardened as did her resolve. If they wanted her so badly, they would have to settle for a corpse. "Show no mercy!" she seethed as she forced herself to her feet.

The area was soon alight with fire's flame, countered only by ice's wintery touch. Shards of earth erupted from cracks in the ground, impaling many of the hounds, while vines served to hold others at bay. Bolts of lightning struck the ground with a deafening crack, searing the hounds alive. The stench of burning flesh that it created hung heavily in the area but their focus was so strong that the wave of nausea was unfelt. The battle dragged on slowly, but their tenacity had begun earning them the upper hand. Falling back behind Luna and Myst, Tara took a chance to look around.

"Ellia! Look out!"

Tara's head shot to her right, just in time to see a hound leaping from the shadows at one of the mages who had followed her. Everything was suddenly happening in slow motion as her mind raced for a way to save the girl. One of her runes would be ideal, but from her prior visits, she knew that it would take too long to cast. As the hound neared Ellia, Tara could feel her body tense. In an instant, she saw what she wanted and closed her eyes tightly. "Rune of binding, protect her!" From the ground shot tendrils of energy which wrapped themselves around the hound, pulling it down instantly. Ellia dove out of the way just as the hound began to yelp and cry as it was crushed. And then, all was eerily silent as the group began to come together.

"Tara! You're injured."

Tara tilted her head then looked down at her arm. "It's nothing, really." By this point she couldn't tell if her arm was bleeding or if it had stopped. Her clothes were a saturated mess. "I'm all right." She tried being assuring, but her protests were met with unlistening ears. As they fussed over her, however, she couldn't help but feel that things were far from over.

"Tara, relax. With the ordeal over, we can focus on finding Trista and Tristan."

"It would have been easier if the others had decided to come with us." another student commented with a sigh and a frown.

Ellia took a seat in the grass close to Tara. "I dunno. I think we did really well, all things considered." Her gaze then became serious as she glanced at Tara. "Thank you for saving me. You're a great leader."

Tara's brow arched. "Eh?"

"You are!" Ellia protested.

"Sitting around wasn't going to get anything done. That doesn't qualify me as being a good leader." She then looked at the ground, watching as blood soaked into the earth, staining it for generations to come. "Besides, if I was so great, everyone would have come with us."

"Not really," Ellia corrected. She leaned back and stared into the sky. "People will do what they will do in life. There's nothing to be changed about that. But look at us. We're still following you. So you must be doing something right."

Lifting her head, Tara looked at everyone around her, seeing each of them nodding. For a moment, a brief smile crossed her lips, but as she looked toward the other end of the clearing, her smile faded. "No."

Everyone else followed her gaze, staring in horror as the form of a huge bulldog came charging toward them. "What . . . is that?"

"He really did find me," she breathed.

"Who?"

But Tara only shook her head. It wasn't fair. Why did they have to be pulled into her personal hell? Everyone cowered behind her and the two wolves, watching as the distance between them closed with every bound. "Do something!" Ellia pleaded.

Tara pushed to her feet, her gaze frozen as she stood between the dog and her classmates. "You took him from me!" she snarled. "You took him from *them*, from everyone!"

The students exchanged confused glances. "Who is she talking about?" one student asked, receiving a shrug in response.

"I won't let you hurt my friends!" And with that, her arms shot out in a sweeping arc. Taking hold of her element, she began freezing the water in the air, creating a barrier just as the dog lunged for them. Again and again the barrier was charged, and every time, it held. "Where is your Master!" she demanded.

Everyone looked around, shrugging shoulders and exchanging confused glances. "Who?"

But Tara knew. All too well did she know. "Durion! Where are you, you coward!"

The student's eyes went wide. "Did she just say . . . ?"

"Mm . . ."

The group collectively paled. How could Tara be so demanding of someone so horrific? They had learned very little about him in their studies, except for the ruin and death he was known to cause, but all had heard tales of him since they were small. "Tara are you insane?"

But their voices were lost to her. "How odd," she mumbled, her brow creasing. This dog was his pride and joy. He would never leave it on its own like this. The sound of a deep crack drew her quickly from her thoughts and she soon found she had much more to worry about than Durion's whereabouts. Before her, she could see her barrier begin to give way under the constant battering and knew that she had to do something, and do it soon. "But what . . ." As her mind raced for what she hoped would be a quick solution, she remembered the rune that she'd used against Raiden when she first arrived to Nimost.

"Tara, do something!" Ellia shouted, huddling close to the center of the cowering group.

Tara shot a look back over her shoulder. "Why is everyone counting on me all of the sudden?"

"Past experience?" one of the students answered nervously, which made Tara's brow twitch.

"And you really don't seem to be afraid of them," another student added.

Tara's brow nearly shot up into her hairline at the last comment. She almost spun around to face the entire group, but as she moved, the group collectively gasped and screamed, which served to irritate her further. "I'll deal with that little comment when we're out of this mess," she vowed, turning her attention back to the barrier and finding herself eye to eye with the large dog as he rammed the shield once more. She braced herself, feeling the reverberation through the energy and closed her eyes. Focusing was a bit harder with everything that was going on, but as she did, she was able to see what it was that she wanted, and as she willed it to be, an image bearing a resemblance to an exploding star appeared as a glowing orange mark upon the center of the dog's chest.

"Let this rune send you back to the hell that spawned you," she hissed through clenched teeth. "Rune of Destruction, detonate now!" Everyone watched as the deep orange glow that the rune had was changing, giving birth to a piercing white hot light, but that was all they saw. As the runes of energy came to a head, the protective warmth from the blessing Christine had given her once again made itself known. Her head fell forward, her body trembling under the exertion. "Protect them," she whispered. As her eyes shot open, the rune did just as she had commanded, just as the fire left her to create a wall between herself and the rest of her classmates. She knew she was too close to the release and her barrier was already damaged and wouldn't hold so she braced herself for a violent impact. When the dust finally settled, Tara was lying face-first on the ground at her wolves' feet where the barrier had manifested itself. Blood gushed from the reopened wound in her arm and from some fresh wounds in her chest where the shards of ice had made their mark thought they had melted under the heat of her blood. Where the dog once stood, a small indent was left in the ground, the only proof that remained of their encounter, or that anything had happened at all.

* * *

It was days before Tara came to. "Why, hello there."

Tara's eyes flickered open, confused and a bit disoriented. She tried turning her head to see who was around her, but saying the small action hurt was putting it lightly. "Don't try and move."

She stared at the ceiling, unable to recall just what had happened to put her in so much pain. She wondered how much school she'd missed. School . . . instructors . . . Her face paled, and she shot up in her bed. "Trista! Tristan!" She regretted her movements instantly as her head began to swim, causing her to fall back against her pillow in a cold sweat. "We couldn't find them," she groaned. Her voice was so distant as the flood of failure set in. "The attack . . . the others . . ."

Arcainous sat on the edge of her bed and took her hand gently. "Everyone is fine," he assured.

"But—"

"That mission," Yukino began. "That was your final exam. You weren't supposed to find them."

A sudden knock at the door interrupted the conversation. Moments later the doctor in charge of her care entered the room followed closely by the twins. "Oh good . . ." Trista breathed. "You're awake."

"You pack quite the punch," Tristan added, leaning against the door as it closed.

"Yes, yes," the doctor said as he began the task of looking her over. "However, this packed the punch back." He pulled open her shirt to examine the bandages covering the wounds on her chest, applying a healing salve before new bandages replaced the old. He cleaned the cuts on her face and neck, then moved to her hands and arms. He bandaged the cuts on her hands before turning his attention to her arm. He tsk'ed and sighed, turning her arm over. "It's showing signs of infection."

"From an illusion?" Trista asked as she looked over his shoulder.

"Illusionists strive for perfection, but not even the most perfected illusions can imitate the bacteria and other parasites that exist within what they are projecting. There are always subtle flaws in every projection though it takes quite the keen eye to spot them."

"So you think that."

"It's largely possible that one of his hounds got through the barrier."

The doctor cleared his throat as he bandaged her arm before placing it in a sling. "This is hardly the place for such a conversation." He then gathered his things together and rose to his feet. "I'll return in a couple of days to check on your arm. Everything else, however, is healing quite nicely." He nodded to the group and headed off to his other appointments.

Tara sat in the silence, looking at everyone that was around her. But something was missing. "Where are Luna and Myst?"

"The Watchers are looking after them until you're healed," Arcainous assured. "Though pulling them away from you was no easy feat at all."

"They attacked and snapped at the others involved with your testing when they tried to get to you."

"They're quite protective of you," Trista said with a smile. "You've become a second mother to them."

Tara nodded and looked down at the bandages that covered her. "I guess the final didn't go well."

"That's not true," Tristan countered.

"He's right," Trista said as she sat across from Arcainous. "You did very well."

"I don't know how this is well," Tara answered dryly as she held up her bandaged hands.

"It was a duel final," Tristan explained. "The mages against the illusionists. A test to see how you handle combat and how well you can think on your feet."

"But also dedication and conviction," Trista added. "You showed amazing leadership when it came to finding us."

"No, I didn't. Not even half the class followed. How did we succeed?"

"You might not have all been together," Trista began.

"But you did all fight."

Tara looked past the group to Tristan. "What do you mean?"

"The group that stayed behind was defeated almost instantly," Arcainous explained. "Your group survived and was victorious against your foes."

"How many of the others got hurt?" Tara asked.

But Trista only shook her head. "We don't know how, but you managed to will another element to protect them." The look of confusion apparently warranted further explanation. "You summoned a wall of fire that protected everyone from the power of your rune. We asked the fire mages that were with you, and neither of them created it."

"They were all very worried about you," Trista said as she joined Tristan at the door. "They said that if they had to choose again, that they would follow under your leadership without question."

Tristan nodded. "Speaking of, Elder Fisonma has asked to see you when you're able."

"Me? Why?"

But Trista just gave a small shrug of her shoulders. "Ours is never to question the will of the Elders. We are, after all, nothing more than instructors."

"And on that note," Tristan began as he stepped to the side to open Tara's door.

Trista nodded as she approached the bed. "We have another class to prepare for." She hugged Tara gently. "We're all so proud of you." And with that, she was by her brother's side within an instant, both disappearing through the door.

With their absence, the room again fell into silence. Tara stared at the door for some time before she chose to spoke again. "I wonder . . ."

Arcainous shifted a bit. "Wonder what?"

"Why Durion?"

"What about him?" Yukino asked as she took a seat in a nearby chair.

"Why pick him, his hounds, his prized bulldog." Something to her just didn't seem to sit well with the whole thing.

Arcainous looked to Yukino for help. They all knew, but if she were to ever find out. "Next to the Generals of the Shadow Lands, Durion is the most feared. Confronting everyone with something so fearsome makes all other encounters much easier to sort out."

This made sense to Tara and she nodded. "I understand. Thank you, Yukino." She then kicked her blankets off and scooted to the edge of her bed. "Guess I should see what Fisonma wants."

"She said when you were able," Arcainous protested, steadying her as she began to topple.

"I'm awake and moving aren't I?" Tara asked. "I think that qualifies as being perfectly able."

"I just think you should rest more," Arcainous replied, turning his back as Yukino assisted Tara in getting dressed.

Tara's brow creased. "What's with you today, Arcainous? I'm assuming that I was out for a while, yes?"

"Yes."

"Then I think I'm pretty well rested."

"He was just worried about you, dear," Yukino's voice was always so calming. "We all were."

Tara looked up at her as the three left her room. "But I'm fine," she protested.

"We didn't know that earlier," Arcainous said, his voice a bit harsher than he'd meant it to be.

Tara stopped, watching as he continued walking, looking up only when she felt the warmth of Yukino's hand upon her shoulder. "He never left your side. The two of you hold a special bond stemming from your first visit here when you were little. He holds that quite close to his heart."

Tara blinked, looking back at him, watching as the distance between them grew. She continued on in silence until they reached the courtyard. Yukino excused herself to tend to other business, leaving the two alone in an awkward silence. "Where are we supposed to meet her?" she asked, wishing not to broach the subject of what had happened without someone else around.

"She'll be here shortly," Arcainous replied, remaining standing as he looked around. "Are you sure you want to do this now?"

Tara scowled as she looked up at him. "I'll be fine."

"Nothing is ever as easy as a simple conversation here. You know this."

Tara mumbled under her breath. "Will you quit worrying and let her know I'm here."

"I don't need to," he said as he took several steps from her. "She already knows you're here." And with that, he gave a deep bow. "Elder Fisonma, Raiden."

"Hello, Arcainous." Fisonma greeted. Her smile was warming, and even Raiden seemed a bit relaxed. The two looked upon Tara. The patches and bandages. The cuts, scrapes, and bruises. And of course, the sling that encased her right arm. They exchanged glances before Fisonma decided to speak. "The doctor tells us that your arm is a bit infected."

"There is suspicion of something foul happening during their test," Arcainous confessed. "The watchers are investigating and a full report will be available to you as soon as it's completed."

"Dutiful as always, Arcainous."

He gave a single nod as Raiden's gazed fixed upon Tara. "I hear you did well during your final."

"That's what everyone tells me," she answered with a shrug.

"You have a different opinion then?"

Tara just shrugged and turned her attention to the ground. "How can freezing be considered doing well?" Every fear came back to light in that moment. "A soldier needs to be focused and able to deal with their fears."

Fisonma took a seat beside her, resting a hand upon her knee. "Even the best of fighters will freeze. Tara glanced quickly from the corner of her eye before staring back at the ground. There was a reason she froze, but there was no way she could explain why. Feeling the wall begin to build itself back up, Fisonma squeezed her knee gently. "There was a reason we had the illusionists focus on Durion's hounds."

Tara blinked as she lifted her head. "Huh?"

Arcainous stiffened, watching closely, relieved only when he watched as another image sphere appeared before them. In it, they watched as a small child found friends, discovered enemies, was attacked and chased, the images fading only as she toppled through, back to her world, the door slamming closed behind her. "It is important that we face our fears and learn to overcome them. In this realm it will be much easier for Durion to find you so you must be prepared for whatever may come your way."

Tara just stared blankly at the sphere and nodded. "But I haven't been chosen by anyone, so, I'm probably going to wind up going back to my world. It'll be harder for him to find me there."

It was only then that Raiden stepped forward. "Actually, I was thinking about taking you on myself to finish your training." The look that crossed Tara's face was one of complete confusion as he continued. "We will fine-tune your magic and runic abilities as well as school you in the art of weaponry."

Tara's jaw hung open in unmasked awe as she looked between Fisonma and Arcainous. "Me?"

"We will' of course, have to wait until your wounds are completely healed," Fisonma added as she rose to her feet and gave a shallow bow. "Arcainous, please escort her back to the dorms so she can rest."

"Of course, Elder." He bowed, watching the two depart before he turned to Tara and held his hand out to her. "Shall we?"

Tara just stared, her mind off on its own. She looked up at him and nodded, placing her hand in his as the two headed back to the dorms. "How are they?" she asked, wishing to distract her mind. Without the two wolves around, things were a bit too quiet.

"They're perfectly fine. Until we knew the extent of your injuries, we thought it best to keep them away. But they're being taught to hunt and how to fight. You know, things that all wolves should know."

Tara nodded. "Everything seemed so real. I really thought he had found me like he swore he would."

Arcainous just nodded. With the state of infection in her arm, it was highly possible that one of his hounds had, indeed, found her, but he wasn't going to alarm her with that. When they entered her room he stayed near the door. "You needn't fear about them. We've been keeping a close eye upon them. They're nowhere near Nimost."

Tara was relieved to hear that as she sat on the edge of the bed. Arcainous moved across the room to sit in a nearby chair, his hands resting comfortably in his lap. She didn't know what she wanted to talk about, if there was anything left to talk about, and the silence became unsettling enough that she began to fidget. Arcainous, however, was calm, and used the silence to thank his stars that Fisonma hadn't revealed that they had dug through her room to find her diaries. His attention shifted only when Tara rose to her feet and walked over to the window. "Arcainous?" She looked back over her shoulder, her expression confused and troubled. "Can I talk to you?"

His brow arched slightly as he pushed to his feet and moved to stand behind her. "You know you can come to me about anything. What's on your mind?"

She turned to face him, unsure if she could do this, but the overwhelming weight of keeping things so tightly closed within herself was starting to take its toll on her. Their final exam was just the catalyst that was starting to make things feel like they were closing in around her. "There's more going on with me than my travels here."

"Oh?" The look that crossed his face was one of surprise, not because of what she had told him. He already knew, they all did. What surprised him, was that she was finally taking the steps to put everything out into the open. He knew that with this step her powers would amplify themselves several fold as would her confidence in them.

She exhaled heavily and turned from him, staring blankly out the window as she began to recount everything to him. What happened after they fled Durion, watching Belzak as he was engulfed in the sea of hounds. The wall that had erected itself around her mind and how Belzak's voice managed to shatter it. She told him about the trio that chased her during her second visit, and the disturbing dreams that she'd found herself caught up in since her arrival. When she was done she felt oddly better, but things were once again too quiet, enough so that she began to tremble under its weight. But then she felt it, the warmth of his arms as they slid around her shoulders.

"You're shaking," he whispered as he pulled her back against his chest. She remained silent though, lost in the peace of his embrace. She wondered if it had always been like this. But if it had, she was probably too closed off to realize it. It was too much to think about though, so she just closed her eyes and laid her head to the side. This of course, made him frown and he scooped her up into his arms. "I told you that you should have waited until you were a bit more recovered." His scold though, was a bit halfhearted as he carried her to her bed.

"I'm fine, really," she protested. "Just a little tired." In truth, she was feeling a bit weak from ridding herself of so much weight. She just didn't want him to worry.

He gave her a knowing look, however, as he set her into bed and tucked the blankets around her. "You shouldn't overdo things."

But as he rose to take his leave of her she grabbed on to his sleeve. The look that crossed his face was puzzled while uncertainty filled hers. "Don't go."

His brow creased with concern. "Are you all right?"

"I don't know," she admitted.

He cupped her cheek gently before the form of a large silver wolf leaped onto her bed. He curled up on the vacant side of her bed feeling the warmth of her hand on his paws. He watched as sleep slowly took her. As it took him, however, his mind was plagued with the very real possibility that the vampiric trio had interfered with the final exam. It was the only explanation since they were master illusionists and the infection in her arm was very real. It was something that would take the work of the Watchers finest scouting party. For now though, he was quite content and had no real desire to move. He licked the back of her hand gently, moving it around slightly with his muzzle before finally surrendering to the sleep that awaited him.

CHAPTER

18

A Diamond in the Rough

"I feel so far behind everyone!" Tara's complaining was cut short as she leaped back into a series of single handed hand springs, coming to rest in a crouch with her right hand tucked tightly to her chest. As she snapped her arm out, however, the air filled with a spray of ice shards.

Raiden dodged most of them quite easily. "You're focusing on too wide an area," he shouted, ignoring the complaint for the time being, even as one of the shards cut into his arm. "It's good for an area attack, but center it more for a single opponent." But he rushed her quickly, stifling any chance for her to use what he'd just told her. "Why do you say you're so far behind?" he asked, his closeness now forcing her to use hand to hand combat, something she was not fond of at all.

In the distance, a group watched in silence as the physical assault began. "I remember going sword to sword against him." Wella said with a cringe.

"It wasn't all that bad," Anon scoffed, folding his arms across his chest.

Elexis rolled her eyes. "That's why you're the leader of the Guardians," she said dryly

"What are you three doing here? Practices are over."

Everyone turned to see a petite blond heading down the corridor. "Kayla," Wella said with a smile.

Kayla, Raiden's second in command in training. On first appearance, the petite blond wouldn't look like she could tangle with the best, but her powers rival Raiden, therefore commanding a great respect from all who trained under her. "Something must be interesting." She reached the group and looked down into the arena. "Ah, Tara."

Back on the field it was business as usual. Raiden was unrelenting in his assault and it was painfully obvious how unskilled she was with a blade. "Is this why you feel so far behind?" he asked, thrusting his blade downward.

She swung her blade up to deflect his, the clash echoing in the silence. The deflection, however, caused the hilt of her sword to twist in her hands, sending a searing pain through her wrists resulting in her yelping. "I've seen what the others are able to do," she answered, constantly moving out of the way of his blade.

He didn't answer her. In fact, his assault became more intense, each move trying to get her to strike back and take the offensive. "I have worked with them far longer than I've even known you," he told her as he finally pushed her back against the wall.

Even from where the four stood, they could see the terror in her eyes. "What a shame." Elexis sighed. "She had such promise."

"Practice will be over shortly," he promised as he hefted his blade into the air. Tara now saw the opening she'd so desperately watched for and took hold of it. With a simple fluid motion of her hand she released a sphere of ice, hitting him in the center of his chest and sending him flying back.

"Maybe she still does have some promise." Anon said as they watched Tara lunge forward.

She was soon upon him, the tip of her blade poised to strike the center of his throat. "Impressive," he coughed, pushing the blade away gently with the flat of his palm. Tara didn't answer, but held her hand out to him, helping him to his feet.

The group stared in awe at what they'd seen then parted ways before they were discovered. Anon lingered for a moment longer, nodding. "Not bad, kid," he mumbled before he too disappeared into the night.

"You show great patience when you are faced with an opponent of greater skill, waiting to seize the perfect moment to strike. Not many possess that kind of a talent."

Tara's brow creased. "I wouldn't call it talent," she mumbled as she rubbed her wrists. "You were killing my wrists. I just wanted you to stop."

"We'll strengthen them up over time," he promised, handing her a towel. "We need to have you in tip-top shape for the Tower Festival."

By this point, Tara was only half listening as she ran the towel over her face. "Yeah, sounds like fu—wait, what?"

"You heard me correctly, child. You will be displaying what you've learned at the end of the Festival in the Tower Tournament."

"What?" She'd never even heard of such things, let alone thinking she would participate in them. "What on earth are you talking about?"

"The Tower Festival is a celebration of the Elementals and those who protect them. At the end of the Festival there is a tournament where the Guardians of each element face off against each other. Normally the last spar of the tournament would be between myself and Kayla, but with us one Guardian short, she will be participating in the main event. Therefore, you, will be standing in for her as my opponent. We need to make sure you're at your best. A lot of important people will be in attendance."

"And on that note, we introduce the politics," she muttered dryly.

"Not really," he countered mildly. "These people will determine your final place with us."

"Eh?"

But Raiden just shook his head. "Nothing for you to concern yourself with. All you have to worry about is giving me your absolute best."

She just scrunched her nose before tossing her towel at him, disappearing into the night with a huff. "She has a lot of spirit."

Raiden tossed the towel aside and smiled. "I hope she didn't disappoint you all Kayla."

"Anon seemed impressed enough." Kayla replied, emerging from the shadows. "She's gained a lot of control over her powers as of late."

"I knew she would. It just took her trusting someone enough to open up about everything that's happened to her."

She nodded a bit. "How do you think she'll do in the tournament? She will be going against you after all." She then began to laugh. "I can't even beat you."

"You will when it's your time to," he assured her.

"You shouldn't talk like that," she scolded. "You haven't been at this for very long."

"Long enough to see to the training of many Guardians."

"And you'll see many more," she told him with a sarcastic roll of her eyes. "Stop talking like you're going to die tomorrow." The two laughed and gave their farewells, parting ways into the silence of a peaceful night.

Tara walked into her dorm room to see Luna and Myst curled up on the foot of her bed while Arcainous leaned back in a chair. "How was practice?"

Tara paused for a moment, actually needing to consider the question. While Raiden thought she was improving, she thought she was lacking. "It . . . was all right." She then headed to her closet for some bandages.

"Just all right?" he asked as he rose to his feet, aiming to follow her just as she emerged from the closet and sat down at her desk.

She held up the bandages to answer his question before she set to the task of wrapping each wrist. By now they had begun to ache and show mild signs of bruising. "My wrists are too weak to face him in hand to hand combat."

"I can always help you with that you know."

She lifted her gaze to him, scrunching her brow slightly. "I'm sure you have more important things to do than to babysit me. You are after all, the leader of the Watchers."

"I am," he answered simply. "However, I've been asked by Elder Fisonma to watch over you until we are able to find out what exactly happened during your final to give you such an escalated infection through your arm."

She sighed heavily. "Do I really need a babysitter?"

In retaliation, his expression became soulfully wounded. "Is that all you think of me as?" Even as she met his gaze his eyes seemed just as wounded as his voice.

"No! Of course not," she sighed, tripping over her words in some attempt to rectify what she'd just said. "It's just . . ."

But the echo of his laughter stopped her midsentence. "I kid, I kid. Try not to take things so seriously."

Her expression darkened, finding this less than amusing and with a single fluid motion, she snatched a nearby pillow and launched it at his head. "I'll make you regret wanting to teach me weaponry," she snipped.

In spite of her empty ended threat, Arcainous made good on his word and the next day he had her in one of the training arenas while Raiden worked with others under his charge. "Get used to its weight and how it feels in your hand," he told her, watching as she stared down at the dagger in her hand. "Find the balance point in the blade and use that to move it around in your hand."

Tara was obviously less than pleased at the small weapon in her hand. "Um, no offense, but Raiden comes at me with swords, not daggers."

"If you don't start light then you'll do some real damage to your wrists. When you understand one," he began, moving the dagger easily within his hand. He flipped it easily in his grasp, tossing it only to create a thin veil of energy across his finger which gave only slightly as the tip of the blade pushed into it. ". . . then you pretty much understand them all." And with that, he gave a gentle push of the blade, catching it by the hilt once more.

"And now you're just showing off," she scowled.

But that's how her time passed. If she wasn't training with Raiden then she was training with Arcainous. If she wasn't with either of them, she was in her room tending to cuts and bruises or lost in her meditations, focusing on manipulating her energies to better aid her in her training. Sometimes she would create something and it would fail almost instantly, but those that had the potential of lasting she focused on, making them better, more potent. One such manifestation was a whip handle created out of the same ice energy that she'd made the medallions from for Luna and Myst.

Before she knew it though, the festival had arrived and the streets of Nimost were alight with torches and colored lights. But as Tara stared out over the throngs of people, the dancers and the singers, the booths and the patrons, she could only wonder. "Will all my training be enough?"

CHAPTER

19

The Tower Festival

Down on the streets Tara was able to better see just how elaborate the colors were. Brilliant, striking, and bold. Nothing pastel or soft. They were accented only by the flickering flames of the torches lighting the night. Luna and Myst stopped, watching as a group of women danced down the street dressed like old time gypsies from her home. The sounds of bells jingled pleasantly with their movements while wandering musicians played their tunes.

"Take that!" The sound of a child's voice instantly broke the hold that the dancers held Tara in. Shaking her head lightly, she turned to see what was going on.

"You think that will hurt me?" another child scoffed. "I am the great Alex!"

"And I'm Eaden!" the girl shouted. "I summon a monster to eat you!" She then thrust a triumphant point in Myst's direction. He gracefully accepted the role of the fiend and leaped around on his hind legs, snorting in an attempt to seem ferocious without scaring the both of them. With a single thrust though, the fight ended, and Myst flopped onto his side, playing dead as he was slain.

When it was obvious that the act was over, Myst sat back up just as the two children hugged him around the neck, giggling as their faces were licked. Even passersby who had seen it stopped to comment on how tame the two were. "Thanks, ma'am. That was fun!" They waved and soon disappeared in to the swelling sea of people.

Tara just stared, her head tilted. "Alex? Eaden?" She didn't remember hearing their names before, and wondered if perhaps they were old Guardians who perhaps had passed on in this life. Even as lost as she was to her thoughts, however, she was still aware enough to move to the side as Arcainous failed miserably to jab her in the ribs. "You'll have to try better than that," she told him, her gaze still lingering where the children had disappeared.

Trying to recover from an obvious mishap, he cleared his throat as if nothing had happened. "To answer your question," he began, his hand finding the small of her back as he gently guided her forward. "Alex and Eaden are Captains to the Fire and Nature armies." He paused as a girl passed by, who was selling flowers. "This is as much a celebration for them as it is for the Guardians and the Elementals."

Tara nodded as he talked, looking over the different food venders, scanning over the selections completely. Luna and Myst were delighted when she stopped at a meat vender and chose what anyone could assume were the two largest turkey legs anyone had ever seen. "I didn't realize it was such a big deal," she commented, handing over the treats which were gratefully accepted. The two then trotted off to a nearby clearing to chew on their prizes.

"To those outside the hold of the Shadow Lands this is a very large deal." He chose something small for the two of them to eat and led her to where her wolves rested. "Everyone fights their best in order to protect the people. This is their way of showing their thanks."

"I didn't realize the conflict was that intense."

"Normally it isn't. As of late, however, things have increased and there are a growing number of reports from the outposts of activity from the Shadow Lands borders." He then gave a soft sigh and shook his head. "You shouldn't worry about that though."

But she did worry. No matter how small the scope, whatever was going on, involved her. But to make him happy, she changed the subject. "So are there any other celebrations?"

"On this grand of a scale? No. Each town has their own celebrations such as those celebrating the birthday of a Guardian, Captain, or other person of note, all depending on the town they hail from, but this is the only festival that Nimost is directly involved in."

She nodded and stared up into the night sky. As the hours passed, things had begun to slowly wind down and people were making their way to their respective lodgings for the night. She too thought it was best to call things. She had a rather long week ahead of her. "Thanks for showing me around the festival." She stood propped against her door frame as Luna and Myst muscled their way passed her and onto the foot of her bed.

He just smiled and gave a shallow bow of his head. "I thought that with what you have coming up, that I would show you the key points. Perhaps at the next festival you'll be able to enjoy yourself a bit more."

She just exhaled and stared back at the window. "Yeah. I think I'm just going to lay low until my match with Raiden."

"Oh?"

"Yeah . . . I need to be focused, and well rested." Her shoulders dropped as she gazed back up at him. "Even with all the training I've gone through with you and Raiden, I still feel like I fall short of his skill."

But he just chuckled and kissed her forehead, something Tara was beginning to look forward to at the end of their evenings together. "Raiden has trained many Guardians, but not even they can best him. He is good at what he does. Worry about your skill and how well you do, and you will be just fine." He left things at that, and took his leave for the evening.

The next few days Tara stayed shut in her room in intense meditation. She focused on her runes until just the simplest thought brought them forth. She was also able to dispel them just as easily. Deciding to work on her weapons after a well needed break she pushed to her feet and walked to her window. Like the days prior, she stared out over the swarms of people, but this night seemed different. Everyone was so "in love."

She looked down at the picture of her mother and Mark then stared up at the full moon that hung low in the sky. Even still, after so much betrayal, somewhere in the deepest part of her heart, she still missed him. And why not? They had been together for the majority of their lives. She sat heavily in her chair, the moon now centered almost perfectly in her window. Large enough that she felt that she could reach out and touch it, but far enough away that she felt the icy shun. Putting pen to paper, she allowed her gaze to become distant as forgotten emotions began to creep back to the surface.

Full Moon

The full moon is the lovers' moon
But where are you? Not here
The light cascades not over me, not us
But on those in eternal embrace
Where is that touch that I often sought
The kiss from a moonbeam pure
The pale blanket of innocence white
Igniting passions true
The secrets held though in darkened sky
Elude such seeking light
Mystery surrounding always the moon
Such a brilliant hanging sphere
Hiding always the plans it may hold
Forever the lovers' moon.

When she set the pen down she felt very drained. Once again she looked out the window into the crowds and sighed. Why did she have to take part in this tournament? All she needed was to make a complete fool of herself in front of so many people. "You're over-thinking things."

Startled, she turned around and gave a faint smile before turning back to the window. "There's no way I can compete with any of them." Her voice was distant as she traced her fingers down the window, staring into the night.

"Now what kind of attitude is that?" Yukino scolded. She walked up behind Tara and looked out the window over her gaze. "I know I've taught you better than that."

"I just don't understand why I'm the only one participating in this tournament that isn't someone of station. I know I trained with students that were a lot better than I was."

"I don't know, dear," Yukino answered softly. But she did know. A small part compared to what Fisonma and Raiden suspected, but to tell her anything would be more overwhelming that what she could currently handle. "Perhaps you're a good-enough student that they want to display his talents as a teacher and trainer, and yours as one of his best students."

Tara sighed, relenting the discussion. "In front of all those people though?" she asked, looking over her shoulder. "That really isn't the place to prove them wrong about my skills."

"Then prove them right," she said simply. "Release your tension and take hold of the power I know you possess within you." She turned and headed to the door, stopping just outside the door way. "You have more power within you than you realize. When you can unchain yourself from your past and take hold of it all, you will understand."

Tara watched her door close, leaving her once more to stand in the soft echo of the music she had been playing. She looked off to the side and gathered her weapons together, placing them into a draw-string bag, leaving only the small crafted handle laying on the desk.

"I have to make sure this works." Taking it in hand, she closed her eyes, giving only the smallest through as to what she wanted. When she looked down at it she could see the icy tail of the whip coiled at her feet. A frost blue aura pulsed gently from the solid core that was the main tendril of the whip. For now, it was good enough to know that it worked. Everything else would have to wait until the next day. Dispelling her energy, she slid the handle into the bag and pulled the drawstring closed and flopped onto her bed.

Folding her hands beneath her head she stared at the ceiling, her mind constantly going over a mental check list she'd made to assure that she was ready for the next day.

"Not that anyone can be ready for something like this," she mumbled. But as she fussed over the things to do the music she was listening to filtered through to her once again. Turning her head, she stared at her MP3 player. Her brow scrunched. "I don't remember this music ever being on here." But the more she listened, the more it wrapped itself around her mind and before she was aware, she was fast asleep and for once, a peaceful look crossed her face as she slept.

Yukino opened the door enough to poke her head through and gave a tender smile. "You wouldn't know that music," she whispered. For she had put it there days earlier before she began her preparations. "But it was important for you to sleep." She exhaled softly and shut the door once more. "Good night my dear."

"Tara . . . Tara, wake up." Arcainous shook her shoulders gently, but got nothing in response. "Tara the tournament is going to start soon. You're going to be late for your registration."

Her mumbling became more coherent as she tried shoving his hands away. "I don't wanna go, Mom." She rolled onto her side, and the sounds of light snoring once more rose from her chest.

Arcainous sighed. "She's exhausted." But she had to get up. After such a long week, the highlight of the festival was finally upon them. "Tara, please, wake up. We have to go."

Tara rolled her shoulder, moving her arm from his grasp. "Don't make me go back . . . He's going to be there."

He stood up and stared down at her. "He?" The look that crossed his face was perplexed to say the least, wondering if this "he" person she was talking about was Darius. What he'd read in her journals about the two of them was nothing short of volatile. There weren't many details, but what she'd written was enough to give an overall image. That, however, was neither here nor there. They had to get moving, so he grabbed her bag, her MP3 player, and her, heading out the door with Luna and Myst trotting behind them.

As soon as the sun hit her eyes, however, she was quite awake, although still a bit groggy and uncoordinated. "Umm . . ." She looked around, seeing that she was being carried around. "Why are you carrying me? My legs do work, y'know." She then began the process of squirming free from his arms, grateful that no one really saw them and what was happening.

He just rolled his eyes at her and took her by the wrist. "You wouldn't wake up, and the tournament is getting ready to start." He led her through side streets and various short cuts, making it to the registration tables just in time. "Tara," he announced. "She will be facing off against Raiden in the final match of the tournament."

"Ah, yes." The man eyed her closely. "It's not often that a student competes. You must be something rare indeed."

"Thanks," she answered quietly. "I'm nothing great though, I assure you."

The man just sat back and chuckled, waving them through. Tara looked back over her shoulder then back up at Arcainous. "Why is everyone making such a big deal about me fighting Raiden?"

"Because what he said was true. Very seldom does a student fight in the tournaments. You should consider this a great honor."

But she just scrunched her brow and looked at the stands seeing that they were quickly filling. "Is this an all-day thing?"

"It can be. The longest tournament I've seen took three days to complete. It all depends on who gets paired against who and how well they can use their skills." He led her through a corridor to a room that overlooked the arena.

She saw that they were the only ones there, a fact that the two wolves enjoyed as they sniffed around. "Why can't I wait with everyone else?"

Arcainous arched his brow. "Um, no one waits together. It allows the Guardians to prepare for their match. There's a room where they all meet though after the matches are over."

But a knock on the door interrupted their conversation. Tara peered from behind Arcainous, watching as a young man entered the room followed by two others.

"Pardon us, but we were asked to present the young lady with a gift."

The two exchanged looks before Tara crept further behind him. "What sort of gift exactly?" he questioned as he looked over the one, then the other two. Though it was quite common for the Guardians to receive gifts both before and after their matches, Tara's involvement was known to just a few select people.

"Please forgive us," the man began with a swift bow. "We don't mean to cause you any unrest." He then stepped aside, allowing the other two to pass, each holding pieces of an intricately carved set of armor. "Our master asked that we present this to the young lady in hopes that she would wear it."

Arcainous's gaze hardened. "And just how did you happen to know about Tara's involvement in the tournament today."

The gruffness in his voice made all three stumble backward, but the apparent head of the trio cleared his throat and stammered on. "He . . . he happened to be leaving the forges late one night and caught her training with Raiden."

"That explains nothing. Many students are chosen to train under him."

"He did some digging . . . Please, sir, we know nothing more than that. All we know is that he studied how she trained and crafted this specifically for her."

His gaze narrowed. "Does this master of yours have a name?"

"Yes, of course he does." But he turned his attention to Tara, wishing for the interrogation to end. "He is an apprentice under the head smith to the Ice armies. He found out that you are to face Raiden, and that when you do, you will be without armor. He is hoping that if you choose to wear this and are victorious that you will take him on as your personal armorer."

"Those are really tall if's," Tara replied. She turned from the group and stared out the window, watching as Wella faced off against Nao. "Even if I do manage to win, nothing says I'm going anywhere. I might just wind up in the armies."

"It is something to consider though, my lady." The three respectively bowed then took their leave before Arcainous could question them further.

Standing once more in the silence of the room, Tara and Arcainous stared first at the armor, then to each other. Tara was obviously a little shaken, knowing that there were people outside of the close-knit group that knew of her impending bout against Raiden, but she would try and remain positive.

"There really isn't any harm in seeing if it fits . . ." She stepped forward and picked up one of the gloves, seeing for the first time the intricate pattern of woven snowflakes that moved with great ease as she shifted the piece in her hand. Her questioning gaze then returned to Arcainous as she held the glove a bit tighter. "Right?"

His gaze was more scrutinizing, however, as he lifted the chest plate into both hands. It was rather light as far as weight went, but further investigation showed the chance it had for durability in a fight.

Impressive, he thought as he set it back onto the table. He then turned to Tara, seeing the questions racing through her gaze. "No, there's no harm in seeing if it fits," he assured her.

Any possibility of a threat to her were nulled the second he picked up the piece of armor. There was no ill energy within it. *Perhaps they were telling the truth*, he thought, watching as Tara began to dress herself. 'Maybe he did catch her training with Raiden.' But they had every right to be suspicious.

"How do I look?" Her question drew him from the never ending train of thoughts and he had to chuckle as he watched her turn from side to side, trying so hard to see every inch of the armor now that it was on her.

"If only it was that easy to get you into a dress," he laughed, patting the top of her head as she glared up at him. "You look . . ." He watched her, how her demeanor changed. She looked so much more sure of herself, determined. "You look like you could be one of the Guardians."

She tilted her head and shook it, turning her back to him as she walked back to the window. Before her now, she saw the raw power as Elexis faced off against Ashton. Bolts of lightning struck the ground with a force that sent pieces of earth spraying out from the point of impact while walls of fire cast everything in a smoldering glow. All joking now cast aside, she exhaled a doubt filled sigh. "How do they expect me to compete with that?"

"No one is expecting you to be as good as they are." He placed his hands on her shoulders, the two watching as attacks collided and exploded. "It takes ages to even get to where they are now. All you have to focus on is what you've learned. Forget everything you're watching now, forget the ideas of having to be as good as they are. Clear your mind and you'll do fine."

By this point she had quit listening. Her gaze remained forward, watching as that matched blurred into another, and finally blurring into the fourth, the match just before she was to fight Raiden. Anon and Oron seemed so incompatible as opponents, but watching as Oron wove the flows of air to catch what Anon could throw at him was nothing short of amazing. "Excuse me." But Tara was so far gone that she didn't even realize that someone else was in the room.

Arcainous turned around and gave a shallow bow. "I assume you're here for her?" he asked, motioning to Tara with a nod.

She nodded. "I am."

By now, Tara had registered the third presence and had turned around to acknowledge the woman before her. "Tara, she's here to escort you to the staging area."

"Already?"

"I'm afraid so."

"You'll do fine," Arcainous said softly. He kissed her cheek then motioned for Luna and Myst to follow. After a bit of whimpering they finally relented and the three disappeared to wait with the others.

Tara stood there for a moment before deciding to shuffle off after her escort. With nothing interesting to look at, she focused on the woman's armor, taking note of the glowing symbols etched into key points along her armor. Down the outsides of her arms, on her back, and the backs of her hands, the tops of her feet and the outsides of her legs. "Those are runes, aren't they?"

The woman smiled and gave a soft nod. "You are correct. The guards throughout Nimost are trained with a certain runic capability. Wherever we show significant strength, we are given runes to amplify it. When it all comes down to it, no two sets of armor wind up being the same." Her heart went out to Tara though. It was obvious that she was trying to keep the silence at bay, as well as steady her nerves, distract herself from what was about to take place. When they reached the staging area she opened the door, stepping to the side to allow Tara to pass through. "Good luck. I have a feeling that we will see something spectacular from you today."

Tara turned to thank her, but she was already gone and she was once more thrust into an unwelcomed silence. Pacing the room, her nerves began to get the better of her. Deafening quiet was broken, however, when the guards came into the room. "Excuse us, ma'am, but your match is ready to start."

Those words thundered in her head and she felt her stomach bottom out followed by the sudden urge to vomit. "Please, don't call me ma'am." Her voice was shaking, even as she tried to keep herself composed. "You make me sound old." The guards just looked at her, and she sighed at the failed attempt of humor. Shuffling after them, she stepped through the doors and into the uncertainty that awaited her.

CHAPTER

20

Letting Go

"For the final match of the evening, we have something special indeed." The MC's voice seemed oddly loud, and she began to rub her ears as he continued. "In past tournaments, the final match has always been fought between Raiden and Kayla, and they have never failed to impress." This was met by thunderous applause, and the MC had to wait for it to die down before he could continue. "With the unfortunate disappearance of Marcus, Kayla was able to take part in the main event. Standing in for her in the final match of the evening, coming to you from the Physical Realm, may I present to you, Tara!"

The crowd erupted into cheers, and the discomfort of everyone's eyes falling upon her only served to make her stomach tie itself into more knots. "I expect you to give me all you've got!" Raiden's voice broke through, drawing Tara back to the present. "I'll know if you hold back," he told her as he slid into a fighting stance.

Of course he would know. It was his job to know, to be able to read his students, to know the intentions and scopes of their power. But even as she vowed to hold nothing back, she could feel her nerves getting the better of her and her stomach churning with ideas of its own.

Raiden could read her like a book and he knew how scared she was. But what better cure for that fear than to face it head on. "Whether you're ready or not, here I come!"

"Huh?"

But before Tara could register anything, Raiden's arms had swept out in a centered arc, mirroring how she had attacked him when they'd first met in Nimost. But nothing happened. People began to murmur, and Tara was beginning to think that maybe, just maybe, she could take him on. That was, until she felt the entire arena floor begin to churn. She watched as it began to liquefy, bulging and rolling like the beginning of ocean waves. They pulled back, gathering at Raiden's feet before a final flick of his wrists sent the muddy wave racing toward her with a consistency of liquid concrete.

From the room where the Guardians and their Captains rested, they were able to watch as the fight began, but Nao was already disappointed. "He started too easily on her," he scowled.

"Well, look at her!" Elexis snapped. "Poor thing is scared out of her wits."

"I think it's safe to say that she'd never participated in anything closely resembling this tournament, or any other outside of sports." Oron sighed.

With that comment now in the open, Arcainous could feel everyone's gazes upon the back of his head. "Yes?"

"You've watched her train," Wella began.

"Is she any good?" Ashton asked.

His shoulders dropped noticeably as he looked back out the window. They watched as the wave crashed around her only to become a frozen dome as it collided with her shield. "She has seen the seven of you fight. She sees the respect that your Captains command. She's unsure of the reason for her involvement in the tournament, especially since she feels that she doesn't measure up to your level of skills." He lowered his head. "If only she would let go and relax."

"Well, how do we do that?" Eaden asked. All they were seeing was just a repeat of the beginning of the match. Raiden always holding the offensive while Tara did her absolute best to avoid any and everything he sent her way.

"I've watched her practice with her music," Anon offered.

Aaronel chuckled. "Just like the leader of the fearsome Guardians. Always sizing up any potential hopefuls."

The look across his face was hard as stone and he opened a small panel that allowed them to hook her MP3 player into the arena speakers. "I'm not surprised that she needs a trigger still. That should change though, the more she trains."

Elexis listened for a while before her head started to bob in beat with the music. "She has the best taste in music!" she squealed. "Remind me to talk her into copying it for me."

Everyone looked at the Lightning Guardian and shook their heads before returning to the sad sight in front of them. "What happened to the fire I saw in you!" he growled, rushing her, only to hear the clashing of metal echoing throughout the stands. With the repeated clashes, Tara was unaware that the ringing in her ears had suffocated the music that was playing, but it didn't stop the energy it was written with from reaching her, seeping through to every nerve. "You disappoint me, Tara."

Her brow twitched. She didn't ask to be thrown into this fiasco. She didn't *want* to be thrown into this fiasco. She watched as he hefted his blade, thinking he was about to end their match when she struck. Just like in practice, she summoned a pulse of energy strong enough to send him flying backward. "Are you now?" she hissed. She leaped toward him after stabbing her sword into the ground, eyes locked as he drew his own and swung toward her.

"Is she stupid?" Ashton asked.

"Looks like it," Keshou mumbled.

Timing was key for this to work perfectly. Tucking her legs as she leaped, she used the momentum of his swing coupled with the power from her legs to send herself flying straight into the air. As she reached her peak of assent she removed the handle of her whip, bringing it to life with the simplest flick of her wrist. Soon, gravity reclaimed her and began to pull her back to the ground. Before she would be taken though, she shot the body of her whip out, watching as it snaked around the length of Raiden's blade. "Bleed." The word was whispered, but it was enough to set things into motion.

Everyone watched in disappointment as her whip faded, and while they thought it was a failed summoned attack, she could only smile as she landed on the ground in a sinking crouch to absorb the shock of her impact. "It was a nice attempt," Raiden said as he rushed her once more. She barely had enough time to retrieve her sword before the assault started anew.

But she would only smile, sliding around easily, answering each blow with a well-placed counter. "Attempt nothing." She grinned as the pulse of energy that was released from their weapons sent them flying back from each other. This time it was Tara who was first to her feet, rushing him with a set glare to her eyes. She leaped, watching as Raiden prepared for it. She had something else planned though and dropped to the ground, sliding between his feet and pushing back to hers. "Shatter." Another simple command that would hopefully yield the effect she'd been waiting so long to see.

In a single instant, the energy that had bled from her whip into his blade began to seep through every molecule, coating them, freezing and expanding, forcing the metal apart on a scale that no pair of eyes could see. One final blow would hopefully be all his weapon would now allow him as their blades met. The expulsion of energy was enough to make even the Guardians take notice. Jaws hung open as the outline of small cracks were illuminated in a brilliant blue, branching from the point of impact with her blade through the entire length of his.

"What has she done?"

Everyone just stared in disbelief, shaking their heads as the sword finally gave way, sending shards of metal in all directions. "I have no idea."

"No one should be able to break it," Wella said. "The amount of times it's been folded and tempered during its forging—"

"Should have made it shatter proof," Ashton finished.

"Apparently, she found a way." But as everyone marveled over the broken blade, the match continued before them, becoming the spectacle that everyone was expecting from the great trainer of the Guardians.

Magic and runes flew like the wind. For every attack that Raiden could throw, Tara easily found a counter and vice versa. The crowning gem of the match, however, began to manifest itself in the form of a towering golem carved from the most solid of ice.

"What the—!"

"Oh, I hated my golem fight," Elexis said with a visible cringe.

"I don't remember ever fighting a golem," Wella mused.

"Not all of us did," Anon remarked as he moved to get a better view of the fight. "To be put against your own element, now that is a challenge."

Tara stared up at the towering figure feeling the color draining from her face. "It should be easy enough though," she mumbled. "Ice can break ice. Just look at the icebergs back home." This gave her confidence a boost and her fingers flexed, sending jagged shards of ice jutting from the ground. Gasps escaped as the crowds watched the ice impale through the golem's legs. The crack that resulted reminded her of branches breaking from the trees during a violent storm, but even as the pieces of ice fell to the ground, she took several steps back from her target, her confidence wavering.

What she thought was going to be easy turned out to be anything but. Everyone watched as the golem slowly took in her energy, using it to mend the broken limbs and, to her surprise, using her energy to grow larger. A rumbling roar reverberated through the area as it lumbered toward her.

"Nice try," Raiden commented.

He took to leaning against the far wall, his arms folded as he watched. There really wasn't much to do when it came to the golem. They were rather sufficient fighters, and this would give him the perfect chance to rest.

"No way!" she breathed. How could it have possibly gotten bigger! But right now, that thought was neither here nor there. She had to find a way to bring it down, and quickly. In truth, she barely had enough time to erect a barrier to keep from getting flattened by a massive chunk of earth that had been thrown at her. The kinetic energy, however, found its way through the barrier and sent her flying back into the wall. Dazed, she slid to the ground, groaning as she held her head. "Owww . . ."

"If Raiden is good at anything," Oron began as he leaned against the window, "it's knowing how to work his way around energies."

"It was impressive to see her energy actually have an impact on it," came the quiet reply of the Plasma Guardian.

Back on the field, Tara was quickly finding herself running out of options. Everything she could throw at the golem only served to either heal him, or make him bigger. She'd even gone so far as to freeze the moisture in the ground, creating a sheet of ice that she hoped the golem would slip on. But as she feared, he only absorbed the energy and slammed his fist into the ground, the rippling of it causing her to lose her footing and she stumbled back, catching herself to try and stay on her feet. "How?"

Everyone watched as her shoulders slumped in apparent defeat. "Do you yield!" Raiden asked.

From a booth nestled in the center of the stands, The Elder Council sat, watching the events unfold. "Do you think she's given up?" Fisonma asked.

"I hope not," Yukino replied quietly. "But there's so much conflict still within her that it's clouding her sight."

Fisonma sighed as she turned her attention back to the arena. "All we can do then is to have faith."

Tara was breathing heavily, smearing blood across her cheek as she wiped it from her mouth. "Yield? Are you crazy! I'll never give up!"

"You have to admire her tenacity," Aaronel remarked.

"Yeah, but sometimes you just need to know when to call it," Wella said.

Tara stared at the hulking giant before her. She wouldn't give up, but she couldn't see any real way to win either. "There just has to be a way to beat it." But her ponderings left her open and she soon found herself doubling over in pain as she was once again sent into the wall by way of a fearsome abdominal shot. Coughing violently, she spat out a mouth full of blood as she hit the wall. Her vision was blurry and her head spun whenever she tried moving. It was in this disjointed sight though, that she saw something she had apparently missed before. Flowing as an altered shade of blue she saw it, the flow of her own energy that had been absorbed during the duration of the match. "Let go . . ."

Tara looked around to find the owner of the voice she had just heard. It sounded like her mother, but the idea of that bordered the insane. "Let go of what?"

"Let go of everything in your heart." The voice was whispered, but a soothing warmth began to surround her.

She stared forward feeling everything drain from her. "The energies are changing," Fisonma replied.

Staggering to her feet she began a renewed assault, deliberately attacking with ice based attacks. The golem didn't grow, but she could see the slow expansion of her energy, like some odd blood stream flowing rapidly through it. "Has she learned nothing!" Anon grumbled, his fist hitting the wall. "All she's doing now is wasting everyone's time."

"I dunno 'bout that," Wella said as a slender finger pointed in Tara's direction.

"Wella is correct." Arcainous leaned forward a bit to examine the situation. "Look at her eyes. The fire is back. She's determined now, more focused.

"We'll see," was all the Earth Guardian would give as a response.

Tara was back against the wall, eyes narrowed, always keeping her flow of energy in sight. As her mind worked her eyes shifted, fading from their brilliant emerald hue to the calming glow of first lights ice. The bluish white glow was easy for all to see as she took hold of her energy. Feeling it bend to her once again, she willed it as she saw fit, watching as frozen tendrils shot forth from arms and legs, branching into the ground, spreading out like roots to anchor the golem into place. Even as it bellowed in agony its cries were lost to her. She was determined that the match would end, here and now.

"Impressive." Raiden's voice broke through to her, cold, foreboding, confident that she would fail. "But how long do you think this will hold before you see the same results as earlier."

She was now away from the wall, her slow, deliberate steps taking her ever closer to her opponent. "It will hold as long as I will it to. I am in control of my own energy!" she declared. With each step forward, her eyes became mudded from their icy hue to one of an explosive orange, which caused the flow of her energy to darken slightly.

"Hey, Keshou, that's almost your color, isn't it?" Oron asked with intrigue.

"Too dark," he replied simply.

"No, it's not the color of plasma," Arcainous said. He knew that color all too well.

"You know what she plans to do then?" Ashton asked.

"I do," he sighed. "It won't be pleasant."

The roar of what most thought to be distant thunder echoed around the area as Tara's energy became more distinct from the golem itself. In truth, they were nothing more than small explosions as thousands of exploding runes began setting themselves off, the beginnings of a chain reaction. Starting from the tendrils that held the golem in place and working toward the center, the runes becoming progressively bigger until they all triggered the large rune burned into the center of its chest. Fine cracks gave easily beneath the power of her runes and as the large one detonated, the golem disappeared into an icy mist that sank to the ground like the glitter from a snow globe.

Everyone stared in disbelief. No one expected such a display of power from a mere student and the stands soon erupted in applause and cheers. But in her quest to defeat the golem, she forgot that her true opponent was Raiden himself. Her chest heaved under her armor as she gulped down breaths of air, but he was on her like a blur. She was able to match him blow for blow for a time, searching for that second wind, but she had overdone herself well past her limits and he was able to take her easily. With a single, well-placed blow, he sent her sliding across the ground. This time, however, her body remained unmoving. She had finally succumb to the battle.

"I really thought she had it," Alex said, the group watching as Raiden was once again declared victor.

The Council rose to their feet, nodding and talking among them. "There will be much to discuss in upcoming days." Fisonma's gaze shifted to Yukino, seeing the smile that now graced her features.

"I think she finally let go."

Fisonma placed her hand on Yukino's shoulder. "It just takes a little faith. She always had the ability to do it. She just needed a bit of help. But why don't we go congratulate her, hm?"

Tara stared blankly as Raiden approached her and helped her to her feet. As she stood though, she felt her legs give way, and he wound up catching her, supporting her weight as he slung her arm over his shoulders. "Easy there, champ."

His voice vaguely registered to her as her gaze fell. "I didn't do that well, did I?" she said with a wry smile.

"Your display of power was greater than you let on," he replied as they vanished into the tunnels that would take them to where the others waited. "You broke through the walls that were holding your energy. The end was impressive, to say the least."

She just nodded. Trying to walk on her own was still out of the question so she leaned against Raiden as they rounded the final corner. "Sorry about your blade."

He could only chuckle, which caused her to stare up at him questioningly. "It's not often that I learn a lesson from my students. I underestimated your energy. I thought you simply didn't have the will to keep your weapon manifested, but I see now that it did exactly as you had commanded it to."

Their conversation faded, however, as they reached the room where everyone waited. When the door opened Luna and Myst were the first to the door, their happy whines a welcomed sound. Next, and almost as eager to see her, was Arcainous who took her carefully from Raiden. His arms encircled her, allowing her head to sink against his chest.

"You did well," Elexis said with a warm smile.

"Thanks," Tara answered, pressing closer to Arcainous. She knew she was in the presence of the Guardians and still felt a bit inadequate in their presence.

Raiden cleared his throat. "Allow me to make some introductions." He motioned with a sweep of his hand, beginning at one end of the room. "This is Anon, Guardian to the Earth Elemental, and his Captain Elsia. Next we have Ashton, Guardian to the Fire Elemental, and his Captain Alex." He continued introducing them, Nao and Eaden, Elexis and Rayne, Keshou and Katsuro, Aaronel, Oron and Eiricka, and finally, Wella and Adam.

Each pair stepped forward, giving a shallow bow before stepping back. Tara nodded to them, looking past them, out the window where the festival was brought to a close with a grand fireworks display coupled with demonstrations from the Towers Dragon Riders. "Pretty impressive aren't they?" Adam asked, seeing the transfixed state in which Tara was watching them.

"Dragons . . . exist," she breathed in complete awe. She'd learned about them in class, but it was only when she saw them before her that she truly believed in their existence.

"She's so cute." Eiricka giggled. She then looked back to the riders as they brought their display to an end and gave a dreamy sigh. "They never cease to amaze me."

Adam chuckled. "She has her head in the clouds again."

"As it should be," Oron replied, defending his Captain. "She is Captain to the elusive armies of Air after all."

It was with the warm hearted jabbing at one another that their time together ended. Each said their good nights and parted for the evening. Stepping into the pale light of the moon, Tara took her first look around Nimost now that things were over. With the multitudes of people gone, it seemed like such a ghost town. "I'm so proud of you."

"Eh?" She shifted her gaze to see Yukino's warm smile. "Yukino, Fisonma." She smiled happily to them, though the others that were with them, she did not recognize and her smile faltered just slightly.

Fisonma stepped forward and swept her right arm out. "Please allow me to make some introductions. These people to my right are the members of the Elder Council."

"Good evening, Elders," Arcainous gave a shallow bow of his head.

"Arcainous, a pleasure as always," came the reply from beneath one of the hooded cloaks. "We have much to discuss concerning your current task. Please speak to us when you are able."

"Of course, Elders," he replied with another bow of his head.

Fisonma then motioned to the two on her left with Yukino. "The woman you see before you now is Vonri. She is the master armor smith to Aaronel's armies. The young man beside her—"

Before he could be introduced, however, he rushed forward, causing Tara to step back a bit. "A thousand apologies." But he seemed in his own world at the moment. His eyes almost seemed to glow under the moon, much like the bluest ice of ancient ice bergs and what she could only assume was sandy-blond hair that seemed almost white under the unforgiving light that bathed over them. He found the small cracks, dents, and scuffs from her encounters. "It held up better than I could have hoped." It was easy to hear the excitement in his voice, but the sound of Vonri clearing her throat brought him back from the clouds he'd found himself in. "Pardon me." His posture soon became erect as he bowed his head. "My name is Leigh." He then leaned in allowing their eyes to lock as he studied the wolven features within Tara's eyes. "I hope you will sincerely consider my offer."

Tara tilted her head then gave a soft sigh. "Like I explained to your friends earlier—"

But she was tactfully cut off as Fisonma cleared her throat. "We can discuss this later." Her gaze fell softly onto Tara. "You look very tired dear."

Tara scrunched her brow. "I feel—" But her own sentence was cut off by a rather large yawn. She made a face, unaware that she was so tired. "I guess I am . . ." Her tone was bewildered, but she wasn't going to argue.

The group turned to take their leave. "Do come find us Arcainous."

"As you wish."

Tara watched them leave, brows merged before calling out after them. "Leigh! Where can I find you to give you back your armor?"

Leigh and Vonri turned around to face her once more. "It's yours. Keep it, but I'll have someone pick it up so I can fix it." The two then turned to join the others, leaving the four standing in a tranquil silence.

"The Council doesn't say much, do they?" Tara looked up at Arcainous as they walked back to her dorm.

"They converse," he told her. "Theirs is just more of a mental conversation than verbal."

"So like, telepathy?" she asked as they climbed the stairs to her room.

"In a matter of speaking."

"Well, as long as they keep out of my head." She opened her door, allowing Luna and Myst to lay down and rest. She then walked in, her eyes falling upon the armor stand now placed in her room. 'Well, that answers that question.'

Arcainous walked up behind her, laughing softly as his arms circled around her waist. "I don't think it works like that," he assured her as he leaned in and kissed her cheek.

"As far as you know." She grinned, leaning back against him.

He had to give her that one. Even he wasn't sure how it worked, but he had more important things to think of, but the more he thought about her, the colder he realized he was becoming. Stepping back, he realized that the chill racing through his arms and chest was from her armor. "Forged from ice is an understatement," he said as he ran his hands along his arms.

"You're the one who touched it," she teased as she began the process of changing out of it and placing it on the provided form. "You should know better," she laughed.

"Yes, yes. I know." He slid his arms around her once again and kissed her forehead. "Now rest. I'll see you in the morning."

"All right." She really didn't want to sleep, but once he'd left, her head hit the pillow and she was gone.

But as Nimost slept under the watchful light of the moon, news was being shared that would change lives forever. "Are you absolutely sure?" Arcainous asked.

"We've gone over the footage of their final many times," Fisonma explained. "A summon brought forth by the Illusionists have no aura, but the one that first attacked had an aura that was identical to Durion's hounds."

"I didn't know that they could mask themselves."

"We've talked to the illusionists who participated in the final. No one remembers creating the image of the woman on the ground."

One of the other council members stepped forward. "Our greatest fears are coming to light. It's possible that the Shadow Lands somehow managed to interfere with the final exam."

"So what do we do?"

"Continue to protect her," Fisonma said. "There is still much that the Council must discuss."

"Of course." Arcainous bowed and took his leave. He joined the Watchers to relay the message, instructing them to be extremely careful and to let him know at once if anyone from the Shadow Lands was spotted.

CHAPTER

21

The Birth of Darkness

While Nimost rested in moonlit serenity, deep in the heart of the Shadow Lands, things were all but peaceful and calm. "How is our progress?"

"The darkness has almost consumed him," came a reply from the depths of the shadows in the room.

"Almost?" Vonspar slammed his fist against the table. "Giving himself to the darkness was his idea. He was willing to accept the Shadows as his own! So why do you give me the answer of ALMOST, Dante! I really do expect more than that of you three."

"Of course Master, and you shall have the results you desire." Dante stammered.

"Then WHAT is taking so long!" he demanded.

"There is a light in the core of his heart, an energy that is not his own. It is preventing him from being truly ours."

"A light?"

There was silence while Dante carefully chose his words. "At first we believed it to be his mother's energy," he began.

"But?" came the impatient reply.

"After extensive testing, the nature of the energy was determined not to be his mothers, though it does stem from someone close to him."

"The girl," he seethed, refusing to speak her name aloud. In his twisted delusions, she betrayed his friend, the catalyst that had begun Darius's descent into the dark abyss, and it was this greatly altered fact that he would hold fast to. It was the corner stone of his darkest ambitions.

"It is possible that it is her." Dante replied. "The energy she possessed when we encountered her resembles the signature of this light. If it is her, however, it would appear that she is unaware that this power even exists."

To Vonspar this all sounded more like excuses, though the notions of a hidden power did strike a chord in his mind. "Go through his memories of her. Warp them to aid our cause. He will destroy that light himself. When he does, our Angel will be born!"

Dante bowed. "As you wish, Master. We will proceed immediately."

He vanished instantly, leaving Vonspar to think on what had transpired. "A hidden power?" He paced in small lines, chewing on the nail to his right thumb. It could mean a great many things including the possibility of her being their rival. "How absurd," he chuckled. If his information from previous encounters with her was correct, she was nothing more than a scared lithe child that could never hope to amount to anything, using nothing more than parlor tricks to run and hide.

"Master?" The timid voice of a woman interrupted his thoughts.

Lifting his gaze, the figure of a woman with jet black hair tied into a high ponytail and lavender eyes glowing beneath her bangs bowed. "Oni, my most treasured pet." His voice was truly affectionate and she was at his side in an instant, purring as he ran his fingers along the back of her head. "I know you'll always have information for me."

"Always, Master," she muttered, resting her head on his knee as he continued stroking the back of her head.

"What have you found out for me?" he asked, pulling her head back so that she met his gaze.

Adjusting how she was sitting, Oni folded her hands in her lap. "She is quite skilled in the element of ice, far better than she was before."

"Oh? How did you find this out?"

"She participated in the tournament held in Nimost."

His brow arched. "Did she now. How did she do?"

The look crossing Oni's face was disinterested. "She wasn't very good." She then went about telling him about her bout against Raiden, how she was before and after they had played her music, the fight against the golem, and the ultimate end. "It was all quite disappointing if you ask me. To still need a trigger to set your powers into motion . . ."

He chuckled and patted the top of her head. "Always so critical," he said. "Especially of those so under skilled in comparison to your own training. Now, is there anything else?"

Her chest puffed out with pride as she was praised. There's was truly an intimate relationship rooted in service. "There is!" she exclaimed as she retrieved several pictures

Removing his arm from around her shoulders, he took the pictures and began to riffle through them. He glanced from the photos to Oni, then back to the photos. He stopped at one where Arcainous had his arms wrapped snuggly around Tara while he kissed her cheek. The look that crossed his face was one of pure cruel intention. "We can use this information." He leaned down and kissed her. "I need a bit more information though my pet."

"Yes, Master, what do you need?"

He held up the picture, his finger tapping the form of Arcainous. "I want you to find out why he is always around her. We might just have the perfect weapon for destroying him and getting to her."

"Shall I get him prepared then, Master?"

"Not quite yet. Patience will yield the results we desire. Now, go find what is so important about that girl that she needs to be protected by that mutt."

"As you wish, Master." And in an instant, she was to her feet and darted from the room.

Vonspar tucked the pictures away, his mind turning as dark plans fell into their perfect place. "A constant thorn in my side," he growled. To him, since he had run into Darius, she had always stood between him and the goals he desired. At this moment, what he desired above all else, was the birth of the Dark Angel. "You will not interfere!" His fist was clenched, hitting the wall just as another presence broke through. He composed himself quickly and turned to the shadows of the room. "This had better be important Durion."

The form of a bulldog broke through the shadows quickly followed by Durion himself. "My Lord," he greeted with a shallow bow of his head. "You are wise in waiting to send the watcher after the girl and her guard."

"Oh?"

"The link he has to her is nothing we have seen before. He has a pathway to her mind, a link that breaks the energy from Nimost that protects her."

"He has served us well by luring her back here. I know he still poses a use to us, but I digress, what news have you."

"As I had stated before, the energy of Nimost protects her, preventing Dante, Toran, and the others from entering her dreams. Since their last attack against her there seems to be a constant light surrounding her mind."

"Again with the light?" Suddenly, the idea that seemed nothing more than a fool's notion was becoming quite a real threat.

"Again?" Durion asked, his voice slightly puzzled.

"Nothing."

Durion nodded. "We should consider the possibility."

"No! I will see her destroyed before I'll entertain the thought," he snarled. "We will attack her from every possible angle! I want her broken! No, I want her shattered! I want the hope and light snuffed out from her very soul! If Belzak is the only one who can reach her, then send him! Destroy her! Do I make myself clear!"

Durion chuckled. "It shall be done." Spinning on his heels, he took his leave while down in the bowels of the Manor progress was finally being made.

Dante, Gabriel, and Malik circled around Darius's unconscious form, their fingers submerged deep into his thoughts as they changed his memories to suit their dark purposes. Stumbling upon the day that he'd revealed the secrets he believed Tara was keeping from him, Gabriel began to laugh. "This will work perfectly."

They read carefully through the messages sent between the two, altering things where they saw fit. Instead of being on the offensive, they played him as the victim, a friendship turned to love on his behalf. Accusations turned into questions about what he had found in his mother's journals. Instead of defense, they warped Tara's text into nothing short of mocking pride, belittling him where ever she could. They added what they wished, making an apparent break up nothing short of violent. "If this doesn't work . . ."

"I have something that will."

"Vonspar," Malik stammered. "What brings you down here?"

"Wake him."

"But, Master Vonspar, he's not ready yet," Gabriel protested.

The look he received made him shrink behind his brothers. "You might be as old as time, but you will do well to remember who rules over you," he snarled. "Now wake him!"

Bringing Darius back from his comatose state wasn't hard, but it was lengthy. Over time, eyes flickered open, clouded with such hatred and malice that the vampires backed away with unease. "Is it over?" Darius's voice was mellow, betraying the darkness warping his heart.

"Almost," Vonspar assured.

"Is something wrong?" Darius asked as he slid from the table and approached his friend.

"There might be," Vonspar admitted, motioning for Darius to follow as he began to walk. "Tell me, what do you remember of your past with Tara?"

Darius closed his eyes and thought back. Warped memories came to the surface and the expression on his face twisted. "A lot of secrecy," he mumbled. "Secrets between her and my mother about this place . . . about the change I saw in her eyes when we were kids. She always said she had no recollection of it, that she didn't see it. But I always knew she was hiding something."

Vonspar took note of the ease in which he spoke of such betrayals. Calm manipulation. Such gifts could be used in the future. Reaching into his pocket, he removed the photos, holding them between his index and middle fingers. "Eyes like this?" he asked, taking a seat and setting the pictures onto the table.

The picture that Darius saw first was a picture of Arcainous, his Lycan-born gaze staring at him from the glossy paper. "Similar to this man's gaze, yes."

Vonspar watched as he looked through the remaining images, watched as his aura grew ever darker with the intimate poses captured between this man and the one his warped memories had led him to believe he'd given his heart to. Continuing the role of the ever concerned friend he leaned forward, elbows propped on the table, hands folded. "As soon as I saw these, I knew I couldn't wait until you woke. You deserved to know why she was so cold toward you."

In his heart, the final light began to crack under the weight of the growing hatred now flourishing throughout his heart. "Thank you, Vonspar. You have always been a true friend."

"You are a brother to me."

Darius blinked. Brother. Family. Honor where he had only known betrayal and lies. Betrayal. His mother, his lover. A woman he gave everything for, but turned to this . . . creature instead of returning his affection. Now he had family, people he could trust, people who trusted him. His eyes flickered and flared as he felt Vonspar touch his arm.

"Are you all right, my brother?"

My brother. Such odd words to have echo through his mind, but a measure of comfort all the same. Allowing the energy to transfer seemed to be all that was needed to allow Vonspar's darkest dreams to come to light. Light shattered, starting a series of convulsions that gripped Darius with both pain and power. By now, the trio had joined Vonspar, watching as darkness seeped from every pore in his skin. It floated to the floor like fog, building around him and concealing him as his features began to change. Concealed within darkness, a great metamorphosis began to take place. The sound of tearing flesh and breaking bones resonated throughout the room with a sickening echo that would turn the stomachs of any normal person, but here, all watched in anticipation. Gnarled screams drowned out the sopping sound of wings breaking free from their prison. From within the confined depths of darkness came the sounds of rustling as blood began to establish flow through the new appendages. As they came to life, they extended, drinking in the darkness around him until the mist was no more.

"In all my days . . ." For the first time, Vonspar found himself without words to express what he now saw before him. It was still Darius who stood before him, but different, better in his opinion. His appearance was altered slightly, more muscular, defined by the armor he now wore which gleamed like newly polished onyx. His delight, however, was watching the destruction of light as it reached Darius's armor. Though light fell with Durion as well, there was something special about this. Darius was their Angel, the very definition of darkness.

Darius stared down at his hands, feeling the intense energy that coursed through his body, the burn, the tingle that attacked and took over every nerve. "What is this feeling?" he asked.

"That is the power of darkness in its purist form."

* * *

Tara tossed and turned almost violently, shooting up from her bed as the light planted in Darius's heart shattered. She was soon on her feet pacing the length of her room, the look in her eyes wild and distant. The intensity of her movement caused Arcainous to awaken. He yawned, returning to his human form, watching as she stared into the empty moonlight. "What's wrong?" For a time she was silent, his voice failing to reach her. Only when he touched her shoulder did she react, spinning to face him, allowing him a full glimpse into the emptiness her gaze held. "Tara?"

Blinking, her gaze once more became her own. "Huh?"

"Are you all right?"

"I don't know," she said, her arms folding and unfolding, only to refold once again. "Something feels . . . off." Her eyes squinted before she returned to stare out the window. "Something is very wrong."

"Can you tell what it is?" he asked, running his hands along her arms feeling the unnatural chill.

"It feels like something's died." She sighed, pulling away from him as if his touch caused her harm in some way. She fell silent again and stared back up at the moon

The look on his face was one of both concern and wounded from having her pull away from him. "Perhaps we should consult the Elders."

Things were silent for a great while. "No," she replied as she returned to her bed. "I'm sure it was nothing more than a bad dream." She pulled the blankets up and wrapped herself in them as tight as she could. Even with as assuring as she was trying to be, a sense of foreboding began to creep into her heart. "I hope it was just a bad dream."

* * *

Everyone stared in respective awe at the being that now stood before them. "Everything I have worked for. Lifetimes have passed, but now I have found him." Bringing himself back to the present, Vonspar cleared his throat and looked to the trio beside him. "Malik, you three will train him. Teach him all that you are able to. You are timeless and have a vast amount of knowledge that he will need if we are to be successful."

Darius looked up at his friend. "You won't be training me?"

"I will fine-tune all you have learned. Together we will teach you what you will need to rule over this cursed land. People will cower in your presence and that whelp will beg for your forgiveness."

The prospect of revenge against those who had betrayed him was a very satisfying idea and he relented to the three who would train him. "Until then, my brother."

"Until then, brother," Vonspar repeated, watching as the four of them exited the room. There was no need for him to worry. With his fingers so deep into Darius there was no chance he would rise against him. His control was absolute. Soon the most sinister laughter echoed throughout the room. "So much patience for this moment." But there was still more that had to be done. "Belzak!"

From the shadows emerged the towering form of a black wolf. "Yes?"

"Walk with me." The two walked slowly, discussing what had recently transpired. "Tell me, do you still have access to Tara's mind. The link that is created when a Watcher imprints is unknown to me."

"The bond created when a Watcher imprints cannot be broken."

"Even when one serves Light where the other serves Darkness?"

"You are correct. The bond is stronger where the Watcher is concerned. We have access to their mind. We are even able to feel when they are in distress. In fact, when Darius defeated the light within his heart, Tara reacted with a heavy amount of distress."

"Interesting . . ." His mind began working again, and he gave a sound nod. "Continue to follow her, and keep me informed of any news."

"Of course." And with that, Vonspar was once again in silence.

He spun on his heels, walking toward the opposite end of the room. He stopped at a rod iron cage where a hunched over figure sat. "You have seen what has just transpired. Will you not reconsider my offer for you to join us?"

A man stared up from beneath disheveled hair, his body littered with shadowed scars where they had attempted to infuse him with their energy. "Your path is the path chosen by cowards. You under estimate the powers of Light and truth. That will be your downfall."

Vonspar's eyes grew hard, his body tensing with the desire to lash out at their captive. With a single breath, his facade was again calm though his eyes revealed the brewing storm. "I should kill you," he began, jaw set and teeth close to being clenched. "But I have decided that I'll let you live long enough to see just how wrong you are!"

"You will be the one who is wrong." For even as beaten and scarred as this man was, his voice, his gaze, they were very determined, and very confident.

"I will make you regret those words," he vowed.

"I will regret nothing," he replied. "You, however, will regret more than you realize."

Vonspar found himself losing his patience rather quickly with their captive. His jaw was clenched to the point of pain radiating through his teeth as he spun on his heels. "Double the energy," he growled, hearing the scurries from the shadows. "I want him to know the meaning of suffering." And with that, he stormed from the room, the echo of grunts and screams fading into a distant thought.

Field Training

Time passed quickly for Tara. She had settled into a steady routine of going on patrol with various platoons from the armies of Ice to further sharpen her skills. It was on one of these missions that she was informed that they would be assisting a far off outpost who had recently been attacked by a group from the Shadow Lands. "I'll be back before you know it." She tried to be assuring to the two wolves who were forced to remain behind. "I have from every other trip right?" But she was met only with more whining and whimpers of protest. She pushed to her feet and sighed as they slunk back, their displeasure clearly splayed within their features.

"They'll be fine after a couple of days," Arcainous assured. His hands ran along the length of her arms as he stared down at her, taking her in. "Come back to me in one piece," he said softly. But as he leaned in to kiss her she pulled away with an almost annoyed look on her face.

"Why is everyone suddenly so worried about my safety?" She slid the gauntlets to her armor over her hands and backed away to join the group waiting for her. "I've always come back safely, we all have. This time will be no different." But before anyone could inter-ject, the call of one of the officers broke the conversation, giving the orders to move out. "I'll be back soon, and in one piece. You'll see." And with that, she spun on her heels and caught up with the depart-ing group.

This trek, however, would prove to be far different than the more non-eventful excursions she was used to. More than once one of the other rune casters had to use a rune of cloaking to allow them to pass through different nesting grounds. One cast failed, however, as they were making their way through an area where the monstrous bats she'd learned about were known to make their home and she found herself using her binding rune to ground it before any harm could be done. "Put it down and harvest what you can," came the order of one of their officers.

"What?" Tara spun around, staring as the orders were carried out. "Why can't we just release it once we're far enough away?"

"One of the things they leave out in your classes is that once these bats take in your scent and begin their assault, they will follow you until either you, or it, are destroyed."

That would have been helpful knowledge, she thought.

Her thoughts were interrupted, however, as she felt something hit her in the head. "Here." came the reply of one of the expert skin-ners. "Trim the tendons away and roll that up. We're going to make camp here tonight so we can treat the pelt and the webbing while the cooks dry the meat."

Tara blinked as she looked at the large piece of webbing around her. "You didn't have to throw it on me," she mumbled. "That just felt gross." But she did as she was asked. The tendons were carefully trimmed away, used by the weapon smiths to experiment for new bow strings for the archers. The webbing was cleaned and treated with a special blend of oils to keep it malleable and to protect it from eventual cracking.

The scent of the meat was fragrant as it was treated with various spices and dried over a low flame to preserve it. The pelt was cut as needed, scraped and treated with the same oils as the webbing was treated with. Even some of the fangs had been harvested to create curved daggers or arrow tips. "Make sure to get some of the stomach acid. One of the alchemists needs some for a poison for the archers' arrows."

They broke camp with the rising of the sun, but as they continued their trek toward the outpost, Tara couldn't shake the feeling that they were being watched. It wasn't like she was the only one who noticed either. She watched as trackers broke away from the main mass of the army, disappearing as they began their silent hunt. Every report was the same though. No tracks, no activity. Day after day passed this way, but the night before they were to reach the outpost seemed to be the most oppressive. Tara sat apart from the main groups, a steaming bowl of stew cupped in her hands, her mind searching and probing the darkness around them. "What are you doing all the way out here? Surely you're not hiding to get used to the bat meat."

While it was true that the gaminess of the meat took some getting used to, she sighed over the bowl, watching the steam curl into nonexistence. Only then did she look up at the man beside her. His name failed her as did most, but she remembered him as one of the officers that had been sent with them. "An uneasy feeling," she replied, sweeping her hand to the side, offering him a seat.

He took the offered seat, studying her as he pressed for a more detailed answer. "Any specifics?"

Tara sucked some of the thick broth from her spoon as she regarded the question. "We're being followed," she answered simply.

"Are you certain?" he asked. While it was true that the trackers were feeling the same thing, no one else outside of the officers really felt anything.

"No," she said simply, her mouth now full of potato and carrot. "But why else would the scouts and trackers be out as much as they are?"

"For the same suspicions," he sighed, allowing her to finish her meal in silence. And just as before, the reports that came back were empty. There were no signs that anything had been, or currently was, following them. The air around the camp for the remainder of the night was one of unease, but as dawn broke the darkness it broke the tension as well. Gone was the feeling of eyes watching them from some dark shadow, replaced finally with an air of hope and peace. Things remained quiet, however, as camp was broken down and a small breakfast prepared before they headed out.

Shortly after they started out, they reached a densely wooded area. "The outpost is just through the trees." their commanding officer said. "Move quickly and silently." And with that, they disappeared into the brush and shadows. The echoes of fighting soon began to reach then am their pace slowed, their movements becoming more deliberate as they picked their way through the trees. Hand signals gave the orders, some staying back with the cooks and smiths while the rest snuck to the tree line to assess the fight. Bodies from both sides lay everywhere and the smell of death hung in the air like a stagnant blanket.

The mages and rune casters snaked into the open while the archers hid in the trees acting as snipers. As the order was given for them to attack it was answered with great pride and decimation. Tremors shook the ground as destructive runes reduced several mages to nothing more than a fine red mist. Ice soon flew, quelling sparked fires or impaling the random soldier. Archers covered them as they recovered, proving time and again why they were a silent force to be feared. This in turn gave the main bulk of the army a clear window in which to attack.

Being flanked by their enemy was less than pleasing to the now dwindling group, and a wall of flame soon shot up from the ground separating the old group from the new. This, however, brought the nauseating stench of burning flesh as dead bodies were set aflame. Startled at the intensity of the flames heat, Tara stumbled back only to find herself flanked by two additional mages. "Just watch." one assured her as he brought the moisture up from the ground. He then began to freeze it, allowing the flames to melt what was needed to extinguish the flames. The other mage, however, targeted the mage responsible for the wall of flame and encased him in a solid sphere of ice.

Hell's fire seemed to surround the mage with an aura that pulsed against his prison. The interior slowly began to melt, but no one seemed particularly worried about that. Now, Tara knew, that because of their split nature, the 'Outer Elements' had a slight edge over the Primary Elements. But as time continued to pass, it was becoming more of a factor as the interior of the sphere continued to melt. "Shouldn't we do something?" she asked. "It looks like he's about to break through."

"Everything is under control," she was assured. "Just look."

Tara turned and stared, her gaze taking in the nature of the sphere, the reinforced wall that was untouched by the aura. She stumbled back with a startled gasp, however, as she looked to the spheres interior. Gone now were the protesting flames and in their place were small bubbles, the last of the mages breath as it escaped, aiding in his own drowning. The sphere then dropped, breaking the hold it had as the contents spilled out across the ground. As the battle continued, Tara became very aware that she was with a very battle hardened group. Death didn't seem to outwardly faze them, and it was with that tenacity that they began to take the upper hand.

By the time the battle was theirs, not a single member of the Shadow Lands remained standing. Tara busied herself by helping to tend to the wounded while priests saw to the funeral rites of their fallen. Outside the borders of the outpost the bodies of their foes were piled and set aflame while some prayed for their souls, hoping that in death, they would finally accept the light that they spent their entire existence trying to destroy. Officers busied themselves with the task of dispatching replacements while the trackers went out to assure that no one was waiting for their guard to be lowered to attack.

Dinner that night was quiet, most eating only after the wounded had been fed and cared for. Again, Tara sat away from most everyone, picking at her food and watching those around her. She went to bed shortly after, falling asleep quickly though her sleep was anything but restful. Images of burning and drowning foes haunted her dreams, so much so that she woke up in a cold sweat. Her eyes adjusted quickly to the moonlit room, and she saw that the others with her were sleeping quite fitfully. She pushed to her feet and picked her way carefully outside into the waning moonlight.

"Trouble sleeping?"

She wasn't all that surprised by the guard's presence and nodded some. "Kinda," she admitted, casting a glance back over her shoulder.

"You'll get used to it," he assured with a comforting smile. He watched as her gaze drifted to the forest line. "The group you are with is very battle hardened. They know their job and they do it well."

"A little too well," she confessed.

"True," he admitted. "But I'm sure there was a reason you were sent with them." They all knew she was new to their ranks and to be sent out with such a veteran group, something great had to be expected.

Things were quiet for a few moments before Tara chose to speak again. "Has anyone ever left?"

"Left?" the guard asked. "Oh, you mean quit?"

"Yeah."

"Well, the training we go through allows the Guardians and their officers to see the scope of people's skills. From there, they are able to select those who would best be able to serve in their armies. But no matter how much training one goes through, there is just no substitute for combat. Some people are unable to handle the demand, and others still are unable to cope with the sights and smells of death. These people are released from service before it takes a mental toll." He then leaned in and studied her closely. "Are you thinking about leaving?"

"No way," she said with a bit of a laugh. "There would be a long list of people waiting to beat me if I did with Raiden leading the mob."

The guard just smiled as he straightened back up. "Yes, he is a force you don't want to cross." His smile faded though as he regarded her features in the pale moonlight. "You should try and get some sleep though. I've heard that you're on the morning tracking team."

* * *

It was several days before the replacements arrived, a welcome sight to all. "Are we not staying?" Tara asked as she helped load the wounded into wagons.

"Our orders were to help retake the outpost and stay until reinforcements could arrive."

Tara spun around seeing her commanding officer, her body becoming stiff almost instantly. "All I meant was—"

But the raise of his hand silenced her. "Do not fret, child. You will not find a finer group of warriors. This outpost is well protected."

"Yes, sir."

"Good. Now, I must contact Aaronel and let him know we will be heading back." Tara watched him leave, her posture returning to normal as she assisted the last of the wounded. The officers emerged just as the last of the horses were hitched to the wagons and the last of their gear was packed away. Instructions were soon given out as to who would be taking which position for the march back. This gave Tara a prime opportunity to tune a few things out since she'd really only been brought to sharpen her skills as a fighter so when he announced her name she didn't hear him. "Tara!"

"Yes, sir," she stammered, hoping for a quick recovery.

"You will be riding flank to the rear point."

"Yes, sir," she answered with a quick bow of her head.

* * *

And that was how her time was spent, moving from one patrol to the next. If they intended to have her work on her tracking she was allowed to bring Luna and Myst, much to the delight of the two wolves. Every time they returned they were always greeted by Fisonma, Aaronel, and Arcainous, each sure to convey their pride in a job well done. "Well?" Fisonma asked.

Aaronel's arms were folded as he watched her play with the two wolves one fall morning. "She's become more confident in both her actions and especially in her abilities. The officers never have anything ill to say about her. They're always impressed that she's willing to do whatever task they give her, and she's always asking to learn something new."

Arcainous stood with the two as they talked, only partially listening as he gazed upon the young woman with a great fondness. "So does this mean that she will be knighted into the armies. I know having a place to finally call home will lift a hidden burden from her mind."

"It is quite possible. A great many things can happen," Fisonma replied. She glanced to Aaronel, watching his features, almost studying him as he watched Tara feign death beneath Luna's looming form. *Even under such a comforting energy, so many things remain unclear,* she thought with an audible sigh.

"Is something wrong, Elder?" Aaronel asked, casting a glance over his shoulder.

"In two weeks, there is to be a meeting with the Guardians, their Captains, and the Elder Council. I have already asked that Yukino be there." Her gaze then shifted to Arcainous. "Will you be in attendance?"

"Of course, Elder Fisonma. I will attend on behalf of the Watchers." But the look on his face became puzzled. "But what will we be discussing?"

"Why, Tara, of course."

CHAPTER

23

An Elemental's Decision

The next two weeks passed by terribly slow for Tara. Without an explanation, she was taken off any patrols she had been scheduled for until further notice was given. She leaned against the wall of her dorm, staring blankly at the shimmering tower in the distance. "I guess I just wasn't what they were looking for," she said with a heavy sigh. She thought she had finally found her place, dreaming of a home in the grand Tower of Ice. She was drawn from her thoughts though as she felt Myst's cold nose against the back of her hand.

"I highly doubt that," came a voice from behind her.

Tara looked over her shoulder as Arcainous entered the room, quickly returning her gaze to the window. "And just how do you know?" she challenged.

"I don't," he answered calmly, his arms circling around her waist as he held her close. In truth, he only knew part of what was going on. He knew there was to be a meeting held concerning her, and that for her own safety during this meeting it was suggested that she be kept from her rounds with the armies. She remained quiet, enjoying the small shivers that made their way through her muzzles as he kissed along the side of her neck. "I don't have long," he said softly, his embrace tightening slightly. "I've been summoned to a meeting with the Elders."

Tilting her head back she stared up at him. "You sure have a lot of meetings lately."

"Unfortunately, that is one of the many downfalls of leading any faction. We quite often find ourselves in some form of meeting."

"So you don't have to keep watching me then," she said as she snuggled into his arms, her gaze still fixed on some distant point on the other side of her window.

"No," he corrected, tapping her nose. "I have my duties to you as well. Now more than ever with your excursions taking you into contact with armies from the Shadow Lands. We still don't know what they want with you." But that wasn't a conversation for the present moment. To his dismay too much time had passed and he found himself reluctantly pulling away. "I have to go," he said softly, kissing her jaw near her left ear. "I'll come back when the meeting ends."

She watched him go then stretched. It was one of the rare nice days for the season to stay cooped up. "How about some time outside?" she asked, receiving the excited yips as the two circled in front of the door. She grabbed her cloak and the three headed out to the vast lawns of the dorms.

The Guardians and their Captains entered the White Tower, descending into the hidden lower levels where a secret meeting hall had been constructed long ago. The walls were ornately carved with pillars depicting each Elemental. Strong figures, each bearing a torch burning with the color representing their element. This also included the fabled Elemental of Light that legend told would appear with the revelation of the White Angel of the Realms. The floor had a beautiful marble inlay of an eight pointed star with colored spheres settled between each point, their colors also representing each Elemental.

"The energy is quite strong here," Yukino said as she, Raiden, and Arcainous entered the room, staying near the door.

"This place is very old, created after the Shadow Lands were driven from Nimost. Much council has been sought here, and many

Guardians have been chosen here," Fisonma replied as she and the rest of the Council gathered in the center of the grand star. Each Guardian stood in the center of the sphere that represented their respective element while their Captains stood to their right at each point of the star.

"Shall we begin?" one of the Council member asked, seeing that everyone was now in place.

Fisonma nodded extending her arms as the Council joined hands. "Spirits of the elements, we come before you now as protectors of peace throughout this Realm and those beyond." She continued, giving their collective thanks for their abilities, insights, and strength needed to fight against the Shadows. She asked for continued guidance, allowing them to be the leaders they are meant to be. With thanks given and guidance sought, Fisonma broached the subject that brought the group together, asking the Elementals to reveal themselves. In the end, Tara's fate was ultimately in their hands.

Silence soon fell upon the room as they waited for a response. The Guardians looked around, fearing that the silence was, in fact, their answer. Choosing to remain hopeful, each member in attendance fell into a deep meditation, reaching out with their hearts, sharing their hopes and desires. Resolution and closure for a friend now lost to them, and completion as a team. These feeling echoed through space and the room was soon filled with the feeling of peace and a soothing warmth that could calm any unease. Slowly, one by one, each of the spheres beneath the Guardians began to glow. Dimly at first, but the room was soon alight with a rainbow of color. "Your words have reached us, Children of the Light."

Everyone's eyes shot open, beholding the most radiant beings anyone could have ever imagined. "The Elementals . . ." Yukino breathed. Never before had she seen them, having only heard rumors from previous meetings of such a secret nature.

"Where is Marcus?"

Fisonma turned to regard the ice Elemental, her striking beauty accented with the hard edge of her element. "I do not know," she admitted. "He has long since fallen from my sight. We hold out a slim ray of hope, but we do expect the worst."

"This is indeed very troubling," came the almost whispered voice of the Air Elemental.

"We have exhausted all means of finding him." Fisonma replied. "Which is part of the reason we have called upon you."

Raiden stepped forward, clearing his throat. "We have been looking at a possible replacement."

The attention of eight turned to the trainer chosen to teach the Guardians, each pair of eyes holding him in great respect for his skill. "Raiden," came the flowing voice of the Water Elemental. "You have done a fine job in your duties." Her smile radiated a warmth that betrayed her normally cool nature. "You are to be commended."

"Thank you," he replied, giving a deep bow.

"We know of your prospect," came the voice of the Earth Elemental.

Everyone turned to see an image of Tara floating above their heads. "We did doubt your choice at first," came the quiet voice of the Plasma Elemental.

"We understand," Fisonma answered. "We had our own doubts that she would find a home here at all with the clouds that had surrounded her heart."

"Her heart was darkened with the desire for revenge against those responsible for her mother's passing," the Nature Elemental replied. "Revenge is a very dangerous seed to harbor, for whatever reason."

Another image appeared beside Tara, bearing the images of Luna and Myst. "These two have helped a great deal in quelling the hatred in her heart. In them she sees herself, an orphan. But as they have chosen to trust again, so has she."

"She chooses life above all else," came the added input from the Fire Elemental. Further proving his point, he brought up what they had observed on the platoons march to the outpost. Everyone saw her bind the large bat, fighting with her commanding officer to allow it to live. She had only relented to its destruction once its true nature was brought to light.

In spite of the positive changes she had made in her life, her fate was in the hands of the Elementals. The gaze of the Earth Elemental fell upon the form of Ice. "The decision is ultimately yours. Your word is final, and all will abide by the choice that you make."

This was never a decision to be made lightly. Freedom and peace always hung in the balance of every choice that was made. Everyone waited in a tense anticipation as unheard discussions dragged on, but a collective nod revealed that they had come to a conclusion. The Ice Elemental strode forward, everyone's gazes fixed and waiting. "I foresee a great many things in her future. While her past may have clouded her heart, the structure she has found with all of you has given her peace and her value for life has excelled."

"But this does not mean that she will be without her trials." came the insertion of the Water Elemental. Her gaze, as well as the gaze of the others, fell upon Arcainous. For an instant, a sense of grieving filled the room, as if a premonition was being realized. But it was gone as quickly as it had come, their gazes returning to the group as a whole. "She takes the values held by the Guardians to heart, and we believe that she will serve us well."

Wella and Elexis exchanged excited glances, but Fisonma stepped forward, her gaze meeting Aaronel's. "Is their decision all right with you? You have been Captain to this army, and if you feel that you would make a better Guardian, now would be the time to voice your opinions."

Aaronel bowed. "I was chosen by Marcus to be Captain of his armies. If permitted, I will gladly continue to serve under Tara."

Fisonma nodded, her attention again returning to their guests. "We will begin preparations immediately. We owe you ore deepest gratitude." They were released with a collective thanks and one by one, they faded. The last to take their leave was the Ice Elemental, her forlorn gaze lingering upon the empty space. The bond between an Elemental and their Guardian ran deep. A piece of them was given to their Guardian when they were accepted by the Council so a loss hit very hard. "We will find him." Fisonma vowed. "One way or another, he will come home."

"I know." Her form began to fade from the room. "You have all served us with honor and are a great credit to those who have lead before you."

When they were alone Fisonma looked around to everyone, focusing on Aaronel. "Are you sure this is what you want?"

"It is."

"Then prepare her room. We will move her and proceed immediately." She then looked to everyone in attendance. "Please keep what has transpired here to yourselves." Even with the energies of Nimost protecting her, protecting them all, the Shadow Lands were still finding ways to reach into her dreams and her mind. "Captains, please escort your Guardians back to their rooms and take care of them. This has been a taxing day for everyone."

Arcainous and Yukino followed behind the Guardians while Raiden approached Fisonma. "What now Elder?"

"You will need to speak to Vonri and Leigh. Armor and weapons will need to be forged for her."

"I'll go speak to them now," he assured, bowing before taking his leave.

This left the Elder Council alone, each staring at the image of Tara that was projected before them.

"She will bring about a great change," one of the Elders commented from beneath his hooded cloak. Everyone nodded as they took their leave. So much had to be done, and Fisonma's first stop was to see the head Priestess of the Ice temples.

CHAPTER
24

A Guardian Forevermore

The next few days found Tara staring at a flurry of motion even though she felt quite stationary. Arcainous had returned to his clan without a word as to why. Yukino, and even Fisonma had even withdrawn from her company, telling her that there were important issues that needed to be dealt with. "If it's the Shadow Lands, I can help!" She remembered the discussion she had earlier in the day, trying so hard to get some form of information from anyone.

"It's not that easy," Fisonma had told her. "Please believe me when I tell you that you're not ready."

The urgency on her face as she took her leave stayed in Tara's mind as she walked back toward the dorms. "I am ready," she muttered beneath her breath. She would prove that she was ready for a life with the armies of the grand Tower of Ice. "I just have to sneak into the next patrol." She looked down at Luna and Myst, hearing the whines of disapproval. "This is as much for you two as it is for me," she assured. "I want to give you guys the best life possible." In response, the two ran circles around her before Myst tackled her to the ground. They soon began licking her face before laying in the grass beside her, nuzzling the sides of her neck affectionately.

"With the two of you, who would need kids." She laughed, scratching the tops of their heads vigorously. She looked up into Luna's face and that's when she saw it. Unconditional love, and the highest level of trust that they placed in her. Her hand slid down Luna's neck, her mind lost to her moonlit gaze. "Still though . . ." Her gaze shifted to the sky. If she were to become a member of the armies, it would mean that Arcainous would be around her much less than he had been in the past. While the thought saddened her, she was happy. "He has a pack to lead after all. He can't always be shadowing my every move." She had become used to his presence, and having him curled up beside her at night always gave her a measure of peace, especially with the darkness that would occasionally plague her dreams.

Her daydreaming had put her off schedule quite a bit, however, and she pushed to her feet, motioning for the two wolves to follow her. "Come on, guys. We have to see if there are any details going out today and how to sneak into them." Their tails dropped, clearly displeased with the idea. They wanted to continue playing and rolling around in the grass. Reluctantly though, they followed, making their protests audible. "If we go back now and there are no patrols going out, we'll go hunting once night falls, okay?" This of course changed their attitudes like the flipping of a switch and they were soon leaping and bounding in circles around her. "It really doesn't take much to please you two does it." She laughed.

But as they reached the main walk to the building she was staying in, they saw Raiden exiting the building. Tara's brow scrunched as she studied him. "I wonder what he's doing here . . . Raiden!" Pleased that she had caught the attention, she jogged up to him, brushing her bangs from her face. "What brings you all the way out here?"

"Looking for you actually."

Tara stopped, her expression becoming quizzical as Kayla joined him. "Me? Why?"

"I need you to come with me. Kayla will look after your wolves while we're busy."

"Uhh . . . Did I do something wrong?"

Kayla giggled and Raiden just shook his head. "Must you always think on the dark side of things first?"

"Well," she began, cut off as Kayla revealed two rather thick cuts of meat.

"You two go do what you need. I'll be fine with these two," she assured as Luna and Myst rolled through the grass tearing into the treats they had just received.

As they walked, Raiden continued scanning the distance. "What are you looking for?" Tara asked.

"Not what," he calmly corrected.

"Okay, then who?"

But it seemed that her question was lost to him as he spotted the person he was looking for. "Aaronel!" Catching his attention, he waved him over.

Aaronel gave a shallow bow in greeting. "Hello, Raiden, Tara." His gaze soon set upon Raiden specifically. "What can I do for you?"

The gaze the two shared revealed all that needed to be said. "I am entrusting her to you. Please see that things are ready."

Tara looked between the two, her brow creasing. "What things?"

But she was again ignored as Aaronel bowed his head. "I understand, sir. She will be ready," he assured.

With a single nod, he gently pushed Tara forward. "I will see the two of you later on then. There are still several things I have to attend to." And with that, he spun on his heels and took his leave of them.

Tara watched him go then spun around to face Aaronel. "And just what was that all about?" she demanded.

But he just chuckled. "It was nothing."

"That seemed a bit to cryptic to be nothing," she challenged.

But he just laughed and swept his arm forward, wishing for her to walk with him. "Come on, we have to get you ready."

"For what?"

"You're so full of questions," he teased as the two entered the tower of the Ice Elemental.

He led her through a large hall that she didn't remember seeing during her last stay and he noticed that her pace had slowed.

Large tapestries hung from the walls depicting great events through the Realms history. Banners bearing the symbol of the Ice Elemental hung from the ceiling, stirred by a chilled breeze.

But Tara's attention was elsewhere. "Who are these people?" she asked, her gaze fixed upon the row of paintings that lined each side of the wall.

He stood behind her, staring up at one of the portraits. "These are paintings done of every Guardian that has ever served the Elemental of Ice."

"Why are there different armors in all these cases?"

"These were their sets of armor. When a Guardian is chosen, the armor smiths are given a glimpse that not most get of their heart and spirit. With these images, they are able to craft a suit of armor tailored specifically to them."

Tara walked to the end of the hall, her gaze fixed upon a single portrait. "Who is this? And why isn't his armor here?"

His posture and expression changed as he followed her gaze. "That is Marcus."

Her eyes widened. He was the one that Christine had mentioned to her. "Oh . . ."

But he just shook his head and guided her from the hall toward a grand spiraling stair case. "Come on, we don't have much time."

Her brow arched some as she followed him. "Time for what?" she asked, keeping his pace easily enough.

"You'll see," he promised as they reached the first landing. "This is where the Officers and I stay." When they reached the end of the hall he opened the door, Tara was instantly taken aback.

"This room is huge," she breathed.

"This is the room where you'll be getting ready. Clothes are in the closet, and the bathroom is through this door here." He motioned to the door to his left with a nod. "If you feel like cleaning up a bit." He then stepped back and bowed. "There are still a few hours before things begin so there is no rush. I'll be back by then to get you." And without another word her door close and the echo of his footsteps faded into silence.

Tara turned slowly, taking in the cold elegance that surrounded her. The colors were various shades that ranged from a frosty blue to white, but to her, it all seemed to work. The walls looked frosted, and the floor tiles looked like squares of ice, heat treated for that constant wet look. Heavy velvet curtains were pulled back to reveal a balcony much like the one from the room she had stayed in only with more ornately carved railings. Drawing her gaze from the balcony, she walked over to the canopy bed, her fingers running along one of the bed posts.

"It's like glass," she breathed.

Encasing the entire bed were sheets of a flowing mesh material, soft to the touch and toning down the deeper tones of the bedding, allowing it to blend better into the rest of the decor.

As much as she would have loved to jump onto the bed, she knew that she would almost instantly fall asleep if she did. Instead, she returned to the entrance of the balcony and stepped out onto the cool marble flooring. Leaning over the railing she could see everyone bustling about, rushing back and forth, driven by some hurried energy. Her eyes brightened though as she spotted Arcainous.

"He's been gone for so long," she sighed, watching as others joined him.

She recognized Yukino, Raiden, Fisonma, and some of the members from the Elder Council. "But who's that?" she wondered, her eyes squinting as she tried to get a better look at the stranger. His hair was white, and almost as long as Arcainous's was, but that was about all she could see from the distance between them.

She watched them disappear inside before pushing from the railing, heading back inside and into the bathroom. Frozen flames carved from frosted glass curved into an oval to frame a large mirror in which she stared at her own reflection for several moments.

"This is all way too fancy for a knighting ceremony."

But she shrugged her shoulders. It wasn't like she was an expert on what went on here, so she decided to go with the flow of what was going on around her. Stepping from the mirror she turned on the hot water, breathing in the steam as she stepped under the spray.

The force of the water as it hit her shoulders was amazing. As she rested her forehead against the wall she could feel the knots slowly being worked from her muscles. Her eyes slid closed as she lost herself in thought. She couldn't help but wonder why she was here, and why everyone was being so cryptic with her. Exhaling heavily, she blew water from her lips as she lifted her head.

"Unless I'm completely overthinking this." Which was probably what she was doing. Nodding, she finished her shower, wiping herself down with a towel before tying a plush robe around her waist. As she ran a smaller towel through her hair she realized that the only things with her were her MP3 player and speaker, which were currently playing. Realizing she was now at the mercy of what was chosen for her suddenly made her uneasy.

She gripped the door, taking a shallow breath as she opened it. Her shoulders dropped instantly as she saw the contents. "Dresses?" Her brow twitched as she looked at the array of formal attire. Different styles and lengths, some clearly meant for the red carpet, while others were less fancy, but still formal. And all she could see as she stared ahead of her was the smug look on Arcainous's face when he vowed that she would wind up in a dress. "Not in my lifetime," she snipped. She pushed the door closed and went to retrieve her street clothes. "Hell will freeze first," she vowed.

Only the sudden knock on her door drew her from her moment of brooding. When she answered it, she stepped back at what she saw. Standing before her was Aaronel, dressed in his finest armor. He in turn, had the look of unmasked confusion splayed clearly upon his face. "Why aren't you dressed?"

"Nothing to wear," she stated flatly.

"What?" He was assured that clothes were brought up for her to change into. He rushed over to the closet and opened it, turning to face her. "There are plenty of clothes to choose from," he protested.

"Those are not clothes," she corrected quickly.

"You can always wear the robe from your shower," came a reply from the door. "It's a bit unorthodox . . ."

"No," Tara stated bluntly, cutting the woman off.

Aaronel chuckled. "Kiara, a pleasure as always."

Kiara strode into the room wearing armor that was equally stunning as Aaronel's. She bowed her head to Tara and smiled. "I am Kiara, second general to Aaronel." She then looked past her and to the assortment of dresses. It only took moments before she snatched one from the middle of the bunch. "This will do," she announced as she pulled Tara behind the changing screen by the wrist.

"Do I really have to?" came the rising protest. "Can't I just wear a nice pair of jeans and a top?"

Kiara stared blankly before poking her head around the screen. "She doesn't know, does she?" The look she gave Aaronel was knowing, and a devious smile crossed her face.

"No, she doesn't. You know as well as the rest that things are meant to be under wraps."

"Somebody better tell me what's going on!" Tara snipped.

"After you get dressed," Kiara promised, crossing her fingers behind her back as she handed the dress over. She then poked her head back out. "Hey, Aaronel, find me some shoes. Something strappy with heels."

"Heels?"

Aaronel just smiled to himself as he shuffled through the closet. "You're better off not arguing with her." Even he rarely challenged her.

"But . . ."

"Going barefoot isn't an option," Kiara interrupted, flicking Tara on the nose.

"Hey!"

"I warned you," came the reply from the closet. Moments later he emerged holding just what Kiara was asking for. Heels with straps that looked like slivers of ice and small, clear crystals across the strap crossing the top of the foot. "Will these do, Kiara?"

Kiara poked her head out from behind the screen. "Perfect!"

Tara sighed again just before another audible thwack echoed through the room. "Owwwww."

"Don't bruise her."

Kiara, of course, ignored him and soon stepped from behind the screen. "She cleans up well," she said with a triumphant grin. She looked behind the screen, her expression becoming cross. "I will pull you out from behind there," she threatened.

Tara mumbled under her breath. The thought of being pulled into the open and the possibility of finger shaped bruises along her arms were enough to make her compliant. Aaronel gave a low whistle. She was wearing a semiformal gown, off the shoulders with an ice crystal cluster in the center of the form fitting bodice, flowy skirt with a slit that came midthigh. "Someone will need to keep Arcainous on a leash," he chuckled, watching as she was lead to the vanity and set in the chair.

"If he's wise, he'll stay away from me," she scowled.

"Oh, come on. It's not that bad," Kiara assured. She then looked at Aaronel. "There's just a few more touches, then we can spend the rest of the time helping her walk in those." Receiving no protest, she began to rummage through the drawers of the vanity. Finding what she wanted, she went to work brushing out her hair before sectioning it out into three cascading ponytails, tiling off each section with shimmering ties. "I'm surprised that you have your ears pierced," she teased as she placed a pair of ice cycle ear rings in her ears that matched the straps on her heels. "Now for the finishing touches," she mumbled as she slid in front of her to apply the makeup. When she was done, Tara looked like the embodiment of their element.

The remainder of the time they had left was spent trying to teach Tara to walk in heels. More than once she'd taken a spill, but they were always there to catch her. "You know . . ." Aaronel teased. "You remind me of one of our newborn foals trying to walk." But even as he laughed, he soon found himself rubbing the side of his head as he was hit.

Only a soft knock on her door signaled that their time had come to an end. Kiara answered the door, stepping aside to allow one of the servants to enter. "Everyone is beginning to gather downstairs," she said with a deep bow.

"Thank you," Kiara replied. "Please inform everyone that we'll be down shortly."

"Of course." With another bow, the woman disappeared down the hall leaving the three in a peaceful silence.

Kiara turned to Tara and smiled. "Don't keep us waiting." And with that, she too disappeared down the hall.

"What's going on?" She'd asked so many people, but no matter who she asked, she would never get an answer.

"Something wonderful," he assured.

"What?"

He sighed heavily, looking at her as they descended the stairs. "I'm simply a Captain to the armies of this Tower trying to maintain enough hope for the armies to do their jobs."

"I know, I know. You can't tell me," she finished with a wry smile.

"Are surprises really that bad?" he asked with an upturned brow.

"I don't remember ever having one," she answered with a shrug.

He just shook his head and fell silent for the remainder of the walk to the grand hall. To Tara's delight, there weren't a lot of people, but out of those who were there, she recognized only a handful. "Tara, you look absolutely stunning."

Tara turned carefully and smiled. "Yukino." She accepted the offered hug, looking around from the protection of her arms. "Who are all these people?"

"Well, there are the members of the Elder Council. The Guardians are here, as well as their Captains and Officers." She looked around to see who else she could recognize before continuing. "The high Priests and Priestesses from the temples are here, the Smith masters, dignitaries from the towns, and the Alphas from the Watchers."

Tara had to admit, that was a lot of people. But just as she was about to ask why she was invited to such a formal event, Fisonma and Raiden called for things to settle down and everyone began to file into the banquet hall. Each group seemed to know where to sit, and as they did, smaller conversations began, too garbled for her to understand. Aaronel escorted her to their table, seating her before being pulled into another conversation. "I wouldn't try to follow it," came a voice from the other side of Wella. Elexis poked her head forward, eyeing them as a purple strip of bangs fell into her face. "Once they get together, all they talk about is war and strategy."

"Not all the time," Adam protested.

"Oh yeah?" Wella asked. "Then what are you talking about?"

"Training . . . tactics," he admitted bashfully.

"See?"

But before she could have drilled him further, revealing talk of the new poison tipped arrows, Raiden called things to order. Fisonma rose once things were quiet and thanked everyone for the attendance. One by one, each of the towns gave accounts as to how things were going, and how things had escalated with the Shadow Lands. When everyone was heard, the Elders gave their word that they would ensure the safety of the towns.

As each group spoke, Tara found herself growing increasingly bored. Looking around the room, she found the table that Arcainous was sitting at. Her face brightened, but to her dismay, his focus was elsewhere. She slumped into her chair, wondering if she'd done something to make him angry with her. "Or maybe he doesn't need to protect me anymore," she breathed.

"Hm?"

Tara looked up only to lock gazes with Wella. "Oh, nothing," she replied sheepishly. "I was just talking to myself." The look on Wella's face was confused, but she nodded and turned back to the podium.

"Tonight's gathering is cause for both hope as well as for grieving." Fisonma's voice broke through Tara's thoughts, drawing her from the clouded mass gathering in her mind. "We gather together to mourn the accepted loss of Marcus. His unexpected disappearance is a devastating blow to the Guardians." Her gaze fixed upon the table where they all sat. "Aaronel, you have risen above the call of your station to ensure your armies have not faltered. You are to be commended for your dedication."

Aaronel rose and bowed. "Thank you, Elder."

Fisonma looked over the group once more as the head Priestess of the Ice temples joined her. "But even where there is darkness, there is always a ray of hope. The Elementals have chosen a new Guardian for the Tower of Ice." Fisonma's gaze remained steadfast, trained upon the Guardians and their Officers. "Tara, will you please step forward."

Tara's face lost all expression as she stared blankly at Fisonma. Only Aaronel's nudging brought back any signs of life. "Come on," he whispered. His smile was warm as he rose to his feet, extending his hand out to her. As he escorted her to the front of the hall a renewed energy of hope was beginning to awaken, reaching the hearts of all in attendance.

Tara glanced back at Aaronel. He nodded and stepped back, allowing Fisonma to address her. "You have overcome much." one of the Elders said as he joined Fisonma and the Priestess. "You have shown great courage, leadership, and conviction." He then produced a pale blue sphere from the folds of his robe and held it forward. "In the end, the decision is yours, but the Elementals see greatness within you."

She felt the weight of everyone's gaze upon her like lead bricks. She glanced back to Aaronel once again, then to everyone in the room before looking back at the people before her. "Wouldn't Aaronel be a better choice?" she asked. "I have no history here, and they already know him."

But before she could continue, Aaronel cleared his throat, his gaze trained on Tara as she turned to face him. "The Elementals have never lead us wrong. My place is with the armies, and if you will permit me to, I will continue to serve as their Captain."

The look of confusion was clearly splayed across her face. "What?"

"You are the one who's been chosen."

She looked around, searching for the comforting gaze of Arcainous, but when she found it, it was the same as everyone else's. She felt her heart drop, but Fisonma cleared her throat, drawing her attention once more. "Tara."

She turned back around. "Yes?"

"Have you decided, dear?"

Her breath held in her throat. She didn't know what was expected of a Guardian, nor did she know the full scope of what she was jumping into. But people who knew nothing about her had faith in her. "I have," she replied softly.

"What have you decided?" she asked.

"I'll do it."

There was a collective sigh of relief coupled with an excited energy that soon filled the room. The Elder who had been holding the orb stepped forward, holding the sphere forward. "Then take this. The orb will connect you to your Elemental, as it has with Guardians before you."

Tara looked from the orb to Fisonma with an unsure look in her eyes. "It's all right, child." Her voice was soothing as she continued to speak. "This sphere contains all the knowledge and wisdom you will need to become the great leader we know you will be."

She nodded and stepped up to the Elder, reaching out slowly toward the orb. As her fingers brushed over the top of the orb an expulsion of energy filled the room as the orb itself converted to an icy aura around her. In a matter of seconds, she saw everything she needed to see, knew everything she needed to know. From their place at the side of the room Vonri and Leigh saw everything they needed to craft her a set of armor and weapons based off the characteristics of her heart, as was the custom with all of the Guardians.

When the aura faded into her form, the Priestess stepped forward, gazing at Tara fondly. She took in her features, her energy, the gaze she shared with those who watched over the Realm. "You will lead with grace and civility," she began. "Your heart is fair, and it is just." But as she studied her, something was also troubling her. She stepped closer to Tara, taking her hands snugly. "Value life above all else," she said, her voice dropping so that only they could hear. "Do not grieve. Justice is always absolute." After that, however, she almost seemed lost as the energy between them became tense.

"Tread carefully," she murmured. "You hold a precious gift that can be used against you." But before she could be questioned, the Priestess stepped back, the calm smile again gracing her pale features.

"The Guardians are once again complete," Fisonma said. "This is truly cause for celebration." And with that said, large trays were soon being brought out and placed on every table. Breads to exotic fruits, meats, cheeses, and vegetables. With the movement of the servers and redirected attention, Tara was able to escape back to her seat, sliding in between Aaronel and Wella once again.

"Congratulations," Wella said with a warm smile.

"Thanks," Tara replied, picking at some food in front of her. Conversations began again and she found herself losing interest rather quickly. She slipped from the dining hall easily with a group of servers and made her way back to the staircase she'd come down from. "First things first," she muttered, hiking one leg up, then the other, removing the horrid shoes she'd been made to wear. The slit in the dress allowed her to sprint up the stairs as she went over a mental check list of what she would need to do once she got back to the room she'd changed in. Getting the makeup off, and back into her street clothes were at the top of her list. She did, however, like how her hair looked.

When she walked into the room she saw that her things were neatly placed. It felt like her own. "I still don't get why they couldn't have just told me this." But she shrugged and looked for her street clothes. They weren't in the bathroom where she'd left them. Heading for the dresser, she caught sight of Luna and Myst, sound asleep on new, larger beds. The look on her face softened instantly. "I'm sure Kayla ran you two ragged," she said softly. Not wishing to wake them, she passed on changing for the time being and walked through the open windows onto the balcony.

Leaning against the railing, she took a deep breath of the cool night air, her eyelids blinking repeatedly as small ice crystals fell around her. She finally felt completely at peace. "They're almost as beautiful as you are."

Her eyes slid closed as she heard his voice and a mild smirk crossed her lips. "You really shouldn't lie like that."

"I'm not." The warmth of his breath brushed over her ear as his hands slid along the length of her arms.

"I'm surprised that you're not giving me the lines of 'I told you so.' about me being in a dress."

"I'd thought about it," he admitted, turning her to face him. His gaze was nothing short of adoring as he brushed the backs of his fingers across her cheek. "But you were so stunning when I saw you that it took my breath away."

"Flattery?" she asked with an upturned brow. "Tell me," she began, turning from him and staring up once again into the night sky, "did I do something to anger you?"

He was taken aback by her question and pulled her back against his chest instantly. "Never," he murmured.

"Then why—"

"Haven't I been around?" he asked, finishing the obvious. "A lot has been going on over the last few seasons that affect quite a bit throughout the Realm."

"Like the guy who was with you tonight?" she asked.

"Yes," he replied. "His name is Niako. He has recently been appointed as my second in command of the Watchers."

"Is he really gone then?" There was a level of sorrow in her voice as she turned to face him. Belzak had given his life to save her when she was a child, and she felt slightly responsible.

"I'm almost certain of it." He ran his fingers along her jawline, tilting her head as he stared into her eyes. "Why do you ask?"

"I don't know. Sometimes it feels like he's here, with me, watching me. Like that feeling of being watched even when you know for a fact that no one is with you."

He drew her in closely, his arms encircling her shoulders protectively as he kissed the top of her head. "We won't let anything happen to you. This I swear."

25

Heart of Malice

The seasons passed quickly for Tara. She fell easily into a steady routine consisting of training with the other Guardians, hours of intense meditation where she sought out guidance from her Elemental, and patrols with the armies. But for all of the mental and physical training she endured, there was one aspect of being a Guardian she still had troubles adjusting to. The endless meetings that the Guardians would find themselves in bored her to tears. She knew how important they were, and endured them with her ever present smile as they listened to reports, discussed plans, and discussed the slow increase in activity from the Shadow Lands.

"The Shadow Lands have been quite active lately," Keshou said one cold afternoon as they exited the meeting hall.

"I know," Wella replied, bundling under a heavy coat to keep herself from shivering.

"I'm worried that they're planning something," Tara admitted as she slid her arms through a denim jacket, quite content with the chilled air.

"We have several groups of scouts crossing the borders to gather intel," Oron added as he joined the conversation.

"I hope they're all right." Wella sighed. "I have a bad feeling."

* * *

Somewhere in the bowels of the Shadow Lands, Darius and Vonspar sat watching recent recordings of Tara's fighting and overall conduct since she'd become the new Guardian of Ice. "She handles herself all right." Darius began. "But I can't believe the allowed her to become a Guardian."

"True," Vonspar said as he leaned back, running his fingers through Oni's hair. "But this can be used to our advantage with our prisoner." Deciding to take things back to his prior comment, he studied the images closely. "She will never match your skill, no matter how much she trains." He stared down at the woman beside him, his fingers tangling through her hair now. The fondness in his gaze was all she needed to know that she had pleased him.

Darius turned his head, watching the display with a mild interest. "Have you always had her?"

Oni was the first to react, craning her head to the side to look up at him with a questioning stare. Never before had anyone shown an interest in her on such a personal level. Vonspar chuckled at the look crossing her features as he traced his fingers along her jaw. "Not always," he admitted.

"Oh?" He had to admit as he stared into her lavender eyes, that his interest was piqued.

Vonspar leaned back, recalling the raid that led to his capture of her like a fond memory. "We were trying to expand the Kingdom of the Shadows and her village was one of the first that we encountered. We gave them the same offer that we give everyone. Surrender and serve us, or death. Nothing has ever been simpler. Most fought against us of course, and were killed for defiance." Oni of course had heard the story several times and had rested her head on Vonspar's leg, closing her eyes as she felt the warmth of his hand against the top of her head. "She was just a child when I found her. Five or six by your Realms years. But even with those around her slaughtered by my men, she showed no fear toward me. I asked her if she was afraid and she said no. After questioning her at length, I decided to test her and told her to fetch me some water."

"At such a young age she was bred for service?"

"She was," he replied. "She was so obedient and eager to please, so I took her as my own. I trained her to be the perfect pet. She serves without question, and when she was completely bent to my will, I trained her to be my eyes and ears outside of this great Kingdom of ours. I am quite proud of her."

The look in Oni's eyes brightened as her chest swelled with a silent pride. The greatest reward any proper slave could hope for was praise from their Master and she had just received the highest praise of all. Darius, however, continued to study her, contemplating the affection shown between the two. "Do you love her?" he asked suddenly.

"Love?" he replied as if the concept of such an emotion were completely new to him. "As much as a Master can love a slave I suppose."

Darius sat back, the three of them watching a frozen image of Tara. "She's much different than that foolish girl who is always around Toran."

"That girl is nothing but as posing little misfit." Oni spat out of instinct. She quickly recoiled, however, as the slap from Vonspar's hand met and echoed against the back of her head. Pulling away, she folded her hands tightly in her lap and stared at the floor, falling silent once again.

"While Oni is correct, Toran isn't strong enough to control her either."

"He seems like more of a problem than he's worth." Darius said.

"His downfall," Vonspar began, "is that he's too arrogant. He flaunts his abilities and thinks he is able to intimidate through his show of supposed power. All of that aside, he does have his usefulness. He was, after all, the stressor that finally allowed the wall around her mind to crack enough for Belzak to get through to her again. And through that, she found her way here into this Realm." He stopped suddenly, his gaze shifting quickly to Oni. "I wonder . . ."

"What are you thinking Brother?" Darius asked, leaning forward and watching the two.

"There has been talk about the girl," he began. "Talk that she holds some hidden power, even though no one has seen any hint of such a thing."

"I've heard rumors from the armies, yes."

"Her lack of confrontation will make her capture so very easy."

Now Darius was completely confused. "What are you talking about?"

Vonspar reached out, taking hold of Oni's chin, lifting her head to display her form with newfound pride even as her body tensed beneath his touch. "Capturing and breaking her of course." He then looked at his friend, his brother, as his expression darkened. "Think of it my brother, revenge in its purest, most physical form. Breaking her by true force and using her control over Ice as our foot hold into Nimost."

The thought of seeing her beaten form beneath him, the focus of all his rage. The release against her body, using the darkness itself to crush her. These thoughts brewed an excitement within him that he had felt when he surrendered his heart to darkness. "I don't wish for something fond and intimate as your and Oni, but she will bow before me if I have to shatter bone to put her there."

Excitement brewed within the depths of Vonspar's gaze. "She will learn to bow before your fist," he promised as the darkness which possessed them seeped into the room giving it an unnatural chill. "We will proceed immediately. Oni, have the alchemists prepare a sleeping serum and its antidote. When that is done you are to instruct Belzak, Dante, Malik, and Gabriel to begin their preparations."

"Yes, Master."

"Why them?" Darius asked. He was hoping to be the one to capture her in the beginning.

"Just think my brother, when she awakens in this strange, dark place, and her first sight is of you. Picture the look that will cross her face." He then turned back to Oni, slightly annoyed that she hadn't left yet. "I have another mission for you *my* pet."

Her head snapped up. "Yes, Master?"

"So eager to please." He smiled, tracing his fingers along her cheek. "I need you to sneak into Nimost and monitor the guards. They march in a particular pattern with designated times they stop at each point in their patrol. It is your task to break this pattern, do you understand?"

"Yes, Master."

"I want flawless notes, a clear path from the entrance of Nimost to the Tower of Ice, and how long they will have between passings from the guards."

"I will not fail you, Master."

"See that you don't." The evident warning betrayed the calm tone of his voice as he unleashed his second greatest triumph upon an unsuspecting Nimost.

CHAPTER

26

The Nightmare Begins

For almost a full season, Oni studied the guards of Nimost. Detailed calculations were sent regularly, allowing Dante, Malik, Gabriel, and Belzak to train accordingly. She would also occasionally add small side notes, information strictly for Vonspar which concerned personal notes about Tara's behaviors and routines. It was while Vonspar was reading one of these notes that Darius happened to walk by and glance over his brother's shoulder. "Is that really wise?" he asked, able to read a portion of what was written.

Vonspar looked up with a cool smile. "Letting her know she's being watched?"

Darius nodded as he took a seat beside him. "If she gets caught—"

"She won't be," he assured. "She's not allowing herself to be seen," he continued after a moment. "She is, however, allowing her presence to be felt." He shifted some in his seat, his smile twisting to cruel delight. "Think of it. You know you're being watched. You can feel their eyes bearing down upon you, but any inspection tells you that you are alone. She will be quite wound up and paranoid by the time the other group moves in that capturing her will be simple."

"You are truly twisted." Darius chuckled.

"Are you complaining, brother?" Vonspar asked with an upturned brow.

Darius shook his head, raising his hands in defense. "I'm sure she wears terror well," he said as the two shared a laugh at Tara's expense.

* * *

Tara stared out over the courtyard of the towers of Nimost as the prickly feeling of unease slowly crept its way up her spine. 'I wonder if the others feel it too.' she thought as she ran her palms along her arms to warm them.

"You sure do enjoy staring out at the stars lately."

Tara spun around, her eyes narrowing slightly. "I'm not stargazing," she muttered.

"Do you still think you're being watched?" he asked, sliding his arms snugly around her waist.

"There's no thinking about it Arcainous," she sighed. "I know I'm being watched." She then turned around, her eyes fixing upon the shadows. "I just can't prove it."

"If you're that worried about it, then let's go to the Elders."

"It's late," she sighed. "I'll go talk to them in the morning." She could feel his eyes boring into her. Spinning around, she met his gaze. "Yes?"

"If you're so worried . . ."

"I said I'll go in the morning. I promise." She slid past him and into her room, flopping onto her bed as Luna and Myst watched her with tilted heads.

"You're so stubborn," he mumbled as he followed behind her, sitting in a chair and watching as she fell into a restless sleep.

Oni watched from her place in the shadows, gathering the last bit of information that was required. She was then given the order to return and retreated from the White City with no one being the wiser.

* * *

The next day, and for days after, the energy of Nimost returned to normal. No longer feeling that she was being watched, Tara decided not to seek out the Elders with her concerns. She did, however, meet up with Wella and Elexis to discuss plans for a march north to investigate rumors of several disturbances near the resting grounds of the dragons. "Why would anyone want to bother them?" Wella complained through pursed lips.

"Do the Shadow Lands have nothing better to do than bother those poor creatures?" Elexis grumbled.

"They lose their riders, or are gravely injured. The lands to the north are supposed to be a haven for them." Eiricka sighed.

"I talked to Keshou," Tara offered. "He told me that he and the rest of the Guardians have their groups ready to march."

"It's a fair-sized army that we're sending out," Wella mused.

"Well, it's a large area, right?" Tara asked.

"It is," Elexis answered.

"With this size of an army, who's going to be leading them?"

Wella raised her hand. "That one's easy," she said with a smile. "Eiricka, Adam, and Katsuro are going to be leading them."

"And on that note," Eiricka began, rising to her feet, "we should probably get the final preparations underway. I hear they're wanting to leave at first light."

* * *

"How are our plans?" Vonspar was now pacing the floor while Darius and Oni sat and watched.

"Things are moving along nicely," Toran answered. "Durion is to the north of Nimost, causing problems with their dragons. The vampires have just finished the serum that will drug Tara, and all that is left is your order to march."

287

"Then tell Belzak. He's working on the link he has with her. I want this done quickly, and I want this done with no mistakes."

"As you wish."

Vonspar watched him leave before turning to Darius. "Are you ready for this, my brother?"

The look on his face was puzzled. "What do you mean?" he asked. As far as he was concerned, there was nothing to be ready for. As soon as she was theirs, he would make her regret everything, including her own existence.

"When she comes, and we begin the process of breaking her, she will likely resort back to how she was before, trying to lure you in so that you feel pity for her and free her." He clasped his hands on Darius's arms. "Can you stand up to that?"

"The person she was then is tied to the person she is now. I know this, brother. I will not soon forget what she has done, nor will I forgive it."

"I will be there for you," he assured. "I'll begin her breaking process. Nothing short of pure force of course. When you are brought in, she will see you as a form of salvation, timing you to your past together. She will reach out for you, her gaze likely hopeful, and you will be able to crush that hope to dust."

"Torture. It sounds fitting." Darius mused. "I like it."

"I knew you would." His attention then turned to Oni. "Please see that a guest room is prepared, my pet. One of the rooms near ours that can be altered with a door for easy access to her."

"Yes, Master."

* * *

Tara stared up at the sky like she did most every night. As she folded her arms on the railing, she reflected back on how far she had come in her life. From a child who broke the rules who grew into a teen looking for the bitter taste of revenge, and now, having become a part of something great. But as her reflections lifted her gaze skyward, she suddenly felt shunned as her gaze rested upon the moon. She had usually felt such comfort in its haunting glow, but tonight she felt almost betrayed. She pulled back, retreating back to her room and sitting at her desk. She reached for one of her journals but before she could even begin writing, she felt the warmth of Luna's and Myst's heads as they rubbed against her sides.

She leaned back in her chair, her arms dropping as she stroked the sides of each of their necks. "You two are such good kids." But even surrounded by such a loving aura, a glance to the side brought back the feeling of foreboding which made her shrink back in her chair. "I thought things had returned to normal," she sighed as she leaned forward to pick up her pen. With the questioning whine of the two wolves she looked down at them fondly. "Everything will be fine. I promise." Seeming content with that, the two wolves trotted to their beds and curled up on their plush pillows. She leaned forward, resting her cheek on the back of her hand as she watched them. "I love you two so much," she whispered, twirling her pen between her fingers.

The ease of their energy set her soul at rest, and diminished the desire to write in order to free her heart. She placed the pen back on her desk before sliding from her chair and walking back onto the balcony. She stared out over the courtyard once more, watching the guards patrolling beneath her. The more she stared, the more she felt her focus slip away until she was staring blankly into absolutely nothing. "A little more, Belzak," Gabriel whispered.

Belzak's eyes glowed from within the cover of an illusion, his mind slowly seeping into hers, wrapping it, warping it, drawing her focus carefully enough that she wouldn't detect that he was with her. He nodded, knowing that his voice would echo to her if he spoke and he was unsure how she would react. He was just about to give the signal to drug her when another's presence appeared behind her.

The warmth of his arms circling her waist drew her mind to the present. Though she was a bit startled, she turned in his arms, smiling as she rested in his embrace. "I didn't hear you come in," she whispered.

Belzak growled. "We were so close," he snarled.

"Be calm, my friend." Malik gripped his arm, keeping him in place so their position would not be compromised.

"We can use this," Dante whispered while Gabriel continued to enforce the illusion they hid behind.

"How?" Belzak snapped.

"With her distracted by Arcainous, you will be able to grab her with more ease than you would have if you were still within the depths of her mind. We just have to wait for the right moment to strike." Malik assured. This seemed to sate the wolf for the time being and he settled further into the shadows to wait.

* * *

Arcainous ran his fingers through Tara's hair and stared into her eyes. "You seem distracted tonight my dear."

Tara gave a bashful smile as she slid from his embrace. "I'm just worried about the army we sent to check on the dragons," she admitted.

"They were some of the most experienced soldiers that all of you have sent out. They will be fine."

"But that doesn't mean that I won't worry," she said with a soft sigh. She planted her hands on the railing, turning her arms outward as she allowed them to take the weight of her upper body. "You know how I am," she added, tilting her head back to stare directly into the glow of the moon."

From their hiding place, a ripple of energy was released as Gabriel saw their mark. "There it is brothers," he whispered. "Aim for the vein along the inside of her arm."

The mode of deliverance was almost as important as the serum itself and several devices were created to handle a multitude of situations. A fine needle filled with enough serum to do the trick and as it entered her arm, several small straps unraveled, wrapping around her flesh. A single yelp of surprise was the only indication that something wasn't right. "What's wrong?" Arcainous asked as he rushed to her side.

Her eyes were wide as she began to dig at her arm. "I don't know!" She held up her arm, pulling at the thin straps around it, catching a glimpse of the end of the needle as the moonlight reflected off of it. "What is that!"

Expectant eyes continued to watch from the shadows. The more she panicked, the faster her heart would beat. This, in turn, would spread the serum like venom, taking effect much quicker. Arcainous gripped her arm and tried to guide the needle from it. "I don't know what it is," he admitted.

The commotion roused the two wolves who were soon on the balcony, pacing and whining. Suddenly, Tara stopped struggling and just stared. "I don't feel well," she mumbled as her body began to go slack.

"Tara!" Arcainous grabbed her as she slumped against the railing. "Tara, stay with me." He was patting her cheek, staring at her eyes that were quickly glazing over and rolling back. Not even the warmth of Luna and Myst were reaching her.

Angered by the small set back, Belzak began to growl. "Easy my friend." Dante whispered. He then removed a hair thin needle and in a blur of motion it was gone. Arcainous felt the unseen bite to the back of his arm closely followed by a rush of liquid fire consuming his nerves. From pure instinct he recoiled, watching in horror as Tara's form fell over the railing.

"Guards!" He shouted repeatedly, unsure if there were even any within hearing distance of his pleas for help. Fighting the fire in his arm he reached for her, missing her by mere inches. In that instant, reality struck with the possibility that he was going to watch her die on the frozen ground below. From empty space, however, a figure raced toward her. Long, bound, black hair accented the darkened features of a face long considered dead to the realm of Light. "Belzak!" he snarled.

He caught her with great ease, pushing from the face of the tower to land on one of the jutting crystals. "Hello, Arcainous." His eyes were cold, and emotionless as he addressed the one he once called brother.

"What have you done!" Arcainous demanded. "Release her, now!"

"I'm afraid I can't do that," he replied with a cruel smile. "Vonspar has plans for her."

Luna and Myst growled and snapped as they paced the length of the balcony. Arcainous felt his muscles tighten, the fire in his arm slowly losing to the rage he now felt as he continued calling for the guards. "Did you forget the vow you made to her? Look at her eyes!" he demanded. "You imprinted to her! A vow of eternal protection!"

Belzak stared down into the vacant gaze. "Such a wonderful path to her mind and her dreams," he chuckled.

Tara stared up blankly. The man before her now, she did not recognize, but she did not have the conscious will to fight. "Who . . . are you . . . ?" she managed.

"Belzak! Come back to your senses!" Arcainous ordered.

The commotion was beginning to draw the attention of approaching guards who were beginning to sound the alarms. "Belzak, will you hurry!" Malik growled.

Belzak looked over his shoulder and nodded before jumping back to the ground. Spinning on his heels without a word, he began to walk back to his group until the cracking of the earth echoed around him. Stopping suddenly, he saw himself face-to-face with the large silver wolf. The look that crossed his face was amused. "Such a splay of power," he taunted.

"I'll kill you!" he growled.

The air around them grew colder than the energy emitted by the tower as the look across Belzak's face darkened to pure cruelty. "You're just jealous," he spat. "I imprinted to her, and you couldn't. She will never be truly yours." His gaze then changed, staring down at the woman he held in his arms, touching her cheek with mock affection. "She and I will always have a sacred link, a fact that you are well aware of." Arcainous lunged toward him, but even with Tara in his arms, Belzak was able to avoid him with ease. "Blind rage suits you," he said, retreating to the safety of the illusions as the guards began to move in.

"Inform the Elders," Arcainous ordered. His nose caught their scent easily and in an instant, he was in pursuit. "I will return you home," he vowed.

CHAPTER

27

Evil's Dark Intention

D ays passed as Tara stared blankly through her drugged state. She vaguely registered that they would stop to alter her dosing of the serum coursing through her veins so they could rest. "Do you think this will finally convince him to join us?" Belzak asked one night as they hid in a group of trees just miles away from the border to the Shadow Lands.

Dante kept watch, listening and sniffing the air to make sure they were far enough ahead of their pursuers to rest properly. "I'm not sure," he answered. "If what we have learned over the ages so is correct, once a new Guardian is appointed, the powers of the previous Guardian become null and void."

"Wouldn't these be different circumstances?" he asked. "I thought that only applied when the Guardian had passed or left service."

Dante thought for a moment and shrugged. "There's only one way to find out," he said at length. "We'll have to get her there and hand her to Vonspar personally before we can speculate on anything."

"Get some rest." Malik hissed. "They aren't far behind us."

"We'll be safer once we're behind our own borders, but until then, Malik is correct. We should rest." He then looked at their young captive. "She won't be a problem. She should need only one more alteration to her dosing before we reach the Manor."

As Belzak rested in the crook of a branch he couldn't help but hope that Arcainous was close behind. He wanted so much to destroy him, but thank him for allowing him access to such immense powers. In these thoughts he found a bit of rest, disturbed only when Gabriel shook his shoulder. "It's time to go. We are no longer safe here."

By the time he was ready with Tara, the trio was already on the ground. "How far are they?" he asked as he leaped to the ground.

"Only a few miles." Malik was, of course, disappointed by this as he spoke. "They're moving faster than expected."

Belzak looked down at Tara. "Do you hear that?" he asked, knowing that she couldn't reply. "Your lover really thinks he can save you."

Dante laughed. "Torment her after we're safe."

"Just letting her know there's no hope for her to be rescued," he replied as the four moved closer to, and finally across the border to the Shadow Lands. It took two more rises of the sun for them to finally breach the borders of the Manor. "Oh thank God," he huffed as he fell to his knees letting Tara fumble onto the ground.

The trio had only the faintest hint of fatigue as they circled around the other two. "You did well Belzak," Malik commented.

"I'm sure Vonspar will be pleased." Gabriel added as he picked the girl up from the ground. "Brothers, help him. We should not keep them waiting."

As they ascended the stairs to the Manor, Vonspar emerged into the dim light to greet them. "Well done." His gaze fell to the former Watcher and he nodded to himself. "Escort him to his room please. I will have Oni see to his needs while we are busy with our guest."

"Of course, Vonspar," Dante replied as he and Malik escorted Belzak down one of the side halls.

Vonspar watched them leave before turning to Gabriel. "Come with me." It was all he said as he walked along the main hall. "I am anxious to get this started."

"Of course," Gabriel replied as he followed behind him.

When they reached the large study, Vonspar pointed to a nearby chair. "Set her down and tie her to the chair," he ordered, tossing some rope to him.

Gabriel nodded and set to work, binding her legs and arms to the chair before wrapping the remainder of the rope around her mid-section. As he rose, he noticed that most of the lights were off, casting a rather dark shadow over a portion of the room. "I don't remember it being quite so dark in that corner."

Vonspar nodded as he approached the chair, needle in hand that held the reversing agent to the serum that sedated his guest. "That's because it normally isn't."

Gabriel watched as the rim of Vonspar's irises began to glow a sickly jade. He placed the pad is his thumb upon the center of her forehead, directly on her third eye chakra point, watching as a green mark appeared beneath his thumb. "What is that mark?" he asked, abandoning the issue of lighting.

"It's a magical block," he explained. "This will keep her from using her powers until I am sure she will use them to our benefit." When they were sure that she was bound properly, Vonspar injected the serum through the needle in her arm before removing it with a solid yank. This action of course, caused a thin trickle of blood to snake down her arm, but Vonspar considered it the beginning of the end for their captive. "Go now," he ordered. "Inform our prisoner that we have something that will force him to change his mind about helping us."

Gabriel looked surprised. "He still can?"

"You think that just because there is a new Guardian, that all others lose their power?" He sighed heavily, unwilling to let him answer. "I will explain later. For now, allow me to see to our guest. Find Oni when you are done with your previous task and see if she has the room ready. When it is, tell her to come here and wait outside."

"Yes, Vonspar," Gabriel bowed and ducked out of the room quickly.

"Now, my beautiful captive," he began, circling around her chair like an animal circling its prey. "It is time for you to awaken." He returned to his desk, taking a seat upon the edge as he placed his hands on either side. He didn't have to wait long for the countering agent to take affect and the sounds of soft whimpering soon filled the room. "How nice of you to join us."

Her head was drooping down, her eyes opening slowly, but not fully. What she saw was nothing more that blurs that made no sense to her. Then she heard a voice, but her muscles were slow to respond to what her brain desired from them. Still more mumbles and whimpers fell from her lips, her mind crying out for the waking world and the warmth of Arcainous's arms around her. When her sight finally returned to her, she saw that she was bound. A chill ran the length of her spine and she suddenly began to fight against her restraints. "I wouldn't fight it if I were you."

She lifted her head, her eyes staring forward as she tried to freeze the ropes around her. But her powers wouldn't come to the surface. She could feel it within her, sleeping, but it wouldn't respond to her summon. "What . . . what's going on?" Her gaze shot to the side when she heard movement. "What did you do!"

The sound that came from Vonspar's throat was scoffing. "I'd be a little more respectful if I were you. Especially given your current situation." He then strode up to her, landing a single slap to the left side of her face. "Now, if you would kindly pay attention. I would honestly watch myself if I were you." He smoothed out his shirt and walked back to his desk. Taking a seat upon the edge, he folded his arms loosely across his chest. "I have something for you."

"I don't want anything from you." She spat, literally spitting in his direction.

His eyes became dark and hard as granite as he resisted the urge to strike her again. 'There will be time for that.' He reminded himself. "Brother, would you please join me."

"Brother?" Her eyes shifted to the darkness in the room, squinting as she tried to make out the outline of the figure that was slowly emerging into the light. Onyx armor shone in the dim light of the room, its destructive ability currently at rest. Her gaze lifted as his face came into view, an audible gasp falling from her lips. "Darius." She breathed.

"You seem surprised to see me." His voice was amused as he moved to stand beside Vonspar.

Tara's brow creased. "I, I don't understand."

"Of course you don't." Vonspar chuckled.

"Your mom is worried sick about you. She's been looking all over creation for you," Tara continued, ignoring Vonspar outright.

"Yukino?" Darius asked. "That woman is dead to me now." The tone of his voice seemed too dismissive, and Tara couldn't believe what she'd just heard.

"You see," Vonspar began as he slid from the desk with ease, "I have offered him a life free of betrayal and broken promises."

"What?" Her gaze narrowed as she stared at him. "You gave him delusions, not a better life." She snipped.

But her comment would bring her too close to the monster, and he was upon her in just seconds. His fingers tangled through her hair, tugging her head back and forcing her gaze to meet his. "Why don't you ask him what I gave him." He snarled. Expecting an answer from Darius, he jerked her head so that her gaze was upon his brother. "Tell her, my brother, what did I give you."

The look across Darius's face was calm, as if he'd found something he'd long searched for. "He has given me peace and completion. He's given me family and power. But most importantly, he'd given me truth. A truth that will soon be beaten into you."

"Darius . . ."

"You see," he began again, yanking her head to once again meet his gaze, "I've taken him in as a part of my family to repair the damage that you and that woman have done."

"You're the one doing the damage." She hissed, only to feel the sting of yet another slap.

Darius made no attempt to stop Vonspar from inflicting any sort of pain upon their captive. He remained against the desk, arms still folded, as he watched what was transpiring. After a moment, Vonspar released a gruff exhalation before stepping back. He regained his composure and stared thoughtfully at their captive. "I have an offer for you," he said flatly. "One I heavily suggest you consider."

"Like I would ever consider anything from you unless it was my release." She growled.

"You really won't have a choice," he corrected. "Disobeying me will have dire consequences."

"Do your worst," she challenged.

"Oh, I intend to do just that." He chuckled. "We will make you wish for death by the time we are done with you." Seeing the defiance in her eyes he knew he would get no further with her. "Oni!" His voice was loud as he called for her,

Tara saw his features soften as the woman entered the room. She was at his side in an instant, accepting the offer of his open arm. She purred as she was pulled close to his chest, her gaze shifting from Tara to Vonspar. "Yes, Master?"

"Master?" Tara's face twisted in disgust as she spoke to Vonspar. "How can you let another human being treat you like nothing more than property?"

Oni remained quiet, scowling as Vonspar began to laugh. "I wouldn't expect a child to understand the complex relationship a Master has with their pet." He kissed Oni's forehead before stepping from her. "You will understand though, in due time." The look he gave Tara was laced with cruel thoughts before he returned his attention to his beloved pet. "Please take her to her room. Have the guards escort you in case she gives you any troubles."

"Of course, Master, right away." She replied with a quick bow. Her venomous gaze then shifted to Tara as two guards entered the room and pulled her to her feet after removing the binds from around her legs and midsection.

Once they had gone, Vonspar returned to his brother's side. "I will teach you how to break her. When she realizes that there is no one to save her, she will give us what we want."

"Do you think she can be broken that easily, brother?" Darius asked as the two finally exited the room.

"Everyone has their breaking point. We just have to find hers." He thought for a moment, reflecting back to the looks of defiance that she would give them. "She is strong willed like you had stated earlier." He said at length.

"She got that independent streak from Yukino," Darius muttered.

"I see . . ." Vonspar replied, his mind off on some other string of thoughts. "I think we will have to revise our tactics with her." He said at length.

"How so?"

"Since she now knows that you have surrendered to the Shadows, she will no longer expect you to come to her 'rescue.' Instead, I am thinking that we crush her hope outright. I'll have you in the room with me while I begin the process of breaking her. Once you are comfortable with the tactics, I will teach you, then I will turn her over to you. You will be the one to destroy her spirit and get her to help us."

A dark delight crossed Darius's face with this prospect. "I will not fail you, brother."

"I know." Vonspar chuckled. "We will begin in the morning. We must prepare mentally for what we are about to undertake."

"Of course, brother." And with that, the two departed to their own rooms, each anticipating what the next few days would bring them.

Meanwhile, Tara was anything but pleased, though when she saw her room, she had to admit that she was a bit surprised. "What, no dungeon?" she asked in a scoffing tone.

"I can arrange one." Oni hissed. She then turned her attention from her to admire her handiwork. "It's nowhere near as nice as my Master's room," she said with pride. "But for you, I suppose it will do."

Tara looked around a bit. There was a Japanese-style bedroll set off to one side, an open door that led to the bathroom, a chair, and a few small tapestries hanging on the walls. "And what's to keep me from leaving?"

"Easy," Oni replied with a cruel smile, pointing to one of the doors. "That door leads to Darius's room. The other leads to my Master's room." She then dismissed the guards who exited and locked the door that they had come through. "I suggest you get some rest," she said as she approached the door to Vonspar's room. "You'll never know what the morning will bring."

And with an almost childlike giggle, she disappeared through the door, leaving Tara to contemplate her fate.

CHAPTER

28

Hell

Tara woke with a start as she heard the crack of a door as it was slammed against the wall. "Get up!" came the boom of a stern voice.

The look that crossed her face was anything but pleased as she was woken up. Her vision was still a bit fuzzy, but the voice was unmistakable. "No," she replied bluntly, scowling as she rolled onto her other side, facing away from them. Hearing silence, she gave a silent nod, sure that they had left, leaving her the victor of their little spat. Her body began to relax into the mat, once more warmed by the blanket that was draped over her, but she soon found herself being hoisted into the air. "Hey!" she protested. "Let go!" she demanded.

"Very well," came the cool reply. Darius arched his brow, but the look that crossed Vonspar's face was twisted as he threw her into the wall. The only thing heard after that was the thud of contact followed by her groan as she hit the floor. "I let you go." He stated simply. "Now, I will tell you again. Get, up!"

Tara slid her arms beneath her and pushed up enough to rest on her elbows. "In what delusional world do you think I would listen to you?" she hissed.

It would prove to be a statement better left unspoken, but realization came too late for her. He was upon her in an instant, his speed catching Tara off guard. The sting of an open slap, however, brought her back to the grim reality of her situation. "I will beat that attitude from you." He vowed, kicking her solidly in the ribs, which sent her once again into the wall.

Tara rolled onto her back, her arms wrapping tightly around her torso. "I'll be dead before you can." She wheezed, gulping down small mouthfuls of air.

But Vonspar just laughed as he moved to stand over her. "I could never let that happen." He chuckled, picking her up by the front of her shirt. "You're far too valuable to us."

"Whatever." She snapped, only to feel the knuckles of the back of his free hand against the bridge of her nose. This was closely followed by the warm flow of blood as it gushed down over her lips and chin. Her eyes watered, but she allowed enough blood to gather between her lower lip and jaw before spitting it into Vonspar's face in a misty spray before narrowing her eyes at him.

His brow twitched, feeling the vein in his forehead begin to throb. He lifted his hand once more, slapping her before drawing the back of his hand across her other cheek, throwing her toward Darius. "I don't know how you put up with such insolence." He growled in fury.

"It wasn't easy," he muttered, catching her firmly by her right bicep, yanking her toward him. His cold gaze fixed upon her, his voice dropping to a predatory growl. "You will show him respect."

"And what if I don't," she snarled, spitting her own blood in his face as well.

The room grew dangerously quiet as the two looked at her. Her jaw was set, refusing to back down, but Vonspar's laughter soon broke the tense quiet. "Spitting blood at me is one thing, but you really shouldn't have done that," he said as he walked toward his room. He stopped in the doorway and turned to Darius. "Make sure you clean up when you're done with her." And with that, he closed the door, hearing nothing more than the echoes of painful cries and vengeance.

And that was how her time was spent. The subject of the most ruthless violence. Time had been lost to her, and as it continued to pass, her hopes of being rescued began to dwindle. Even with as weak as she was, she remained defiant, refusing to break and become a target for unwarranted hatred. It was after one of these hellish encounters where she heard a conversation that would simply strengthen her resolve to fight them. "If we have her," Darius asked. "Then why do we still have him?"

"Leverage," Vonspar replied with a wicked grin. "As long as he's alive, we can still convince her to aid our cause."

Tara lay on the floor, shaking from the extent of her injuries, listening to the conversation. "Who are they talking about?" she whispered

"He's still secure in the dungeons though," Vonspar assured with a shrug. He then looked into the room, seeing the smears of blood throughout the room. Sighing in disgust, he looked down at his beloved treasure. "My dear Oni . . ."

She looked up at him with adoring eyes. "Yes, Master?"

"Be a good girl and clean up the mess in there."

The look that briefly crossed her features was one of bewilderment. It wasn't her blood on the floor and walls, and to her, the woman on the floor was far inferior to herself. But as she trained her sight upon his gaze, she could tell that he was awaiting an answer. Looking into the room once more she cringed. He had treated her with nothing but kindness and affection and she didn't want to start going down the path that this woman had obviously gone down to receive such wrath. "Yes, Master, I'll do that now."

"Good girl." He petted the top of her head before sending her off. Turning to Darius, he motioned for him to join him as they tried their luck with their captive they'd just been talking about.

Oni stepped into the room, looking back over her shoulder to make sure that they were gone before shutting the door to Vonspar's room. As she approached Tara she could hear the ragged breathing and as she knelt beside her, she could finally see the extent of the damage that had been done to her throughout the course of her stay. Her left eye was swollen. Blood, both fresh and dried, was smeared across her skin and clothes, and matted throughout her hair. There were cuts and bruising across her form in various stages of healing. But what was frighteningly noticeable was the intense shaking of her body having gone into shock. "You really shouldn't speak out against them the way you have."

Tara's right eye quivered with the inability to focus. "Why do you care?"

Oni's first reaction was to take offense to the statement, but the more that she viewed the woman, the more her heart seemed to go out to her. For whether she wanted to admit it or not, the two were sisters now. They were servants, though they rested on opposite ends of the spectrum of slavery. So instead of reacting to the outburst, she simply helped Tara sit up. "We must get you into the bath. It will be the quickest way to warm you." But as she wrapped her arm around her side, Tara cried out in pain. She sighed heavily as she led her to the bathroom. Her nose scrunched as she saw the blood soaked clothing and tsk'ed. "Let's get you out of these."

Tara slumped into a chair, watching as Oni ran the hot water. "Why are you doing this?"

Oni turned to face her. She reached for the hem of her top then stopped. With the pain she was feeling, removing them traditionally would only inflict more, and she was nothing like Darius. Instead, she reached for a pair of scissors and began to cut the blood soaked garments away. They would be going into the trash anyway, so she saw no reason to be kind to them. "We are sisters now." She answered simply.

"You were ordered to. We aren't sisters," Tara corrected as she was helped to her feet and into the steaming water.

"I was," she said easily as she helped Tara sit in the water. To her delight, her shaking began to lessen, but to her dismay, the water quickly turned a sickly crimson. She drained the water and ran the shower, pulling down the removable head to wash the blood from her body and hair. She set to the task of washing her hair, watching the shampoo turn a pale pink, but as the conditioner sat she washed

Tara completely. When she was done, she again filled the bath with water, adding some salts that would help calm and relax her.

"Why do you let someone treat you like that?" Tara had to ask. The idea of someone owning another human being. It wasn't right.

"Treat me like what?" Oni asked as she gathered the shredded remains of Tara's clothing.

"Like a dog." Her head fell back as she focused upon the ceiling. "How can you stand to let him treat you like this? I don't understand how anyone can subject themselves willingly to this kind of torture."

"Torture?" she asked, dropping Tara's clothing into the trash. "My Master has never treated me with anything but respect and affection."

Tara rolled her head to the side, taking in Oni's flawless features. There were no scars, no bruising, cuts—nothing that would even hint at the hell she found herself going through. "None of this makes sense." She groaned, sliding further under the water.

Oni knelt beside the tub, her hands folded in her lap. "I don't think I can explain it, but I will try." Her eyes closed as she looked inward, searching for just the right words to put her relationship with Vonspar into a perspective that Tara would grasp. "The bond between a Master and their submissive, it transcends any normal bonds of love that you would be accustomed to. A submissive surrenders herself fully to her Master. She has no will. Her mind, her body, her spirit, actions, thoughts. They are all His to mold, shape, and direct as He sees is needed. The bond is developed from trust. A submissive trusts her Master to protect her from all harm and to make the decisions for her that will make her better."

Tara stared, seeing the glow that seemed to surround Oni as she spoke. There was such a reverence in her voice, and she truly did seem happy in the life that had been dealt to her. "It seems kind of one-sided."

"Not at all," Oni corrected. "A Master must place just as much trust in His submissive that she places in Him. He trusts her to be flawlessly obedient, and to act as an extension of Himself. He trusts that she will defend Him with her very life." She opened her eyes and turned her head, regarding the young Guardian once more. "Do you understand now?" she asked. "Do you see why this bond is so much stronger than something so small as love? Yes, there is a degree of affection, but it is born from duty and a desire to please Him."

Tara had to admit that she was still a bit confused, but she did have a better understanding of her situation. But she couldn't help but ask. "How did you find yourself in this situation?"

She stared ahead of her, recalling the night she was found. She wasn't ashamed that it was during a raid to expand the Shadow Lands territory. Even from the time she was small she was taught to obey those who were over her, no matter who they were. "My Master was looking for someone who was unafraid. Someone He could train to be His eyes and ears. Someone He could mold into perfection. Everyone ran when they saw Him and His armies ride up, but I wasn't afraid. I think that's what made the first impression on Him."

"What about your parents?" Tara asked. "Didn't they try and protect you?"

But she shook her head. "From what I remember, my parents sold me when I was just able to walk."

"Sold you?" Tara sat up, staring in disbelief. "But if your town was under the protection of Nimost, something like that shouldn't have even crossed their minds."

"We were on the fringes of the borders. The armies of the Elementals did what they could, but there were duel influences. The people who sold me were obviously driven by something more material." But how she arrived to her current locations meant nothing to their current conversation. "Submitting to Him was as natural to me as breathing, and that's how I was brought up. But you, you were brought here at the request of my Master and Darius. Where my submission was of my own choosing, yours will be forced. You are to be an outlet for Darius's anger and rage. They will wear you down until you finally submit and surrender your powers to them."

"Well, they're not going to get it," she snapped.

"That's what he said when they caught him," Oni replied softly as she rose to her feet. "If you think what they have done to you is torture," she began, holding up a robe for Tara to slip into, "then you are truly blind to the true scope of their ambition."

Tara slid her arms through the sleeves of the robe and tied it around her waist. "He?" she asked as the two returned to the aftermath of her ordeal. "Wait, you mean Marcus?" She sat in a nearby chair as Oni began cleaning the room. "He's alive?"

"They told him the same thing that they told you. Defy them, and they will make you wish for death." Within moments, the room was cleaned and looking as it did before this hell had begun. "He will be kept alive until one of you cave to their demands."

"He's alive." Tara sighed in relief.

Oni rose to her feet, casting a look of concern upon the young Guardian. "Do not try to be a hero," she warned. "For as much as they want your power, they won't hesitate to kill you and try again with someone else."

Tara blinked as Oni tossed her some clean clothes. "Why do you care about what happens?" she asked.

"I don't," she corrected. "We might be sisters now, but you will always be inferior to me. What I said is nothing more than advice."

Seeing that her duties were done, she walked to the door that would take her to Vonspar's room. "For your sake, I wouldn't leave."

And with that, she was gone.

Tara sat in the silence of the room contemplating everything she'd just found out. "I have to find him." She decided. "I have to tell him to stay strong." She moved from the chair to a dresser to find some clothes, leaving the clothes that Oni had given her to fall onto the floor. To her dismay, everything she found was too short, too revealing, things she would just never wear. "They look like things Oni would wear," she said with a sigh.

But even these would be better than wearing a robe to find Marcus. Rummaging through the clothes, she decided on a pair of short black shorts and a black halter top. Her movements were sluggish, but she knew she would be able to find him if she could be sneaky. But as she walked past a mirror she had to stop. With all the blood cleaned from her body, she was finally able to see the extent of the damage caused by Vonspar and Darius. "I'm so glad that Arcainous isn't here to see this." Her voice was small, filled with disbelief as she stared at the horrific reflection.

Tearing herself from the mirror, she made her way to the third door. Holding her breath, she opened the door, ever so slowly as a mix of hope and fear consumed her.

CHAPTER

29

Marcus

To her surprise and relief, there was no one by her door. "I was sure there would have been guards or something," she mumbled. "Unless they thought I wouldn't be able to move." But that was neither here nor there at that point. What mattered was finding Marcus and trying to escape. Hugging the walls for both support and stealth, she made her way through one hall after another. "There have to be stairs somewhere that lead down." But as she rounded another corner she froze, the color draining from her face.

"Well, well." The look that crossed Toran's face was one of amusement. "I knew we had a visitor," he continued, his eyes raking down her form, taking in both her clothing choice as well as the bruises and cuts scattered across her exposed flesh. "Now what are you doing out of your room?" He asked, pinning her to the wall by her shoulders. He enjoyed watching her wince in pain at the applied pressure to her swollen joints. "Wait until Darius finds out about this," he said with delight.

But she didn't care. She was on a mission, and no one would stop her from achieving it. "Where's Marcus?" She spat only to feel the sting of his slap across her face.

"I see they have been unable to break that attitude of yours." He grumbled. "You were nasty then too," he added, referring back to when she was in high school and their encounter when she was in college.

"Duh."

But she would only succeed in angering him, and to prove that, he dug his thumbs further into the joints of her shoulders. "Does it hurt?" he asked after a while, his eyes reflecting the glee in his voice as she writhed beneath the pain in his touch.

"Where . . . is Marcus." She demanded again. Even with her mind swimming in absolute agony she would see her goals to completion.

"Now what do you want with that old-timer?" he asked, staring intently into her eyes.

"I didn't have to explain myself when we were in school, and I sure as hell don't have to explain myself now." She snipped. "Now where is he!"

Toran was enjoying the little game he'd started with their new guest, enough so, that he was unaware that he himself was being watched. "I might tell you." He teased, his grin truly sinister. He pressed himself firmly against her, taking in the scent of the soap used to clean her. "But it will cost you." He whispered against her ear.

But before things could progress further, Toran's little moment was interrupted. "I knew it!" came the shriek from a female voice from the shadows.

Tara looked past Toran to see the blond that was always with him. She was red-faced, hands balled into fists as she stormed toward them. In spite of the pain, she couldn't help but laugh. "Busted."

"Shut up," he growled. He then looked over his shoulder, turning his attention to the blond. "I told you to stay in your room!" he snapped.

The anger she felt burned in her eyes as she shot an accusatory finger toward them. "What are you doing with her!" she demanded, ignoring both his statement, and the tone it was spoken in.

"It is none of your damned business," he snarled.

"I really don't feel like being in the middle of this lover's spat, so if you'll just tell me where Marcus is . . ." Tara mumbled.

"I said shut up!" And with that, the back of his hand struck the side of Tara's face again. He then turned his attention back to the blond. "I'll not tell you again. Go back to your room!"

"I knew you liked her more!" she yelled. "That's why you're always following her around!"

"I'd kill the both of you in a heartbeat." He growled. Spinning around, he threw out his left arm, sending the girl sprawling across the floor with a single pulse of dark energy. "But I know how much that will be frowned upon." He continued with distain. "Now, I won't tell you again, you filthy little mutt. Go back to your room!"

Tara was completely appalled by his actions. He was showing himself to be too much like Darius, and even though she didn't know this girl, she knew that Toran, like Darius, would show no mercy. "Please listen to him," Tara mouthed. "This isn't worth getting hurt over. Get away from here."

The look on her face was now one of confusion as she tried to figure out why an enemy would care about her well-being. But only after moments of thought, the look in her eyes became hard. "Fine!" she shouted. "But you just wait until Darius finds out what you're doing to his girl."

"Eh?" Tara's brow shot up as Toran moved to strike her once again, but the blond was on her feet and gone.

"Stupid girl." He growled, turning his attention back to Tara. "So you want to see Marcus, do you?" He took her roughly by the arm, pulling her along a narrow hall that led to a spiraling staircase. "Keep up," he ordered as he dragged her down the stairs.

Tara did her best to keep up, tripping several times as he pulled her along. He glared over his shoulder at her and she would scowl in return. "What do you expect!" she protested. "It's not like I'm in the greatest shape to be pulled around in."

"Maybe you should learn to listen to your betters." He retorted as the two reached a vast room.

"If there was anyone here better than me, I might." She hissed. But as she looked around the room she did fall silent. She stared in horror at the cages scattered through the room and the chains dangling from the walls. There were bloodstained tables and machines she could only guess the natures of. "What is all this?"

Toran just chuckled, ignoring her as he led her to a cage that was kept away from the others. "Consider yourself lucky," he said in a gruff tone as he shoved her forward.

She landed on the floor with a yelp, pulling her legs tightly to her as she peered forward. She saw the shadowed figure in front of her and squinted her eyes trying to see better. "Marcus?"

Only when she spoke his name did he move. He lifted his head, staring at the woman before him. "Who are you?" he asked.

With his movements, Tara could easily see the dark scars that littered his exposed flesh, but before she could answer, she was spoken for. "Oh, you mean, you don't know?" Toran asked. "Marcus, this is your replacement, Tara." He then looked down at the woman on the floor. "This is your predecessor, not that he was any good. Neither of you are actually."

But Tara refused to listen to any of the garbage spewed from his mouth. "We'll get out of here." She promised, reaching out a hand to him.

But she was stopped cold as her breath was taken from her with a single swift kick to her ribs. "Can't have you doing that," Toran interrupted as he pulled her back by her hair. "You two have visited enough anyway," he added as he began to pull her back toward the stairs.

"Let go!" she shouted, clawing at his hand as she kicked her feet across the floor. Her eyes were wild as she stared back to the cage. "We will escape!" she yelled. "Please be strong!"

Marcus watched as the two disappeared before leaning against the back of the cage. "Something in her eyes makes you want to believe in the impossible," he mumbled. But he had been there for so long, and his body was beginning to show the desired signs of fatigue that Darius and Vonspar were hoping for. "She's nothing more than a child." He added as his body slumped further. "Elder Fisonma always did say to have something to hope for though. Maybe now is the time to have such hope."

Toran had just reached the hall that would lead to Tara's room, but as he drew near, he could feel the chill of a dark presence. "Darius." He stammered, seeing the dark glow in his eyes. He then looked past the Dark Angel to the blond who was hiding behind him. "You . . ." he growled.

But she would not be afraid. "See?" she asked, looking up at Darius. "I wasn't wrong. He had her."

"Thank you for being quick to inform me," Darius said as he gently rested his hand upon the top of the girls head. He then looked over his shoulder. "Belzak."

He stepped forward, eyeing Tara coldly before returning his attention to Darius. "Yes?"

"Take her with you. I want her protected from any form of retaliation from this insect."

"Of course," he replied with a shallow bow of his head. He then placed his hand upon her shoulder, sweeping his free arm to the side to escort her away.

Darius then turned his attention to the two before him. "Dante."

"Yes, Darius," came the reply of a hooded figure as he stepped forward.

"Bring her here." Wordlessly, Dante obeyed, pulling her from Toran's grasp before returning to the small group with their captive. "Thank you," he replied quickly, gripping her wrist tightly. "Now then . . ." His eyes focused entirely upon Toran. "Why did you have her?" he demanded.

"She escaped!" Toran argued.

"I'm not impressed," Darius began. "Why didn't you just take her back! Where did you take her!"

"She was asking about Marcus," he began.

"You took her to see Marcus!" He shifted his gaze to the vampire trio beside him. "Take him and show him how we deal with traitors." He ordered. "I'll deal with our guest."

"Right away." The three answered in unison. Darkness soon consumed Toran, blinding him and making escape impossible as they took him away.

He stared down at Tara once they were alone. "So you met Marcus, I see." But she was silent, refusing to even look at him. But he just smiled as he escorted her into her room. "Would you rather be down there?" he asked. "I can arrange it for you." He chuckled. But again, he would receive nothing but silence in response. His smile faded, and his fist connected to the back of her head. "You'll learn your place soon enough." He remarked as he left for his room.

CHAPTER

30

Two Lives for One

Tara could only assume that days had passed since she'd seen
Marcus. Elation filled her with a renewed sense of hope that
they would escape the hell they presently found themselves in. "If I
only had access to my powers," she whispered as she slid into a deep
meditation.

Like every other meditation done since that moment, she found
the green covering which blocked her third eye chakra point. She
had also discovered the tether that led to the same kind of covering
that kept her powers from her. But every time she tried to pry the
coverings away, she was met with lock after lock that kept her at bay.
As much as she tried, she could not figure out the words that would
allow her to progress and eventually escape.

"I told you not to leave your room!"

The sound of Oni's voice scolding her broke her meditation,
and she allowed herself to come from her trace like state. "I haven't
seen you in a while," she remarked, ignoring the look she received.
She saw her holding a tray of food and arched a brow slightly. Usually

her food was already in her room once she'd woken up, so it was a bit of a surprise.

Oni scowled as she set the tray down before taking a seat upon the floor. "You really made them angry," she said in a hushed tone.

The look that crossed Tara's face was confused. "So?" she asked, wondering if she was supposed to care about this small bit of information.

Oni sighed in frustration. She hadn't come across someone quite so willful and it irritated her. "Darius and my Master are talking about killing the both of you," she said in a harsh whisper. "They have done worse to Toran. They have completely taken his will away from him."

Though the small notion of information intrigued her, her mind was still frozen on the fact that Vonspar and Darius were actually talking about killing not only her, but Marcus as well. "Why are you telling me this?" she asked at length.

Oni pushed to her feet and stared at her for a moment. "So you can prepare," she said flatly. "Your actions affect more than just yourself," she added as she exited the room before she too felt the wrath of the two rulers of darkness.

Tara sat and poked at her food clearly displeased with the lecture she'd received. She was in no way responsible for what happened to Toran but she couldn't help but wonder if they would really kill Marcus because of her. "No . . .," she said after a while. "That's stupid. They wouldn't kill either of us if they thought they could use us to get into Nimost." She looked at the door, her eyes narrowing as she heard voices on the other side. "I just wish I could get out to make sure he's okay."

She hadn't touched her food at all. She'd just pushed it around on her plate when the door swung open. Startled, she dropped the fork onto the plate and scooted back when she saw the leering gazes of the guards that approached her.

"You've been summoned," one of them said as he yanked her up by her arm. Even with her skin showing the sickly yellow signs of her bruising on the mend, her muscles and bones were still in the beginning stages of their healing and the yelps of protest of her manhandling were proof. "Stop your whining." He growled. "They'll do worse to you than this."

Tara's eyes widened. Oni had spoken the truth, and she was about to meet her fate. She began to pull against the guard's grip on her wrist, but the second was directly behind her, a large spear tip pressed uncomfortably into the center of her back. "I wouldn't do that," he warned.

It wasn't long before they reached a large set of double doors. When they were pushed open, they revealed a grand hall, much like the throne rooms described in children's fairy tales. "Vonspar, Darius, we have brought her as per your orders."

Darius remained seated while Vonspar rose and approached them. "Darius tells me that you have met Marcus," he began, his eyes piercing into hers. She remained silent, staring at him in defiance. But he simply chuckled as he ran his fingers along her jaw, gripping it tightly as she tried to move from his grasp. He turned her head from side to side, examining the yellow hue to her skin before looking back to Darius. "I believe you have redefined pain my brother. Her internal injuries are severe I'm sure."

"She wouldn't listen." Darius said with a shrug of his shoulders.

"Indeed." Vonspar was quiet for a moment before he looked at another guard who was standing his post in the grand hall. "Please see to the final preparations we had discussed earlier and return to me when they are complete," he instructed.

"At once," the guard replied, taking his leave through a side hall.

"Now then," Vonspar began.

"What do you want!" she hissed.

"What do I want?" he asked, his grin becoming quite devious. "I have exactly what I want," he chuckled.

"We won't help you!" she shouted. "And when the others find us!"

But that's as far as her threat could go before Vonspar slapped her once more across the right side of her face. "That will be quite enough," he stated calmly. He looked back at Darius before returning to his seat. "She has no idea, does she?" he asked.

"It doesn't appear so," Darius replied.

Vonspar nodded with satisfaction, his fingers echoing a loud snap. In an instant, Oni was kneeling at his side, her head resting on his leg as he ran his fingers through her hair. "You are such a good girl, Oni."

Hearing those words made her chest swell with pride. "Thank you, Master."

"I actually expected you to tell her what is going to happen."

Oni looked up at him in wide-eyed disbelief. "I would never," she breathed. "Besides," she began, casting a cold gaze toward Tara, "she said herself, we aren't sisters."

Vonspar chuckled as he smoothed his hand against the side of her head. "Do not fret, my pet," he said softly. "You needn't waste your time anymore on such an inferior specimen." He then looked to his side at Darius to see if he might have crossed a line, not that he cared, but his reaction intrigued him.

Darius just sat there and smirked. To him, she was nothing more than an outlet for his anger, and soon they would see what possibilities she would hold for them. He rolled his head to the side and looked at Vonspar. "Shouldn't things be ready by now?" His energy was becoming restless once more and he again desired the satisfaction of taking his wrath out on his childhood friend.

"Actually, yes, they should." His gaze drifted down to his beloved treasure. "My dear pet," he began, stroking his fingers beneath her chin. "Please be a dear and find out what is taking so long."

"Right away, Master."

But as she rose to her feet, the guard returned. He approached, giving a deep bow. "Our apologies, Vonspar, but the preparations are now complete."

"It's about time," Darius grumbled.

"Now, now, brother." Vonspar chuckled. "Since the guard is back Oni, will you escort Darius? You know where to go. Please help him get ready."

"Yes, Master," Oni replied with a bow before following Darius from the room.

"Now then." Vonspar rose to his feet, approaching the three before him. "Do you know where to go?" he asked, casting a serious gaze toward the two guards.

"Yes, sir," came the reply from the guard with his spear poised at the center of Tara's back.

"Good." He chuckled, clearly enjoying himself as he placed the pad of his right thumb against the center of Tara's forehead. Once again his eyes began to glow an eerie shade of jade and Tara could instantly feel the pain of the invading energy. "Do take her there with haste," he said. "The bind holding her energy at bay will last only a few more minutes." And with that, he took his leave of them.

The guards of course, were less than thrilled about the news they had received and ushered her through the halls quickly. Almost nothing was said as they maneuvered through the maze, but little by little Tara could feel the intense pressure against her forehead. She knew that it was her energy fighting for its own freedom against the invading energy and the fight made her quite uncomfortable. "Finally." one of the guards remarked as they reached their destination. "Shove her through," he told the other as he opened the door.

"You don't have to tell me again," came the reply as he shoved Tara forcefully through the open door.

"Hey!" she cried out as she stumbled, tripped, and fell onto the ground. Pushing to her feet she looked around, the pit of her stomach churning when she saw where she was. As if on cue, throngs of people booed, loud enough that she almost had to cover her ears to drown the sound from her mind. She had found herself in yet another stadium and a horrific thought crossed her mind. "What if she was right?" she whispered, the color draining from her face. "But instead of killing us outright—" She couldn't even finish her sentence as a wave of nausea hit her. She stared ahead blankly as the thoughts of her having to fight Marcus to the death began to flood her mind.

But as these thoughts began to send her into a near panic, the cheers she heard drew her from the edge. Looking up, she could clearly see Vonspar, but Darius was not with him. He raised his hands for quiet and as soon as things had settled, he thrust an accusatory finger toward her. "This woman!" he began. "She is to be tried for crimes against our homeland!" This of course led to roars of demands calling for her immediate death, but Vonspar once more quieted down the masses before he continued. "I understand and feel your anger and frustrations!" he continued. "With her powers we will be able to launch an attack against the White City!" Again cheers erupted throughout the stands, and still his finger remained aimed at her.

"However!" The beginning of a new statement seemed to hold everyone as an oppressive hush fell over the area. "I have decided to give this to you in entertainment. A fight!"

Tara couldn't help but notice their want for violence. "They're nothing like the people in Nimost," she whispered as she looked at all the people, feeling the palpation of their energy as they again called for her death. The last of her energy was breaking through the binds that held it and she could feel the welcomed chill as it once again seeped through her body.

But relief was short lived as the doors on the other side of the stadium were flung open. Demands for death were quickly replaced by ground trembling cheers as Darius emerged into the ring. Ebony wings flared out as the very essence of light was crushed as it neared the polished onyx armor. "You will fight me," he told her. "You have no choice in the matter."

Tara stood with pride. "I will not."

"You will either fight me or die."

"You can try," came the cool reply. "I'm not a puppet that dances on your strings. I don't dance on anyone's strings. I am my own person. I am a Guardian of Nimost! And I will make my own choices as to what I do or do not do!"

"Coward!" Tara heard the voice from the stands and turned her head just as a large object was thrown in her direction.

She swept her arm out, encasing the object in ice before allowing it to shatter into a fine mist that glittered around her as it fell. "I may be a great many things, but a coward is not one of them," she growled as her attention once again turned to Darius.

"Then you will fight me," he stated simply. And to prove his point fully, he swept his arm out, unleashing a wave of dark energy.

Tara threw her arms out, erecting a dome of ice around her, watching as energies collided. "Why does everything have to be about fighting?" she asked, watching as the dome slowly began to crack under the pressure of his anger.

"Ever since we were young," he began, diluted and twisted memories fueling his growing hatred. "You always had to show just how much better you were, how much quicker you were, that you were always the best."

"I never said that!" she protested.

"Quiet!" he demanded. His energy responded, cracking against the barrier until it finally broke through and sent her flying back against the wall. "You and her," he growled as he walked toward her.

"Yukino showed you nothing but unconditional love!" Tara protested as she scrambled to her feet.

"Lies!" he shouted, sweeping his arm out once again as another wave of darkness was released.

"They poisoned your memories!" she shouted, just barely able to get out of the way as the energy crashed into the wall. This time, however, it formed into a large mass before sinking onto the ground and giving chase.

"Where is the greatness that the grand Guardians of Nimost are known for!" he demanded. "Where is your power, your gift from the Elementals!"

"We don't fight because we want to!" she shouted, building yet another barrier around her as the energy crested up to crash down upon her. "We fight to protect those who chose peace over this!" Her convictions gave strength to her energies and the shield began to freeze the darkness now surrounding her. With a push of her hands, the shield exploded outward allowing her to watch the fragments of darkness fall to the ground around her. "You used to believe the same." She then thrust her own finger at Vonspar. "He's the one who changed you, not me."

"Insolent wretch!" Darius snarled. Vonspar was on his feet, his gaze hard as stone as he watched Darius rush toward her.

Tara froze the ground, relieved at the desired effect as she watched Darius fall and slide across the ground. "Don't you see what happens when your mind is clouded by hate?" she asked, trying so desperately to get through to the person she knew before.

At this point people had begun to murmur, voicing great disapproval at the lack of fighting. This in turn made Vonspar increasingly angry. "If she won't fight willingly," he muttered bitterly, "then I will force her hand." Still standing after Tara's previous accusation against him, he raised his hands, demanding silence. "If she will not fight to prove she deserves the powers she holds, then we shall give her incentive to do so!" Tara looked up as the crowds began to cheer. "Open the far gate!" he demanded.

Tara looked to the far end of the arena as the doors were opened. She had to squint as a cage was brought onto the grounds, but as soon as she recognized the figure within the confines of the bars, her face went pale. Darius laughed as he pushed himself to his feet. Using a sweep of his arm he shattered the ice covered ground before brushing himself off. "Have you realized yet?" he asked.

"Arcainous . . .," she breathed, racing to the far end of the arena, but all she could hear was the cruel laughter around her.

Arcainous lifted his head slowly, the torture evident in his features. "They told me you were dead," he murmured as she reached the cage.

"Now let me make this perfectly clear to you." Vonspar snapped. "You give us what we want, and we let them go free."

"A two for one deal," Darius added as he took several steps toward her.

"What are they talking about?" Arcainous asked.

"They have Marcus."

"What is your answer!" Vonspar demanded. "Surrender to me and the two of them will be released. Defy me and you will be made to fight for their lives as well as your own."

"Marcus is alive?" he asked, staring up at the face of the woman he adored.

"Yes," she whispered, ushering him away from the bars as she took hold of them. Her eyes glowed with the frosty hue of her element as she repeated what she had done to Raiden's sword during the tournament.

"Answer him!" came the enraged voce from behind her as Darius released wave after wave of electrically charged energy.

"Break the bars when the energies collide," she instructed. Her back was pressed to the cage as she brought up a barrier strong enough to withstand the first two waves of energy, but the electric current coursing through Darius's attacks shattered her barrier with more ease than expected. Her jaw clenched in pain with the convulsions of her entire muscular system as the energy reached her and sent her through the bars she'd just frozen.

Dazed, she stared skyward, her body still twitching as the current ran its course. "Tara!" But she just sat up and pulled free from Arcainous's grasp, sliding back to the ground.

"You leave them out of this!" she growled. Her fingers curled tightly, causing tendrils of energy to erupt from the ground, wrapping themselves around Darius's arms and legs. "You should have released them when you had the chance!" she snarled. She rushed forward for a full out attack but as she reached him, the energy that had bled from his armor caused the tendrils to die and a hand to hand assault began.

"It's good to see you come alive with the false sense that you can defend them." Darius chucked.

She weaved around his attacks with great ease, but her physical attacks did little against the armor he was wearing. *I have to break through his armor*, she thought, crossing her arms in front of her as he brought a newly manifested weapon down toward her heard. She winced with the connection, feeling the bones in her wrists begin to bruise almost instantly but a move from her training in the martial arts came to mind and her hands turned, gripping his wrist. She allowed a portion of her energy to bleed into his armor as she spun around, thrusting her hip into his and throwing him over her shoulder. "With any luck," she whispered as she brought spikes of ice from the ground, watching as they pierced into his armor. "This·didn't need to happen!" she yelled, watching as his armor gave way to the invasion.

Declaring this fight over, she walked over to where Arcainous still lay. "Tara . . ." he mumbled, resting his palm against her cheek. "I was afraid you were lost to us."

"It's all right," she assured. "We're all going home." She then looked up at Vonspar. "I believe I have bested your champion. Now, we will be taking our leave of this pit and I *will* be taking Marcus with me!"

"Think again," came a chilling voice from behind her.

In an instant Tara felt her head being pulled back by her hair as Darius's arm secured itself firmly against her throat in the same fluid motion. "How?" she squeaked out, trying so desperately to alleviate the pressure that was constricting her airway.

"Stay right there, dog," Darius sneered, leveling his sword at the Watcher. "You really had no chance against me," he whispered, his lips brushing against her ear. "Did you honestly think you could defeat darkness?" he asked as he pushed her forward. He kept a firm hold of her hair though and as she reached the length of his grasp he yanked her back.

As she fell back she felt it. A pinch that became a slow steady burn, her pain soon equaling the horror clearly splayed across Arcainous's face. Suddenly finding it increasingly difficult to breathe she looked down, her face becoming ghostly pale as she saw the tip of a blood stained sword glistening from the right side of her chest. She lifted her head, her gaze transfixed. "Arcainous?"

The cruelty of their laughter echoed far too loud as Darius pulled her closer to his chest, impaling her further onto the blade. "I told you there was no hope for you to ever be my equal." And with that, he shoved her away from him, watching as she fell into Arcainous's arms. But as her body left the blade, the only thing sustaining any kind of life, blood began to rush like a torrent into her lung, around it, and out both puncture holes.

There were no words that could be spoken. Any attempt of speech was met with the sputter of blood spraying in a mist from her lips as it continued invading places it had no place calling home. All she could do was stare into his eyes as regrets came flooding to the surface. Words she had never spoken, actions she wished she could have taken. "Don't," he whispered, his voice broken as he brushed his hand across her cheek. He rocked her gently, his mumbled voice continuing to fall to her ears until her injuries finally claimed her and the once vibrant spark of life died. Her body went limp as that final breath gurgled from her lips and Arcainous's world began to implode as he stared down the man responsible.

CHAPTER

31

The Birth of an Angel

Glassy eyes stared up, fixed in the gaze of death. The look her final moment held, however, was not one of malice, or even anger, but one of pity, sorrow, and regret. Arcainous held her lifeless form close to his chest, smoothing his palm over the side of her head as if the small symbol of affection would bring her back to the world of the living. "How can you have such a disregard for life!" he growled. "The two of you were destined for great things, and you just threw that away!"

"I have obtained my greatness," Darius replied calmly. He stared down at the blood dripping from his blade with a deranged sort of fondness as he traced his fingers through the thickening substance. "She was weak, and greatness was not meant to be hers." Pulling his gaze from what he was doing, he leveled his blade toward the Watcher. "I'm feeling merciful." This of course, elicited a wave of murmurings from the stands. "Hear me out, fair people!" he declared, his gaze moving through the stands. "We have the former and current Guardians of Ice! We can extract her powers and force them into our captive! What better way to deliver despair and hopelessness than to send this dog back to the White City with his tail between his legs to tell of their Guardian's demise!"

"I'll do no such thing," Arcainous declared.

"Won't it seem odd then? Returning without her?" Darius asked, his fingers caressing the blade once more.

* * *

As the argument continued, Tara found herself in a cold darkness. She knew she wasn't in the depths of her subconscious, but where she was, she had no idea. "If this is death," she began at length, "then I'm really disappointed." She had wished so much to be back with her mother, thinking death would offer her such an opportunity. "Perhaps there really is nothing after death." But that did little to explain where she was.

"You are in limbo."

Tara looked around. The voice was everywhere, but the darkness around her reminded her of the darkness of Darius's armor. The thought made her cringe and she ran her hands along her arms to warm them. "Who's there!"

"Do not fear my child." came a soothing voice from the darkness. Slowly, a warm light began to aluminate the area, surrounding Tara in the most welcoming embrace.

Startled, Tara looked down at her feet, then to her arms. "What is this?" she asked before movement caught her eye. Squinting against the light she leaned her head forward. "Who are you?"

"I am the Elemental of Light," she replied softly. "I have watched you for so long. You have a strong heart and a caring spirit."

"Watching me?" It was obvious that she was more than just a little confused.

"Your desire to defend and protect life is what caught my attention. Luna and Myst, even your defiance to fight Darius. Your heart understands the need to live," she admitted.

"Only because I've seen life taken away when it shouldn't have been." Tara replied almost bitterly.

"Your mother." There was a sorrow creeping into her features at the mention of Senia's passing. The subject seemed so raw to her even after so much time passing.

"I want to be with her again," she said suddenly. "I'm dead right? That means I can go and be with her. So why are you keeping me here?"

The pain manifested itself in her voice now as she begged to be with her mother. "Your time to rest has not yet come child. I have stopped your passing over to offer you a gift."

Entangled in the desire to be with her mother, Tara's mind became clouded. "I don't need another gift. I couldn't even use the ones I had to save Marcus and Arcainous!"

"I didn't raise you to think so negatively."

The injection of a third voice drew Tara's attention and she once again squinted against the light. The Elemental looked back over her shoulder with a welcoming smile. "I had planned on saving this for after you had heard my offer out and made your decision, but perhaps this will help smooth things over."

But it didn't matter. Tara was already in the warmth of the embrace. "Mom . . .," she murmured softly, burying her head into Senia's chest.

Senia ran her fingers lovingly over the back of Tara's head. "Please listen to her, my dear. You are needed much more than you realize."

Tara shifted her gaze to look at the woman. Once the Elemental was sure she had her attention, she continued. "What I offer you is the chance to regain your life. I want you to rise from the ashes of death as my Champion."

As Tara stepped away from her mother, an image was shown to her of Arcainous defending her lifeless body. Senia took Tara gently by her shoulders as she stared in horror at what was transpiring. "You have always been so strong, but there are people who still need you to be strong for them."

Seeing her mother so vibrant and full of life gave Tara an extreme measure of comfort and peace. "I wanted to be with you so much," she began. "I hated that I couldn't make you better."

"There is nothing that could have changed what happened," Senia assured.

"The choice is yours as to which path you take," the Elemental replied.

Tara turned to face her. It was obvious that her energies had once again calmed. "I want to protect the people I treasure."

Relief appeared upon the face of the Elemental. "Then take my hand," she began. "Accept my gift and become the Angel of Light."

Tara stepped back from her mother and looked between her and the outstretched hand. "I always knew you were destined for great things, and I know it's too late, but I'm sorry I never believed you about this place. When you don't see something, it is often hard to believe it is there."

The smile gracing Tara's features was broad and her heart swelled with both pride and love. "I love you so much, Mom."

"I love you too," Senia replied softly. Cupping her hand around Tara's cheek, she kissed her forehead then stepped back. "Always let love guide you."

Tara nodded then turned to the glowing Elemental. Taking a deep breath, she placed her hand into hers, inhaling sharply at the surge of energy that raced through her body.

* * *

Arcainous lay on the ground, blood gushing from several fresh wounds sustained from his attempts to leave with Tara's body. "I told you, Watcher! There's no—" But his statement was cut short as a faint aura began surrounding Tara's fallen form.

Moving his head to the side, Arcainous was able to see what had startled Darius. Awe filled him as he watched the woman he cared for began to show renewed signs of life. A warm pallor began to return to her features as the wounds made by Darius's sword began to mend themselves. In time her chest rose allowing air to flow through her lungs. Movement, however, was prolonged as her spirit was returned to her physical body. As the joining completed, she was entombed in a blinding white sphere. "Tara?"

Her voice was that of a warm breeze, soothing to those who would accept it and hot as hell's fire to those who denied her. "Thank you." Such simple words that moved him to the brink of tears.

Everyone watched as the sphere began to condense itself around Tara, splitting in half to form a brilliant pair of wings. Eight glowing orbs nestled themselves in the crook of a multipointed star, each resembling a different element. "How are you alive!" Vonspar and Darius exchanged glances. "Kill her!"

But as Darius rushed toward her, she threw her arm out in an arc, sending him flying back with nothing more than a pulse of energy. Pulling Arcainous to his feet, she held him close as her attention turned once more to Vonspar. "We will be leaving, and we will be taking Marcus with us." And with another flicker of energy the two disappeared.

"I want every available guard down to the holding cells! I want her dead!" Vonspar was furious as he raced down the halls with guards all around him.

When Tara and Arcainous appeared, there were only a handful of guards who had been ordered to watch him while the whole fight was taking place. "You can't be in here!" one of them said as they all approached her.

"I believe I can," she replied calmly. Sweeping her arm out in yet another arc, she sent the guards flying back into the walls before approaching Marcus's cage. "We're getting out of here," she assured. It was easy to break the door and all that was left was for him to take her outstretched hand.

"I can't walk," he told her. "All I would do is hinder your escape."

"No one said anything about walking." With determination set in her features, she leaned in and grabbed hold of his hand. Instantly she regretted it, feeling the rush of the darkness that had been forced into Marcus suddenly being absorbed into her own body.

Arcainous saw the shock on her face and shook her shoulders. "Tara?"

Instantly a war began as her newly acquired energy tried desperately to destroy the darkness that was now invading her. She saw the endless torture, the forced infusions. "We have to go." Her voice held a tinge of panic to it as she pulled Marcus from the cage. With the two on either side of her, she closed her eyes wishing so desperately to be back in Nimost and as Vonspar reached the room they were in, the three disappeared only to appear in the center of Nimost.

Everything was soon nothing more than a flurry of motion. It barely registered to her that both Marcus and Arcainous were taken from her, each being rushed to the infirmary for a complete work up. Such commotion drew the attention of Fisonma and the Elder Council. "Thank the Gods you've returned!" she exclaimed with relief as she rushed forward to greet her.

But Tara simply moved back, shaking her head. "Stay back. Something's not right with me."

Stopping, Fisonma studied her closely and gasped, covering her mouth instantly. "By all that is holy," she breathed, finally seeing the engraved image upon the chest plate of the armor she now wore. "The Elemental of Light has awakened."

"Something is not right Elder." one of the council members murmured.

* * *

Vonspar paced the width of the great hall in a blinded rage. "She's gone!" he howled. "And not only that, but the Watcher and the prisoner are gone as well!" No excuse was good enough to quell the growing anger and those who tried found themselves unable to move after receiving his wrath.

Darius sat in quiet contemplation, his eyes closed and his ears blocking most of what his brother was spouting off about. Only when he was completely sure of his own silent findings did he dare speak. "Brother." His voice was calm and even, waiting patiently for Vonspar to acknowledge him, but it soon became apparent that he was lost to his own ranting. "Brother!" This time his voice was louder, more commanding, and in that single instant the room fell deathly quiet.

Vonspar turned slowly. The look clearly splayed across his face was one of certain death. "What." His jaw was clenched and his arms were rigidly at his sides.

"There is still a way to make her ours."

The ease with which he spoke infuriated Vonspar and the ever changing expressions crossing his face did little to hide it. "And just how do you know this?" he demanded.

"I command the darkness," he began calmly. Proving his point, dark shadows seeped around him in the form of mist. With idle movements of his fingers the mist took shape, taking forms he wished for it to before retreating back to the confines of his armor. "I hear it," he continued. "It speaks to me and tells me what I desire to know."

"And just what does it have to say?" Vonspar asked.

"It seems that our newly awakened angel somehow drew in all of the energy we had forced into our captive. Her soul is currently doing battle to contain and destroy it."

Vonspar stopped his pacing and stared intently at Darius. It was obvious that his mind had switched gears and was now thinking of ways to use this newfound information to their advantage. "Can you control it from so far away?"

"I can control all darkness throughout the Realm." Darius assured.

His back to the others, he snapped his fingers sharply. "Belzak!"

The former Watch shifted his gaze. "Yes?"

"Are you able to sustain a link long enough for Darius to travel to her subconscious?"

"If her conscious mind is kept at bay. Any encounter we've had with her was best achieved during sleep or states of unconsciousness."

"What are you planning?" Darius asked as he leaned forward to better study his brother.

"A full on assault." Vonspar stated simply. "Since you can control the energy within her, I want you to make it volatile enough that we are able to establish a link into her subconscious. Once you're there, you will destroy her, once, and for all."

Belzak chuckled as he rose to his feet. "She's with the Elders of Nimost," he informed. Sharing her sight when it suited him was a useful gift. But his gaze turned serious as he stared at Darius. "If you can control the shadows, no matter where they are, how come the Guardian we kidnapped didn't fall to our power?"

Vonspar looked back, then to his brother once more. "I have to admit, I wonder the same."

Darius gave a simple shrug of his shoulders. "I really wasn't that motivated to destroy him," he admitted. "I wanted him to willingly accept the energy. It makes the transition smoother and the power greater." His gaze then focused completely upon Vonspar. "Wouldn't you agree Brother?"

But he just glared, his gaze ever darkening. "Just get it done!" he ordered.

* * *

Tara shook with the confrontation raging within her. Everyone tried so desperately to approach her only to watch her keep her distance. "What is going on, Tara?"

Tara could only look at Fisonma, her arms clutched around herself, holding whatever was within her at bay. "It's inside of me." Her voice quivered, echoing the terror etched into her features.

"What's in you?" Fisonma asked.

"The energy they forced into Marcus." With this admitted, she began the tale of what had happened when she took his hand and the images she'd seen as the energy transferred to the core of her being.

"There must be a way to expel this energy," one of the Council members said, thinking back to the many tombs that were housed within the great libraries of the White Tower. But with that statement made, the energy contained within her body seemed to react, attacking random nerves and muscles. A chain reaction began that forced her body into a state of rigidity so severe that her conscious mind slipped away once more to find an escape from the searing agony.

* * *

When her eyes opened again she knew exactly where she was. The depths of her subconscious mind were becoming all too familiar to her, but as she became more aware, she could hear what sounded like distant rolls of thunder as the two energies warred around her. "I know I can beat this." Her voice was soft but determined, but even as she continued to assure herself, she came to the realization that she had never felt something so cold, so, evil, and her confidence shifted slightly.

"Do you feel that?"

Her head jerked from side to side, her ears listening, shifting as she tried in vain to locate the origin of the voice. Darkness distorted it, warping it to nothing more than a taunting echo but she would not be swayed. "Who's there!" she demanded. Even in such a diminished state, she would prove that she was a force to be reckoned with.

A chuckle echoed through the darkness. Centered at first, but moving with great ease as it detected her focus. It soon began to surround her, closing in to the point of suffocation before moving to the side of her and taking on a more solidified manor. The energy soon gave birth to a sickly light which cast a haunting glow through the immediate area, revealing the face of her visitor. "Such a fool you were, thinking you could take on the darkness."

"Darius . . ."

"You sound surprised to see me," he stated simply as he approached her. His attention soon turned to the battle going on around them, his arm sweeping out, motioning to it as if it were a living entity. "Did you really think you could defeat us?" he asked, casting his gaze down to her. "You are truly foolish to believe that you can."

Tara pushed to her feet, listening to the clash of energies around her. "Why are you doing this?"

The gaze in which he looked down upon her with feigned contemplation while disgust crawled its way through his muscles giving his face a truly cruel look. "Why does anyone do anything?" he asked, turning fully to face her. "Why do you bow down before the Light?"

"I don't bow down to anything," she corrected with a snap, ducking to avoid his hand as he lashed out to strike her.

"One of these days you will learn your place," he growled. With a snap of his fingers he watched as some of the energy began to solidify, forming tendrils that quickly bound themselves around her ankles, wrists, and neck. His gaze was cold and emotionless as she was subdued, and only then did he choose to continue. "You ask why I do this as if it was a choice," he began. "So on your level, I suppose I do this for the same reasons others would if they were in this situation."

Tara coughed in disgust. "You're so full of yourself," she spat, only to feel the sting of a firm slap.

He ignored her, however, and continued on with his preaching. "I do this for power, revenge . . ."

Power? The Darius she knew had no desire for power, but this change that he had undergone had warped any sense he might have had. She squinted as she studied him closely, concerned with his desires for revenge. "Revenge?" she asked cautiously. "Revenge for what exactly?"

Being bound made access to her painfully easy and within the quickest instant he was upon her, attacking without a second thought. The force and speed of his blow knocked her to the ground and the tendrils binding her were more than yielding as they shrank, keeping her under his whim. The gaze consuming his eyes was one of pure hatred as he stood over her. "Do not act so innocent that you don't know why I've done this," he snarled.

In this delusional state Tara knew there would be no reasoning with him. But this didn't mean that she was going to sit there and accept the treatment he was giving her. Her gaze was hard as she stared him down. "Do not sit there and blame me for the choices you made with your life!" she snapped. Her chest swelled with the heat of her energy, her finger seeking out the bodies of the tendrils to burn them away. "Where you are is a result of your own actions, and I will not be at fault for that!" True or not, her statement did derive a reaction from him and she barely had enough time to erect a barrier to deflect his attack.

"You and my mother," he seethed, anger quickly consuming him. "All of your secrets, all of your lies." He began laughing, his mind twisting with ideas of torture, remembering times from their past. He leaned down and stared at her, the cruel smirk still crossing his lips. "I can't believe you thought I could love you." He then stood back up, chuckling at his dig into her heart. "Just look at you!"

"You wouldn't know love if it slapped you in the face and said hi," she snipped.

He stared at her with an upturned brow. "Oh really."

"You're just mad that I moved past you and don't obsess over you like you think I do," she hissed.

His muscles twitched, and the tendril around her neck reacted, tightening around it. However, he was hell bent on staying in control and his composure regained itself. Struggling to breathe, their gazes locked in a fiery embrace, but she made no attempt to free herself, even as she gripped the body of one of the tendrils firmly. "I see the anger brewing within you." His voice was almost seductive as he spoke, breaking the gaze the two shared. "Take hold of it and fight me," he dared.

"I'll never bring myself down to your level with needless fighting!" she spat in open defiance.

He stared at her, his expression becoming hard as untouched stone. "Then here, is where you shall die!" And with that simple statement, the air around them came alive with an electrical charge strong enough to elicit a scream of agony that no one would ever hear.

* * *

In the conscious realm, many stood watch over Tara's comatose form. Feeling much better, Arcainous paced while physicians looked her over. "Arcainous, sit down." Yukino watched him from her seat at Tara's side, stroking the back of her hand gently.

"What was she thinking?" he murmured. "She should have known better than to take that energy in."

"From what we were told when talking to Marcus, it happened the instant she touched his hand." one of the doctors replied.

"You see?" Yukino asked. "It wasn't intentional, but if she's going to overcome this, we have to believe that she will."

As they continued to talk, however, a series of small tremors began to race through her nerves. They grew steadily stronger until a single pulse of energy threw everyone away from her. "Tara!" Arcainous was to her side in an instant as her body once again went limp into the mattress. Gripping her shoulders, he began shaking her vigorously. "Tara! Wake up!"

* * *

Darius laughed at the sight of her limp form supported by nothing more than the tendrils that bound her. Her head moved sluggishly as her chest tightened with a series of coughs. When her vision was once again focused, she stared back up at him. "Why don't you just kill me since you claim it would be so easy for you to do."

"Now what fun would that be?" he asked as another current raced through her nervous system. Around them the energy flickered and crackled with the charged atmosphere creating a volatile environment.

"I . . . I still won't fight you." Her forehead creased as she scowled. "What will it prove?"

"Must things always have to have a point?" he huffed with an exasperated sigh. But he received no reply and the scowl once again returned to his features. "You're so weak," he finally declared in irritation.

"You're the weak one," she shot back. He moved to strike her once more but she was only able to partially manifest a barrier to keep him from reaching her.

He grabbed her throat, listening with delight to the chokes for air as he squeezed tighter and tighter. He felt the chill of the energy from the tendril that had secured her neck as it snaked along his arm, finally sinking into the depths of his armor. "I'm weak?" he asked, turning her head slowly from side to side, examining the remnants of injuries she had suffered at his hands. "All I have to do is squeeze, and everyone will be planning your funeral."

"Then do it, you coward!" she hissed.

"Vonspar would like that," he began at length. "But I don't believe I'm quite done with you yet." Moving his fingers, he pressed down on precise points through her neck, almost paralyzing it, forcing her to keep his gaze.

"Don't act like you're doing me a service," she snapped, only to feel the sting of his hand across her face once again.

"Oh, I'm not doing you a service, believe me." He chuckled. "As I stated before, you are weak, and I want your death to come in glorious battle."

"Barbarian!" she yelled, only to feel her head being yanked back as the fingers of his free hand tangled itself into her hair.

"I will show you pain," he continued, as if she had never spoken. "I will show you torture, and when I am done I will make you wish for death." Using great caution to control her head, he leaned down to whisper into her ear. "I will take great pleasure in killing those close to you."

"You leave them alone!" she growled.

He laughed as he threw her to the ground. "Such a noble ideal, thinking you can defend them," he challenged as he rose to his feet. "You needn't worry though. I won't kill them just yet. I want you to become stronger. I want you to think that you actually stand a chance at defending them." Holding his hand out, he began to draw the darkness back to his armor, a sign of good will in his mind. "Do not disappoint me," he ordered, giving her a final shock before he departed from her mind to plan his attacks on those who meant the most to her.

CHAPTER

32

Solstice

It was hours before her eyes finally opened and she was once again part of the waking world. This of course was met with the elation of Luna and Myst, who began eagerly licking her face. "Yes," Tara mumbled. "I missed you guys too." She scratched the tops of their heads before sitting up, groaning as she felt her head swim with a wave of nausea.

"Don't rush things." Yukino was always so sweet, and worried greatly about her. But it was that sweet nature that made her heart sink. The horrible things that Darius had said about her still rang clear through her ears.

"I'll be fine," she answered quietly, allowing her gaze to drop to the blankets covering her. Darius's threats and desires continued to haunt her, and as Arcainous touched her arm she drew away quickly.

The look that crossed his face was one of confusion and concern. "Perhaps we should give her some time."

Everyone looked to see Fisonma standing at the far side of the room, her hand sweeping toward the door to usher them away and allow her to rest. As Fisonma herself was preparing to exit, Tara lifted her head quickly. "Elder?"

She stopped, surprised at having been addressed so formally. "Yes?" As her gaze fixed upon the young Angel she could see the terror carved into her troubled eyes. She moved quickly to sit upon the edge of the bed, resting her hands upon the backs of her arms. "Child, what is wrong?"

With her rebirth, it was impossible for her to show Fisonma her wounds, the evidence of torture, and what had happened during the time of her capture. "Marcus," she began.

"Marcus is fine. The scars of his ordeal will be permanent, but we owe you a debt of gratitude for returning him. Most had accepted the fact that he was dead."

While the news relieved her, she still remained distant. "Darius attacked me."

"We know. The release of energy sent the physicians and Yukino flying from the side of your bed."

The mention of her name made Tara's entire posture drop. "She's going to be so devastated."

"About?"

But she couldn't even bring herself to look up as she elaborated on her ordeal. Her body shook as she once again relived every horrific memory, told every second of the hellish torture she had endured that led to her death and ultimate transformation. "After that, we retrieved Marcus and wound up here," she said softly. "The next thing I knew, I woke up in darkness watching my energy fight against the energy I took in from Marcus."

"Is that where Darius found you?"

"Yes." She went about telling her about the confrontation, the attacks, and the dire warning that he had issued to her. For a moment she was quiet, reluctantly lifting her head before she chose to continue. "I have to become stronger. I have to protect everyone. But he will be watching me and he'll know when I'm at my peak. That's when he'll strike out at us."

"Tara, you do know that all of Nimost will fight alongside you. There's no need to take this on by yourself."

"But that's just it," she began. "I don't want to fight. I didn't want to fight him when we'd been captured, but I had to protect Arcainous and Marcus. There has to be a better solution."

"Your heart desires peace and preservation. I'm not surprised you were chosen as the embodiment of Light. However, it seems that Darius is very set in his ideals. We might not have a choice but to fight. You have to be prepared for that." She then rose to her feet and stared down at her. "Do not lose your desire for more peaceful solutions. They will make you a great leader someday." And with that, she took her leave.

* * *

It had been days since her talk with Fisonma. Tara sat on the balcony of her room staring out into the late afternoon sun. The weather was warm and the scent of flowers hung gently in the air. "Tara! Where are you!"

Leaning forward, she looked behind her as Luna and Myst disappeared into her room, yipping happily as they were greeted with treats. "I'm out here, Wella," she called back as she rose to her feet.

"Girl do you know how worried you had us!"

Tara's shoulders dropped as she sighed. Elexis quickly clamped her hand over Wella's mouth. "What she means to say, is that we're all glad you're safe and back in Nimost."

"We also owe you a debt of gratitude for returning Marcus to us." Anon began.

"Everyone had feared the worst," Keshou added with a hint of a smile.

Tara studied the usually quiet Plasma Guardian with interest, but before she could probe, Marcus stepped forward. "I owe you my life," he told her. "I don't know how much longer I could have held out before caving to their demands."

Tara looked up at him and tilted her head. "We're family. I would have done it for anyone here."

"And that is why you are who you are," Oron said with a genuine smile.

"We are complete," Nao commented. "We are united in both spirit and cause. We will be unstoppable against the Shadows."

Tara, however, didn't share their enthusiasm. She scrunched her brow at the group and fell silent. If only they knew even the smallest taste of their true power. Would they be so confident then? "Well, we won't beat anything if we stand here." Ashton's voice broke the destructive train of thoughts she'd begun having and she trained her gaze upon him. "Raiden will make things worse on us if we're late."

That night, as Tara was preparing for bed, her room was illuminated by a warm glow. Luna and Myst pressed against her as she turned, curious of their new visitor. "You have proven yourself quite strong in the short time you have been awake."

Confused, Tara squinted. "I didn't expect to see you again," she admitted.

A soft laugh fell like a warm breeze. "The powers of Light have long been lost to this world. Because of this, I will oversee your training." Turning a bit to her right, her arm swept toward the curtains. "I have brought you something," she continued. The small group watched as the curtains ruffled, eventually parting to reveal the form of a small white dragon. "She will grow to be the dragon to your tower." the Elemental told her as the small dragon ruffled her wings.

Tara watched the fledgling closely. "Her wings are like mine," she noted.

"She is the Dragon of Light. It is only natural that she have some of your characteristics."

Tara studied the small dragon as she made her way toward them. With a single leap, she was soon perched comfortably upon her shoulder with her tail wrapped securely around Tara's torso. "I guess I'm just confused because the other Guardians have their own riders."

"That is because I have been dormant for ages while I waited for someone worthy enough to bring Light back into this realm. Now that it has awakened through you, those with light in their souls will begin to awaken as well, and we will be able to form an army for this tower." She approached them, tucking her fingers gently beneath Tara's chin. "It will be imperative that you be undisturbed by anyone while you are forming the bond with your dragon. The two of you must be an extension of one another. You must learn to read the others body language as if it were your own. In essence, the two of you must become one in both mind and spirit. Do you understand?"

Tara stared up at her and nodded. "I do understand."

"I knew you would," she said with a warm smile. "There will be a seal upon your door that only you will be able to open. Your meals will be left outside your door. The Elders are already aware of these instructions, but I must see Raiden so that I might give him the knowledge to continue your training while I am away."

"Away?" Tara asked as she ran her fingers along the side of the dragon's neck.

"Yes. We are beings of energy, and the more we are visible to the waking world, the more that energy is used. Very seldom are we out so regularly, but I am to begin your training. When Raiden begins where I leave off, I will return to my plane of existence to rest." She stared into her eyes seeing an uncertain fear within them. "I know that there is one who shares their gaze with you." She ran the pads of her thumbs gently over her eyes as she spoke. "While I cannot completely block him from you, this will at least make things much harder for him to get through. He will not be able to see you train, nor will he know about your dragon. But I'm afraid that he will have access to the rest of your time spent."

Tara forced a smile. "It's all right. I truly am grateful for the help you've been able to give me."

"You are welcome, my Champion."

Tara watched her fade away before looking at the wolves who now studied their new companion with interest. Tara knelt carefully on the floor, beckoning Luna and Myst to her. "Come meet your new sister." She ran her fingers soothingly through their fur as they approached and watched carefully as they interacted. "When she gets older, it will be up to the two of you to teach her what the Watchers have taught you. You'll have to teach her to hunt as best you can." She then looked to the golden eyes that watched her. "Once you get bigger I'm sure you'll adapt things to better suit you." She was met with a croon and a tired yawn that revealed tiny but rather sharp teeth. "I suppose we should all go to bed. We have a long road ahead of us."

As days passed, Tara would catch brief images as she watched and bonded with the white dragon. Images of space, a horizontal line of stars with the sun at both its highest and lowest points of ascension. But as each night faded into memories, without either knowing, their hearts began to sync in beat and rhythm. One humid summer morning Tara woke to a rather extreme pressure in her chest. Pushing her hands forward, they were met with a solid mass.

"Solstice . . ." she groaned. "You're getting too heavy to sleep on my chest."

This, of course, was met with great protest as the dragon moved to the floor. Tara sat up and stretched before staring blankly. "Did I just call you Solstice?" She stared once more into the golden eyes that peered back at her. At once she seemed transported to the depths of space, watching as comets raced along their path. Asteroids collided with barren planets creating life, and shooting stars raced across the heavens. "The heavens truly do you justice," she whispered.

"They define us both mother."

The echo of yet another voice to her mind brought her vision back to her room, once again staring into the adoring eyes of the dragon before her. "You talk?"

A soft trill echoed from the depths of the dragon's chest. 'We are synched as one.' Solstice began. 'As long as our bond remains strong, we will be able to communicate.'

Tara stared in realization. "Do you understand now?" came a voice from behind her.

She was on her feet, spinning around in surprise. "I do," she answered with a deep bow. "The bond between the dragon and their rider is so strong. No wonder when one is lost they don't try to imprint them upon another."

"You are so quick to understand," the Elemental replied with a warm smile. "But now it is time that we begin your training."

Tara nodded. "I'm ready."

* * *

For months, both she and Solstice were pulled into the depths of her subconscious to train for hours on end, lost in deep meditation. In the heart of the Shadow Lands, however, events were taking a less honorable path. "There had better be an update!" Vonspar demanded as the door to Belzak's room was flung open.

The former Watcher growled as he was jarred from his probing. "If you keep interrupting me like that I won't find anything!" he snarled. He was soon to his feet, tossing long strands of bound ebony hair back over his shoulder. "There is a white fire barrier that is keeping me from breaching her mind and her gaze."

Darius craned his head before poking it into the open room. "A white fire?" he asked, intrigued by the bit of news.

Belzak nodded. "Everything I've used to break through it only burns away."

"There's no way she's that powerful yet," Vonspar grumbled.

"Then it leaves us with only one other option," Darius replied with a dark chuckle. "It means that she is training."

"And why is that funny!" Vonspar snapped.

But the smile remained. "Because she's only training because she thinks she can defend those around her. This is actually the news you have been waiting for. She is still weak. If we strike soon, we will crush them."

Vonspar paused for a moment as he contemplated what he had just been told. He stared at Darius. "My brother, gather the Necromancers." He then looked to Belzak. "Gather enough people and go in search for dragon corpses!"

"Yes, brother," Darius replied with a sweeping bow.

"Right away, Vonspar," Belzak answered.

Vonspar watched the two depart, following behind them slowly. "Your time is nearing its end, Angel," he spat. "You have signed your undoing!"

CHAPTER

33

On The Edge

In an area that was the very definition of unholy, Darius, Vonspar, Belzak, and the vampire trio gathered behind a group of black cloaked figures. Darius looked out over the multitude of corpses, seeing the various stages of decay that they were in. "Are you sure this is going to work Brother?"

"If things are timed the way I have planned them out, then yes, we will be successful in our desires." He then turned his attention to the group before them. "You may begin when you're ready."

Things were quiet for a moment before a series of chants began. Spoken in some forgotten language, Vonspar didn't even try to understand it. He stared intently, his fingers curling and uncurling as he waited, certain that this would secure a victory against Nimost. In time, his waiting would pay off, and a being of energy began to appear in the center of the chanting group. "Who has summoned me?"

Delight shone in Vonspar's callous gaze as he heard the raspy voice. "I did," he answered, stepping forward and giving a shallow bow of his head.

"Why have you summoned me?" the being asked.

"I am seeking information," Vonspar stated plainly.

"What information?"

"Soon we are to wage war against Nimost and reclaim our rightful home. I want to know if we will be victorious."

A sigh escaped like a hiss as the spirit stared directly at the group. "There are unknown factors that make your answer hard to find."

Vonspar's brow twitched. "Like what!" he demanded.

"The one he seeks to destroy," the spirit began, his slender finger pointing directly at Darius. "She is protected by Holy Light. The extent of her power is lost to my sights, so therefore, I cannot give you a valid answer to your question."

"That is not what I wanted to hear!" Vonspar's demeanor changed suddenly, and with a swift movement of his hand, the summoned spirit howled as it found itself bound to one of the many corpses that had been unearthed. Runes began to glow a sickly jade hue as they appeared in various locations along the newly animated corpse. "You are mine! You will help me bring my desires to fruition!"

"You will not win . . ." The spirit's voice faded as he was swallowed by the energy.

Vonspar watched as the essence of the spirit was dispersed throughout the dragon before finally seeing the fruits of his labors. Bones creaked as the dragon slowly rose. Hollow eye sockets held the same sickly glow as the runes that bound its essence of life. Still in the late stages of decay, ooze leaked from what remained of its internal organs, landing upon the ground with an acidic hiss. "This is perfect." Vonspar laughed. He then turned his attention to the vampires beside him. "Take this abomination away and find it a rider. Soon we will be ready to exact our revenge against those who stood against us."

"Right away," Gabriel answered with a sweeping bow.

And for several phases of the moon that's how things progressed. Slowly, an army was built that would overpower the armies of Nimost and plunge the realm into everlasting darkness.

* * *

Finally free from the confines of her room, Tara enjoyed a training session with the other Guardians while Solstice rested with the other dragons. "You've really come a long way," Anon commented.

This was the first time Marcus had seen her in action, but even he had to admit that he was impressed with how easily she moved. "Thanks," she replied, unable to say much more as she created a thin veil of energy between herself and a spike of earth that soon erupted from the ground. The attack crumbled as it met the barrier, but she used the energy to propel herself into the air. She floated in a suspended state, arms crossed, but as she fell back with gravity she thrust her arms to the sides. Large needles of energy punctured the ground before exploding, sending the Guardians scrambling for cover.

"Nicely done," Raiden commented as he watched the group practice.

"She's not supposed to try and blow us up!" Wella protested.

"You have to anticipate everything," Raiden continued. "Now continue!"

Wella sighed heavily, but they all attacked Tara at once, aided by the force of wind generated from Oron. Tara in turn, held out her arms, generating a barrier around herself that leached out, taking hold of each of the attacks. She could feel the force compressing against her shield and the desire for an impact. With a single thrust of her muscles, she sent the attacks colliding back toward their respective casters, concealing herself in the multitude of dust clouds. But as she hid, something revealed itself to her that chilled every inch of her being. The images drew her in, so much so, that she found herself surrounded by a tangle of lightning and vines. The jolt of energy erased the images from her sight and she soon found herself writhing in a searing pain.

"Tara, how could you miss that!" Raiden shouted, putting a halt to the practice session.

Tara was on her feet looking to her left, then to her right. "You guys didn't see that?"

"See what?" Elexis asked.

"Are you feeling all right?" Aston added.

But as she was about to explain the horrific images that appeared before her, Solstice's shadow loomed overhead. In seconds the white dragon landed, lowering her head to the ground. 'Mother, did you see that?'

"I did," she whispered, running her hand gently over the dragon's forehead as she turned to the others. "We have to go back to Nimost." There was an urgency in her gaze. She was afraid of what she had seen. She knew that war was on the horizon.

CHAPTER
34

The Final Confrontation

Solstice landed with a ground quaking thud as the Guardians followed behind. "Tara!"

But Nao's voice would not register. She simply motioned for them to follow her as she raced up the steps to her tower. "Fisonma! Yukino!" Her eyes scanned the area around her, the stair cases, and the rooms that were in close vicinity.

"I believe they're in the central library."

Tara stopped, looking at a passing servant and gave a quick bow. "Thank you." She raced up the first flight of stairs and down the hall. The doors to the library gave a low echo as they hit the wall upon their opening.

"Tara." Fisonma rose to her feet, seeing the trouble clearly splayed across her face.

"Tara, calm down." Yukino was soon at her side, her hands grasping Tara's firmly. "What has gotten into you, child?"

Tara created a sphere, doing her best to show the others what she had seen. They all stared as the vision played out to its completion before repeating over, and over again. "What is that?" Nao asked.

"The reason you and Elexis were able to catch me off guard," Tara replied dryly.

"Those poor dragons." Wella pouted. "Why can't they just leave them alone!"

"They haven't raised them," Fisonma explained, highlighting a section of a frozen image. She brought to light a series of runes, pointing to each one as she spoke. "These are runes of binding and control. These are troubling indeed." She turned to the small group. Her expression was serious as she held each Guardians gaze. "It appears that we are on the cusp of war."

Everyone exchanged glances. "We have to warn everyone." Anon said at length. "If they travel through any of the towns, it will be a massacre."

"I will address the towns on the outskirts of our borders," Fisonma assured. "Meanwhile we must prepare Nimost for those who choose to flee." And that's how their time was spent. In the span of days, Nimost changed from a capital city, to a refugee camp.

"Here come the first evacuees!" came the call of one of the guards. In those spoken words, Nimost became a flood of motion. Families were directed to camps, temples, even the school dorms were converted to living quarters for those fleeing the darkness. As more people arrived, tales of a darkness most foul began to circulate.

"It doesn't look like we have much more time." Wella sighed.

"It's like the darkness was right at their heels," Eiricka said with a frown.

Tara seemed distant. She didn't want to find her childhood friend. She had hoped that she could reason with him, make him see the mistakes that he'd made, but it seemed that the time for talk had long since died. "We should seek advice from the Council," she said at length. "See just where they are, and plan accordingly."

But even with such dire circumstances staring them in the face, Anon couldn't help but show a small smile. "You're learning quickly how to be a wise leader."

But she just looked over her shoulder at him and rolled her eyes. "You lead us, not me," she reminded him as the group disappeared down the hall.

* * *

Days later, everyone stood outside the central tower of Nimost. The crowds of evacuees watched as the armies gathered and fell in line. The rumble of dragon trills echoed like closing thunder as the riders took their place. "They would follow you to the maws of hell if asked."

Tara looked up at Oron as he spoke. She was silent, nervous, and unsure. Her gaze fell upon those standing at the entrance to her tower. Fisonma, Raiden, the Council . . . Her eyes fell upon the woman who had become a second mother to her and she almost broke. "I don't want to fight Darius," she began. "I can't take your son from you."

"Tara." Her voice was calm and soothing as it always was, and the smile that graced her lips was welcoming and instantly calming. "That man, he is not my son. His heart and soul are no longer human. You must fight him so that we are able to keep the peace we've fought for so long to maintain."

Before she could reply, the group retreated to the entrance of the tower and her gaze once more found itself resting upon the throngs of people before her. A touch to the back of her neck drew her from the growing storm in her mind as loving words found their home in her ear. "As long as your heart is light, and your mind is focused, we will be victorious."

"Arcainous . . ." She turned around, staring at him with glistening eyes.

"You are stronger than you realize," he murmured, kissing her forehead. Drawing back, he stared fondly into her eyes, but in that fondness, she could feel a growing sorrow.

"What's wrong?" she asked, her voice anxious.

"Nothing at all, my love," he whispered. He seemed to be studying her, memorizing every flawless detail about her. At length he cupped her jaw, his fingers applying a gentle pressure to hold her head in place. And it was with that gentle pressure that he leaned in and kissed her.

Their first true kiss. Her body felt hot and cold, numb and awake, alive and surreal. Tears slipped down the contours of her face, bombarded with the heavy sorrow that had transferred through such a simple action. "Arcainous . . ."

He rested his forehead against hers, a soft smile soon gracing his features. "You must be strong," he began. "All of Nimost, and those under our protection, are putting their faith and hope in you. If nothing else, you must survive so that our tale might be told and so that Light may prevail and continue to bring peace."

She was almost horrified with what she'd just heard. "Arcainous!" Her body shook as she tried to pull away from him. He held her firmly and she finally relented and stared up into his eyes. "Why are you talking like we'll never see each other again?"

"Shh, shh." He pinched her lips together lightly. "I meant nothing ill by it, my love. There will be many more cherished moments between us. But there will be those who fall."

She stood straight, nodding as she felt his lips upon her forehead once again. "We will come home," she promised, her voice raising so that all would hear. "We will all tell the story!" Spinning around to face everyone determination flared out around her, even as the sorrow from her kiss continued to envelop her. "We will drive the Shadows back from our lands! They will fear the fire in our hearts knowing that we will not fear them! We will serve with pride, and we will return with honor!"

Cheers arose throughout the masses, loud enough to drown out the rumbles of the dragons. Moving from her love, she stepped easily onto the top of Solstice's head as the dragon riders took to the skies. Niako joined Arcainous as they watched the dragons float over the armies as they moved out. "So much rides on her shoulders."

"She'll emerge victorious. I'll give my life to ensure it," Arcainous replied, his gaze fixed forward.

CHAPTER

35

The Beginning of the End

Darius and Vonspar stood on an altar of debris from their most recent excursion into the lands protected by Nimost. "My brothers and sisters! Today marks the beginning of the end for Nimost! This is the day we take back what rightfully belongs to us!" Vonspar had a charisma about him that was almost infectious, and those under his command rallied for a cause they saw as just. Most knew the tale spun from the old times, and revenge against Nimost and the Elder Council ran deep for many generations. "This town is one of many that will fall to our might!" he continued, preaching about the victory that was foreseen.

Dante looked at his brothers and nodded. "The energy is building. They are marching."

Vonspar heard this and he lifted his hands once more. "Even now the armies of Nimost march against us! They intend on denying us what we rightfully deserve! I ask you now brethren, will we stand for this!" Delight shone on his face plain as day as he heard those around him shouting their backing of his cause. "Then I say, here and now, that we send them to the hell they sentenced us to so many lifetimes ago!" With roars of approval, the small group watched as the massive army marched toward their destiny.

* * *

It took several days of marching before they reached the field that they felt was suitable. "At least it's far away enough from any civilization." Wella commented as she scanned the vast horizons.

"How do we even know that they will meet us here?" Keshou asked.

"Our collective energies will draw them in," Anon explained.

"Like moths to a flame," Adam added.

"That's the hope."

Tara looked around the landscape, pointing things out to groups of archers. "Those outcropping of rocks will provide excellent cover for sniping. I think what will be key, is having small groups scattered throughout the rocks."

"It will provide us better coverage," one archer remarked.

"I will leave you to it then. I'm going to go see how the alchemists are doing with the poisons you'll all need."

As she made her way toward the tents where the alchemists we busy making poisons and potions, she was stopped by a couple of the illusionists that had accompanied them. "Excuse us," came the almost timid voice of the obviously younger illusionists.

Tara paused, confused that, even after the amount of time she'd been in the Realm, that people would still approach her with caution. *I guess everyone is nervous though*, she thought. She was certain that no one around had ever, in their wildest dreams, pictured they would be here, in this moment, ready to tackle something short of pure evil. "What can I do for you?" she asked, giving a warm smile that seemed to put them at ease.

"A lot of people have concerns for those who will be working behind the scenes of this fight," she began. "We're worried that we'll all be too exposed." To illustrate her point, she pointed around where everyone had set up. "We're too open to attack. Even if we are able to mask our existence to the opposing armies, if one of us is found . . ."

She didn't need to go any further for Tara to realize where she was going with this. "Anon! Oron! I need you guys!"

The two jogged up from the meetings they had been conducting. "What can we do for you?" Anon asked.

Tara explained the concerns that had been brought up to her, asking if something could be done. "I'd also need pillars brought up with holes in the sides to allow the illusionists a place to hide so they aren't losing concentration." She then looked at Oron, her finger pointing to the skies. "I need your dragon in the air. He can take the appearance of the clouds right?"

"He can," Oron replied with a nod.

"I need eyes on the Shadow armies. I need to know how much time we have to finish everything."

"Consider it done." the two answered in unison before setting to their tasks. Oron gave instructions to his dragon rider while Anon set to the task at hand. The ground rumbled as pillars jutted from the bowels of the earth housing carved out spots for the illusionists to hide while the concealed their camp and treatment areas they had set up for the wounded they knew they would receive.

"What do you think?" Anon asked as he inspected his handy work.

Tara looked, motioning the illusionists over. "Well?"

They each settled into the cave like hole that was made for each of them, finding more than enough room for what they needed. "It's perfect!" one exclaimed.

"Everyone from this point back will be well hidden." another assured "We'll get to work immediately on setting up the illusions."

"Now that that's out of the way . . ." she sighed as she ran her fingers through her bangs.

"Tara?"

Looking up from her thoughts, she saw the small group who had slowly become her family. Nao stood before them, concern showing in his expression. "Is something wrong?" Inside she feared that they had run out of time, and that the time to fight had finally come.

"They're still a day away," Anon assured. "We'll be ready before they get here."

"But that's not why we wanted to talk to you," Wella said quietly.

Tara's brow arched as she looked at them. Everyone looked to Anon to continue and he slowly stepped forward. "We have discussed things and have decided that you are going to stay behind once things start."

"What!" She felt instantly wounded and had gone on the offensive. "I'm part of this army too!"

"But we need you to keep an eye out for Darius," Elexis pled.

"If he decides to attack, and you're busy . . ." Ashton didn't even need to finish his sentence for the message to get through.

"I'm the only one who has a chance against him," Tara finished.

"You're an amazing warrior," Marcus assured.

"But you hold enough light to rival his darkness," Keshou added quietly.

Her shoulders sank knowing that she would not be standing beside the armies as they fought, but at the same time, she understood the position they were all in. With great discontent, she relented to their wishes. "I will stay back."

Anon rested a hand upon her shoulder and squeezed it firmly. "I know this is not what you wanted, but it is what will give us the greatest chance for victory."

"I understand," she replied with a small smile. Looking at the group she lifted her head some. "I did have an idea that I wanted to run by you. I don't know if it would help, or hinder us, but I think it will keep everyone fresh and ready to fight."

"Any idea is always welcome. You know this."

"What I was thinking is staggering the armies." She saw the perplexed looks on everyone's faces, so she continued. "Divide them into thirds, and have them attack in waves. Have each wave fight as long as they are able then fall back allowing the next to fight, so on and so forth. This will give those who have fallen back before to get proper care and rest."

"It will allow us to last longer." Keshou commented as his gaze shifted toward Anon.

Anon nodded "Thank you." Turning to the others, they began to implement Tara's plan. "Brief everyone on what's going on. Divide your armies and have the two spare waves fall back behind the lines. This war will be ours!"

With a victorious cry, the group disbanded to set their plans into motion leaving Tara feeling very much alone. Catching glimpse of a swift moving cloud, she watched as Oron's dragon landed. "They're hours away." The report gave their position being much closer than she had anticipated and things were beginning to feel very real. "Their bone dragons breathe a toxic vapor though. If that gets anywhere near our forces . . ."

"Don't worry," Eiricka assured. "If they start breathing that stuff, we'll be ready."

"They're over the next ridge!" Everyone heard the call and looked toward the horizons. "They'll be upon us within the hour!"

Tara felt a chill race through her body as the echo of Anon's voice rang in her ears like a bell. "Everyone ready! Our advantage is rest and preparations! Let's show this scum why we are to be feared!"

Tara stepped slowly behind the protection of the barrier. "Please be careful," she whispered.

"Do not worry child."

Tara spun to see one of the Priests that had come with them. "Things should not have come to this point," she said as she looked out over the battle as it began. "There should have been a better way."

"You have a good heart." the Priest replied. "But sometimes, those corrupted by power will only seek resolution through violence, and even those who protect peace must give in to that desire of battle and lust for bloodshed. Your faith in your friends will see them further than you realize."

"I hope so," she mumbled, watching as the incarnated bone dragons hung over the horizons. She cringed and stepped back feeling the palpation of evil that had become their breath of life. As was suspected, they did breathe out the foul clouds of acid but Oron and his armies were ready and answered with howling winds that sent the mists back over Vonspar's armies.

"Give them hell my brothers!" Vonspar shouted as darkness was unleashed.

"Show them that we will NOT quake in fear, and that we *will* be led by the courage in our hearts!" Anon's reply to Vonspar sent a shiver through Tara's body and her heart swelled.

"Maybe we can do this," she whispered, but even with great faith in her friends, there was still fear gripping at her knowing that Darius would not stay out of the fray of battle for long.

"Where is she . . ." Darius growled as he scanned the depths of the battle. "I feel her."

"Belzak!"

"Yes, Vonspar?"

"Find her. If she is hiding, we will force her to fight!"

"It will be my greatest pleasure," Belzak replied as he stared out over the battle. "Where are you hiding?" he mumbled as he eyes seemed to glaze over. He knew it would take much longer than it normally had because of the Light that surrounded her, but he was also sure that it was that Light that would help him find her.

As the days dragged on, Tara busied herself with helping tend to the wounded. Her calming nature coupled with the light that radiated from her helped their fighters heal much faster than most would expect. But not even light could help everyone and more than once Tara would mourn the loss of those who had fallen. "I'm so sorry . . .," she murmured as she took yet another body to be prepared for its return to Nimost. "You served bravely," she whispered, wiping a tear from her cheek.

"Child of Light, I have finally found you."

Such evil laughter at her discovery sent a sharp chill straight through her spine. Her head shot up, eyes wide as she stared into the distance. "Belzak?"

He delighted in hearing her voice catching in her throat. "Where are you hiding, my child?" He was genuinely curious, but only so they could destroy her. "Show me where you are."

Instantly he was blinded as she sent a flood of light to mar his sight. Running through the camp, she reached the barrier just as Darius appeared. "No . . ."

Waves were changing as the front forces were falling back to rest when he struck. "You are hiding her!" he yelled, releasing a mass of dark energy of the converging forces.

"Not this time!" she growled, creating a film of energy above her armies, protecting them from the explosion of energy.

"So she is here." Darius chuckled, attacking over and over, only to meet the same resistance. "Where are you!"

Tara grabbed two of the illusionists that were preparing to relieve the ones keeping their barrier. "I need you," she plead.

"Of course. What can we do for you?" one of them asked.

She looked at one. "I need you to make me and Solstice invisible." She then looked at the other. "I need you to create an image of us in the distance. I don't want him knowing where everyone is." She stared at them for some time before speaking again. "Can you do this?"

"You know we can," they assured in unison.

"All right. Let's do it then." She signaled for Solstice who was at her side in moments. "This will at least get him away from you guys so we have a chance."

"Good luck."

She nodded as she took her place upon the top of Solstice's head. Floating into the air, she could feel the energy surrounding them, concealing them as they breached the illusion that hid the majority of their forces. As they moved away from where the armies were hidden she continued shielding those who were fighting from Darius's wrath. With a safe distance reached, her mirrored image appeared slowly, drawing Darius's attention with a roar of her dragon. "There you are!" he hissed, sending the large attack he'd been charging directly toward the illusion.

Tara watched as the attack decimated the illusion which was the key for the other illusionist to drop the shield around her and bringing them into the depths of the battle. "You have poor aim!" she shouted. Though her gaze was hard, inside, her nerves were beginning to toy with her stomach. "Why don't you leave them alone and chase after someone who can fight back!"

Turning around, he saw his prey, but he had destroyed her and he looked back to where she had been. "What is the meaning of this witch!"

With a touch of her hand the skies were soon ablaze with white fire, driving Darius from the fray battle. "Follow him!"

Solstice lurched forward, maneuvering easily as the two gave chase, following him to the edge of a nearby cliff. Staying back far enough, Solstice lowered her head, dropping Tara off near a grouping of trees. "Please be careful, Mother."

"I will be," she promised. "Now, go help the others." Solstice gave a shallow nod before floating away from her and returning to the battle. Tara looked up seeing Darius standing on the edge of the cliff, brushing off the arms of his armor. Knowing that Solstice had hit him, she ran forward, charging up to face her destiny. "Darius!"

36

A War Between Angels

Darius glared down the embankment as Tara ran up to face him. "This is your fault," he growled. "You know that, right?"

Tara stared in openmouthed disbelief. "How is any of this *my* fault! You attacked *us*! Not the other way around!"

"If you had just given us what we wanted . . ."

Tara's gaze soon held an intense edge to it as her jaw clenched. "I refuse to see this world plunged into darkness," she seethed.

"Then it appears that we are at an impasse," he said with a hint of boredom. "One that you have created mind you. And this is why we find ourselves in our current situation."

The echo of an open slap stopped him from saying anything more than he just had. He laughed as he rubbed his cheek, staring down at her, seeing the unmasked anger that flared in her eyes. "Take ownership of your own actions!" she spat. "I know it's hard for you to do, but once you get used to it it's pretty damn easy!"

His body tensed with the great disrespect that she spoke to him with. There was no way he would allow it, especially by someone he saw as gravely inferior to himself as he saw her. With the speed and power equal to that of a snake, the back of his hand found its home against her cheek with enough force to send her sprawling backward. "This is where you will learn your place . . ." he vowed through clenched teeth.

"I have a place!" she shot back, rolling out of the way as a pulse of dark energy hit the ground. The dust settled, revealing the small indent into the earth where she had been. Instantly, she was back to her feet, only to take to the skies as Darius seemed to flee her. She chased after him, the two weaving through the others energies as attacks collided and exploded behind them.

"You've improved," he admitted. "But you can never hope to be my equal."

Tara sighed in frustration. "I'm not trying to be your equal!" But any further conversations were quelled quickly. Crossing her arms in front of her, she had just enough time to erect a barrier around herself to deflect several rays of dark energy that Darius had sent toward her. When they faded away, she dropped her shield quickly and retaliated. Catching him with her own speed, she hit him with several blasts that sent him plunging to the ground. "I want you to wake from these childish notions you have of power!" she yelled as she dove after him.

Just as she was about to reach him, however, she was met with a dome of almost solid black energy. Feeding from the growing anger that continued brewing in his heart she could clearly see leads of electricity begin to form, arcing across the surface of the barrier before lashing out at her in random intervals. "Come and get me now, wretch!" he dared. "I swear to you that it will be the last mistake you ever make!"

From what she could see, she had been able to wound him. He sat, crouched on the ground with his arm securely across his chest when the impact of her blast had hit. She closed her eyes tightly and backed away as one of the tendrils of electricity came dangerously close to striking her while the rest struck like coiled whips being unleashed. It was also in this state that she was able to feel just how deeply Darius hated her. 'Where is the friend I grew up with.'

she wondered, her eyes opening slowly. "There has to be another way . . ." she murmured. "This isn't the answer."

"Coward!" he howled as blinded rage continued to feed his energy through her calm demeanor. "If you're so good, and so pure, then you have nothing to fear from me!"

But she wouldn't listen this time. There was no way she would let him into her mind like that again. "I will find a way . . ." she whispered, and as her heart sought out a means to an end, it connected with those who desire the same as she. A nonviolent conclusion to a meaningless child's tantrum. These hopes soon filled her with a warmth that she had never before felt and her body was soon at peace.

"Release their energy."

Her head lifted as she was drawn from her thoughts. "What?"

"You have begun to awaken those with Light in their hearts." The voice was welcome in her mind and Tara offered a small smile. "Release the energy they have given to you and allow them to awaken."

Tara's expression changed slightly as the echo of attacks around her began to intensify. "How?"

"Relax," she whispered before her voice faded from Tara's mind.

Knowing there were those who shared her views about senseless bloodshed gave her a great measure of comfort. Hearing her wings rustling caused her gaze to shift to her side and she watched as they became illuminated in the most brilliant light. "The energy of peace," she murmured. She knew what she had to do and her gaze hardened as she thrust a single finger toward Darius. "I will not let you destroy what they have spent centuries striving to protect!" Her declaration fueled her energy, sending it racing from the outermost feathers of her wings as thick tendrils that pierced through Darius's barrier with great ease. Her energy burned away the shattered remains of his barrier as they ripped through his wings and punctured the ground. Though he was now unable to flee, the two were now tethered and very much open to the whims of the other.

His howls of pain failed to faze her, but the threat he made next struck its mark with her. "Release me, or by all that is dark and unforgiving, I will show you true pain."

She only stared back at him, unwilling to allow him to affect her as he had in the past. "I will release you when you listen to reason!"

The light of her heart had now begun scalding him as her energy began seeping into his body, burning away the darkness that had ensnared him so long ago. "What are you doing!" he snarled.

"Trying to make you see what a fool you've been," she replied calmly.

But the energy that owned him had other plans and with her distracted, it was the perfect time to strike out. A pool of black ooze began to form beneath her, and as she spouted on about truth and Light, it struck. From the depths of that pool shot a single, thick tentacle of energy that quickly wrapped itself around her. She screamed, struggling against the tar like consistency only to find herself being pulled back to the ground with an unneeded force that knocked the air from her lungs. "Much better . . .," came a hissed whisper as it continued to pool and froth around her.

Darius just laughed as he pushed to his feet. Watching her struggle against his energy was like watching a fly try to free itself from the web of a spider. Allowing it to shock her at its whim he brushed off his armor. "Submit, and surrender your power to me!" he demanded.

"I will not!" she shrieked.

He growled, snapping his fingers as the ooze delivered one final shock before retreating back to where Darius stood. Shooting up around him, tendrils of energy broke through the energy that tethered the two together before sinking back to the ground and seeping into his armor. Once absorbed, the energy quickly went to work healing the burns he'd received at the hands of his foe until every trace of what she had done was wiped away. A single strand of energy shot forth from his hand, wrapping securely around her waist as he yanked her back to her feet, allowing it to be burned away by the Light in her armor. "Do you remember the vow I made you?" he asked, watching as her body tensed, but he wanted verbal acknowledgement of his question. "Do you remember!" he shouted, striking her where she stood.

Tara staggered back, wiping the blood from her mouth, feeling it smear across her cheek. "I remember!" she growled.

He only chuckled, looking down at his fingers as he rubbed her blood between them. "Today is where everything ends for you," he began, looking back up at her. "One by one, everyone you hold dear will die."

"You leave them alone!" she seethed.

"Then defend them by fighting me!" he challenged. "Deny me and they will all die!"

Her shoulders dropped as she faced away from him. What she saw before her was nothing more than needless fighting, and her heart sank. "What choice do I have?" she sighed. To ensure minimal loss of life, she would have to give in to his demands. "If I fight you, you will leave everyone out of this! Things will go no further than you and me!" Her gaze shot back to him suddenly. "Do you understand me!"

The echo of his laughter was as chilled as winter's night. "So noble," he teased. "But as long as your blood spills, I will honor your request." He took a predatory stance as he faced her fully. "Now, show me what you're made of, Angel of the White Tower!"

His response was so cold, almost as if he enjoyed what was about to happen, but there was no backing down anymore. To protect life, she would risk her own and pray for victory. In unison, the two thrust their arms downward, manifesting swords created from their own energies. "This will all end here!" she vowed. The two soon charged toward each other with great speed, the cracking of their weapons creating such a massive blast of energy that it all but halted the war entirely.

It was later written that in that moment, the power released when two warring Angels clash was enough to cast the whole of the Realm into silence. Those two beings showed just how true that statement would become. Small craters were carved into the earth with each expulsion of energy, and it was quickly realized that neither had an equal. Thunder cracked as weapons clashed, showering the two with sparks that would slowly fade to nothing more than smoldering embers. "This! This is what I wanted to see!" Darius exclaimed with absolute glee.

"Don't get used to it!" she snapped back. "I'm only doing this to save everyone from your cruelty." She tucked her arm tightly against her side before striking out at him, firing a pulse of energy directly into his chest. Lunging, she was soon upon him, blade poised to strike. "What happened to you?" she asked. "What made you think that this was your only way out!"

Her question found her rolling across the ground with a well-placed kick to her gut. "You can't get inside my head," he informed coolly, his shadow looming over her. With a sadistic grin he placed the toe of his boot into her throat and began applying a steady pressure, delighting greatly in the sounds she made as she gasped for air. "Don't you understand?" he asked, staring into her eyes, drunk off the panic that slowly began to fill them. "This is my destiny, one that I welcome with open arms."

"What . . . What about . . . your . . . mother . . . ?" Her voice was raspy as she fought for breath. "What do you think . . . this . . . will do . . . to her?"

The laughter that hit her ears was nothing short of dark. "Yukino?" he asked, tracing the tip of his blade along her jaw, watching as a thin line of red trailed in its wake. "Do you honestly think I care what hurts her? That woman is already dead to me."

Shock crossed her face as she continued trying to move his foot from her throat. "She . . . did everything—for you!"

"Oh, don't act so surprised!" he snarled, flicking his blade and cutting into her cheek. "She may be dead to me, but soon, soon, you will be dead to everyone!"

"No!" There was no way she was going to lose to him. Not here, not now, not ever. Since she couldn't move him, she was make him move. Gripping his leg tightly, she released a flood of energy, letting its heat do what it had done before.

"Bitch!" he howled, leaping away from her as he felt the searing pain radiate through his armor and into his leg. She rolled away quickly, coughing violently and gasping for breath. "Do you think I'm done with you?" he shouted. Tendrils of energy broke through the ground, wrapping around her wrists, ankles, and her neck. "I will enjoy spilling your blood over this god forsaken land!"

"Come to your senses!" she wheezed, but even as she burned away the energy holding her captive, there was always more waiting.

But he had heard enough of her voice, her proclamations, and sent wave after wave of electric currents coursing through her. He delighted in the sight of the tremors racing through her nervous system, almost causing her to convulse. "Darius! Stop this at once!"

The two turned seeing Yukino riding ahead of the Elder Council. Fear flooded Tara's expression instantly, knowing full well what would happen if they even through of interfering with their fight. "Go back!" she shouted. "Please . . . go back!"

"Shut up!" Darius ordered, sending a shock through her so powerful and continuous, that her body became paralyzed. Her mouth was frozen in the beginnings of a scream, her body hovering in a semiconscious state. Nothing responded as air floated into her lungs keeping her literally on the edge of life. "I'm in control now," he snarled. "And if you want her to live you'll listen to what she said and get back!" In his darkest desires, however, he longed for them to make the mistake of trying to free her. He wanted so desperately to spill all of their blood and plunge his former friend into a never ending despair.

"This won't change anything Darius." Yukino remained cool against her son. "With or without her, you will lose."

He just laughed as he turned his attention back to the woman at his feet. "You're so certain in your ill placed faith in her," he began. "Just look at her!" her ordered, drawing the tip of his blade across her throat, watching as yet another thin line of red awoke in its path followed by thick drops of blood trickling down in random intervals. "Does this look like a champion to you?" he asked as he returned his gaze to those before him. But the brewing confrontation allowed enough of a distraction and he soon felt a sudden surge of pain explode in the back of his neck. The break in concentration released Tara from his hold, made evident from the ear splitting scream that fell from her lips. "Damn you!" he hissed, wiping the blood from his neck and flicking the droplets to the ground. "I will kill you all!" he declared.

Arcainous crouched protectively in front of Tara, fangs exposed while blood stained the fur of his muzzle. "You idiot!" Tara choked.

"I will not let him harm you!" he growled.

"This was supposed to be between us!" she yelled. "You have to go!"

"I'm not leaving you like this!" he snapped.

Her heart quivered knowing exactly what could, and most likely would, happen. "This is my fight . . ." she told him. "I'll be all right."

"This is not all right!"

"You should have listened to her." All conversations stopped as a deathly chill filled the area. When their eyes fell upon Darius, he had his hand leveled toward the two with the look of hellfire burning in his gaze.

"Darius stop!" Tara begged.

"You took a family bond from me," he began. "So in return, I will take the bond of love from you!"

"Darius, no!" But even as fast as she was to try and put herself between Arcainous and Darius, the two found themselves encased once more in the tar-like energy.

Yelps and whines faded to the sounds of screams of a human male as a reversion was forced. "I told you I would kill everyone you hold dear." His tone was so matter of fact as the energy brought Arcainous to Darius's feet. Tara had managed to burn away enough energy to free her head and body, but her arms and legs were still bound by the now hardening energy. Darius laughed as his fingers tangled through the silvery strands of the Watchers hair, yanking his head back and forcing the two to look at each other. "Now doesn't this look familiar," he chuckled.

"Let him go!" she demanded. "This fight is between us!"

"You are in no place to make demands of me!" he snarled. "The rules of engagement changed the second they interfered! And now, he will die."

Tears ran down her cheeks, mixing with the drying blood before falling silently to the ground. "Darius please? Don't do this."

"Only now do you show the truth of your heart?" he asked, yanking his head back further. "How pathetic," he spat. "You are no warrior."

"Shut up and let him go!" she demanded.

"Oh no, I'm afraid I can't do that. But I will extend my offer to you one final time. Give me what I want, and I will let him go."

"What?" Arcainous stared at Tara. "Whatever he's talking about, you have to refuse him."

Her voice broke as pain and fear began making themselves present in her gaze. "I can't lose you," she whimpered. She shifted her gaze directly to Darius as she continued trying to pull from the energy that held her. "If I agree, you let him go, and you leave!"

"Your life for his. I will release him—that is all I have ever promised to you," Darius corrected.

Arcainous stared in horror. "You can't be serious!" he shouted. "Tell me you're not honestly entertaining such a foolish idea!"

"I don't have a choice!" she protested.

"You have a choice!" he shouted. "This Realm needs you!"

"And I need you . . ."

"Enough!" While Darius did enjoy the torment shared between the two, he also desired an answer to his demands. "Choose!" he growled.

"I . . ."

"Don't . . . do this," Arcainous whispered, his body trembling.

She gave a quivering smile as her body slumped with the weight of the situation she was now faced with. "Forgive me," she mouthed before looking up at Darius. "I surrender."

"Tara . . ." Yukino gasped, looking quickly to Fisonma and the Elder Council.

Darius laughed uncontrollably. "Then come and take his place, Tara!" he ordered.

"Release Arcainous!" she demanded.

"When I have you, then I will release him," he corrected.

Tara felt the energy fall away from her, allowing her to rise slowly to her feet. Her body felt weak and more than once she tripped as she made her way toward her end. "Stop being foolish," Arcainous choked.

"Shut up!" Darius snapped, striking the side of his head with the hilt of his blade. "You should be grateful. Because of her, you may continue with your existence, knowing that it was her death which made it possible." He stopped only as he saw the shadow of his prize standing before him. He shoved the Watcher to the side and took a firm hold of Tara's wrist. In a single movement, he spun her around, her back pressed against his chest so that she could see the looks on every face that would be made to watch her undoing. "Are they worth it?" he whispered.

She brought her free hand tightly against her side, refusing to give him the satisfaction of an answer. Instead, she looked to each person before her, holding their gaze as she tried to silently convey her message. "Please understand why I have done this," she begged. "We must do everything within our power to protect Nimost and the people who depend on us for their safety."

Darius looked physically ill from the emotional farewell. "How touching," he spat. "Now die!"

She rose onto her toes with the upward force Darius applied to her arm to keep her in place. As Darius lifted his blade to end her life, Arcainous dove toward them as Tara was releasing her attack. Hitting the ground with a crashing thud, everyone watched as Tara's attack exploded in the skies above them. "Oh no . . .," she groaned. "Arcainous . . . what did you do . . ."

Everyone felt the air become heavy and electrically charged as Darius's mood grew ever darker. "You really thought you could best me?" he asked with an eerie calm to his voice. He looked down at the two and lifted his blade. "Two lives for the price of one. Love is fleeting and fatal. In the end, we will still get what we desire." Seeing the end closing in their favor, Darius once more brought forth the ooze of his energy to hold them in place.

Tara's eyes were wild as she fought against their bindings, but for everything she was able to burn, there was always more bubbling to the surface. When it all failed, she tried manifesting a barrier around them until she was able to free them. Before she could do anything, however, the echo of metal upon metal froze her mind in mid formation of the barrier. He had struck with enough force that the tip of his blade broke off, becoming lodged in the chest plate of her armor. Darius ripped the blade from Arcainous's torso, stepping back to admire the work he had done, laughing as he watched blood spill onto the armor of his lover. Tara looked into the eyes of the man she loved, seeing his body shaking over her. "No . . ."

"Tara . . ." he wheezed, blood dripping from his mouth onto her neck.

"Stay with me!" she ordered, but it was no use. Gravity soon won and his body gave into the loss of blood and soon fell on top of her. "Noooo no no no no no." She scrambled from beneath him, tremors racing throughout her nervous system. His blood was every-where as she rolled him onto his back, patting his cheek repeatedly. "Open your eyes," she prodded, moving strands of hair from his eyes. "Arcainous?" she whispered, now shaking his shoulders. "Arcainous, please, you can't go."

A violent cough erupted from his chest sending a spray of blood across her face. His eyes opened slowly seeing her hovering over him and he gently cupped her cheek. "I'm . . . glad . . . you're all right."

Tears ran down her cheeks and she gave a quivering smile, see-ing that he was still with her. She quickly scanned his body, finding the wound he'd received. "I can fix this for you," she assured as she placed her hand over the puncture wound. As her hand settled in the pooling blood she grimaced at the sticky consistency his blood contained as it began to dry in the open air.

He took her hand gently, moving it to the side as he shook his head. "No. It's too far gone. My time has come."

"I . . ." She tried to speak but her voice failed her, and her mind couldn't form the words she wanted to say. "You . . ."

He gently placed the tip of his finger over her lips. "Shh." He then ran his fingers over the side of her head, holding her gently. "My destiny has always been to protect you. Just remember that I will always love you."

She grabbed his hand, burying her face into his palm as he fell silent. "I love you too . . ." she whispered. When she received no answer, she let his hand drop and gently shook his shoulders. "Arcainous?" But there was no reply. Her vision blurred, the tears escaping with greater ease. "You can't go!" she cried, pulling his head into her lap. She rocked back and forth with him as she rubbed her cheek over his matted scalp. "Please don't leave me," she pled, but it was too late. His essence had already slipped away. Staring down with a distant gaze she gently laid him back on the ground, and with quivering lips, Life and Death shared their final kiss.

Everything she wanted, everything she had worked so hard to create, it all lay dead before her. A sickly chill found its way around her as gnarled vines of hatred began to suffocate the light from her heart. An acidic taste began to rise to the back of her throat as desires of revenge began to burn within her. "Tara, do not lose control. You can't."

Tara knew the voice now speaking her name and as she pushed to her feet she cast a single glance to her side. "Save him," she stated bluntly.

"I can't, you know I can't. We are not allowed to interfere with the plans of the Fates."

"You saved me!" she yelled.

* * *

"What is she talking about?" Eiricka asked as the captains and Guardians joined the Elders.

"When we were captured in the Shadow Lands" Marcus began, "Darius had killed her in a fight to save both myself and Arcainous. Her Elemental was able to bring her back because she had accepted her destiny as the White Angel."

* * *

"I saved you because it was your destiny to become my Champion, and you accepted it."

"He's dead because of me!"

"You cannot think like that. He can use that against you, and he will."

But at this point, she had quit listening. Everything she felt was pooling to the core of her soul, surrounding her with the most uncomfortable pressure imaginable. Darius laughed, watching as her body shook under the weight of energy until, with a guttural scream, it was released. With her body as its epicenter, a wave exploded outward covering the entire battlefield. "Tara!" Wella shrieked, watching in awe as the armies of the Shadow Lands were decimated into nothing more than ash. Vonspar and the others fled but were quickly caught by the dragon riders. At Vonspar's order, however, Oni slipped away into the darkness. Each were bound, their energies sealed away with incantations spoken by the Elder Council before being led back to where the guards were waiting to escort them to the dungeons of Nimost. Darius, however, had no intentions of being taken. Though wounded, he unleashed the full powers of darkness against the armies of Light.

Tara's gaze was hard as stone. "You won't harm them," she vowed as his energy collided with a newly erected barrier that spanned the length of the armies lines. When the dust had settled, the symbol that glowed upon the ground was evidence of a new rune.

"That symbol . . ." Yukino breathed as her gaze shifted to Fisonma.

"The Star of the Elements." Fisonma replied. "I didn't think it was possible, especially in her current mental state."

Everyone's attention turned, however, as each of the Guardians stepped forward, their armors glowing brightly as they added to the strength of the barrier. "Don't worry Tara." Elexis assured. "We have this."

"Clear your head." Tara looked at Keshou. His voice was always so calming in spite of the volatile nature of his element. "Please end this for us," he continued. "Only you have the power to defeat him and bring peace back to our Realm."

But even with as soothing as his voice was, Tara was losing the fight for her own sanity. Hatred ripped at every fiber of her being as the acidic taste of bile moved from her throat and began to pool in her mouth before being expelled as spit onto the ground. "She can't help you." Darius laughed. "Look at her!" he shouted, pointing his finger toward her. "She can't even control her own emotions!" He then approached her, each step so deliberate as he kept her gaze. When he reached her, his hand was instantly around the back of her neck, pulling her close, delighting in her broken state. "Your corruption will be my finest triumph," he whispered. "The hatred that burns within you, your want of revenge for destroying what you truly held dear. You're no better than I." He then pulled back from her, sliding his fingers over her cheek, puling at, and reopening the wound she'd received earlier. "When you are mine, the others will be free, and we will rule over this cursed land."

His laughter seemed so distant to her, and everyone could see that she was slipping from them. "You have to fight this!" Keshou yelled, still trying to break through the wall that had been placed around her mind. "Remember everything we've ever stood for . . ." he added, his voice softening as the group continued to strengthen the barrier protecting them.

"She can't hear you anymore." Darius laughed. "She is mine!"

But Darius couldn't have been more wrong. Though she was fighting her own demons, she did hear him, and his words had brought her a small measure of comfort knowing that they still stood behind her. Her head dropped, her gaze fixed upon the ground and the man she loved. His blood was pooled on the ground, smeared across her armor, dried to her skin. It was all too much, and in a blinding movement, she sent him sprawling away from her as her gaze lifted. "I am nothing like you . . ." she began. "I do not, and I will not, kill needlessly." Her heart quivered with both pain and determination as she strived to fight off the poison he tried infusing into her soul. Her head fell again as her arms wrapped tightly around her chest. "Please," she whispered. "This is not me. Help me . . ."

A being of light began to manifest itself beside her, wrapping her arms around Tara's fragile form. "My child . . ." she whispered. "You are not alone." The Elemental drew her head back before placing her hand over Tara's chest. "Allow me to ease your pain." Her very essence crushed the hatred that had ensnared Tara's heart into nothingness, driving a rather large crack into Darius's foundation.

That simple action seemed to cause Darius great pain and as he attacked, Tara knocked it away with a single sweep from the back of her hand. "I will no longer fear you!" she declared over the echo of the exploding attack. "You can take everything from me, and I will still rise against you!"

"I will take great pleasure in killing you!" he snarled as he charged her.

"We give you our power . . ."

Tara straightened as she heard the voices of her friends. She was soon filled with the welcoming warmth of both their energy and the love in their hearts. A gust of wind suddenly surrounded her before pooling around her hand. With a single movement, she sent Darius flying, crashing into a pillar of earth that jutted from the ground. Taking advantage of his dazed state, she was upon him like a blur. She planted her hand firmly upon the chest plate of his armor as ice's touch crept through every molecule. With that area frozen, it was easy for her to break through and expose the flesh of his bare chest. With the warmth of skin at her fingertips she released Elexis's powers. "Tell me how it feels," she whispered through clenched teeth.

His body twitched as his nerves were assaulted, but the basis of his energy was electric and he was able to recover with moderate quickness. "About as good as this," he coughed as he smashed a large rock against the side of her head. She was on the ground in an instant, dazed and barely able to move. "This will all end now!"

Unable to fight back, such a close ranged attack would mean her certain death, but as it was unleashed, a barrier appeared around Tara. "I will not allow you to harm her."

Tara sat up slowly, feeling her head swim as a pulse of energy sent Darius flying away from her once again. The air around him began to glow an almost neon orange as plasma took his armor. His screams of agony filled the air as the superheated energy burned his flesh. "Coward!" he howled. "You can't even fight on your own!"

"Because I'm not alone," Tara said softly. She could feel the blood running down the side of her face as she slowly rose back to her feet. "I am part of a team who looks out for one another. I am a Guardian of Nimost, but more importantly, I am a Guardian of Light, and protector of its Elemental!"

"How weak," he spat. "I need no such help!"

Tara sighed. "Even after all of this, after all that you have put your people through, you still haven't realized have you." Lifting her hand toward him, she encased him in a sphere of white fire. "Since you refuse to see, then burn in Light for all of eternity!" With her declaration made, she shot her arm out to her side, sending him colliding into the side of a far off mountain, forever to be forgotten among the rubble.

Cheers erupted around her, but it all seemed like nothing more than a distant roar. "Tend to the wounded!" Aaronel ordered.

"Gather our dead," came Adam's voice, sending those who escaped unharmed scattering to carry out their orders.

A look that was eternally lost crossed Tara's face as she took in everything around her. But when she heard the pained cries of dragons she turned. Several groups had the bone dragons grouped together in an attempt to dispatch of them. "Wait!" she shouted, racing across the field to where they were being held.

"But . . ." one of the mages began.

"No," she answered, shaking her head slowly. "These dragons are not born of darkness." To prove her point, she waved her hand across the breast bone of one of the dragons, the group watching as lines of glowing symbols appeared. "They're trapped souls ensnared in Vonspar's disgusting trap."

"You'll never free them!" he shot back, fighting against his own bindings.

"I will free them!" she snapped back. She then stared back up at the group of dragons, feeling the pain they endured with their binding and their desire for eternal rest. "Please . . .," she whispered as tears ran down her cheeks once again. "I know you couldn't save the man I love, but these souls have done nothing against us. All they want is to be at rest once more."

"Dear child . . ." The voice that answered filled her with a peaceful warmth. "Even when faced with great heartache, you still seek peace for those around you." The warmth spread through the core of her chest, through her arms, and gathering in her fingers. "Free them, my Champion."

And just like that the presence was gone from her. With determination shimmering through tear stained eyes she swept her arm up in an arc. Strands of energy shot from her fingers, infecting and destroying the runes that bound the spirits caged within the bones. "Be free, and be at peace!" she shouted, watching each rune shatter. As each spirit found its freedom, the skeletons began to tremble before finally falling to the ground with tremor like force.

One spirit stayed behind, the first seer that fell victim to Vonspar's intentions. "You truly are blessed by the Light," he whispered. "This Realm and every world bordering it, they are lucky to be protected by your heart." And with a low bow of his head, he too returned to his resting place.

Drained, she turned from the pile of bones and walked from the small group without a word. She returned to the fallen form of her beloved and sank to her knees beside him. "We did it," she choked. Her smile quivered as she scooped him close to her chest, rocking back and forth as her cheek found its home in the tangle of blood matted hair.

"Tara?"

She looked up to see the faces of her friends standing around her, shielding her from those who were trying to see what was going on. "Honey, let's go." Wella's voice was calm as she extended her hand out to her friend.

"I can't leave him here," she mumbled, staring blankly at the offered hand.

"He won't be left here," Anon assured. "Besides, you need to get that gash on your head looked at."

"I'll be okay," she protested.

"That's right, you will be okay," Anon began as he scooped her into his arms. "Right after you get your head looked at." Looking back over his shoulder, he watched as Keshou lifted Arcainous's body before they headed toward the waiting medics.

Anything after that was almost impossible for her to bring to recollection. The herbs she had been given did well to sedate her. "Mother?"

Tara's head rolled to the side, her eyes barely opened. "Solstice?" Her mumbled voice drew the attention of those in charge of her care, causing them to pay closer attention to her actions.

"Is it over?" she asked. She'd been away from the main body of the fight, having joined some of the other dragon riders in pursuit of small groups that had tried to attack Nimost directly.

"It is over," she whispered, feeling the joy that swelled in her dragon's heart.

"I look forward to your return, Mother." Tara could hear the excitement in Solstice's voice, and it gave her a small measure of peace. "Will Arcainous be with you?" she asked.

But the mention of her fallen lover moved the young Angel to tears once again. Sensing the growing distress, she called out to her repeatedly, but the medics saw the free falling tears as a sign of pain and sedated her once again. The last thing Tara would remember was the echo of Solstice screaming her name.

CHAPTER

37

Forever Alone

The haunting sound of bagpipes lingered within Tara's mind as funeral after funeral were held for those who had fallen in defense of Nimost. "You should be proud."

Tara looked over her shoulder as Yukino entered the room. "Why?" she asked, turning her gaze back over the balcony's railing as her bandages were changed.

Yukino sighed as she approached. Looking out over the railing she could see the multitudes of people gathered for the funerals. "Because without you, there was no way the armies would have survived."

"Why didn't he listen?" she asked suddenly, listening as the doctors left her room.

Yukino took a seat beside her, resting her hand on Tara's arm. "Who, dear?"

"Either of them?" She didn't know. Her mind hurt, her memories were haunting her in vivid nightmares, and she really hadn't dealt with anything that had happened.

"Darius had many opportunities to change his ways and stop what he was doing," Yukino began.

"But what about Arcainous?" Tara's voice escalated as anger began to creep in. "I told him that I had everything under control, and he didn't listen!"

"In that instant, we all feared for your life." The two turned, seeing Fisonma entering the room with two members from the Elder Council. "He acted on instinct when he put himself between you and Darius."

"I could have saved him," she began.

"He knew the destiny that the Fates had planned for him. He loved you from the first moment he saw you, and he would have done anything to protect you." She then turned to face Yukino directly. "Please help her get ready, it's almost time."

Yukino rose and bowed. "Of course, my friend." Once the small group had gone she turned and held her hand out to Tara. "Come along dear, we need to get you ready."

Tara allowed herself to be pulled to her feet, looking at her second mother with a questioning gaze. "For what?"

"We've waited to bury Arcainous until you were able to attend."

Panic set in almost instantly as she tried to pull away. "No! Please, don't make me go out there." Her eyes were wild, and she began to hyperventilate as the very idea of having to face the Watchers filled her with terror. "I can't face them. I've cost them the lives of two of their leaders!"

Yukino sat her down quickly and tried to calm her. "They do not blame you, Tara. Belzak, like Darius, made his choices."

"Belzak didn't make his choice!" Tara argued. "He was taken trying to save me."

She had begun going into a complete breakdown and Yukino grabbed her shoulders securely. "Listen to me." She waited until she had her full attention before continuing. "None of this is your fault. Now, we need to make you a little more presentable. They're all waiting for you." Rising back to her feet, Yukino busied herself with brushing out Tara's hair, cleaning her face and arms, and dressing her in a white gown and robe. "The other Guardians are in full armor, but yours is so damaged."

"Do I really have to go out there?" Her eyes were pleading, wishing so much to just stay in her room, the only place she felt safe, the only place where she was sure she wouldn't feel judging eyes upon her.

"We will all be with you," Yukino assured. "Come on now." As she led her through the halls they were met by several servants giving their condolences and giving their best for a speedy recovery. Stepping through the main doors Tara froze. So many people were gathered. Citizens, guards, armies. Her stomach turned as she saw Niako standing with the rest of the Watchers, their eyes trained upon her. Her skin looked severely discolored against the purity in the color of the clothes she wore, but she was greeted with love all the same.

"We were so worried about you," Wella said, hugging her tightly, letting go only after she felt Tara wincing.

"Welcome back," Anon added, offering his hand as he helped her down the steps.

"Thank you," Tara replied quietly, watching as the other Guardians fell in place around her. The masses fell in line behind them as they walked toward the cemetery where Arcainous was to be buried. Looking up, she could see the dragons perched upon the tops of each towers, their low cries echoing throughout the area. The sounds of bagpipes again echoed in her ears as they walked, but all she could see was their last blood filled moment together.

Everyone gathered as the coffin was placed. "The Fates have plans for us all," the priest began. "Arcainous personified the traits that all of Nimost strived for." But as he continued Tara felt herself breaking all over again. Her body shook as tears streamed down her cheeks. Her fists were clenched so tightly in a vain effort to maintain control that wounds on the backs of her hands were reopened and blood began to seep through the bandages covering them.

"Tara?" Elexis looked over seeing the young Guardian grasping for any form of mental stability.

Wella looked over seeing the same and gently took her arm allowing the calm flow of water to surround her in an attempt to calm her. "Honey, take slow, deep breaths. You're starting to hyperventilate."

Tara looked up as she felt the calming energy surrounding her. The look in her eyes was fractured and lost. "I miss him . . ." Her voice cracked as she heard the creek of the pulleys lowering the casket into the ground.

"Oh, Tara." Wella's arms wrapped around her as she fell against her and cried. Once more the other Guardians closed protectively around her, keeping her from the view of those paying their last respects. "Shh, shh. It's okay, we're here," she whispered, running her hand over the back of her head gently.

"Excuse me."

Everyone looked up to see Niako and the rest of the Watchers standing before them. "Yes?" Anon asked, his gaze shifting from person to person.

"Might we have a word with Tara?"

Tara clung closer to Wella, shaking her head feverishly. "Please no." She looked up at her friend with a look of absolute horror.

"It's okay," she assured as the group parted, but they did not leave her side.

"Tara?" Niako stepped forward, watching her body language, and shook his head. She looked more like a terrified child instead of the great warrior that had fought back the shadows. "Fisonma told us about your fears and your concerns about how we might view you."

Tara looked up at him, at them all. "I'm so sorry. I could have saved him. I wanted to."

"I know," he interrupted. "But he wouldn't let you."

Tara nodded slowly, and Niako just smiled.

"He knew when we went to war that he was going to die. Mourn his loss, but do not blame yourself for his passing. He loved you deeper than I've ever seen anyone of our race love another. We will mourn the loss of our brother, but know that we hold no ill feelings toward you."

Releasing her grip on Wella, she stepped forward and bowed deeply. "I will mourn his loss until my dying breath."

Now that she was away from the others, he could see just how wounded she was. "We will continue to watch Luna and Myst until you are healed." But before she could thank them, he looked back to the other Guardians. "Please escort her back to her tower. We have all endured much, but I see that her hands are bleeding."

* * *

Once in her room, Tara began to pace. Everywhere she looked were nothing but reminders of the small amount of time the two had together. Her head swam in both pain and memories as she made her way to her bedroom door. "I can't be in here." And with that she slipped into the empty halls. There were enough libraries for her to get lost in, so that's where she headed. Stepping through the grand doors she grabbed the first book available to her and found and oversized chair to curl up in. What she'd found was an early history on the Realm that dated back to Nimost's struggle against the shadows and their eventual salvation. Intrigued by the notion that there was another Angel that existed, there was little information that existed about them, leaving her slightly disappointed. It did raise new questions for her, and as she dwelled upon them, she slid deeper into the chair and drifted off to sleep.

And that was how she spent the next few days. Lost in isolation, delving into whatever book she could get her hands on. Most had to do with the history of the Realm, giving her a greater understanding of her new home. Yukino and Fisonma stood off in the shadows as they watched her, both concerned about her wellbeing. "Do you think she's going to be all right?" Yukino asked. "I can only imagine how hard this is, losing both her mother and Arcainous."

"Her heart needs time to grieve. It will heal in time," Fisonma assured.

"Because of her, we have that time," Yukino said with a smile.

"Indeed we do."

Hearing voices, Tara leaned forward seeing the flurry of disappearing robes. She gave a small smile, knowing that they were concerned for her wellbeing and settled back into the chair to finish the book she was currently reading.

"At least they can all return to a normal life," she sighed, hugging the book tight to her chest. But the days spent lost in the pages she read gave her a small sense of clarity and she began to feel that she could finally close another painful chapter in her life.

Once she reached her room, she sat at her desk and pulled out a pen and paper. Letting her mind slip away, she allowed the energy to write itself, and when she was done, she stared at what was written, feeling tears sting her eyes once again.

In Loving Memory

In spirit, I'll always miss your touch
The protection in your gaze
As your arms grow cold my heart will die
Unable to let you go
Your life sacrificed so that I might live
To set all things in Light
But with you gone, I know I am lost
Your laughter, in echo's past
Will you remember to watch me from where you rest
Will you be my silent guide?
I don't want to go on, knowing you're not here
I don't want to face solitude
A world to watch, a life to lead
All points that seem so small
I hope though, that we will meet again
When my world has faded away
With my mission done, with a torch that is passed
Would you even know who I am?
In shadows I wander, but they will be lost
A heart torn by duty and love
All things though, will happen in time
Of this, I must have faith

The hope of your smile, your tender touch
These must spur me on
Until at last I am laid to rest
With you, my dearest love.

Feeling the drain that writing had taken on her energy, she curled up on her bed, clutching the stuffed wolf her grandparents had given to her, and fell into a more fitful sleep than she had experienced since their ordeal had begun.

EPILOGUE

It would take weeks before any sense of normalcy returned to Tara. She soon felt stable enough to return to her duties as a Guardian of Nimost, though very seldom did she leave the city. She did go and see Solstice, assuring her dragon that she had recovered, though she could still sense the pain in her mother's heart. "The Realm is at peace, Mother," Solstice crooned.

"It is," Tara replied with a soft smile.

"Arcainous would be proud at what you have done," she added, her head laying on the ground against Tara's leg.

"I know . . ."

Before she could say anything further, she was interrupted by the sounds of elated baying and yipping. "You can be a hard person to find."

Tara turned before feeling her back meet the ground as she was tackled by Luna and Myst. "Hello my loves," she whispered, scratching each behind the ears. "Hello Niako."

"You're looking well," he commented, helping her back to her feet.

"I won't lie, it is hard. I still miss him."

"I'd be worried if you didn't."

She just nodded as she leaned against Solstice's head. "Accepting his death had gotten easier with time though."

"You were the center of his world," he began, shifting his gaze as he gave the dragon a gentle pat along the ridge of her left eye. "He would have gone to hell and back just to prove his love for you." Turning to face her, he reached into one of the pockets of his coat and produced a small box. "He left explicit instructions that I give this to you once you had come to terms with his passing."

"What is it?" she asked, taking the small box.

"Open it. He said that if the Fates were kind enough to alter his destiny, he was going to ask you to be his mate."

Flipping the box open, the first thing that caught her eye was the dazzle of an ice blue diamond. "It's beautiful," she breathed.

"Look closer," he told her, making a small gesture to the center of the diamond.

"Hm?" Lifting the ring closer, she stared into the center, seeing a tiny metal wolf. As she turned the ring the wolf appeared to run through the multiple faces of the gem. "How . . ."

He allowed himself a small chuckle as he took the ring from the box. "There are some secrets that are better left to the imagination," he said, slipping the ring onto her finger. "There we are."

She hugged him tightly. "Thank you."

"You are most welcome." He stepped back and gave a shallow bow. "I'm afraid I must take my leave. There are things I must attend to."

"Yeah . . . me too," she replied warily, casting her gaze toward the dungeons where their war criminals were being held.

"You are strong," he began. "All they can do is speak and yell, and blame you. Do not let their words affect you."

"I won't," she promised, watching as he walked away. She then turned her attention to the two wolves who were now staring intently at her. "I'll be back. Why don't you guys go play." She was met with happy yips as they ran off toward the courtyard, playing their own version of tag.

"Will you be all right, Mother?"

"I think I will," she said with a smile. She watched her take to the skies, returning to her roost. Taking a deep breath she turned her attention toward the dungeons. It was part of her duties to assure that everything was running smoothly for the guards, and that, while they were considered war criminals, they were still treated properly. As she approached, she was met by the Captain of the guard. "Things are going well?" she asked as the Captain fell in step beside her.

"As well as can be expected," he replied dryly.

"What do you mean?"

"Just the usual yelling, threats. Things we expected from them when they were brought in."

"Is it safe to go inside?"

"Always. They are chained, they're in individual cells, and they all have markings across their bodies suppressing any powers they might have."

"I'll only be a moment," she assured.

"If you need me, I'll be right outside."

She nodded and ventured inside. It was cold as a chill seeped from the stone walls. She remembered being told some time ago that the chill was used to keep their prisoners subdued and quiet, but as she was spotted by one of the prisoners the noise began to escalate. She tuned most of them out, but a low chuckle drew her attention. Turning, she saw the figure of a man bound in energies so foreign that she couldn't make them out, even if she tried. "Does something strike you as interesting?" Vonspar asked, staring at her from beneath his dark bangs.

Silence.

"I asked you a question woman!" he bellowed, his eyes filling with unmasked hatred.

"Is it really so necessary to speak like that?" she asked.

"Oh, my apologies." His voice was so overly exaggerated and she just rolled her eyes at him. "I forgot we were in the presence of the great Angel," he spat, addressing her with such irreverence that it made her skin crawl. But he was not who she had come to find. "Come back here!" he demanded as she walked away. "I'm not finished with you yet!"

It made sense that they were all separated and kept in various cells throughout the prisons, but she wanted to spend as little time as possible down here. "Well, look at you."

She turned to face the cell to her left. "Belzak . . ."

"Why do you sound so sad for me?" he asked. "When we are free, we will be more powerful and we will destroy this abomination, and since you and I share the same gaze, you will be easy to find, and you will be ours."

Could this really be the nature of his heart? she wondered as the echo of his laughter hit her ears.

"You are mine!" he snarled.

The deliberate tone he used made her stiffen. "We may share the same gaze," she began, "but the gaze I bear is nothing but a reminder of a friend long since gone to this world. A friend who risked his life to save a child from the shadows!"

And with that she walked away, listening to the fading growls and snarls coming from his cell.

"I have a question for you."

Tara stopped, looking over her shoulder into Vonspar's cell once more. His voice and movements had calmed, but she was still wary. "Yes?"

"Do you really think that you destroyed Darius?" he asked. "He is the embodiment of all darkness, with powers far superior to your own."

"I will not stoop down to your level and feed your self-absorbed ego, Vonspar," And with that, she walked back into the lingering warmth of the evening sun.

"Are you all right?"

Tara looked to see the Captain waiting for her and smiled. "Just cold," she admitted.

* * *

That night, she stood out on her balcony, staring in the direction that she had buried her childhood friend. Reaching out with her energy, she could feel the sphere, still strong with her convictions and it set her at ease. "I'm sorry, Darius, but you really left me no choice."

* * *

In his own pit of hell, Darius writhed in the agony he now found himself in. His skin was burned and blistering where Keshou's power had taken his armor, almost fusing it to his body. "I will destroy you," he choked as pain sent his mind reeling into the depths of his subconscious.

"Darius . . ."

Darius heard the hiss speaking his name. "Who's out there!" he demanded.

A figure appeared, clad in a dark robe. "I am the birth of all your power," she stated with great pride. "I am darkness itself."

"What do you want?"

"The hatred in your soul coupled with your desire for revenge against those who betrayed you. Well, let's just say, your emotions gave birth to me. I merely pushed things along at key points. I want to free that energy, mold it, grow it, and then release you upon those who imprisoned you in this hell." Holding out her hand to him he could feel the weight of her gaze. "Will you accept my gift?"

He wanted salvation from his Holy prison. The pain, blisters that would burst only to reform and burst again, it was all too much for him to endure. "If I agree to this, what will you expect in return?"

There was no hesitation in her answer. It was always clear what she wanted. "When you are mended, and your mastery of the Shadows are complete, I will set you loose upon this Realm, and once it is destroyed, we will rule in absolute darkness."

The idea of ruling an entire Realm, more power than even Vonspar could wield. Her smile broadened within the shadows of her cloak as she felt his heart become further corrupted. "All right, I accept your offer."

"I knew you would," she cooed. "Now, take my hand, my son, and be reborn in the image I have created for you!" As he took her hand, the fire that had once consumed and tortured Darius began to fall away, being replaced by fire black as night. "Let the energy heal you," she whispered. "When the process is complete, you will find me at the Manor."

And with that said, she disappeared, and a lengthy rejuvenation process began.

ABOUT THE AUTHOR

Originally from Southern California, Kari now calls a rural town in Colorado home. She is the eldest out of six with a background as an EMT, a passion she excelled at before an accident forced her to change career plans. Now she thrives with a new company, and when she isn't helping run the store where she works, she spends her time writing both stories and poetry, painting, sketching, gaming, listening to music, and genuinely just enjoying life and exploring the state she calls home.

9 781642 984330